Wonders will never cease

by
Judi Moore

By the same author

Ice cold passion and other stories
Little Mouse: a novella
Is death really necessary?

Published by Moo Kow Press

in conjunction with FeedARead Publishing

Copyright © Judi Moore 2017

First Edition, 2017

The author asserts her moral right under the Copyright, Designs and Patents Act 1988 to be identified as the author of this work.

All rights reserved. No part of this publication may be reproduced, stored in a retrieval system, or transmitted, in any form or by any means, without the prior written consent of the author, nor be otherwise circulated in any form other than that in which it is published and without a similar condition being imposed on the subsequent purchaser.

British Library C.I.P.

For more information please go to:

www.mookowpress.wordpress.com

www.judimoore.wordpress.com

www.johnlakehobbs.net

This is a work of fiction. The characters, places and events which inhabit it are either the product of the author's imagination or are used in a fictitious context.

Thanks

This novel has been a long time in the making. Thus people name-checked below may be surprised that I have remembered their contribution, made perhaps 30 years ago.

The reason I began this book (or, at any rate, completed it) was because of the first writing group I ever belonged to. It arose spontaneously out of our need to write, and to have support from other writers. I think, for all five of us, it was the first time we had ever shared our work or our aspirations as writers with anybody else. The members of that group were Lydia Chant, Pat Coombes, Ruth McCracken and Marilyn Ricci. Thank you, girls.

I am very grateful to Peter Skelton for sharing with me some of his knowledge about Wagner's *Die Meistersinger* and the sort of things audiences get up at performances of it.

I am also very grateful to John Hobbs for the delightful covers.

Errors of fact or typography which remain are mine own.

Wonders will never cease

Contents

Thursday 3 December 11
Friday 4 December 19
Saturday 5 December 27
Sunday 6 December 36
Monday 7 December 42
Tuesday 8 December 56
Wednesday 9 December 63
Thursday 10 December 67
Friday 11 December.. 71
Saturday 12 December 78
Sunday 13 December.. 81
Monday 14 December... 87
Tuesday 15 December 95
Wednesday 16 December 113
Thursday 17 December 129
Friday 18 December 146
Saturday 19 December 161
Sunday 20 December 180
Monday 21 December... 188
Tuesday 22 December 207
Wednesday 23 December 224
Thursday 24 December 228
Friday 25 December 231

1985

Thursday 3 December

The final Faculty Board of the year proceeded at its customary funereal pace. Fergus Girvan wriggled in his chair and wished its sagging, clammy plastic seat in hell – the moist warmth was playing merry murder with his piles.

Fergus and far too many other people were currently crammed into a single room in one of Ariel University's tatty, prefabricated buildings. Wan December daylight barely glimmered through plate glass windows already running with condensation.

1985 had been as dull as this meeting, for Fergus. For much of the rest of the country it had been perfectly bloody under the ruthless government of Margaret Thatcher. This year she had finally smashed the miners' into submission. Socialism was a dirty word. Greed was encouraged. The Welfare State was being dismantled. Public services fell by the wayside almost daily as their funding was slashed. Even at the university savings had had to be made. These were gloomy days indeed for anyone who'd ever voted Labour. And after seven vicious years there was no sign even of revolt from within the government. Thatcher cried 'on!' and the vegetables in her cabinet simply echoed her cry. Where and at what speed were questions they consistently failed to ask.

Now she had time on her hands Thatcher might well turn her attention to Ariel University. The Iron Lady hated anything Harold Wilson's government had put in place to make easier the lives of citizens not born into privileged families (never mind that she herself was a grocer's daughter). And Ariel was a soft enough target, being funded differently from conventional universities: it stood out from the crowd. It wasn't wise to stand anywhere the Leaderine's steely gaze could see you clearly. Yes, Thatcher's next quarry could well be Ariel. She might cut its funding until it ceased to be viable. Or she might try to snuff it out altogether.

Well, they'd just have to keep their union dues paid and man the barricades if the Gorgon's stony gaze were to swing their way next year. How bad could it really get? Surely in the civilised Eighties even the Mad Axewoman couldn't excise a whole university and get away with it? Looking ahead as far as Christmas, now less than a month away, was hard enough for Fergus. It was not his favourite time of year, not least because it was the one day when the pubs were shut in the evening. But at least the bloody phone didn't ring.

In an attempt to get something done while the meeting droned on, Fergus mentally worked his way through his diary for the rest of the year.

There was the faculty Christmas party yet to endure. That had historically been a ripe and ribald event, but more recently had become marred by limitations placed on duration of the festivities and the quantity of alcohol provided.

Some days before the Christmas party a meeting of the Architecture course committee was scheduled. Fergus was looking forward to that. He intended to present them with a pitch for a chapter on ancient architecture which would make their eyes water. He wanted to make one more visit to the British Library before giving Marion his draft outline for typing. It was yet another scintillating Girvan non pareil. Ground-breaking results from research into the sort of subjects covered by the term 'Classics' was difficult – the ground had been pored over so minutely by so many for so long. But Fergus had discovered something truly original about the Pharos of Alexandria in the bowels of the British Library and he couldn't wait to share it with his colleagues. The wonders of the ancient world had long been a favourite area of Fergus's study. Not so much was known about them as one might suppose. For instance, many scholars disputed the very existence of The Hanging Gardens of Babylon.

Which reminded him of a third professional duty remaining in the year. He was due to meet with a Hungarian PhD student who had a fascinating theory about those very hanging gardens: that they were, in fact, the hanging gardens of somewhere other than Babylon. This would explain much. And was certain to make for a fascinating thesis. He was looking forward very much to meeting Ms Jardanyi.

But as for the Faculty Board – all was, as usual, obfuscation and pettifogging. He didn't know why he bothered coming, except that people who didn't turn up tended to get lumbered, 'by a show of hands', with the faculty's shittier tasks. The last time there had been anything of interest to him on the agenda was when they'd agreed to fund his trip to Alexandria in the autumn. He permitted himself a smug little smirk. They would certainly find *that* had been money well spent.

Reliving the glories of an autumn spent in Alexandria, Fergus slumped into an almost pleasant torpor. As the lengthy business of recording apologies began, his mind finished revisiting Alexandria and segued into a replay of his fiftieth birthday celebration the night before. It began to rove pleasurably over the hills and valleys, some thickly wooded, of buxom Sukie, with whom he had spent that exhausting and rejuvenating night. What a quim – velvety as a mouse's ear and tight as ...

The sneeze caught Fergus by surprise, and his ears popped painfully. His body might be a temple, but recently it had begun to feel like a ruined one. He still hadn't been able completely to shift the sinus infection he'd picked up on the plane coming home from Alexandria the month before.

He glared at the window wall, running with condensation. What did the administration here think they were – guppies? This saturated atmosphere wasn't fit for human occupation. He could feel the bacteria which had taken up residence in his upper nasal cavities expanding gleefully with every minute he spent in this soupy air. The teasing pain in his backside wasn't improving his temper, either.

He wished he'd been able to stay in Alexandria for Christmas. His hotel had been comfortable, the food excellent, the weather balmy. The Corniche had been swarming with sophisticated young women. Of course, it being a Muslim country, alcohol wasn't too plentiful, but he'd managed.

The wearisome present intruded as the Professor of the Classics Department, Petra Stavrou, came in late and squeezed her way noisily past the massed knees of the faculty to reach a conspicuously vacant seat next to the Dean, Patrick Redman. Petra was always a top table person – all the department heads were – but she did not usually rate a seat so close to the godhead. Petra being his head of department, Fergus's curiosity was immediately piqued.

Petra was an ambitious woman, this reflected in her dress. Those fashionable padded shoulders, aggressively tailored suits, and gravity-defying stiletto court shoes were worn to show she meant business. She had joined the Classics Department several years after Fergus. Nevertheless, she had steamed past him in the promotion stakes, receiving the single, fiercely coveted, Professorship available to the department two years before – and becoming Fergus's boss in the process.

Petra was an able enough scholar, but completely preoccupied with the location of the texts and artefacts that were her specialism and the staple of her study. She had a Greek mother but had never lived in Greece. This combination of circumstances made her, of course, obsessively Greek. She had changed her surname to her mother's patronymic by Deed Poll as soon as she was old enough to do so. Greek artefacts should be in Greece was her primary thesis. That so many of them had been removed by the British, Petra felt as a personal affront. Any and all campaigns for the return of the Elgin marbles and similar collections to their country of origin could be sure of her support. About other areas of Classical study she was rather less concerned which, thankfully, left Fergus to get on with his own work unmolested much of the time.

Why had Patrick placed Petra at his right hand like this? Faculty politics was a deep stream, but not a broad one. It took Fergus mere moments to recall that a new Dean would be elected in the New Year. It was Not Done to campaign openly – one hoped to be *asked* to stand by one's peers – but it did not do, either, to depend *entirely* on reputation and respect. A little oiling of the wheels was allowable, even expected. So, Petra had ambitions in that direction did she? And, by the look of it, Patrick's support.

In her absence the Department would require an Acting Head. Ted was too old and Veronica was due to go on maternity leave in the New Year. There was no-one but himself! Fergus Girvan (Acting) Head of Classics. That had a nice ring to it. He could easily manage the extra work load – his current research project would be written up by the spring and his writing commitments too. He could see his way to helping her out. She had only to ask. He could hardly wait.

Fergus's career had been treading water for some time. His doctoral thesis on the Twelve Stages of the Hero's Journey had been an academic best seller. At his appointment in 1969 to the academic staff of the new, innovative, distance-teaching Ariel University (motto 'the university of the air') he had felt like a duck finding water for the first time. He and his new employers quickly discovered that he had a gift for creating course materials which could be taught at a distance. But his star did not rise. His Chair, which everyone considered a foregone conclusion when they hired him, had not materialised.

Not least because Petra snaffled it. She had worked out where in Greece a cache of very ancient marble statues had come from, and insisted they be disinterred from the bowels of the British Museum (where they had been mouldering for a couple of centuries) and repatriated. The Greek government had been effusive in their thanks and had established both a Research Fellowship and a bursary in the department as a result. After that coup her Chair was a foregone conclusion.

His only recourse was to submit a case for a personal Chair. He was particularly hopeful of success next year. He had ground-breaking research in the pipeline, nearing completion in fact, concerning his longstanding area of interest, the wonders of the ancient world. In addition, Ms Jardanyi's research, into the same area of study as his own looked very exciting. The result of his interview with her next week was surely a foregone conclusion. Her résumé was outstanding. To supervise her, surely exceptional, PhD would be a solid asset to his case. And now it looked as though he would be Acting Head of Department if – oh, let imagination reign – *when* Petra became Dean.

It looked as though his luck was finally about to change.

*

They nipped smartly through the agenda, penny pinching here, compromising there, until they got to the art historians' request for funding for a trip to Florence to help develop their forthcoming course on Renaissance sculpture.

At this point Patrick lumbered to his feet. The trip was being planned by Nick Bonetti, the senior Art History lecturer. Nick had obviously expected to be asked to introduce the item. He was trying now to catch Patrick's eye without having to put up his hand for attention like a boy who needs to leave the room. Patrick, on his feet rummaging around for his spectacles and shuffling notes, was resolutely not meeting Nick's eye.

Give him his bloody trip, thought Fergus, and let's get on. He glanced at his watch. The Vaults Bar would be open by now, and the bottle of half-decent burgundy which Chris, the Steward, uncorked for him on Faculty Board days for just this sort of eventuality would be breathing nicely. He could almost taste the first soothing glass.

Patrick was an imposing figure. Six foot three in his Hush Puppies, with a mane of silver hair and matching, luxuriant moustaches, he looked like some legendary ancient Celtic hero. His appearance, however, was deceptive. Patrick was more worrier than warrior, and these days used his considerable intellect to smooth the way for the government's frequent cuts to the university's budget. Instead of standing up for distance education, bloody banner raised, he did the work of the university's fiscal and administrative imps of darkness for them, arguing that a thrifty approach now would reap rewards when things got really tight. When Patrick thought the rainy day he was saving the faculty's pennies for was going to dawn Fergus couldn't imagine. It had been chucking it down in stair rods ever since Thatcher had become Prime Minister six years before. He had begun to fear that they would have to prise the doorknob of No 10 out of her cold, dead hand.

Patrick had got his glasses and notes in order at last, and was in full flow, setting the merits of the Renaissance Room at the Victoria and Albert Museum against the time and expense of actually going to

Florence. The administrators were smiling and nodding, Nick was becoming apoplectic. The rest of his department (two girls and a boy) were whispering. None of them had expected this hatchet job.

Patrick ahem-ed his way to his coup de grâce. He said,

'So I don't see how we can support you in this, Nick – you see it just isn't ...'

Fergus sighed. It was time for action.

'If the Dean will indulge me? I have a few points to make.'

'*Must* you, Fergus? I really wasn't intending to open this up for debate. We still have a lot to get through ...'

He trailed off, in the pseudo-vague way he had cultivated over the years to turn wrath, and started shuffling papers again. Fergus was on his feet at once. Nobody told Fergus Girvan the matter wasn't for debate.

'I'm afraid I really must, Patrick.' Fergus whipped his own specs out of his top pocket and on to his face with a flourish, the better to watch the expressions on the faces of those present. His blunt common sense flooded the room, bringing balm to the souls of the beleaguered members of the Art History Department (pretty girls they were too). He unfurled his tattered and bloody banner, veteran of many a successful campaign, and spoke beneath it, straight to the heart and to the point. He said what needed to be said, neither more nor less, then he sat down.

Nick was right behind his standard,

'As Fergus has so ably pointed out, Patrick ...'

And it was clear the Florence trip was on.

*

In the Vaults Bar Fergus was expansive – this mood enhanced by a couple of bottles of the almost-passable burgundy, the first purchased for him by a grateful Nick, both shared with the whole art history department. Fergus drank deeply and relaxed into the warm, smoky fug.

It was good to be a hero again. Largesse brimming over he poured the remaining burgundy into the youngsters' glasses and waved to Chris for another bottle. The kids demurred. He let his hand fall. He did have things to do this afternoon, and it didn't do these days to be too diddled driving home, especially with the M1 greasy with wintry drizzle.

And just like that he felt the euphoria of the meeting drain away, to be replaced by the reality of his life in which the lows rather seemed to exceed the highs these days. There was no getting away from it, drunk or sober. Despite the gratitude of the Art History Department he, Fergus Girvan, had never really fulfilled his potential.

The iffy cartilage in his left knee squeaked painfully as he rose to go. Ageing was a bitch and no mistake. The quartet of art historians had their heads together over his wine, engrossed in planning the Florentine trip. Didn't they understand what Patrick's attack on it meant? Nick was old enough to know. The young ones thought this was the way things had always been – having to do battle to get a few quid to do essential research. It had been the envy of the world, the British education system. Now look at it. He almost turned back to try and make them see the storm clouds gathering: they should be knocking nails into an Ark *right now* in anticipation of the imminent Deluge. But at least they were going to Florence.

Trying not to limp he set off back to his room.

But by the time he reached it the smile was back on his face. Fergus was not a man to dwell on that which could not be cured. There was going to be a vacancy when Petra announced her candidacy for the Deanship. And he, Fergus, was going to fill it.

Everybody was in, of course, for the Board. Flushed and booming Fergus bestrode the corridors, greeting colleagues cheerily, slapping shoulders, winking at the typing pool. Then he went into his office and shut the door. He had plans to make – which ears could most usefully be bent, which favours should be called in. He would have something new, something unassailable on his résumé next time his case for a personal Chair went in front of the promotions board: Acting Head of Department. Hell, yes.

*

When he got home his answerphone was winking at him. He picked up a message from his daughter, Andy.

'Fergus, I need to see you.' Even on the machine the tinny voice rang with conspiracy. 'Tomorrow's the day you work from home isn't it? Can you come over to the school at lunchtime? Don't call home. I had a major row with Mum this morning and you know she always gets ratty when you phone. See you tomorrow? Please?'

The machine gave the time of the call. She'd only just missed him this morning. Must have called from a box on the way to school. Whatever could it be?

He sighed. His daughter was adept at playing both ends against the middle. It was one reason – of many – why her mother disliked him so intensely. If Mary refused the girl something the first thing she did was go and try Fergus for it. Somehow that always seemed to work, and Mary would rail at him for encouraging her. Whatever it was, it was always his fault.

They'd had these lunchtime assignations before. Lunchtime was good. It meant she wasn't late home. Somehow when they were together time just seemed to slip away and he was always dropping her off hours late, and facing a stormy Mary.

The disembodied voice of the machine said 'end of message'.

Fergus stared at it while it instructed him, as if he didn't know, what to do if he wanted to delete all messages. He had a bad feeling about this.

Friday 4 December

His morning in the British Library did not go well. He found it difficult to concentrate. This surprised him. The material he was translating and cross-checking for provenance was fascinating. The scrolls he was working on purported to be part of a cache of records saved from the library at Alexandria when it burned. They had been languishing in the store rooms of the British Library for at least a century when Fergus happened upon them in the catalogue when looking for material on the Alexandrian library itself.

The scrolls compared the merits and demerits of the various wonders of the ancient world. Some had already been lost when the scroll was written, others were well-loved landmarks of long-standing, others were quite new. The ancient writer was as scathing about the newer constructions as Prince Charles had famously been the year before about the 'monstrous carbuncle' the Royal Institute of British Architects was keen to attach to the side of the National Gallery.

The translation was slow going (the Greek was ropey, the scroll damaged and the photostat he had to work from was fuzzy in places) but fascinating.

Every extrapolation he made from this material, every insight he gained, was utterly original: utterly his own. He was looking forward immensely to writing the first paper, the accolades which would accrue from its peer review, working up the paper into a book. He was currently only a reading member of the team putting together the new architecture course. But he was going to extrapolate from his findings and create a lecture for it, his work was coming together so well. He'd submit an outline to them at their meeting next week. An excellent case could be made for adding something on structures in the Classical world. What better examples of classical structures could there possibly be than an evaluation of the aesthetics and building methods employed in creating the wonders of the ancient world by a contemporary author, discussed and expanded upon by Dr Fergus Girvan?

It would, of course, look wonderful on his case for the promotions board.

Things were, however, chasing themselves around in his head and leaving no room for consideration of the scrolls before him.

The ramifications of Petra's shot at the Deanship plagued him. His subconscious was still working on the angles.

Then there was the imminent, clandestine meeting with his daughter. What mess had she got herself into this time?

And finally there was still a stale taste left by yesterday's meeting. Such a bunch of old fogies they had become. It seemed just a few short years ago that they had been youthful visionaries setting up the first distance teaching university in the world. Ah, the camaraderie there had been then – or was that just the warm patina of memory?

He found he was staring, mesmerised, at the faded blue leather desk top in front of him. The blue desk spaces stretched away from him in both directions – towards the bookshelves to his left and the librarians' desks to his right. They did not demonstrate a warm patina; they looked pretty shabby actually. But the leather smelled good. Which good smell made him think of lunch. Lunch made him think of pubs – and they were certainly open, barely.

He tried to carry on with the translation a little longer but every rustle, cough and sneeze intruded; his concentration was completely shot. He peered along his row trying to spot the noise makers, then realised what he was doing. Only a silly old fogie blames others for his own deficiencies: he was as bad as his colleagues.

He shut the file he had been staring at, told the front desk that he'd be back, and went to deal with his rumbling belly and his devious daughter. Then, perhaps, he'd be able to immerse himself properly in his work.

Outside the museum he walked briskly through the metropolitan bustle and the best of a brightly-silvered winter day. The air was crisp and smelt clean – although that was obviously an illusion. His spirits rose, although he still felt, somehow, unsettled.

He decided he might as well go home as pub-wards. There was a perfectly ripe avocado in the fruit bowl that would serve him for an early lunch. And a nice bottle of Pinot Grigio in the fridge from which he could allow himself a smallish glass.

Then he'd go and find out what trouble his daughter was about to get him into.

*

After a quick lunch it took him half an hour to drive to the school. The kids were just beginning to trickle back. He parked the Jag outside the gates where Andy would be sure to see him – one of the many uses of a distinctive car. Every other vehicle in sight was a wreck; dented 2CVs and Beetles, rust-bucket Fiestas and Metros. He was proud of his XJS in British Racing Green. He had bought it during the oil crisis in 1979, when nobody wanted big-engined gas-guzzlers, because it was cheap and beautiful and had become suddenly out of step with its times through no fault of its own. The V at the end of its number plate pleased him enormously. Holding a V sign up to the world pretty much summed up his own philosophy.

And it certainly pulled the birds.

Andy would probably be late, she usually was. He found *Madame Butterfly* on Radio Three, turned the volume up, then settled back to wait.

And now here she was at his window, tapping. He lowered it and she leaned in.

'Dad!'

He suddenly seemed to be covered in hair and lips. Very pleasant, but he fought a bit.

'For Christ's sake don't call me "Dad" ...'

'Sorry, Fergus. Slip of the tongue.'

She withdrew and he straightened up and became aware of another girl with her. She noticed his glance and etiquette cut in.

'Sorry – Fergus this is Katie. Katie this is Fergus, my ...'

'Let me get out of the car, girl,' he blustered over the last part of the introduction, 'or they'll think I'm an old pervert offering you sweeties.'

The girls both laughed, a spectacular sound like tinkling bells.

Andy stood back and he clambered out, trying not to favour the knee with the wonky cartilage. He hugged Andy and shook hands with Katie. Katie was a stunning girl. Long dark hair, no make-up, classic features that needed none: bee-stung lips, big dark eyes, strong brows, finely modelled nose. What a looker. With difficulty he dragged his attention back to his daughter and gave Katie back her hand.

'Well then, what's the problem? Can we go somewhere and talk?'

'Oh, D..., Fergus, you are a dear. I've got a class, but I can bunk off ...'

'No need for that. What time do you finish?'

'About five today. I've got something I want to get on with in the Art Room after classes.'

'Can you come round to the flat on your way home?'

'Sure. It could take a while, are you going out?'

'No. It can take as long as it takes.' And just like that his attempt not to get into Mary's bad books by keeping Andy out late was scuppered. He kissed her cheek and then held her out at arm's length.

'Give me a clue, though. How bad is it?'

'On a scale of one to ten?'

'Yes.'

She thought for a moment.

'About a six – and I'm not pregnant.'

She laughed again, the stunning Katie joined in, and their silliness was so infectious that he laughed as well, growling along beneath their peals like a liberating cannon beneath victory bells. He was glad he had come.

She hugged him again and was gone. She and Katie waved back at him as they ran, twisting and leaping on their legs like young horses playing.

He drove back with poor Butterfly becoming increasingly desperate on the stereo. Amanda – Andy, as she insisted on being called – was never a waste of time. Of all the things he had done; the research, the books, the papers, the students, Andy was the thing of which he was most proud. And to think that he might never have known her. If Bloody Mary had realised what Andy would do with the information, he was certain she would never have told the child about him.

*

Andy had turned up on his doorstep about four years ago, a skinny teenager in a shabby duffle coat, eyes red and face pale, mouth set, fists clenched.

'My Mum says you're my Dad.'

When he opened the door he had thought for a moment that she was a begging runaway. Her opening gambit had taken him aback. It turned out she *was* a sort of a runaway – had rushed out when Mary had pointed him out on the television that Saturday morning.

'You're always on about your father. Well, there he is, for what it's worth.'

An in depth question and answer session had, apparently, ensued. Fergus could imagine the conversation. But Mary didn't succeed in putting the child off, because Andy had gone immediately to the BBC's Television Centre at White City. She had been armed only with his name, gleaned from the credits of the programme of which Mary had pointed him out as presenter. By the time Andy found anyone to tell her anything it was the middle of the afternoon. Somehow she conned her way into the Ariel Productions Office and had finagled his address out of an exhausted RAT working through the weekend to complete post-production on a new programme scheduled for transmission on Monday. Then his fourteen year old daughter had stormed from White City to Hampstead Heath on pure temper, to turn up on his doorstep and call him father.

She was a creature of impulse, just like her old man.

It had been a difficult meeting. There were lots of tears and recriminations. Then more recriminations (but no tears) from and with Mary when she came to fetch the girl. But before Mary arrived, after he had got Amanda cleaned up and calmed down, fed her and got a little medicinal brandy into her, she had seemed like a nice kid.

It was a novelty to have something of his own flesh and blood to care about. So he had asked Mary if he could see the girl again and obtained her grudging permission. He had taken Amanda out to tea the following weekend, to Harrods, and she had loved it. For a long time they had continued in this fairy tale way – theatre trips, meals out – nibbling round the edges of their very different lives, treading carefully, wanting not to uncover things that they couldn't back away from in time. But gradually they formed a real relationship.

As Amanda got older and turned into Andy, the formality of their meetings had lessened. Andy often popped over to see him on her way home from school now. It was much easier for them at his place, away from her mother. Earlier this year he had given Andy a key to his flat (something he had never given to any other female). It had felt like a big step. It had been a solemn moment between them.

Mary had never forgiven him for the university education she missed out on because of her pregnancy. He had tried everything he could think of to make up for the missing years, offering money in the end in the hope that it would soften her. But she said she didn't need it now and wouldn't take it from him even if she did.

After all those years of it being just the two of them, Mary seemed afraid that he would somehow disrupt her relationship with her daughter. And it was true that some kind of wedge had been driven between mother and daughter by the arrival of the father. Mary maintained it was because he was a untrustworthy, deceitful, lying bastard. He had tried to suggest that difficulties arose partly because of her resentment towards him – if she could, perhaps, be a little less antagonistic? But Mary was adamant, implacable, closed to him.

Still, the fonder he got of Andy the more he thought about the blank space on her birth certificate. He couldn't adopt her – her mother would have had a pink fit at the thought. So he had started a fund for her, quietly, and changed his will in her favour. Under his tutelage, she grew to love books, good wine and beautiful things (which was the greater part of what he had to leave her) and he took pleasure in acquiring a new painting, knowing that Andy would like it, knowing that it would be hers one day, knowing that she would only sell it in a moment of extreme need.

Now she was going on eighteen, and very nearly a woman. Fergus liked young women very much; preferred them to the more mature kind. But a daughter proved to be a very different thing from a lover. He had been on a steep learning curve ever since Andy had found him, which did not appear to be flattening out with time. Just when he thought he'd got the hang of the kind of crisis which was likely to loom, the child would be into something else entirely and all the experience he'd amassed would be useless once more.

But she was a good kid in the main – and a bright one. She was doing her final year of 'A' Levels at the Jennie Lee Academy in Hackney. It specialised in art and Andy's was a heavy syllabus, covering painting and sculpture as well as English, French and Italian. Andy had discovered boys too, so she didn't have as much time for him as she used to. They hadn't had one of their trips for a long time. Her weekends were spent writing essays, going to pubs and discos – and painting. Painting was her passion.

He looked forward to her visit this evening, as he did to all her visits, even if she *was* about to drag him into some mad scheme that would make her mother rage at him. The knee caught him as he changed gear, and he laughed. There were worse ways to grow old. Slipping into old age with his jewel of a daughter was no hardship.

*

She was late. Again. The young led such busy lives. He heard the scrape of her key in the lock and she tumbled into the flat smelling of wood smoke and cinnamon, hair blown all anyhow and her enormous portfolio going before her like a sail. She chucked it down inside the front door, where it fell over; they danced round it trying to prop it against the wall. Then she hugged him, cheeks cold, heart warm.

He got her sat down by the fire with a cup of tea and tried to look stern.

'Now what's the trouble? If you're not pregnant ...?'

It was a fear of his, this – that she would inherit her father's propensity for casual love as she appeared to have inherited his love of the finer things in life. He had trouble imagining her with a man – any father would, surely?

'There's this man ...'

He groaned.

'No, wait. He's a sort of peripatetic teacher who comes to the school once a week. He teaches Katie and me art history. He's seen my paintings I've been doing at school. He says I've got real talent and he wants to see the rest of my portfolio.'

'Because...?'

'He wants to give me extra tuition.'

It sounded like a line to Fergus.

'And you want me to fund it?'

'No. He says he's not going to charge.'

Alarm bells began to ring in Fergus's head. Andy continued.

'He says he tries to find a couple of students every year who could benefit from some extra one-to-one time, a chance to get a different perspective. He says he likes to give something back.'

The bells in Fergus's head became klaxons.

'Mum said you should go and look at his gallery and meet him. His name's David Dunne. He's a fantastic artist – I've seen some of his stuff. He's got a PhD from Trinity, Dublin. He taught there while he was studying for it, then he came to England to make his fortune as a painter. Oh Fergus, it's a marvellous opportunity!'

'Where's the gallery?'

'In Fitzrovia.'

'Is it now.'

'It's a good address!'

'Maybe. Maybe not. You never can tell with Fitzrovia.'

Despite his reservations he knew he would help her. And he knew that she knew that he would. One of his major functions as her father was to conspire with her in schemes her mother wouldn't stand for. He rationalised this function by telling himself that she would start hare-brained projects anyway and it was better for everybody if somebody was keeping an eye on them. This was yet another reason for his on-going lack of rapport with Mary. Not only did the child tell him things she would never dream of confiding to her mother, but all too often Mary discovered him to be at the bottom of something questionable connected with her daughter, apparently egging the girl on.

*

He took Andy out for supper later on and, over some excellent fettuccini, pumped her about Katie. It transpired that Katie was a new student at the school, and that she and Andy had met at the art history classes they both attended (taught by this D Dunne, PhD). One person's crisis was always another's opportunity. If Andy hadn't needed his help he would never have met Katie. And he did, very much, want to meet her again.

Andy plied him with wine, was considerate for his comfort, put herself out to be charming company. Even though he knew what she was up to he was putty in her hands. As she was pouring him the last glass out of the bottle of Chianti, she finally got him to agree to come to the gallery with her the following day to meet Dunne. He grumbled about the bloody awful traffic that would infest the hinterland of Oxford Street area on a Saturday afternoon in December, but it was a vain effort – he knew he would go.

He walked her to the Tube, arm in arm, and kissed her cheek, as cold as porcelain, in the tunnel of warm wind at the entrance. Then he watched her vanish down the steps, back into the other half of her life.

He sometimes wondered what he thought about having just this much of her, but was realistic enough to know that a teenage girl-child, in residence – even if only part-time – would not fit into his life. No, he was content.

He sometimes felt a bit queasy when he thought about what might have happened if they had first met some time soon, and he had not known she was his daughter.

Saturday 5 December

Saturday was wet and windy. Bloody nuisance. He didn't look forward to wrestling with Andy's portfolio in a high wind. With difficulty they wedged it across what passed for a back seat in the Jag and set out for the gallery.

It was not a good address: it was in a down at heel lane off Hanway Street which was, in turn, off the Tottenham Court Road. To call it 'Fitzrovia' was to be creative with its geography, as he had expected.

The building they stopped outside looked as if it had been some kind of warehouse in a better life. There was a very large sign along the front of one of the higher floors which was so tattered and dirty that it was no longer legible, nevertheless Andy was confident that they had arrived at the right place – which he surmised gloomily probably meant she'd been here before.

He left the Jag right outside the building, blocking the alleyway completely. He wasn't intending to be here long. If anyone wanted to get by they could give him a blast on their horn. It might make a useful get-out.

He wondered if his wire spoke wheels would survive the experience as he retracted the car's aerial.

Now that he was out of the car he could see a small sign over a side door that said 'Dunne's Fine Arts' in black Art Deco lettering on a sludgy green ground.

They went in and struggled up three flights of dirty, twisting stairs with the portfolio.

*

Inside, the gallery looked no more inviting than it had done from without. The current occupiers appeared to be proud of its past as a warehouse: all its viscera were exposed, in a manner that was becoming increasingly trendy. Rusty girders criss-crossed the space. Flimsy partitions depended from some of them. The partitions were hung on runners, presumably so that the space could be changed to suit the current exhibition. Some pictures were suspended directly from bits of the skeletal ironwork. These were moving slightly in draughts coming in through the ill-fitting windows in the roof and walls. Fergus saw a couple of nice watercolours that could do with rescuing from the damp atmosphere and paused for a closer look. Andy went on to the office at the back, leant her portfolio against its chipboard wall and knocked on the window that looked out into the gallery.

A man in his forties came out of the office. Away from the light, which was almost entirely devoted to the pictures, it was a job to see much of him. Fergus fumbled out his glasses.

The usual rituals took place. The chap's voice was a pleasant light baritone. He beamed at Fergus as if they were old friends when they shook hands. It was disconcerting. Had they met before? Fergus was sure not. Almost sure. Just in case he was wrong he beamed back. The effort soon began to pain him.

'I feel as if I know you already.' Dunne continued to radiate bonhomie. His smile seemed to be a permanent fixture. 'Amanda's told me all about you.'

Amanda? Andy let nobody call her that. Fresh alarm bells began to ring in Fergus's mind, cutting across the reflection that Andy herself knew very much less than *all* about him – or so he sincerely hoped.

His face was beginning to feel stiff from the aimless grinning, so he dropped Dunne's hand and his own smile with a muttered pleasantry. The man had clammy hands. In Fergus's experience this was never a good sign – but then, the gallery was so bloody cold and damp it was no wonder. Dunne began to play the host.

'Would you like a drink ... wine OK?'

Fergus saw slight salvation. He always thought better with a glass in his hand.

'Please – red if you have it.'

He hoped he wouldn't have to gulp down vinegar, but he was grateful both for the oiling of his gears and the respite he would have while it was produced. While Dunne went to fetch it Andy took him into the gallery's maze and showed him some sub-Hockney pictures which she said were David's work. She, not surprisingly, raved about them. Fergus found them insipid.

The wine appeared and Fergus made inroads upon it. It wasn't too bad – too cold, of course, but welcome.

'Would you like to see around the gallery?' Dunne asked.

Fergus gestured with his glass.

'Lead on,' he said expansively. With a practiced swoop he succeeded in picking up the bottle, and tucked it into his armpit to warm.

*

There was a lot of stuff. Dunne slid the partitions open and closed as they went through. He called it 'the short cut'. It left Fergus seriously confused and in need of sustenance which, fortunately, he carried with him. Finally they came to a space with three large sculptures in it. All the other areas appeared to open off this one although, after Dunne's re-arrangement, it was hard to tell. The sculptures were arranged beneath a skylight, which had substantial holes in the glass. It was properly cold under the broken glass, and rain was coming in. Fergus recharged his glass once more. Bloody hell. Anything on paper left here for more than a month would be ruined.

Nevertheless, he didn't see any damaged work, and Dunne certainly had an eye. There was a theme – a preference – but there was also variety. The palettes were interesting and some of the charcoal sketches were exceptional.

Finally they arrived back at their starting point, which Fergus would have had difficulty locating without a guide. The place was a maze. He realised he had finished the bottle of wine during the tour. He put the bottle down surreptitiously behind a large vase.

Well, speak as you find.

'Extremely interesting. You've got some nice stuff here. In fact ...'

But as he tried to arrive at a decision between the two watercolours he had liked on the way in and the charcoal sketches he had seen ... somewhere in there, his bladder reminded him that a bottle of wine contains a lot of liquid.

'I need to pee ...?'

'Oh, right – down one flight of stairs, on your left.'

Fergus handed his empty glass to Dunne and went in search. It was as down at heel as the rest of the place; the porcelain was cracked, an Arctic draught blew through it and pools of water lay on the floor. He did not linger.

He returned, shaking his hands to remove the water for which no towel was provided. Andy and Dunne were not where he had left them. He hoped they had gone to the office rather than back into the maze – he didn't fancy trying to hunt them down in there. He changed direction towards the office and was brought up short by the sight of the two of them, nicely framed by the office window, in an enthusiastic clinch. He wrenched the door open and stormed in. The two had the grace to stop what they were doing, but stood with their arms about each other, slightly dishevelled. Fergus became aware that his mouth was hanging open and shut it. He was at a loss. Buggeration.

While he tried to think of something sensible to say, and talk himself out of hitting Dunne, the man with his hands all over Fergus's daughter got in first.

'The thing is that the school insists that I meet at least one of the student's responsible adults when I do my mentoring work each year.'

I'll just bet they do, thought Fergus. The words "gross moral turpitude" hovered in his mind, as he was sure they loomed large in the mind of the Student Welfare Officer at the school. He remembered, uncomfortably, that these words had once been applied to his own relationship with a student. His knuckles had been most firmly rapped. The student had been Andy's mother.

Obviously the Jennie Lee Academy was keen they not be blamed if this oddly personable pest seduced their students. Student welfare would be able to bleat that the parents should have spotted the problem. Well, the parent had absolutely spotted the problem. The question was, what to do about it?

'She's told you that I shan't be making any charge for the sessions? It's just a joy to me to help youngsters with talent.' He gestured fondly towards the top of Andy's head which was resting on his chest. 'There's nothing like some serious "one to one" time to bring out the best in them.'

One to one time! How could he utter the words with a straight face? Fergus felt a splutter coming on. It was all too apparent what the "sessions" were to consist of. Fergus had known from the outset what was going on; he took no pleasure in being proved right. The question was, how to prevent Andy from making a serious mistake.

Finally, and not before time, Andy extricated herself from Dunne's embrace and skipped (yes, skipped!) over to Fergus. He in turn put his arm around her and hugged her fiercely. She twisted in his arm to look up at him.

'Fergus, it's ever such a good chance.'

Fergus took a firmer hold on Andy and tried to think. Something needed to occur to him quickly; something witty and irrevocable that Dunne would understand to be the termination of "extra tuition" as a ploy for furthering this inappropriate relationship with Andy. And which would, moreover, cause the scales to fall from Andy's eyes and revulsion for the man Dunne to set in immediately. The daughter in question started to wriggle under his arm and finally, as his grip continued to tighten, hissed,

'Dad, this is embarrassing.'

Fergus looked down at her, a difficult feat because he now had her pinned under his chin.

Andy began wriggling in earnest and Fergus changed his grip from her waist to her arm. Nothing witty was forming in his mind. He was still in a state of shock.

'Ow! You're hurting.'

Fergus was glad Dunne had offered him wine and not whisky. If he had imbibed a quantity of Scotch, Fergus would not have been the calm, rational being who continued to grip Andy's arm tightly and simply said,

'It's been fascinating, Dunne. Andy and I will talk it over with her mother and let you know what we decide.'

He was outraged. But he was also aware that there was a bit of a pot and kettle thing going on here.

He thought about Bloody Mary, she'd better be impressed when he told her how restrained he had been, how responsible – and she'd better be seriously apologetic about permitting this nonsense to get so far in the first place.

'Bring your portfolio, Andy,' he said, releasing her arm so that she could reach it and deftly catching hold of her other hand as she turned to pick it up.

He stiff-armed her through the door and down the stairs. The place looked even seedier on the way down than it had on the way up. Engrossed in constructing the pithy digest of the debacle and its resolution that he would deliver to Bloody Mary when he got Andy home, it was several seconds before he was aware that his daughter was hissing at him.

'No good, sweetheart, can't hear a word,' he said happily.

The White Knight had come to the rescue this time alright – even Bloody Mary would have to admit that. He looked forward to his forthcoming interview with her; a rarity that.

They reached the street and he bundled the portfolio into the back seat, Andy into the front and got the engine running, the car in gear, the handbrake off and the car moving before she had time to say more than,

'You bastard!'

Now that he had scotched any attempt at some kind of Grand Gesture – like jumping out and running back into the gallery – he had leisure to address the situation. So this was parenthood.

'Andy, love – what do you think that man's motives are for snogging you in his office?'

And the rest of the way back to Bloody Mary's was a tearful tirade about how he didn't understand and hadn't he ever been young, and in love, and how was she ever going to become a famous artist now.

*

It was a long time since Fergus had attempted to gain entry to the terraced house in Lyndhurst Close, Tooting where Andy lived. Her mother was a harsh and bitter woman. Fergus supposed there were good reasons for this and Mary made it clear she blamed him for most of them. He was surprised, when he thought about it, which wasn't very often, that Andy never seemed to notice this aspect of her mother's character. Needs must however and, over Andy's protestations that it would only start a row, he followed her up the ratty little front garden in, clutching her portfolio awkwardly under one arm.

Andy let them in and called out for her mother. Mary was in the living room, with Baywatch undulating on the TV, marking a pile of school work. She shot to her feet when she saw who had come in with Andy and he saw her fists ball. Surely she might have expected a report? He held up his hands in a placatory gesture and was relieved to see the fists unclench. Mary, when provoked, tended to throw things. She was easily provoked and had quite a good aim. He held out the portfolio to Andy and said,

'Why don't you put this away and make us all a cup of tea, eh?'

Fortunately Andy made no fuss, fielded the portfolio and disappeared, shutting the door behind her. A closed door would not help, Fergus knew, if Mary started shouting. She had a tongue which could pierce armoured plate. He wanted to try and forestall this, so he got in first;

'Mary, good to see you. Sorry to burst in unannounced, and all that – but I think we should have a very *quiet* talk about Andy, this private tuition and the bloody man, Dunne...'

'What bloody man, Dunne?'

'Ah.' Light began to filter in. 'Andy didn't mention Dunne and his gallery to you?'

'I've just said so.'

'Ah.'

So Andy had not had her Mother's sanction at all. His beautiful Andy had played him for a patsy. If he hadn't caught the two of them snogging, he might even ... He felt queasy at the thought.

'Why don't we sit down, and I'll tell you where we've been this afternoon.'

Mary was dangerously quiet now. The phrase 'eye of the hurricane' came to mind. However, she sat down on the chair by the TV and turned it off. Fergus perched on the chair furthest from her and proceeded to explain what had happened. He ended with,

'She says I don't understand – and she's bloody right, I mean ... .'

He heard, in his mind, the jangling of pots and kettles again, and couldn't find a way to finish his indignant sentence. He suddenly felt rather miserable.

Mary gave a short bark of laughter as he petered out.

'Well, for once, neither do I. I thought she had a boyfriend at the school. Emphasis on the "boy".'

Even this evidence of incipient adulthood gave him a pang, but he repressed it firmly.

'And this Dunne wants to give her private art lessons?'

'I don't know what she wants – tuition from a professional artist, or sex. I know exactly what he wants.' Fergus leant back in his chair.

'Perhaps it's private lessons *and* sex – sometimes things come together in surprising ways. Do you think Dunne has genuine affection for her?'

Fergus snorted.

'Of course not! Nor any respect for her work. He just wants a piece of tail.'

Mary barked again. Then fell silent for some minutes.

'D'you know,' she said. 'I'm inclined to let the mentoring go ahead.'

'Why?'

He couldn't keep the surprise out of his voice. She rounded on him.

'Where do you think Andy gets her talent from you old fool? You? I've touted my work round galleries in the past and done tuition work as well. Sometimes giving a few lessons made the difference between beans on toast for a month and proper meals. And extra, one-to-one tuition from a pukka, professional artist at this point in her artistic development is not to be sniffed at. Even if he is getting paid in kind. Andy is sensible. She won't let him seduce her. Not completely, anyway.'

Fergus felt sure she was wrong, but dared not say so.

'What are we going to do?'

'What *can* we do, you old goat? Do you want me to lock her in her room? She won't get very good 'A' level grades if she's spending her nights braiding rope out of bedsheets will she? The whole thing will soon peter out – and she may learn some valuable lessons from it. About art *and* about life.'

Fergus couldn't help it, it burst from him.

'But he's old enough to be her father. And he's probably got a wife and two tucked away somewhere.'

Once again Mary barked with laughter. The sound reminded him of a vocal Dobermann Pinscher that had guarded a pub he used to frequent. He began to feel very defensive. As he opened his mouth to try again she said;

'I'm not going to forbid her to see him, Fergus. Think about it. What good – really – would it do? She'd only go on seeing him behind my back. At least if she thinks *I* think it's OK I may be able to get her to talk about him, and then it'll be easier to gauge what sort of trouble she's getting into. The whole thing may blow over in a couple of weeks. They may fall out about the tuition. I doubt she'll stand for much from him if he really isn't interested in teaching her. Or if he turns out not to be very good. She's very serious about her work you know.'

Fergus couldn't help but think that he knew more about how easy it was to seduce young women than Mary did – but he really didn't want to go any further down that path. They had had that conversation on more than one occasion. Fergus could still remember, verbatim, the most colourful of their exchanges on the matter. He had said:

'Nobody railed at Picasso when he took up with Françoise Gilot. She was forty years younger than he was.'

'Well, they probably did. But Picasso took no notice, just like you. And he was such a wonderful painter he could do that. Perhaps.'

'Picasso had no problem, Gilot had no problem. Who, then, had the problem?'

'Everyone else. Gilot's parents. The friends she gave up to be with him. The seminal experiences she never had because you can only have them with other young people. And you aren't the best painter of your generation.'

'Nor was he.'

'Of course he was. All right, who was then?'

He had named several, provocatively, neatly heading off the conversation onto other, less thorny, paths. Nevertheless it haunted him. Occasionally.

The subject of young girls and older men was a deep pit – he could see it yawning blackly at him, as it had before. He had always felt his passion for young girls to be a charming foible in himself. Now that he was confronted with it in connection with his daughter it didn't seem so charming. The conversation didn't restart.

Almost at once the living room door opened and Andy came in with a pot of tea. The little minx had obviously been listening. The tea would probably be stewed.

'It's Earl Grey. Do you want milk or lemon?

Andy obviously knew where the conversation had got to. They went over a shortened version of it while Andy poured the tea. Andy was obviously delighted.

'Mind,' said Fergus, 'I am not going to that bloody gallery again. I'll probably lose all control and ... buy something next time.'

They all laughed but there was nothing funny about it really, Fergus reflected as he went out into the rainy evening and into the Jaguar. He knew he would relent – she really couldn't lug her portfolio all the way to Dunne's on the Tube and Mary didn't run a car. He'd stay outside in the Jag, he wouldn't make a scene.

Shit. What a mess.

*

On the way home Fergus felt restless, unsettled. A lot of unused adrenalin was moving around inside him. The night was ridiculously young. He was due to pick up Sukie later for some dinner after which he was going to introduce her to the delights of Puccini, some clean silk sheets and a pair of fluffy bathrobes (his and hers) freshly laundered for the purpose. Somehow he didn't now look forward to the delights in store. He dropped in to The World's End on his way home to try and cheer himself up but the rain had taken its toll. The early evening crowd was as morose as he was himself. The cheery fire in the grate was not taking the chilly damp out of the air. Raincoats steamed, brollies dripped and Fergus's iffy cartilage began to ache. No consolation there.

The excellent pint of real ale he consumed lay uneasily on top of the red wine he had consumed at the gallery. He returned to the Jag and guided it through three narrow streets to his block of flats all of four hundred yards away, where he garaged it in the underground car park. As he walked up the two flights of stairs to his apartment he realised he would have to make his apologies to Sukie, he just wasn't in the mood. As he telephoned her he looked through the window at the darkening common, rain now sweeping across it in sheets. He shivered. Having made his excuses he went and turned on the gas fire for the cheeriness of its artificial flames, then pulled the drapes. Turning, he saw the flickering fire in the twilit room and thought how small a distance man had moved away from the cave. He shook himself physically, shaking out the damp and the thought both.

He could have the Puccini anyway. Soon *Madame Butterfly* soared through the flat as he cooked himself an omelette and let a fresh bottle of Burgundy breathe. He thought about Giacomo Puccini's predilection for writing about young girls abandoned. Such glorious music. All these years he had adored Puccini – and what was it really about? Youth lured, spoiled and abandoned.

Andy was in danger. All her life was there waiting for her to grab it, so what in the name of the Sweet Creeping Christ was she playing at, messing about with a confidence trickster like Dunne? Sure, he was charming, but the stench of dishonesty hung about that man like rotten offal.

In the end he took a turn on the rainswept common to clear his head. The walk helped somewhat, although it made his knee ache worse than ever. On his return he poured a last glass of the Burgundy and switched on the TV just in time to catch the National Anthem. It was about time for Ariel's television lectures to be on. And there was the distinctive jingle with which Ariel's nightly offerings always commenced. After something complicated about mathematical torus, Fergus himself was on, talking about classical Greece. He settled down to watch and his mood began finally to lift. Christ, he was good! The argument was so accessible, the development of democracy in those ancient days related so pertinently to the twentieth century, the comparisons illustrated for the students using primary sources discovered through original research. He remembered that jacket – green with a red stripe just on the right side of vulgar. He looked good too – it wasn't true that TV made you look half a stone heavier. As the credits rolled he raised his glass to himself and, picking up the bottle, wandered off to his clean sheets. What the hell had made him cancel his date with Sukie? Perhaps it wasn't too late to ring her? Shit, it was gone one o'clock. Oh well, he'd call her tomorrow.

Sunday 6 December

The next morning he had barely finished breakfast when Andy rang. She sounded contrite – but she probably only wanted to make sure he really would drive her to the bloody gallery.

'Hi, Fergus, didn't get you out of bed did I?'

He growled – she would have been surprised if he hadn't. She knew that he was usually up and about hours before she was. So what was she doing up at this hour on a Sunday?

'Katie and I are going to the National to draw the Da Vinci cartoon. Do you want to come?'

He'd done a good job on this girl, he thought. Not only did she want to go to a museum on a Sunday, but knew exactly what she wanted to see when she got there. And Katie would be there too. Marvellous!

'Yes. Love to come. I'll pick you up.'

'No, don't bother – we'll get a Tube. It's miles out of your way. We'll meet you in the upstairs bar at The Chandos. Eleven all right?'

'See you there.'

*

Fergus made it a rule never to take public transport in London – or, indeed, anywhere else. It was a matter of pride with him that he could insinuate the XJS into the most emaciated metered space, up any tiny cobbled alleyway, through any gridlock. Nevertheless he arrived late for his appointment with Andy and Katie. The parking had been a breeze compared to the gridlock caused by some bloody fool wrapping an under-powered tin can round a Keep Left bollard on his route. The intersection was still crawling with ambulances and police cars as he crept past the scene of the accident, having been held up for over half an hour. How many ambulances did it take to get one arsehole to hospital for Christ's Sake?

So he was a bit hot and bothered when he hurried from his meter into The Chandos. He quickly spotted Andy, who saw him come in and waved. Then he noticed that there was a third person on the chesterfield with them. A fleeting thought that it might be that bloody Dunne, and that if it was he was going to explode, was pushed out by the realisation that the third person was female. Not Katie – he recognised her wonderful mane of hair on the left; sitting beside Katie, hair short, lots of lipstick, bright scarf round the neck – oh God, it wasn't her bloody mother was it?

It was. Andy introduced them and Fergus made polite, out of breath, noises while thinking blood-curdling thoughts. Why had she come, for Christ's Sake? What sort of a morning could they possibly have with Katie's mother in tow? While his mind raced he missed most of what Andy was saying. The last part of it, however, gave him hope that matters were not as dire as he had feared.

' ... to look around the Tudor galleries.'

'I'm sorry, what did you say?'

'Oh, Fergus, haven't you been listening? I said Mrs Crouch has come with us 'cos her drama group is putting on Schiller's *Mary Stuart* next year, and she's doing the costumes, so she wants to have a look at the Tudor portraits to get some ideas. Let's get you a cup of coffee, you look awful.'

She went to the bar. Fergus wondered what looked so awful. He made his excuses and went to the lavatory to check. He'd looked better. He was very red in the face, and his hair was awry. He made repairs and straightened his bow tie. He took a couple of deep, calming breaths. Then he strolled back to the table. The spare place was beside Andy and opposite Mrs Crouch, so he got a good look at her. She was leaning forward expectantly,

'I've heard so much about you from Andy, Dr Girvan ...'

Holy Hell. He found a smile and attached it to his face.

'Fergus, please.'

'Fergus ...'

She wasn't badly presented he decided, as she wittered on. She had on a smart skirt and jumper that weren't out of the top drawer but weren't from a chain. The jumper was a plummy colour and was good with her colouring – although he doubted that her blonde hair was what she'd been born with. Looked like she spent a lot at the hairdressers. The scarf was flashy but not unpleasant. The jewellery was all costume and not too much of it. Quite nice, if only she'd stop talking.

She'd been gushing all the time he'd been appraising and he realised he'd missed salient facts again. Could he get her to back track without seeming a complete dodderer? He'd work the absent-minded professor routine.

'I'm so sorry, Mrs Crouch – I was momentarily distracted. Could you perhaps repeat ...?'

'Janet, please. Of course, Fergus.'

Yes, she was a Janet all right. Just the sort who would call a daughter Katie and not – well, Tosca or Melisande or anything with a spark of romance to it. Although her options *were* limited with a surname like Crouch to work with (Tosca Crouch? He shuddered inwardly). He assumed she'd been insensitive enough to marry the name. He wondered as to the whereabouts of its original owner.

He smiled encouragingly.

'... I was just saying that I spend my week in a stuffy old office poring over files. I would so love to be more involved in the Arts. Your institution now – those wonderful courses ... so enabling.'

'Mummy's a solicitor,' Katie put in.

Fergus felt a cold hand squeeze his heart.

It was time to make a move. Fergus herded them all out of The Chandos and across the road to the museum. At the entrance there was a lengthy weekend queue to get in because of the usual fuss with bags (the bloody IRA was just so *inconvenient*). While Janet unpacked hers Fergus hissed in Andy's ear that she could forget any idea of going round Tudor portraits with Janet. They'd come to see the cartoon. And when they finished there he had identified several other exhibits that he wanted to show the girls, to would inform their study of it. There was no place for Janet Crouch in his plans.

'Actually, Katie and me decided to come today. *We* invited *you* along 'cos you're *usually* good fun in museums. Katie's mum was a last-minute addition. Don't you like her, then?'

'She's dreadful!'

'She's very nice!'

'She's a solicitor!'

'So?'

They shuffled along in the queue for the cloakroom as Fergus racked his brains for a reasonable explanation.

'I'm not good with authority figures – you know that.'

'You might be glad to know her one day, the way you drive ...' Andy laughed. Fergus scowled.

However, the problem quickly resolved itself when Janet Crouch got a notepad and a book on stage costumes out of her cavernous bag and departed in the direction of the Tudors, saying that she'd catch them up in the tea-room.

Fergus felt himself begin to expand to fill his beloved role of expert and led the way to the cartoon. Properly speaking it wasn't his area, but he had always loved art, ever since he had pored over a juvenile stamp collection when he was a child on the Red Clyde and it was all he could afford of beauty.

*

There was already a crowd of students in the semi-dark cubby hole which housed the cartoon, all copying the drawing. Fergus gave of his wisdom on it freely while the girls sketched it (with commendable skill, he was pleased to see). When he had finished his exposition – which, in his usual fashion, filled the little room – he received applause from those present, muted by the hessian walls and carpeted floor. It gave him a little glow none the less.

They spent a very pleasant afternoon flitting about the gallery to take in Da Vinci's *Virgin of the Rocks*, works by Verrocchio (who taught Da Vinci), some of his lesser known contemporaries such as Domenico Ghirlandaio and Alesso Baldovinetti, and finally one of Da Vinci's best known contemporaries, Sandro Botticelli and his pupil Filippino Lippi. By the time the whistle-stop lecture tour ended Katie was as impressed with him as her mother had seemed earlier. Fergus continued to glow.

They had afternoon tea in the overheated café. The tea and cakes were most welcome. The inevitable party of middle-aged American women were discussing their visit, very loudly, several tables away. They had, apparently, seen nothing in the museum which was of any interest to them. Chittering sparrows. Speaking of which, he noted with pleasure that Janet Crouch had not yet caught up with them.

Fergus finished his Earl Grey, which he'd taken black as there was no bloody lemon available and the little pots of milk-substitute always spat at him when he tried to open them. He was contemplating taking the girls home when there was a 'cooee' from across the room. Fergus's mood drooped. It was either a late arrival for the American table or Janet Crouch. It was Janet.

'I hoped you might still be here. I'm sorry to have been so long. I completely lost track of time. I find one does, don't you? So stimulating ...'

Fergus became aware of sketches being viewed and compliments being exchanged as he realised he would now have to take the mother home as well. It was not often that Fergus regretted his car in London. Today had just become one of those rare occasions.

'Well,' he said, rising, 'I really ought to make a move. I've some work to do. May I offer you ladies a lift?'

'Oh, thank you. I think we said we were going to round the afternoon off with Madame Tussaud's, yes girls? Can we interest you in that, Fergus?'

No bloody fear.

'I'm afraid not. But I could drop you there?'

'Oh, how kind. Come along you two. Mustn't keep Fergus from important things, running us girls around.'

Something suddenly became clear to Fergus: Janet Crouch was flirting with him! A sharp exit was called for. Things were getting far too complicated.

*

Back at the car he installed Andy in the front seat by claiming she got carsick in the back. Andy gave him a look. She was never carsick.

Katie slipped into what passed for the back of the XJS with no difficulty, but her mother needed assistance to alight successfully on the narrow bench seat. Fergus left that strictly to the girls. No way was he going to lay a hand on Janet Crouch. Particularly her rear end.

There was a lot of giggling before she was finally installed and her seat belt fastened.

He got a kick out of driving them, nevertheless. The Jag was looking particularly well at present having been recently valeted. Katie was suitably impressed, he could see in the rear-view mirror. But it was Janet who said,

'There's nothing quite like the smell of leather upholstery, is there Fergus?' A sigh tickled the back of his neck. 'Takes me back to lovers' lanes, long ago.'

She'd had expensive tastes in boyfriends, then. Twenty five years ago leather upholstery was expensive. Unless ...

'It was his father's car, of course. But we had such times in it.' Another sigh. 'Steamed-up windows, and the seat buttons sticking into ...'

Fortunately at that moment they arrived. Fergus drew up on double yellow lines, and clicked on the hazard lights. He kissed Andy quickly and began to encourage them out of the car 'before I get a ticket' so as not to have to listen to any more about Janet's youthful love life. Katie pushed and Andy pulled, Janet popped softly out of the back seat, and they were gone.

He'd call Andy later. They still had that business with the gallery to sort out. He'd have a word with her mother first. Make certain what it was that they'd agreed. For once it would be as well to be in harmony. Dunne, he was certain, was a wrong 'un.

Monday 7 December

Fergus always enjoyed the fifty mile drive up the M1 to the university. For one thing he valued the division which it made between the two halves of his life. For another, he enjoyed driving his Jag: the enthusiasm of its engine when he touched his foot to the accelerator; the way it looked cruising up the motorway, its V registration going before it, giving two fingers to the world; the beauty of its design; its British Racing Green paintwork continuing a proud tradition, glowing among the dowdy mass production colours. Not much passed him of a morning; he was going against the flow of traffic and the road was usually fairly benign. He always gave himself completely to the drive. It set his mood for the day. This, he understood, was a hostage to fortune; sometimes roadworks caused vehicular thromboses, the motorway was stop-go all the way and he arrived feeling irritable. But usually he arrived feeling alive, ready for anything.

That he enjoyed his commute was just as well, for the prospect of living in the new town, in which the government had decided to build Ariel University, had filled him with dismay when he had gone for his interview there. They had driven him round, full of pride in the twin projects – new town: new university. There had been nothing to see but a flat expanse of fields and muddy construction sites interspersed with estates of low rise buildings, shrubberies and roundabouts. It was like a small, cold, LA. It didn't seem to have any culture, decent pubs, nice places to eat, bookshops, museums, nor any sense of community. And, worst of all, the university, which taught its students at a distance, had – ipso facto – no totty. Fergus had known at once that he could never live in such a place.

The bleakness of the new town had been too like the bleakness of Glasgow, his childhood home. True, his childhood home had been high rise where this was like a pancake, and the overriding colour there had been grey, whereas the university was surrounded by a sea of featureless green and brown. He was glad it flourished, but he had never entered it. As far as he was concerned the only road into or out of Ariel was the one leading to its junction with the M1. They had said he could live anywhere within fifty miles, and London just got in under the wire. Many of his colleagues lived there too. Occasionally they would travel up together. Fergus never enjoyed the journey, even if he was driving. Somehow having company impinged on an important, private, time. He couldn't explain it. Many might say that a voluntary commute consisting of a hundred mile round trip each day was madness. There was, after all, a perfectly satisfactory rail service. Fergus knew that the day he agreed with them was the day he would resign his post at Ariel. So far it continued to work its magic.

This morning his brain fizzed with the events of the weekend. He was still worried about Andy and her new relationship with the man Dunne. Nor did he like the resonances with his own life. Girls were delicate, wondrous, creatures and he had always treated them as such. He suspected that after Dunne had lavished attention and admiration on Andy something much less savoury would start. Thank God Andy had no money – that might save her from the worst of it. But that she would be bitterly hurt by the end of the relationship he was certain. He drove faster and agonised deeply as he tried to come up with a plan to save his daughter from herself.

*

When he got to the university he phoned Bloody Mary at her school. Both she and the school frowned on this practice, but he wanted them to be able to provide a united front on this. And Andy was very good at divide and rule.

'What exactly did we agree in the end about this shit, Dunne?'

'We agreed that Dunne giving Andy extra art tuition seemed like a perfectly straightforward business arrangement and that I will sign the waiver clause the school requires so that she may take advantage of Dr Dunne's kind offer. You said that under no circumstances were you going anywhere near his gallery again. We agreed that the necking session you witnessed made the whole thing rather unsavoury, but that censure would do more harm than good.'

'Hmm. I'm not sure we agreed all that. And it's not her that'll be taking advantage.'

'Fergus, don't start. I'm teaching in five minutes. I suppose you're ringing to ask me what you should do when you drive her over there with her portfolio?'

Fergus said nothing.

'I think you should go in with her. If there *is* something "going on" you being there will let him know she's carefully chaperoned.'

'Too late for that I should think. That snog obviously wasn't their first.'

'You would know ...'

'... so he must be aware that she has plenty of freedom of movement. Can't you make her curfew earlier? Insist that if she goes out she's with a girlfriend?'

'Fergus ...' there was a warning in her tone and he didn't pursue it.

'OK. I'll go in.'

'Don't make it sound like some kind of guerrilla raid.'

'I'll try,' he said. 'But I'll probably buy at least one of those bloody watercolours.'

'Nice to know you're a man whose principles never get in the way of his desires,' Mary said waspishly. Fergus let it go.

'Do you know when she's intending to take her portfolio over there?'

'After school today I think. She's worried he may change his mind.'

'Not until he's had his hand up her skirt, at least.'

'And, once again, you would know ...'

'Should I pick her up after school then?'

'That would seem to be a good plan.' Mary was now using her I'm *Really* Running Out Of Patience Voice. Time to go.

*

Fergus almost never got any work done on his days at the faculty. Work was what you did at home, with something soothing on the stereo. 'Meetings, Bloody Meetings' (as John Cleese so aptly put it) were what you came in to work for. Fergus had long ago ceased to roar at the constant opening of his door (often without so much as a knock), the ceaseless tocsin of the telephone, the 'quick word' in his ear sought every time he ventured out of his office.

Even the urinal wasn't sacrosanct. He remembered a particularly bizarre episode during a Deanship election contest some years earlier when Howard Llewellyn, who was standing for Dean, had kept him pinned against the hand driers in the Gents for an eternity soliciting his support, whilst Edith Sutter, also a candidate, had been forced (by her inability to enter the gentlemen's sanctorum) to hang around outside waiting for him to emerge. By the time Llewellyn had released him and Fergus had emerged she had been apoplectic with fury. And with *him*, not Llewellyn! Very trying.

This Thursday was much like any other as far as the level of interruption went, but there was a different kind of intensity about it. It was in the Gents, once again, that Fergus realised the reason for the tension. He was by no means the only academic who felt undervalued and passed over. Thatcher's cuts meant that people had been butting their heads against a glass ceiling for two or three years now. The nomination period for promotion submissions had opened that day. His memory of the date was jogged when he noticed the conversation around the urinals die when he entered the sanctorum. They were obviously talking about him. Did they think he would get his Chair, or wouldn't? Who else had been nominated? By whom? What did they know that he didn't?

He would get Nick to find out what was going on. It was the least Nick could do after Fergus had fixed his trip for him.

On his way back to his office he saw that the notice of the Deanship elections had been posted beside the call for promotion proposals. Sure enough Petra's name was already up; nominated by Patrick, seconded by Nick. She was the outgoing Dean's choice then. Not a surprise.

The name of her seconder was. He hoped Nick knew what he was getting into with Petra. And he hoped he could find some way of making use of Nick's new allegiance himself.

*

Fergus parked outside Andy's school in good time for the day's final outpouring. As Tosca sobbed tunefully over the Jaguar's sound system he reflected that lurking outside places of education like this was liable to get a man an undeserved reputation. He found he was keeping an eye out for passing police cars. Ridiculous. This was what happened when you became a parent late in life. Late in the child's life that was.

At last Andy and Katie wandered across the yard towards him. They looked like peaceful leaves moving through a torrent. Unaware they were observed, they were completely absorbed as they walked towards him; heads close together, willowy, graceful, their long hair caught by the thin December wind. Even wearing the ridiculous fashions girls espoused these days, which were apparently designed to make everyone look like a yob (clumpy shoes, baggy tattered jeans, jackets far too big for them and huge black bags on long straps slapping at their backsides), they still had a pure beauty.

He sighed and beeped the horn.

They ran over to the car when they saw him, smiling broadly. It was good to be wanted, he thought, very good indeed, as he smiled back at the two young faces framed in his window.

'Fergus! Nice! What's the plan?'

He tried to keep his reply nonchalant.

'I thought you might like a lift over to the gallery, get this business with the pictures sorted out.'

'Fergus, you're sweet! Come on Katie, get in. We'll drop you on the way.' She stopped, struck by a thought. 'Unless you'd like to come? You could meet him. He's ... uh ... nice.'

What had she been going to say? How much did Katie know about this? Could a quiet tête à tête with Katie be worthwhile, to see what she knew?

They got into the car, Andy in the front as usual. Katie hefted her bag into the back seat with difficulty. She looked strained Fergus noted, from what he could see of her in the rear-view mirror.

'I've got a pile of work,' she said with a sigh. 'I'd better give it a miss.'

'We'll have to go home and get my portfolio.'

'No problem.'

They went to Katie's home first. Fergus got out with her and carried her bag up to the door. It was as heavy as it looked. The girl would destroy her back lugging all this around. Surely she wasn't going to need all this stuff tonight? While she got the door unlocked he said,

'What the Hell have you got in here? Do they print school books on lead now?'

His sally gained him only a wan smile. He said,

'I wonder if we could have a quiet word sometime? Fairly soon. There's something I want to ask you.'

She gave him a look from under her hair.

'About Mum?'

'No, actually. About Andy.'

'Oh.'

She got the door open and stood in the doorway, obviously uncertain.

'There's nothing to worry about.'

Still she hesitated.

'What *about* Andy?'

'I'd really rather not go into it here. Say tonight? I could pick you up and we could go for a drink.' She took a step over the threshold. 'Anywhere local here, that you're comfortable with.'

From inside came Janet's voice,

'Katie darling? What are you doing? There's a terrible draught.'

'It's alright Mum, it's Dr Girvan. He's given me a lift home.'

Damn! Katie's recent assumption that he might want to ask her about Mother Crouch confirmed his suspicion that the mother found him more attractive than the daughter did. And the mother was a solicitor: somehow he couldn't get past that.

Sure enough Janet Crouch appeared immediately.

'Fergus! How lovely.'

Not always *quite* so wonderful to be wanted ...

'Won't you come in?'

46

Fergus assayed a smile.

'Not just now, er ... Janet, thank you. I've got Andy in the car and we've got to ... er, go home for ... something.'

Christ, he was completely inarticulate! This was what Andy's misdemeanour had led him to. He couldn't even construct a simple sentence of excuse without gibbering. Fergus Girvan did not gibber! This Dunne business had to be sorted out.

He began to back down the path, smiling and waving deprecatingly. Damn it, he hadn't managed to set anything up with Katie. Now, if he wanted to pursue it, he would have to telephone – and that would almost certainly mean another brush with Janet. And require a cast iron reason for him taking her daughter out to a pub on a week night.

He gave a final wave as he reached the gate, shut it firmly and hurried to the car. Inside he found Andy giggling.

'She's really got the hots for you, Fergus.'

'I know. Bloody woman.'

'She's really very nice.'

'You said that before.'

'Divorced.'

'No surprise there.'

'Oh, Fergus! That's just unkind.'

'What time do you want to be at the gallery?' Sadly, the change of subject simply lifted the conversation from one can of worms and dropped in into another: Dunne.

'David said to be there by half past five, but we'll not make that now. I'll call him and tell him we'll be later. I'll do it when we get to my place.'

Fergus suggested, slyly,

'Why don't you use the Crouch's phone?'

There was a calculating silence. Eventually,

'No. I don't want Mrs Crouch listening in. She ... wouldn't approve.'

'She being a very nice solicitor and all ... Do you think your mother and I do?'

Andy turned her most dazzling, big-eyed smile on him.

'No. But you do understand the importance of art. And how important it is to me. You both understand that.'

Which was, unfortunately, true. Without any real hope of wriggling out of the bloody tryst, Fergus tried one last time to put off the evil event,

'Won't Dunne be wanting to shut up shop?'

'Oh, he'll wait for me.'

Fergus could see the scenario all too clearly in his mind's eye. Transact the business, get rid of the father and get the girl on her own. Wine and dine her, offer to show her his etchings (he probably actually had some), get her to phone her mother saying she was staying over somewhere (Katie's probably) and pop goes Andy's cherry.

Well, all that seduction would have to wait for another day, because on this occasion he was going to stick to his daughter like the most tenacious old barnacle ever stuck to a particularly pretty, brand new, dinghy.

'Come on then,' he said, starting the car's engine, 'let's get this over with.'

'You don't have to come, you know.'

'Yes. I do. By the way, can you let me have the Crouches' phone number?'

'Oh Fergus – are you going to phone Mrs Crouch?'

The answer exploded from him before he had a chance to think about it.

'No!'

'You're not after Katie are you? Fergus, that's disgusting, she's my friend!'

'I don't know why her being your friend should make it disgusting.'

'You are!'

Fergus found himself in retreat. Bloody Mary had never painted him in a kindly light to their child. The woman took particular delight in dissing his relationships with younger women.

'I'm not 'after' Katie as you put it, I'm just ...'

'Oh God, you're going to pump her about David aren't you? That's even worse!'

Andy knew him very well indeed, especially considering how little time she'd known him. Fergus shut up. Andy didn't. He cast an eye at the house number as they moved away and noted the street name as they turned out of the road. Andy meanwhile gave him a lengthy justification of the awful Dunne, segueing into how adults never understood and finishing with how she had expected better of him.

If they weren't ex-directory he was alright.

*

Mary wasn't back when they got to the house. Fergus was glad. His normal relationship with Mary consisted of her giving him a hard time, and he felt he was currently getting a hard enough time already from

Andy.

Andy telephoned to re-arrange the time of her meeting with Dunne, picked up her portfolio and joined him in the lounge. Her face was set and she looked rather pale. She didn't seem so pleased about him coming with her now.

'I sort of wish you wouldn't come,' she said.

'I promised your mother.'

'You're usually pretty selective about keeping promises. You could break this one to please me.'

'To please me, let me keep it. I promise I won't hit him.'

'Promises, promises ...'

This made him laugh. What pleasure to laugh at word play with your daughter. It was always a pleasure to laugh with Andy and he didn't hold it in. Fortunately it was contagious. They set off in much better spirits.

The gallery, when they reached it, looked no more inviting than it had on the previous occasion. It had gone dark as they drove across London. The alley was, once again, deserted. Some bits of litter were blowing about. No lights showed. Fergus was glad he'd insisted on coming. This was no place for a girl on her own.

Andy, however, seemed to have no qualms at all.

The downstairs door was locked, but Andy knew where Dunne kept a key (behind a loose brick beside the door). Fergus was even less happy at this latest evidence of intimacy between Dunne and his daughter than he was about the dilapidation of the building.

They went up, turning lights on as they went. The results of their efforts were that sickly puddles of dim light appeared on the landings and left the stairs treacherous. Andy called out a greeting when they got to the top floor. There were no lights on here either.

'The bugger's gone home.'

'Oh no, he'll be around somewhere.'

'Did you tell him I was coming?'

'No, actually; it didn't come up.'

It was the first time he had heard a note of uncertainty in her voice when she spoke about Dunne. He hoped she found it bloody peculiar that a man would ask a young woman – a very young woman – round to a business appointment in a dark, deserted gallery in a dubious part of London. An armouring of healthy suspicion was no bad thing for a girl to acquire. Fergus was beginning to fume – but inwardly. He'd save the fireworks for when Dunne turned up. If he turned up.

'Come on then. Let's find the light switch and get to the office. He might have left you a message I suppose.'

They groped around like a couple of Marcel Marceaux until they found illumination. But it was the picture lights they found, rather than the ones which would have lit their way to the office. The spotlights, pointing nowhere helpful, gave the place an even eerier feel than it had had in semi-darkness, as though ghosts were hanging from the walls. In a sense, Fergus supposed, they were. He told himself firmly that this was no time to start considering the spirit(s) within art. Christ, he needed a drink.

The office wasn't locked – which might indicate that the idiot wasn't far away. There was nothing helpful on the door, like a notice saying 'back in five minutes' or 'sorry, called away'. Damn. Fergus looked on the desk. It looked a lot tidier than it had done the last time he had been in here he thought – almost bare. He tried the drawers. In one there was a cash tin, unlocked and empty. Fergus began to have a suspicion, which lightened his heart considerably.

Did you actually speak to him, Andy, when you phoned?'

'No. I left a message on the machine. I thought he'd just gone to the loo or something. I mean, it was nearly five thirty then, and he was expecting me ...'

She trailed off. The answer machine was on the desk. It showed two messages waiting. Fergus pressed play.

'Dad! That's the same as eavesdropping.'

'Well? I don't recall you saying anything embarrassing last time I heard this conversation.'

'But it might not be my message.'

It wasn't. It really was eavesdropping, and extremely interesting. It was a long message and hadn't been playing long before its burden caused Fergus to search about for some confirmation. It wasn't hard to find. On the desk was a neat pile of final demands. All the utilities were there, as were invoices from journals and magazines which had carried advertising for Dunne. There were also invoices (and some angry letters) from the artists whose work hung on the walls in the gallery. Many were unopened.

The man was flat broke.

On a hunch Fergus wandered out into the gallery, picking his way gingerly among the partitions. Sure enough, on the far side of the big sculpture area was a 'room' that was completely bare. Andy had followed him. He said:

'I don't think he's sold all these since yesterday, do you?'

'Perhaps someone's stolen them. Oh! On top of all his other bad luck!'

Did she really still not get it?

50

'It's more likely that he's taken them to sell to another gallery. Or that the artist has repossessed them. Pity, I think this room had those nice watercolours that I liked.'

'Oh, Fergus! What a selfish ...'

'Not at all,' he said coldly. 'Against my better judgement, I could have helped him with his cashflow problem if they, and he, were still here.'

She brightened momentarily.

'Do you think that's what it is? A cashflow problem?'

'No, love. He's as close to bankrupt as makes no difference.'

'How do you know, just from those few bills?'

'I know.'

But he also knew that, even with the evidence that now surrounded them, she wasn't convinced. As his business was failing, Dunne's motives for mentoring a new artist had to be spectacularly suspect. She still couldn't see it. Kids, particularly female offspring with a crush, still made little sense to him.

And, actually, Fergus wasn't sure he saw the sense of it himself. It wasn't as if Andy had any money she could be parted from to tide the man over. He sighed. He had a nasty feeling this wasn't the end of it.

Fergus was suddenly very conscious that they were the only people on the top floor of a deserted warehouse (where they had no demonstrable business to be) in one of the less salubrious parts of London.

'I think we should go,' Fergus said.

Andy didn't argue. In fact she was very quiet.

'We'll drop the latch on the way out. Does he have an alarm?'

'I don't know.'

'Well, we can lock up, anyway.'

They went back down turning the lights off as they went. The stairs were not straightforward to negotiate in the dark while manoeuvring Andy's portfolio. They were both out of breath when they got back to the entrance, dropped the catch on the Chubb lock, shoved the key back behind the brick and returned to the car.

Fergus hadn't even got the car door open before Andy said,

'There's a pub on the corner.'

'Thank God. I could do with a drink.'

'He might be there.'

Fergus's hopes for an end to this increasingly bizarre affair were dashed. She had been stood up and, like many a one before her, it just made her keener. Damn and blast. But a drink was a drink.

'Which corner?'

Dunne wasn't in the pub. Although Andy had been right about it being his local, the barman confirmed it. Fergus winced inwardly at the thought that she had probably been here with Dunne, gazing doe-eyed at the bloody man over half a bitter. Fergus wished she was looking a bit happier over the half a bitter *he* had bought her. His own pint was exceedingly welcome and he downed half of it in short order. Andy said,

'Something must have happened to him.'

The spooky gallery they had just left had an aura of desertion about it which Fergus's intuition told him not to ignore. He was pretty certain Dunne had done a flit. He tried to avoid smiling about that by sticking his face back into his pint.

'Don't you think so?'

Fergus shrugged, which was not the response Andy wanted from him. They sat in silence for a while after that.

The beer was good, and Fergus had a second pint. It was a rather dreary, plasticky sort of pub. No character. Of course, nobody lived round here, so it was a pub that had no true locals. And it probably closed around seven in the evening. People popping in on their way home, or even at lunchtime, do not a local make. Nevertheless – or perhaps because of this – the landlord kept his beer well.

Fergus realised that his musings on drink, whilst not unusual or without value, were simply an attempt to avoid dealing with what should be done next. There was little option, actually. He would have to take Andy home. She wasn't going to like that. But they couldn't sit here all night in suspended animation waiting for someone who wasn't going to show up.

Unlike Andy, Fergus liked the expedition's outcome very much. But the same intuition which told him Dunne had done a runner insisted that a line had not yet been drawn under the Dunne episode. Something more was going to happen, and he wanted it to happen now. He was in the mood for it now. He had time to deal with it now. He was ready for it now, but it wasn't going to happen now. He was concerned that when it did occur it would find him gone past his current peak of readiness. This worried him. Not least because his intuition murmured that this was how Dunne had arranged matters.

Andy looked miserable. Whether this was because her dreams had been shattered, or because she was worried about the bastard Dunne, Fergus didn't know, and didn't feel inclined to ask. An enquiry might provoke another paean of praise to the man. At that point he would probably lose his temper, which would make things much worse. They were pretty bad already.

Fergus's second pint was finished. Andy was making heavy work of her first half. He felt so sorry for her.

'Want something to eat, kid?'

'No, Dad. I'm not hungry. Thanks anyway.'

That was the second time today she'd called him Dad. She knew he hated it and only called him that to tease, or when she didn't know she'd done it, like her two slip-ups today. After all, he was the only dad she had. Perhaps he hadn't been a very satisfactory one this past week.

They were a silent pair on the way home. Unloading the portfolio when they got there seemed like the most awful anti-climax. He carried the awkward thing up to the house for her, hoping – unusually for him – that Mary would be home. (It was getting to be an unusual day all round.)

Mary was in. Andy took the portfolio from Fergus without a word and began to lug it up the stairs to her room. Fergus manoeuvred Mary into the lounge and shut the door.

'He wasn't there. I think he's done a bunk. Some of the stock was gone, and a pile of final demands was on the desk.'

'Hello, Fergus, nice to see you too.'

'This is important, Mary. She'll be down again in a minute and you know how she eavesdrops. I don't think Andy believes he's gone. She thinks something's happened to him. But she didn't go through the office like I did. She doesn't know the signs.'

'And you do, Sherlock?'

'And there was this message on the answering machine, from a firm of solicitors I think. The chap said he'd left messages at all Dunne's haunts – his home as well – and that if a settlement wasn't made within seven days then "further action would be taken".'

Mary was silent for a moment. Then she said,

'Do you think that's the end of it, then?'

'I don't think so. I've just got this bad feeling ...'

'Well, there's nothing we can do, except wait and see, is there? Did you feed her, while you were out?'

'No. She said she wasn't hungry.'

'Poor kid.'

Conversation petered out, as it had with Andy in the pub. Fergus started to go. As he got to the front door Mary did something that unnerved him more than the rest of the events of the evening put together. She put her hand on his shoulder.

'Thanks, Fergus.' she said. 'You're quite a good dad when you put your mind to it.'

53

Fergus grunted and fled.

*

Fergus felt restless when he got home. It wasn't late, and he hadn't eaten. Adrenalin had been coursing round his body all evening, but had found no outlet. He paced and pondered. He needed company, a nice supper in a little trattoria with a bottle or two of Chianti and some company to share it with. He had just stretched out his hand to the phone to call Sukie when it rang.

It was Janet Crouch – the last person on his mind. However, now he would be able to acquire the Crouches' home phone number quite legitimately and, as a friend of the family be able to ring Katie. But what could Mother Crouch possibly be calling about?

Uh-oh. Would Fergus come to dinner, a small gathering, a few of her more interesting friends.

Thinking on his feet, Fergus reasoned that if he accepted he could easily manufacture an opportunity during the evening to ask Katie what she knew about the bastard Dunne's relationship with Andy.

Dinner with La Crouch's 'interesting friends' was, however, likely to be a high price to pay.

As one who had been fortunate enough (he recognised this) to live his adult life doing almost nothing that he did not like to do, he wouldn't normally have accepted this invitation, not even for the opportunity to be alone with Katie for a few minutes. Nevertheless, these were not normal times, so he put enthusiasm into his voice and accepted for the coming Friday evening. If he kept his ulterior motives clearly in his mind's eye it might not be so bad. He reflected on the anodyne semi where he had dropped Katie earlier and wondered just how dismal the 'interesting friends' were likely to be. He could feel a touch of The Old Complaint coming on already. La Crouch might think she was being artful, but she was dealing with a master here.

'It's fortunate you phoned Janet. I needed a word with Katie anyway.'

'Oh?'

'Yes. She and Andy ... ah ... they're doing a project and they asked me ... you know ... if I could help them with some sources. That's right. So I need to know from Katie what exactly the ... uh ... the thrust of her enquiry is going to be. I thought I might be able to help her sort out a good approach most easily if we could get together for an hour or so.'

Fergus was embarrassed, again, to discover that he was still having trouble articulating falsehoods to this woman. It was Janet being a solicitor that did it. He kept feeling he was under oath.

'Oh how very kind of you. I'll call up to her. Just a tick.'

There was a thud as she put the receiver down and some indistinct shouting. Presumably the girl was in her room. Then there was a slight disorientation on the line and the girl's voice said,

'Hello?'

'Katie? Fergus. Look, what I was saying before, when I dropped you off. I'd really like to pursue it. Can we meet? It needn't take very long. But it's a bit urgent that I ... that is ...'

Damn! He was becoming incoherent again. Sometimes silence was the best policy, so he shut up and waited. Sure enough,

'Well, I don't know what you think I can tell you, but if it's urgent – sure. I can't make it tonight. I've got tons of homework and I've hardly started, but tomorrow should be OK. I suppose you don't want Andy to know about it?'

'Well, rather not.'

'Don't meet me from school, then. Can you pick me up from here?'

'About half seven tomorrow?'

'OK.'

'Don't eat beforehand. I'll treat you.'

'OK.'

She seemed able to summon up about the same level of enthusiasm for their meeting as he had for Janet's invitation to dinner on Friday. Still, the arrangement was made and he doubted that she would cry off. It was unlikely she'd had time to develop either a need or a talent for it at her age.

He hung up and dialled again. Sukie's line was engaged. It stayed that way for over an hour. That was the trouble with the young: no concept of time. If only there was some gizmo which could interrupt her wittering and tell her that he, Fergus, was waiting to invite her out to dinner and ... afters.

He hung up one last time and looked at his watch. It decided him to cut his losses and get down to The World's End before all the steak and kidney pie was gone.

There were occasions – rare, but increasing in number – when he felt his age. Tonight was turning into one of them.

Tuesday 8 December

During Tuesday, at the university, Fergus found his mind straying to Andy and the Dunne problem a lot. As a result neither his morning meeting nor his lunchtime squash match went well.

After a late lunch he decided to work through some of his outstanding correspondence. He had barely ripped open the plastic casing of his sandwiches and picked up the first dusty candidate from the tottering pile in his in-tray, when his door was opened and Nick's head peered round it. 'He never bloody well knocks' Fergus thought irritably, as the rest of Nick slid into the room and started a conversation.

'Ah, Fergus; thought you might be back by now. Good game? Listen, she's being very cagey – even with her soi disant campaign manager,' he pointed to his own chest with what looked suspiciously like pride. 'Wouldn't say straight out. But if you throw your weight behind her candidacy for Dean I think she'll nominate you as Acting Head of Classics. I told her I thought it was a fair quid pro quo. Who else could do it? Ted?' Nick laughed. Poor old Ted had become a bit of a joke in the last few years. 'What was the name of that pensione in Florence again? Better get started on the arrangements before they think of a way to take the money back, eh?'

Fergus broadened his grudging smile to a genuine grin. Wheels were beginning to turn.

'Thanks, Nick. See if you can pin her down before you go off to Italy. It's 'La Primavera'. Mention my name to Madame Laviari and she'll make you very comfortable – might even get you a discount.'

'You old dog! Sure thing, will do, ciao.'

Fergus felt the genuine part of the grin slip as Nick left. There had never been anything intimate in his relationship with Madame Laviari, who was an Italian mamma of the old school resembling nothing so much as an ancient and much-loved sofa – remarkably comfortable but of little remaining beauty. Furthermore he, Fergus, was neither a dog, nor old.

However, the grin re-asserted itself as Fergus assimilated Nick's news, which appeared to be excellent.

Sometimes Fergus wished he could like Nick better; he was a useful ally. Fergus didn't know what it was about Nick that rankled. Academically he was sound. He wasn't a stuffed shirt, he wasn't even dull; he was just ... irritating.

Mulling over his conversation with Nick, Fergus began to munch his sandwiches. There didn't seem to be much meat in either he soon realised. He still wasn't certain how much energy Petra was prepared to devote to his cause, nor how much enthusiasm she expected from him in return. And, of course, if Petra didn't become Dean, then his own elevation would be scuppered also. At least she felt his support was valuable. Perhaps essential. That *was* information worth having.

He eyed the tottering pile of papers with distaste and reached again for the top sheet, but it was too much. Instead he swivelled his chair to look out of the window. The trees across the car park were bare now. The leaves had been a spectacular show this autumn. Their absence improved his view of the sunset, always splendid over the water meadows behind the faculty. Then he realised that the sky was acquiring a rosy tinge, which must mean that sunset was not far off, and suddenly became aware of the gloom in his little room, creeping in from the dull afternoon. It was almost too dark to read. He switched on the desk light.

Cramming the last of his second sandwich into his mouth he stood and tidied away the remains of his lunch. The pile of papers looked bigger now that it was better lit. He straightened the pile. Then he picked up his coat and sports bag and switched the desk light off again. Might as well get home before the rush hour.

*

The flat seemed very, well, flat when he got home. He debated ringing Mary to see if there had been any developments but, of course, she wouldn't be home yet and he didn't like to call her at work. Smacked of an emergency.

Resolution, that was what was missing. Perhaps he would get some useful information out of Katie tonight. Somehow he didn't believe that Dunne was permanently out of the picture. He snorted at his own pun.

He put *Turandot* on the CD, loud, and did several little jobs that had needed his attention for a while. When he had finished the kitchen looked better, and he had three or four envelopes ready to post on his way out. He was still horribly early, but inactivity had never been his strong suit, so he went and got the Jag out. It was a goodish way to Katie's suburb, the traffic might be bad.

The traffic did turn out to be pretty bad, so he was only ten minutes early when he pulled up outside the house. Just early enough to look like a pedantic old fogey, but it couldn't be helped. He'd had Wagner playing for the drive over (Wagner was good in traffic), but that was hardly mood music for the evening he had, however sketchily, planned out. He dug *La Bohème* out of the miscellany in the centre console box and clicked through the tracks to 'Mi chiamano Mimi'. His heart rate was just beginning to slow and the hairs on the back of his neck prickle, as they always did at the melody, when there was a tap on the passenger side window. It was Katie. He ran down the window and received a weak smile of greeting. She looked tired and not at all at ease. He wondered if Andy had said something to her.

'Sorry to be camping outside your house like this. The traffic wasn't as bad as I expected. I'm a bit early.'

She didn't look any happier.

'Look, this won't take long. We could do it driving around the block. But I thought it might be pleasant if we had a bit of dinner at the same time. We can talk about other things than Andy, you know.'

She still looked as though she'd rather be somewhere – anywhere – else, but he reckoned he could get a smile out of her once she'd had something to eat and a glass of nice wine.

'Are you ready to go?'

'Not quite. I'll just tell Mum you've arrived and get my coat.'

Oh God! La Crouch would be out to the car in no time flat.

Sure enough, when Katie reappeared (now wearing a donkey jacket and a woolly hat pulled down nearly over her eyes) she was preceded by her mother. Planting both hands on the sill of the car's, still open, passenger window La Crouch thrust her entire upper body through it, causing Fergus to recoil in alarm. For one awful moment he thought she was going to kiss him.

'Hello,' she said cheerily, her teeth inches from his nose.

Fergus was now in a position where neither escape or dignity was possible. Discomfort and discomposure were not things he enjoyed. He found it hard to be polite.

'Ah, Janet.'

'Won't you pop in for an aperitif before you go? I generally have a glass of something about this time and it would be nice to have company.'

'Ah – hadn't better. Strong drink on an empty stomach – never a good idea! Don't want to be driving around half cut. Perhaps when we get back ...?'

'I shall hold you to that.' She simpered a little and, with some difficulty, extricated herself from the window.

Now that her mother had disengaged from it, he could push the passenger door open for Katie to get in. While she was doing so he switched on the engine and put the car in gear to facilitate a fast getaway. Katie settled and put on her seat belt. Her mother's hands clamped themselves to the window-sill once again.

'See you both later, then,' she said.

Not if I can help it, Fergus thought, letting off handbrake and footbrake and giving the big engine a little encouragement. The car moved away rapidly while she was still talking.

'Right, what do you like to eat?'

'Pizza.'

Fergus gave an inward sigh but injected enthusiasm into his voice.

'Right, pizza it is.'

In Fergus's experience, a lot of young women enjoyed Italian food (it was romantic and exotic without being too far out of their comfort zones) so he knew a several nice trattorias around London and turned right towards the nearest when he got to the end of Katie's road. Doubtless a Pizzaland would have done just as well, but he couldn't bring himself to enter one, even for Katie.

Fifteen minutes later they were tucked into an alcove, and Fergus had his fist around his second glass of passable Chianti from the bottle now breathing on the table. Katie toyed with her small glass. But her unease didn't seem to have affected her appetite. She ordered a pizza loaded with toppings. Fergus was looking forward to a tagliatelle alla salmone. He thought he might as well get the business out of the way before the food arrived. Once they'd dealt with the Dunne thing Katie might finally relax a bit.

'The thing is, Katie – this man Dunne, that runs the art gallery in Fitzrovia. Andy seems to think he wants to hang her pictures, but it all seems a bit dubious to her mother and me. I wondered if she'd spoken to you about it?'

'Yes, she has – he's called David, isn't he?'

'Do you know how she met him?'

'He's running classes on art history, one period per week. We're both taking them. For the first one he gave a talk about Irish women artists. He had some very good slides. I think he's doing a book.'

'So he's an academic then?'

'Not exactly. He gives evening classes. And does odd courses in various schools, I think.'

Oh, God. He could pop up anywhere, in any secondary school or sixth form college in London, doing the same thing to other people's daughters as he was doing to Andy.

'Andy was thought the lecture was awesome. It was certainly very interesting. She stayed behind after to talk to him about it. I had a class so I had to go. I don't know what they talked about. Andy said he was very nice.'

'Has she talked about him since?'

'Yes, rather a lot actually.'

'Anything in particular?'

'Only what you said, that he was interested in her pictures. She took him up to the art department and showed him the recent stuff she's done for her 'A' level portfolio. She's done some at home too. She said he wanted her to bring some of those round to the gallery. Apparently he thought they could be worth a lot of money.'

'But it's only juvenilia, for Heaven's Sake! I know she's got talent, but she's not there yet. Couldn't she see the spiel for what it was?'

Katie looked sullen.

'How would I know? She told me it was a wonderful opportunity and that he was fantastic to take so much trouble over her. She's been going round to the gallery quite a bit. We often do our homework together. But she hasn't wanted to so much for the last few weeks. And I don't know when she *is* doing her homework 'cos almost every day it's David this and David that. I'm a bit fed up with it to be honest.' There was sadness, with an edge of bitterness, in Katie's voice. Fergus recognised her emotion. It's always a sad day when romance first comes between friends.

But from what Katie was saying, the relationship with Dunne was already several weeks old. That was alarming. And it was news which Andy had obviously kept from her mother. Not to mention her father.

'Do you know where Dunne lives?'

'No. I think she's only been round to the gallery.' She paused, then seemed to make up her mind to some kind of revelation. 'He seems to have been pretty cagey about where he lives. There's got to be a reason for that, hasn't there?' She went quiet again. Fergus noticed she was blushing furiously. Telling on her friend wasn't easy for her. 'I think he's married.'

'Almost certainly,' said Fergus, Katie's evidence confirming his fears and producing a sinking sensation in the vicinity of his tagliatelle. 'Or perhaps he's afraid he'll scare her off if he asks her round to ... ah ... look at his etchings.'

Katie gave a short laugh.

'Not Andy. She's not frightened of anything like that. If she wants something she goes for it.'

This was not news, but it was an unhappy reminder.

There didn't seem to be anything left to say, so they turned to other topics. Katie was a bright and engaging girl. She told him that she and

Andy had two subjects in common – history and art history. In addition Katie was doing physics and business studies.

'It's why I have so much homework. Mummy insisted that if I *must* do history *and* history of art, then I must do the others as well, because I'll never make a living from the humanities. She said everyone should have a science, and that I'll never starve if I can do shorthand and typing. Although there seems to be an awful lot more to business studies than shorthand and typing and I have *no* idea what's going on in physics classes most of the time. We moved to London so that I'd be able to choose a good university and still be able to live at home. But it's been a nightmare changing syllabuses. Mummy has no idea.'

It all sounded perfectly dreadful to Fergus. And silly. He'd never had any difficulty making a living from the humanities. The ancient world had been very good to him. Was interesting, well paid, work so much harder to come by these days? It was true that Thatcher's government expected enquiring minds to become entrepreneurs and start up their own businesses. Thinking and knowledge, per se, were out of fashion. The thought of a bright, attractive kid like Katie resigning herself to a life of shorthand and typing and living at home with her mother filled him with gloom. He poured himself another glass of wine. She'd still barely touched hers.

'So you don't get much time for discos, the flicks, that sort of thing?'

'Not much. I've got more homework to do when I get back this evening. Sometimes we – Andy and me – *used* to go out on Saturdays. But sometimes I was so tired I couldn't be bothered.' She looked straight at him for the first time since they'd sat down. 'Sometimes I wonder what happened to my youth, I do really. I wanted a dog, you know. But Mummy said I'd never have time to look after it properly and take it for walks, and she's right. I hardly ever go out, unless it's something connected with school, like when we all went to the gallery last Sunday. And after all this I'll be going to university, if my grades are good enough. Mummy's doing longer hours with the firm to put extra money aside for that, so I hardly ever see her. And I haven't seen my Dad for months. I really miss him. It's beastly.' He noticed that her eyes were brimming and her cheeks were very flushed.

Sometimes it was worse for the bright ones. He couldn't imagine Sukie ever feeling too tired to have fun. Sukie was wonderful – charming, bubbly, enthusiastic about everything he showed her about life and its little luxuries. But she was not Mensa material. He felt so sad for Katie. She was a serious little thing in rather a bind.

'Well then – why don't we go for a walk next Sunday? I live right on the edge of Hampstead Heath you know. Come round for a spot of lunch and we'll go a-roving. People do the darnedest things on the Heath at the weekends. Everything from nudists to people flying kites. We're both missing Andy, given her current obsession – so let's make do without her! And there will be loads of dogs. How about it?'

'That might be nice,' she said. She seemed surprised at the idea.

'And we won't say a word about school, or exams or anything.'

'Great,' she said. She seemed genuinely enthusiastic for the first time that evening.

They had zabaglione for dessert. She spooned up every drop.

When they reached her house, he kept the engine running, pleaded fatigue and an early start, and asked her to make his excuses to her mother. They parted conspirators. Fergus had no fear that she would reveal Sunday's projected walk to her mother – she wanted an afternoon's escape from the routine of which her mother was such a big part.

He slipped the car into gear ready for a quick getaway, as he watched Katie to the door (just in case he saw La Crouch peering through the curtains). He wondered if he could borrow a dog from someone for Sunday. Something tractable and obedient that fetched sticks. Really, he couldn't have asked for the evening to have gone any better.

He telephoned Sukie when he got in. It was late enough that the female chit-chat had dried up and he got through first time. In fact he might have woken her up, she seemed a bit distracted. She agreed to come over for dinner the following evening and Fergus sauntered off to bed with a final glass of wine from his own choice little cellar, feeling much eased. Say what you like, he reflected: like a fart in the bath, he was irrepressible.

Wednesday 9 December

The next day did not go well. The M1 was stop-go all the way and he was half an hour late for his first meeting. He hated to be late: it made one look so sloppy.

The major discussion item was his draft chapter on the historical evidence for the Minotaur of Knossos which was to appear in the forthcoming multi-disciplinary second level course 'Myth and History'.

By the time he arrived they'd done all the administrative jobs on the agenda and were waiting to could feed back their thoughts on his chapter. He felt under-prepared (although he wasn't) and flustered (which he was). 'Irascible' was a polite word for his state of mind.

Those present didn't seem to think much of what was supposed to be the final draft, so his mood did not improve. The only thing they seemed to like about it was the length: they cavilled at his premise, his examples, and his conclusions. They wanted a major redraft and they wanted it by the second week of January. Very aggravating. None of these criticisms had come up when he submitted his previous two drafts. Sometimes he found his esteemed colleagues very hard to understand.

At the end of the discussion a number of heavily annotated drafts came flying towards him. He collected them together, stuffed them into his briefcase and attempted to close it, striving for equanimity. One was supposed to accept the criticism of one's peers graciously. He could, nevertheless, feel his teeth grinding. Why hadn't they said something earlier?

After that Nick came round to whinge about the amount of money Admin had stumped up for his Florence trip. Would Fergus have a word? Fergus found himself thinking of menus for the evening's supper. Something light but sexy – oysters? No, Sukie didn't like shellfish. Something with avocado? Or was it she who had an allergic reaction to it? A salmon mousse and melba toast perhaps, then a green salad with bacon and croutons and cheese? Yes, and then ...

Nick was becoming querulous. Fergus was short with him. The money was enough if he was careful. Fergus had given him Madame Laviari's address. If he booked tourist class seats on a charter flight the money would be sufficient. British academics did not travel first class these days – if they ever had.

'Got to get on, Nick. Things to do, people to see.'

Nick departed, still grumbling. Fergus pondered. It wouldn't do to have his ally in the Petra thing turn against him at this juncture. He thought uncharitably of the effort he had already made on Nick's behalf. The man's gratitude had been short-lived. A bit more self-reliance wouldn't go amiss – academia was a gladiatorial arena these days, you needed to defend your department against attack from all sides. Nick had spent most of his academic life under Thatcher's rule: it was odd that he hadn't got used to the penny-pinching and the endless, bloody, cuts. Had it not occurred to him to inflate his original budget in the expectation of cuts being made to it? Nevertheless, Fergus marched reluctantly up the corridor to the Bursar's office and tried to charm a little more money out of them for a research trip that he himself was not even going on.

*

Fergus's belly began to rumble an hour or so later. Where to lunch, and with whom? Today might be a good day to avoid lunch with the art historians. He recalled that a new secretary had begun work for his department at the beginning of the month. It would be a kindness to take *her* to lunch, give her a few stories from the good old days. You never knew – something might come of it. Sukie hadn't sounded overjoyed to hear from him the night before. He long ago learned to recognise when his girlfriends had had enough of culture, sophistication and his black silk sheets and were about to return to their own world of boys and clubs. Although Katie didn't fit that mould at all. She would never be anything as transient as a diversion. And *her* real world was a dour round of work, work and more work.

Angela, the new secretary giggled a lot, they always did. She began to get rather pink after her second glass of wine, he took pity and escorted her back to work only some fifteen minutes late. He squared it with the senior secretary, who looked daggers but said nothing. Peals of laughter floated out from the Pool all afternoon. It was good to hear them having a good time. The faculty was a sour place these days, no fun in it anymore.

He had his afternoon cup of Earl Grey and then set off for home. He wrestled with Tesco on the way out of town and managed to get most of the ingredients he needed by dint of three monosyllabic conversations with the dispirited young people filling shelves. It seemed a lot of enquiries and walking about for a small basket containing one supper for two. Nevertheless, the bottles of wine clinked merrily in the back of the car as he sped down the motorway. He was looking forward to the evening.

*

Sukie was late. She got to be very late. He tried phoning but the answerphone was on. After the third time of listening to the ridiculous message she and her flat mates had recorded he gave her up and ate the sexy supper himself, washed down with one of the bottles of wine. Unusually for him, he felt slightly dispirited.

A walk down to the pub might help. A couple of pints of decent ale, see who was in, if there was anything worth talking about. Some male company. But when he looked at his watch he realised it would be shutting any minute.

He switched on the television, but it was only spewing out rubbish so he turned it off again.

He found himself pacing the apartment. Buggeration! He had plenty of work to do: apart from anything else, the copies of his draft on the Minotaur, with their myriad comments from his esteemed colleagues, needed to be evaluated. He'd do an hour on the wretched things, then take a turn around the block and go to bed. Bloody women. He wondered what Katie was doing now, probably still poring over her books poor kid. It was tough to be young these days. Not like when he was a young man; there was time for all the boozing, football and totty you could cope with. Was it right to take a sparkling youngster, like Katie, or Andy, and dull them with all this nose to the grindstone crap? Was it fair? Was it, even, productive? With Thatcher's encouragement, the bloody Protestant work ethic had risen again, like the poisonous monster it was, and looked set to keep them all in thrall for another century.

In the end he couldn't face the illegible scrawls on his Minotaur materials, so instead wrote a particularly vitriolic monograph for History Today on the distinction between knowledge and skill in Plato's Greece, juxtaposed with the distinction made in the present decade. Although acidic his argument was irrefutable, ably supported by primary sources and appositely contrasted with late twentieth century British society. It was a bloody good read, witty, pithy, and even a half-wit could measure Plato's approach favourably against the dull teaching of the three 'R's and the meaningless scrabble for qualifications that obtained nowadays. He was pleased with it when he had scribbled the last word and chucked the pages into his briefcase for Marion to type up the next day.

He felt calmer, having vented some spleen on the article, but still felt the need for a period to the day. A walk.

As he strolled along the edge of the Heath he felt his spirits slump again as a little niggling voice reminded him that Sukie wouldn't be coming round any more and he was between affairs. He wasn't lonely, of course. He had lots of friends. His calendar was overfull. He always said he wanted more time at home with his books, his music, his art collection: time to ruminate, to write – but it wasn't really true. He didn't much like his own company. It wasn't that he wanted someone living in the apartment – that would be unspeakable. No matter how fond of the girl he was, no matter how wonderful the night before had been, by the time he had fed her breakfast he was always relieved when she kissed him goodbye. Nevertheless he always found it unsettling to be between girls. Fergus paced the dark December streets and realised that he was what he saw in the mirror of their eyes; reflections in which he could bathe and rejuvenate himself. And now there were no bright, young eyes for him to gaze into. There was Katie, and there was Andy – but he didn't interact with either of them in that sort of way. He spared a moment to wonder when he had realised that about Katie, before he went back to feeling sorry for himself.

Christ! He was a young man inside, the wonky cartilage, the piles, all the other uncomfortable and sordid signs of age meant nothing. He was young still. Young!

Beside him was the incongruous wildness of the Common. There, in the shadows, things were happening; young people's things. Kids were necking and humping, taking drugs, beating each other up. It was vibrant. Almost he turned in, just to walk on the wild side again. But the older man inside Fergus knew that it was a dangerous thing to do. He had to get up in the morning and deal with the motorway, give in his paper for keying, discuss weighty faculty matters with his colleagues, strive for promotion, get and spend.

Even more depressed he turned for home.

The stairs to his apartment left him out of breath and with a familiar burning itch in his arse. He cursed under his breath. Was this all there was left to look forward to?

Thursday 10 December

Thursday was no improvement on Wednesday. It was his squash day. When he checked his bag he realised that he hadn't turned out his kit from the previous week. The grubby, crumpled articles seemed to take up much more room than was logical when they were out of the bag. He shoved them into the automatic and found his other strip from a fortnight ago still in there, unwashed. He slammed the door on the whole lot and set the machine going. It was pathetic to cry off just because one's kit was in the wash, so he scraped about in his cupboards for an alternative. He found an old football shirt, socks and shorts. The shorts were rather tight. He was going to look ridiculous, but he could laugh it off. He pulled a fresh towel out of the airing cupboard and checked his sponge bag. No bloody shampoo either. What the hell had he been thinking of last Thursday when he got home? Oh yes: Sukie. It had been Sukie on Wednesdays recently. Well, she had taken her toll, and now had taken herself off. Good riddance. At least it meant he could get back into a routine. But now he was late. The roads to the motorway would be completely solid by now. Shit.

The day didn't improve. Marion was off sick. The magazine's deadline for his 'Knowledge and Skill in Plato's Greece' article was the following Monday and he didn't like to ask for special treatment (even though he was one of their regular contributors), so he threw himself on the mercy of the typing pool. The senior secretary would have liked to tell him no but the new girl, whom he had lunched the day before, piped up – good kid – to say that she could fit it in. *Occasionally* one is rewarded for one's good deeds, instead of punished.

By the time he had sorted all that out he had only just time to trot over to the Sports Pavilion and change for his game. His squash partner made ribald remarks about his strip and beat him. There were no sandwiches that he liked left in the shop when he got there afterwards and he had to make do with a couple of bruised apples. The bar was closed. He mooched irritably back to his room.

He consumed his meagre lunch with a cup of tea, found his in-tray as intimating as ever and wondered how he could use the rest of the day productively. If Petra was going to endorse his elevation to Acting Head of Classics, then now might be a good time to bend the ears of the faculty's movers and shakers about his personal Chair. He wandered out into the faculty to see who was about. Nick, thankfully, was not in. Patrick was, but Fergus couldn't get past his secretary, who said he'd asked not to be disturbed. Fergus postulated that such injunctions shouldn't apply in an egalitarian faculty such as this – everyone else suffered constant interruptions, why should the Dean be any different – but she was adamant. He could make an appointment, if he liked. The Dean had an opening next Monday morning. Did he want it or didn't he? He did. And the subject of the appointment? He found his mouth opening and shutting, guppy-like. Quizzed like this, he began to feel he might regret something as formal as this carefully scheduled meeting with the Dean on the subject of a personal professorship. He was in the mood for a free and frank exchange of views with Patrick about it *now*. And such a long lead-in time gave Patrick opportunity to work out his position and put together some pseudo-logical response that would make progress impossible. Damn. He might ring and cancel on Monday, he could cite other irons in the fire – that might put the wind up the old fart.

He didn't want to canvas junior faculty members about his Chair yet (although quite a few of them owed him favours). He wanted the Great and Good on his team first. The rest would be his Greek chorus of approval. But nobody else of any consequence seemed to be about. At three thirty he called a halt to his search for ears to bend and headed back along the motorway.

He'd achieved precisely nothing today. It made him edgy. He drove hard down the M1, fast lane all the way. When he got to the North Circular he took advantage of every amber light, every gap in traffic, as if a crisis awaited him at home. But there was no message on the machine when he got in. He made work for himself around the flat until Mary might reasonably be expected to be home.

He was reluctant to phone her, given the mood he was in. If he took it out on her it might be months before she would speak to him again, and he didn't want that with things as they stood with Andy.

He was, apparently, prone to taking things out on Mary, so she said. She herself liked to point out that he had no right to take anything out on her as she was not now, nor had she ever been, his wife. And if she *had* ever been his wife she would jolly soon have divorced him so he *still* wouldn't have any right. He smiled. First of the day. Mary was a likeable bitch. He remembered what it was about her that had led to them making Andy in the first place. 'Feisty' was the word. Feisty had always been a weakness of his. Mary had been ambitious too; had her future all mapped out – before Andy turned up. Mary frequently pointed out that he had completely done for her youth and that if he interfered with her middle age he would be very sorry indeed. He smiled again. Perhaps he would ring Mary after all.

He didn't need to. She called him.

'He called.'

'Oh, God. What happened?'

'I don't know. I could hardly stand there and listen, could I?'

'Oh for Christ's sake, Mary ...'

'She took it on the extension *you* paid to have put in her bedroom.'

Ah, the downside of modern technology, when kids could talk freely on the telephone without their parents hearing every word.

'Well, what did she say he said?'

'I didn't ask her. I didn't want to probe in case it made things worse. We have to trust her, Fergus.'

'Rubbish! Of course we don't. She doesn't expect us to. She wouldn't expect *me* to.'

'Yes, she does.'

'How did you know it was him.?'

'The accent. You said he was posh Irish.'

'Did she go out?'

'No.'

'Is she going out later?'

'She hasn't said so.'

'Well find out if she's intending to.'

'I can't grill her Fergus. She's not a criminal.'

'Maybe not, but I'm reasonably certain Dunne is.'

'Bankruptcy isn't, actually, a *crime* Fergus. Don't you think you're getting a bit obsessive about this?'

'I'm going to find out what's going on, Mary. I can't concentrate with this hanging over ... us. I lost my squash match today! This Dunne thing needs to get resolved. And soon. I'm going to find this bloody man.'

'Us? Ha! You do what you want, Fergus. Just don't make things worse, OK?' She rang off.

But what *did* he want to do? He *wanted* to beat Dunne to a pulp. But civilised people didn't do such things. And anyway, he hadn't boxed since he was a boy. Well, one way or another, he was going to get to the bottom of this.

*

He couldn't settle to anything after speaking to Mary. He paced up and down his lounge like a bad-tempered lion in an overly small cage for a while. But it was no good brooding, so he went down to The World's End. They had a jazz band on which wasn't half bad. The company was good too, for mid-week. He was in a much more mellow frame of mind by the time he got his third pint.

Wandering back past the Park after closing time, he looked in again. The trees were stripped to claws and there was a smell of dampness and cold, wind and rain. Christmas was coming. Already he had a mound of cards on the mantel. He never opened them. He never sent any. Christmas was all right for other people, if you liked that sort of thing.

As far as he was concerned Christmas was a time of excuses and false bonhomie, of parties no-one really felt like attending, of jollity to order and once-a-year caring. He usually bolted his door and toughed it out. He generally got a lot of work done over Christmas.

He walked on, into his building and up the stairs. Back inside his flat, he found his avuncular mood had completely dissipated. He began to pace again.

Tosca might help. It often did. That and something to concentrate on that wasn't David Bloody Dunne.

He put the CD on and got out a paper on Catullus' love poetry that he had been toying with off and on. It needed finishing. He opened a bottle of Chianti, to be in keeping, and gritted his teeth. It was going to be a long night.

Friday 11 December

He finished the paper about three and finally crawled into bed too tired to sleep properly. He had heard the milkman's electric truck and his obscenely cheery whistling and clinking. A dog had barked, then he had fallen into a deep, narcotic sleep and now it was 10.30 a.m. and nothing done. The black silk bedding that he had put on the bed for Sukie's benefit was roped around him. Angrily he stripped the bed, digging out some aggressively patterned cotton bedding to replace the contorted silk.

It was his day for the British Library, and he knew better than to break that routine for anything less than hospitalisation (you don't go once, you don't go twice, then you don't go at all). He got himself sorted out by lunchtime, went in on the overground and had a bite to eat in the Museum Tavern across the road before going in.

He'd not achieved much before he found his concentration had gone, so he stacked his books and files for the librarian and went out for a walk. He was surprised to find it was almost twilight already. Sometimes the individual hours still dragged – but the days, weeks, months and years whizzed by at an alarming rate these days.

All at once he remembered the evening in prospect with La Crouch and her cronies. He *could* still cry off. But on a whim he decided he would go. He stopped off for wine on the way home: he was prepared to bet there would be nothing drinkable at Janet's house. She looked like a cheap Liebfraumilch drinker. Then he realised that, in a masochistic sort of way, he was looking forward to Janet's soirée. He always enjoyed shaking up the status quo. He didn't expect to get a return invitation.

By the time he'd been home and showered it was time to go. In the car he played *Turandot* arias to take his mind off the insane theatre traffic. Forty minutes later the angst of the opera had distilled down into the sublime melody of 'Nessum Dorma' and he had arrived at Janet's house. 'Let none sleep' indeed: he'd make sure they didn't fall asleep over their coffee.

The door was flung open at his knock and he was immediately aware of a sexual tension in the air. Sexual tension was something with which Fergus was familiar; he knew it when it came at him. It was, however, alarming – even for an expert – to have so many pheromones thrust at you before you'd got through the door. La Crouch was looking radiant – the unkind might call it flushed. She was dressed in something fashioned from a great deal of brightly patterned material which flowed in several directions at once and displayed a lot of cleavage. She had obviously Made An Effort. In the background he saw Katie, also dressed extravagantly in very short things and very long boots, with her lovely long hair put into many plaits, which had been looped and piled like a Medusa. Extraordinary.

'You remembered!'

'Of course. And I brought a little something ...' he proffered the bottle.

'Oh, you shouldn't have.' She grasped both the bottle and his elbow and drew him in.

She peeled his coat off him before he was fairly through the door and gave it to Katie, who gave him a tentative smile. The sexual tension was still palpable but he wasn't quite so sure, now, that it was coming his way. Having shucked him out of his coat Janet wasn't getting closer, but moving rapidly away towards what he presumed was the lounge. Sounds of conviviality were coming from it.

'Come through, come through,' she carolled over her shoulder. 'Let me get you some wine and introduce you around.'

Fergus wasn't used to competition. He hadn't known there was a man in Janet's life. And, indeed, a long-standing relationship didn't provoke this kind of behaviour. Her demeanour definitely had 'new man' written all over it. Was it him? Or another? He *should* be glad if the pressure was off him, but somehow he felt a little piqued.

Fergus slipped Janet's tow as she passed the group of people in the middle of the room. She continued towards a dresser upon which were some bottles Two were of red wine, neither of them opened. She attacked his offering with a corkscrew and swiftly returned with a large glass, half-filled. He took the proferred glass and raised it to his hostess, put it to his lips and turned about, with a smile, to find some ammunition about her home with which to make small talk, be pleasant. Only to see ...

Dunne. He and Katie were standing very close together and she was gazing up at the man in a way that Fergus wished she would gaze at him. He feared Andy regularly gazed up at Dunne in a similar fashion. What the hell made the man such a magnet?

Janet, moving like a racing yacht with the spinnaker up, sailed over to Katie and Dunne and obviously insisted that Katie go and do something in the kitchen. The girl went off in an obvious sulk. Janet guided Dunne firmly to a trio of men talking about football and left him there. She returned to Fergus and made introductions at a very rapid rate.

La Crouch actually looked rather good in her voluminous robe picked up, she carefully let slip as they glided about the room, in

Egypt. One could hide a lot in there, he thought uncharitably, but the colours suited her, as did the slight flush on her cheeks.

Fergus's hand was now being shaken by various people who seemed not to be as awful as he had expected. He barely had time to mutter the usual pleasantries, however, before Janet's hand grasped his elbow once more and moved him on.

He was rushed around the room until they came to the quartet of football enthusiasts which included Dunne. Fergus was certain now of the source of that sexual tension he had felt at the front door. Not only was Katie clearly besotted with Dunne, but so was Janet. She transferred her hand from Fergus's elbow to Dunne's as soon as it was within easy reach. The proprietorial gesture was not lost on Katie, returning with the tray of nibbles she had been sent for. She looked daggers at her mother.

'And, last but not least, Fergus, this is David Dunne. He's a ...'

'We've met,' said Fergus heavily.

Her opening gambit stymied, Janet became mercifully silent. Indeed, both mother and daughter became instantly tongue-tied, so it was left to the men to decide what to do with the conversation next. What Fergus wanted to do was shake Dunne warmly by the throat and ask him to step outside, but he contented himself with fixing the man with his most piercing state. Dunne – Christ, the man must have a hide like a rhinoceros – calmly stuck out his hand and said,

'Good to see you again, Girvan. How's Andy?'

Fergus's grip on his glass tightened to danger level. He managed a nod, he didn't trust himself to do more. He took a gulp of wine in the hope of inspiration, but somehow on the way down it took a detour and he found himself, to his mortal embarrassment, choking. The two females fluttered anxiously around him, but it was Dunne, clapping him heartily on the back, who shifted the offending liquid out of the lung it had sidled into and back on track. Despite the discomfort and embarrassment Fergus was glad of the diversion. He wiped his eyes and regained his composure and thought hard. What to do? What to do? Doubtless he could make an opportunity at some point to take Dunne aside and threaten him with – what? What would he, Fergus, do if he, Dunne, ever went near Andy again? And, more importantly, what would Andy do if – no, when – she found out what her father had done? What had been Mary's parting shot earlier? Don't make things worse?

He looked at the scene before him. Dunne was being equally attentive to both mother and daughter. Two women: one man – surely one of them would succeed in bedding the apparently irresistible snake before the night was over? Simple enough then to make sure the news got back to Andy. Could Fergus really sacrifice an innocent young thing like Katie to a rogue like Dunne? Fergus ruminated that he had been meaning to create an opportunity to do something very similar with Katie himself. There were many leggy, intelligent young women with manes of tawny hair in the world. And there were many personable women of a certain age, such as Janet. But there was only one Andy. No contest. Which of them to sacrifice? Or would it, maybe, require both?

Fergus regained his composure as they went in to supper. The meal began well and continued to please, even though he had to put up with a thin white French wine to go with it. He made do, put himself out to be charming – and watched developments. Janet sat at the end of the table nearest to the kitchen with Katie beside her. This part of the seating plan was obviously logistical as the two of them did much flitting in and out to check, serve, and clear away. Dunne had been placed in the seat of honour – beside Janet and opposite Katie. Fergus was relegated to the other end of the table, for which he was grateful, and from where he had a good view of the interesting triangle at the other end. He noticed a tendency for each of Dunne's two acolytes to urge the other into kitchen duties, whilst being quite reluctant to go herself. The meal proceeded slowly for this reason.

On Fergus's right was an interesting couple who had just returned from Nigeria and looked far from well. They didn't touch the wine, which was fortunate, and ate little; but they had plenty of diverting stories about Benin and the bronze work still being made there. On his left was a slightly vulpine-looking television producer with red hair and no tits to speak of. She was currently working on a series examining the reasons for something or other in big corporations. Next to her was a barrister who painted in his spare time. They didn't appear to be an item, although Fergus suspected that the barrister, 'Steph' (who made a thing about the 'ph'), would like them to be. The producer – Fliss – helped Fergus energetically with the bottle of wine down their end. She didn't seem any the worse by the time dessert came, except that she got increasingly sharp with the barrister. Eventually he took the hint and turned his attention to the sick-looking couple and their Nigerian anecdotes.

Fergus and Fliss started a desultory conversation of the 'and what do *you* do' variety, when it quickly transpired that the programmes she was making were for the Management Education Centre at Ariel.

'How is it we haven't met before, then? We have television production studios on the campus.'

'I know. And I was dreading having to move up the M1 to work in them. But because Management Education isn't a faculty the programmes don't have to be made there So I can stay in lovely, lovely London!' She sounded triumphant.

'*I* commute from up from London.'

'Yes, but I don't suppose you go in more than once a week, being an academic.'

He bridled.

'Actually, I go in most days. Except Fridays.'

She laughed.

'I have stalked the corridors of power at Ariel and unless there's some shindig on, all you can hear is the echo of your own footsteps.' She grinned wickedly at him. 'But if you say it's a hive of industry, I believe you.'

'I don't get any actual *work* done. It's all bloody bureaucracy on the campus. I do all my writing at home.'

'How peculiar that a university with no physical students should spend so much time and money providing these invisible people with materials to study. If they were in front of you, you'd simply trot out the same lecture you'd used on that course for the previous twenty years and everyone would be happy ...'

'*I* certainly wouldn't be spouting out of date materials by rote!'

Her eyes twinkled with mischief.

'I'm sure *you* wouldn't. I'm just saying – Ariel is an interesting departure. It works back to front in some ways. In a bricks and mortar university you'd expect your tutor to be right there, in their room, at the end of the phone, whatever. At Ariel – and trust me on this because on a need to know basis I do frequently have a need to know – quite often there isn't an academic, of any kind, in the entire building.'

Perhaps she could see he was getting a little warm under the collar at her heartfelt and even slightly realistic evaluation of the way Ariel's academics functioned, because she changed the subject. She mentioned the names of a couple of business gurus that she obviously thought he might have heard of – Peter Drucker, Edward de Bono – but the name-dropping fell on stony ground as far as Fergus was concerned. He tried to sound enthusiastic but, really, *business* ... it was hardly a proper academic field was it? Apparently he said this out loud, because Fliss agreed with him wholeheartedly. It paid the rent, she said, and gave her something to put on her CV. Female producers were still so rare – less than ten per cent of those working on the whole of Ariel's output. Out in the big bad world of mainstream television it was even worse. She would much rather be making the luscious programmes in a Florentine museum, or at La Scala, that were given to her male colleagues, but what could you do?

Mention of La Scala turned the conversation towards opera, of which it turned out she was very fond, and she and Fergus segued into a cosy conversation on the joys and shortcomings of Puccini.

When Janet began to chivvy them all through to the lounge for coffee, Fergus and Fliss were in the vanguard of the movement. He retrieved one of the two remaining bottles of red wine and the corkscrew from the dresser and settled down on the sofa to share it with her. Halfway down that bottle their conversation shifted to Stravinsky and Richard Strauss – lingering on *Salomé* and *Elektra*. Finally, when Fliss had liberated the last bottle from the dresser, their discussion moved on to the zenith of operatic composers, Wagner.

Whilst enjoying Fliss's company, Fergus kept a calculating eye on the Dunne triangle. He noted a growing hostility between mother and daughter. There would be a row when the guests had gone. Which one would triumph: youth or experience? *His* only problem was how to discover which woman it turned out to be – and how to report it back to Andy so as to cause maximum damage.

The sickly looking couple made their excuses early. The evening wound down quite quickly after that. The barrister obviously had no interest in opera or football, so tried to join the embattled trio of Dunne, Janet and Katie, but could make no headway. He soon left, making 'call me' signs at Fliss which she ignored. The football fans and their partners looked as though they might be going on somewhere: soon after Steph's departure Katie had to relinquish Dunne to her mother for long enough to go and get their coats from upstairs.

The sexual frisson was palpable when they had gone, and Fergus felt it was only fair to give Dunne and his acolytes space for whatever was to come. He enquired as to whether it was feasible to share a taxi home with Fliss and, when she told him she lived in Camden Lock, quickly realised that it was. Rather than phone for a cab and wait an hour, they thought it would clear their heads to walk the short distance to Clapham Common Tube and get one there. Fliss fetched their coats. Fergus made appropriate noises, Fliss kissed everybody, then they were out in the night air. They got a taxi without difficulty and he was back at Heath House in three-quarters of an hour, having had Fliss's card pressed upon him in the dark of the taxi when she got out at Camden Lock.

Back in his flat he stumbled over an occasional table that he had never thought of as being in a vulnerable place before. As he bent down to pick up the magazines which had fallen off it, he realised he was pissed. By God, Fliss could put it away. He put her card on the mantelpiece and looked at the clock there. Half past midnight. Was it too late to phone Mary? Yes, bugger it. Such juicy news as he had needed sharing, but it would have to wait for morning.

Saturday 12 December

In the morning Fergus was up, if not bright, at least early. He had an interesting call to make.

After two large cups of strong black coffee he realised that, without having had to do anything sensible himself, he knew how to drive a wedge between Andy and Dunne. But he couldn't tell Mary about it (as he had intended to do, under the influence, the night before). She would certainly let something slip to Andy one way or another. Given the merest hint of the way the wind was blowing, Andy was quite capable of scuppering Dunne's nascent liaison with the Crouch women (Katie and/or Janet) which Fergus was going to do his darndest to foster, before it ever became useful.

What could he do over the weekend to further his plan? Inaction – even with a hangover – was never his strong suit.

He could follow Dunne next time the man arranged an assignation with Andy. Or Katie. (His courage failed him at the prospect of following Janet Crouch.) His hangover and his conscience both protested at this course of action. It was going too far. And it would be fiercely difficult to find out when any such meeting was to be. At least if he followed the bloody man around all day he might discover where Dunne had his family hidden – which might also be where he was storing the pictures missing from the gallery, as a backstop against penury, if he hadn't already sold them. Fergus would find that information satisfying. However, since the wretched wife and inevitable children were a given, he wouldn't advance the cause of demonstrating Dunne to be a thorough-going shit by being able to point at the marital home. Neither of the girls was likely to be deterred by a wife, or children. The very young believe not only that they are themselves invincible, but that everyone else is too. His hungover brain recoiled into its shell altogether at the prospect of trying to get either Andy or Katie to understand the potential pain Dunne was causing his family with his extra-marital liaisons. One needs to be out of one's teens before one recognises what a betrayal of affection and sexual intimacy feels like.

Which thought gave him an idea. He made a phone call.

'Janet? Fergus. Just calling to thank you for a very pleasant evening. Yes, Fliss and I found a cab, no trouble at all. At the station, yes. Didn't think at the time, should have offered to drop Dunne off, he couldn't have driven home either. Drink flows freely at your parties, eh, Janet? Oh? Oh, right.'

Fergus had to work hard to keep the grin out of his voice.

So the bastard had stayed the night. Perhaps he was running out of bolt holes. Janet didn't strike Fergus as the kind of New Age parent who would permit mixed gender sleepovers, so Dunne must've spent the night on the couch or in Janet's bed. No way to find out which, worse luck. But this was obviously fruitful ground. There was one more thing -

'Could I just have a word with Katie, Janet? About that project.'

He heard Janet call up the stairs, and clicks of phones being lifted and replaced.

'Katie?'

A wonderfully sleepy voice said,

'Who is it?'

'Fergus?'

Her voice in his ear, so intimate with sleep, made his belly contract with desire. He imagined her tousled tawny head, inches from his, on the pillow, as she woke and turned to him and spoke his name. He tried to remember what he had wanted to say to her. He realised he was sweating.

'Ah ... yes ... Sunday! Walk still on?'

'Mmm. Yeah. Great.'

'Two o'clock at my place. Heath House, Flat 31 – third floor, right opposite the lift. Good brisk walk, tea after. You know which bus to get?'

'Mmm. Bye.'

He felt quite odd as he put the phone down. Conflicted, almost. He hoped fervently that it wouldn't rain tomorrow. Rather a lot depended on this walk.

*

He was thinking deeply about Katie and the walk, and the tea, and what it should consist of, and what more she would be able to tell him about Dunne's overnight stay, when his telephone rang. It startled him.

It was Fliss, a very bright and perky Fliss. She had been given tickets for *Die Meistersinger von Nürnberg* at Covent Garden, would he like to go?

He pulled himself together and thought fast. Would he? *Die Meistersinger* was, like so much of Wagner's work, long. Still, a decent seat at the Royal Opera was not to be sniffed at. And the glorious 'Morgenlich leuchtend im rosigen Schein' aria alone was worth much discomfort.

'Where are the seats? They're not behind a bloody pillar, are they?'

She laughed.

'No, you nasty, suspicious man. They're at the front of the first circle. They are, in fact, exquisite seats. They're for Friday next.'

'You've got some generous friends.'

'One or two. Are you coming or not?'

He didn't bother checking his diary. There was nothing in there that couldn't be cancelled if necessary.

'Yes. Delighted. Thank you for thinking of me.'

'No problem. See you Friday, then.'

'Shall I pick you up?'

'No, let me come and get you. I'll probably come straight from work.'

He gave her his address and after a couple more pleasantries she rang off. He found he was looking forward to seeing Fliss again. She was an interesting and capable woman, with a big sense of fun. She had drive too, that was certain. And she had the ability not only to share but, if necessary, *provide* enthusiasm. He usually had to provide his own. It was a new experience for him to be cadging a ride on someone else's. He rather liked it.

He settled into the rest of his day, brain still buzzing, but not unpleasantly. He did his chores; went round to Tesco's and laid in a supply of cakes and things to toast, such as might appeal to a teenager; watched some footie on the TV in the afternoon and spent the latter part of the evening in the pub. A bachelor's bliss. He seldom had a date on Saturdays. Saturday was a man's day, and usually his current friend liked to go out with her mates to a disco or club on Saturday night. Saturdays he liked to recharge his batteries. It was a ritual that suited him very well.

Sunday 13 December

He peered anxiously through his curtains as soon as he got up.

It was overcast and drizzly outside. Hard to tell what kind of a day it would turn into. He hoped his creaky knee cartilage wasn't an omen: it tended to be worse in damp weather. Only two weeks or so of this year left now, but in the new year more gloomy months of winter to come. How was it that the dreary weather always lasted longer than the bright sunny days? How come the world turned so much faster now than it used to? Having made himself thoroughly miserable, he dragged himself into the kitchen and put a pot of coffee on, then headed for the shower.

But by the time he went out to fetch his paper it had turned into a bright, crisp morning. A good day to make the best of.

His way home with the paper lay past his old friend The World's End, and he popped in, just to be sociable. They had a jazz band on, and it was rather good. The bright edge to the music cut through the autumn chill, assisted by roaring log fires in both bars. The place was steamy and cheerful with the raucous music, talk and laughter.

At about half past one he realised that he really would have to make a move if he wanted to be organised in time for Katie's arrival. Outside it was still very crisp, and he wished he'd brought a warmer jacket, but he stepped out briskly and jogged up the stairs to the flat, just to prove he could.

Once back in the flat, he sat down to flick the switch and turn on the gas fire in the lounge, to be warm and cheerful, leaned back to admire the 'living flame', and the next thing he knew the doorbell woke him up.

Shit! He clambered groggily towards the surface of his own mind, wanting to call out ... something, but not sure what the word he needed was; nor completely certain if the doorbell he heard was real, or part of a dream.

His mouth felt like the inside of his kitchen rubbish sack. His eyes refused to open, his mind to function, his body to move. He wondered for a ghastly moment if he'd had a stroke – then remembered that this was the reason he didn't go to The World's End for Sunday lunchtimes any more. Now here he was, lying fuddled in a chair. Katie would think he was a pathetic old codger who needed forty winks in the middle of the day. Jesus H Christ.

With a supreme effort of will he shrugged off the encircling arms of Morpheus and lurched towards the door. Passing the mirror he looked in. His hair was all anyhow, his eyes puffy and bleary, his face red. He must do *something* to repair the ravages.

Finally confident of being able to distinguish between dream and reality, he remembered the word he needed:

'Coming.'

Then he scurried for the bathroom, cold water and a comb.

Looking a little less ravaged he returned to the front door.

But it wasn't Katie. It was Fliss. With a dog. Mother of God! It sniffed him, then wagged a stump of a tail.

'Hi,' she said.

Fergus became aware that he was gawping.

'It's all right – you weren't expecting me,' she said drily.

He could see she wished she hadn't come. However, he had already discovered she wasn't one to back off from situations. So he wasn't surprised when she continued.

'We were passing. We always go to the Heath on Sundays unless the weather's foul, and I wondered if you'd like to join us – no big deal, just an hour or so strolling about while Bracken meets her friends. I could do with a decent stick thrower on the team. Bracken always complains that I'm hopeless at it, get them stuck in trees as often as not.'

Fergus realised he was still gripping the door in a rather hostile 'they shall not pass' fashion. He stood back.

'Come in,' he said, standing to one side and eyeing the dog speculatively. He could, perhaps, still make something of this turn of events if he could find a satisfactory explanation for the presence of Fliss when Katie turned up.

'It's alright,' said Fliss, releasing the dog's lead. 'She's clean. Its afterwards you need to worry.'

The dog took one look at the fire and headed off towards the kitchen.

'If you've got anything out I should rescue it. She reckons anything she can reach in a kitchen is fair game.'

Shit. Fergus made best speed for the kitchen in a bid to save the constituent parts of the tasty tea sitting on the counter in there.

'I thought you might be down at The World's End,' Fliss called after him., 'They had a nice jazz band on. I just caught the last ten minutes of it.'

'I was, but I had to get back ...'

'Oh, are you expecting company? I'm sorry, you should have said.'

She sounded genuinely contrite. Fergus looked at his watch, suddenly suspicious. It was nearly half past two.

'No problem,' he called with a repressed sigh. 'It doesn't look as if ... er ... they're coming.'

Decision time: should he wait for a woman who was already half an hour late, or depart on the same excursion (plus dog) with a completely different woman? He found he was quite unable to resolve his conundrum. But he felt a complete arsehole standing in his own kitchen clutching a bag of buns to his bosom. Bracken looked up at him hopefully, her gaze tracked between his face and the buns, she licked her chops and grinned at him.

It was always the same: no women, or too many women. Buggeration.

It seemed foolish to be shouting the length of the flat, so he returned to the lounge, still clutching the buns. The turbines of his mind were spinning up very slowly. They began to pick up speed, however, when he noticed the red eye of his answerphone winking suggestively at him. It implied, saucily, that if he listened to his waiting message now he might live to regret it but that if he ignored it his afternoon might implode.

Knowing himself to be a man who would have beaten Pandora to the box, he stretched out a determined digit and pressed 'play'.

'Just a minute, Fliss. I hadn't noticed this message. It may explain what's happened to my company.'

It did. A rather breathless voice said,

'Fergus, I can't come after all. Something's happened. It's Mummy and Andy. I'm going round to Andy's now. You were right.'

Thank God she'd been in too much of a rush to go into detail. Fergus smiled the smile of the blameless. Fliss looked intrigued. Fergus said,

'It would take all afternoon to explain, and then we'd miss the sunshine and – what's her name? – would miss her walk.'

'Bracken.'

'I'm not bad with sticks. I'm better with a ball.'

'Balls are good too.'

'I'll just see if I've got an old football in the cupboard, then we'll go.'

The bottom of Fergus's wardrobe disgorged an old football which had gone soft. While he was in his room he thought he'd put on a thick sweater. He had to rummage quite deep for it; he didn't use thick jumpers often. Upon pulling it over his head, he found it rather tight. Odd. In his experience things usually shrank in the wash, not in the drawer. Perhaps he just hadn't worn it since its last wash. No matter. But then he had trouble getting his jacket on over it. That had *certainly* not shrunk. He glanced into the mirror. Ridiculous. His arms stuck out from his sides like a scarecrow. Careful not to rip the straining underarms and back seam he eased out of the jacket and found instead a very old sailing smock. Another glance in the mirror. That was better, gave him rather the look of a debonair old salt. He dug out an old blue paisley cravat and tied it jauntily. Yes, it looked well. He'd be fine if it didn't rain.

A sudden twinge caught him and he sat down quickly on the bed. It was a twinge of conscience. Here he was about to go out and – possibly – enjoy himself when obviously all hell had broken loose in Clapham. He should be burning rubber to get over there. But then, women were such odd creatures, it was a job to know if Katie's message had been a plea for help, or a hint to leave the whole mess alone for her to sort out. Perhaps he should just give Mary a quick ring and see if the shock waves had reached her at Lyndhurst Close yet.

He rolled over and dialled on the bedside phone. The phone rang and rang. He was just going to give up, to avoid constructing something anodyne for the answerphone, when Mary's voice, familiarly curt, said,

'Yes?'

'Mary? It's Fergus. Is this a bad time?'

'Very.'

'Well, it's just ... I had a call from Katie. And it sounded as if she might be headed your way. Is everything all right?'

'No, everything is very far from all right. Katie's here. So is her mother. They're all here. Look – I really can't talk. I'm refereeing. I'll call you later. Bye.'

And she was gone.

Interesting. Fergus hoped, most sincerely, Mary's current occupation meant Dunne had been found out in Spades. Smiling, Fergus disinterred his old sailing cap, to finish off his dog-walking outfit. He clapped in onto his head at a jaunty angle. It would keep the back of his head warm where the hair was thinning. Then he returned to his unexpected guests with a clear conscience.

*

The Heath was bracing. They had a great time. The sailing smock was a godsend, as it rapidly collected several sets of muddy paw marks. The dog turned rapidly from white-and-brown to brown. The football was an enormous success, until Bracken ran off with it and dismembered it under a bush. They retrieved the remains from her after a struggle and put them in a bin, then had to get the dog out of the bin. By this time they were laughing almost too much to throw sticks, but did their best until all three of them were panting hard. Then they watched the kites flying for a bit until they started to feel cold. Then Fergus invited Fliss back for tea.

'That would be lovely – if you don't mind the dog.'

Fergus laughed expansively.

'I'm sure we can get the worst off with an old towel.'

They strolled back to Heath House, a picture of conviviality.

Fergus was glad to have company to eat the carefully planned tea, although he wasn't sure the carbohydrate feast which he had thought suitable for a growing teenager would appeal to thirty-something Fliss. His worries were short-lived. She dried the dog in the hall outside the flat while Fergus slid surreptitiously into his bathroom and made liberal use of the tube of Preparation H secreted there. She came through to the kitchen holding the, now brown, towel. By this time he'd got the kettle on. The cakes barely made it onto a plate before she had her teeth into one. They ate by the fire, with a big pot of Earl Grey. Bracken was almost instantly asleep by his bedroom door. As the room grew darker Fergus put some Chopin on the stereo and opened a bottle of wine. They talked and talked.

He had forgotten what a pleasure it was to talk with an intelligent and experienced woman. Not *sexually* experienced (although there was that too). No, simply the pleasure of another mind that had seen something of the world. Your ideas reinforced and inspired each other; all things became possible. The education of the young was a worthy and entertaining pastime, but the relationships were a *little* two-dimensional. He cast his pearls of wisdom at their feet and each aperçu received the same, wide-eyed, 'gosh' or 'really' or even just a non-committal 'mmm'. His girlfriends learned a great deal, he believed, despite themselves. There was not one, he was certain, who was not at some time say surprised by her own cleverness and said, 'that old bastard Girvan taught me that'. But they didn't give a lot *back* conversationally. They had other attractions. Talking by the fire with Fliss brought home to Fergus the price he had been paying for his pleasures.

His reverie cost him the thread of the conversation, and silence fell. They hadn't known each other long enough for this to be an easy silence. He realised that the only light in the room was the flicker of his ersatz fire, which suddenly seemed quite inappropriate. He leaned over to turn on a lamp and looked at his watch.

'It's eight o'clock!'

Apart from anything else he was hungry again, he now realised.

'Shall we get some dinner?' he asked.

'Eight o'clock? Dinner? Christ! No – I've got to go. Shit. I've got a shoot at Brighton at eight in the morning, and I haven't read the fucking script yet!'

She scrambled to her feet, looking for her boots. Fergus laughed, and rose himself to fetch her coat. The dog got up stiffly and gave a tired wag of her tail.

As he helped Fliss into her coat, Fergus gave her shoulder a companionable squeeze. She turned and smiled at him and he almost kissed her, but found himself unaccountably shy. The moment passed. Fliss bent to put Bracken into her lead.

'It's been fun, ' she said.

'It has.'

'I'll pick you up for the opera,' she said. 'Three thirty sharp.'

'I'm looking forward to it,' he said, and meant it.

She smiled at him once more, then she and the dog were gone.

He closed the door reluctantly on the sound of boots and claws descending the stairs at speed, and returned to the lounge. The small pool of light from the lamp and the flicker of the fire made it rather cosy. He noticed the curtains were still open and went to draw them. The trees on the edge of the Heath were big, ugly, thrashing shadows in a gale that hadn't been there when they'd come in. It was as if a spell had been cast that just encompassed this one place, and elsewhere all was chaos. He shivered as the cold air from the glass in the window found him. Somebody had just walked over his grave. He hoped it wasn't that bastard Dunne. Perhaps Fliss had cast a spell on him? He smiled. She was a good companion, certainly, but she was far too old for him. Bloody good job he hadn't been such a fool as to kiss her. That might have led to serious complications. Christ he was tired. Supper? The pub didn't do food on a Sunday evening and he couldn't be bothered to turn out again anyway. He'd chuck something in the microwave, then get an early night.

Monday 14 December

So complete was the spell his curious, rejigged Sunday had cast over him that Fergus didn't remember the full extent of the chaos embracing his family until the following morning. As soon as he woke it struck him that Mary hadn't phoned back as she had promised she would.

By seven thirty he thought it would be safe to ring her. He poured himself a second cup of tea and dialled.

'Yes?'

She sounded tired. He said so. She sighed.

'So would you if you'd had the kind of Bloody Sunday I just did. Where were you?'

'Everybody kept telling me to keep out of it, so I did.'

'Not like you to do as you're told. Must be incipient senility.'

It was too early in the morning for true irritation to take hold, but Fergus felt stirrings.

'I've got a meeting at nine. Just bring me up to speed. What happened yesterday?'

'Janet Crouch – you know, Katie's mother – turned up here at lunchtime with David Dunne. He said he'd come to apologise to Andy for not being there like he'd promised when you went round. I got them settled in the lounge and called Andy down. When she knew who it was she flew down before I could say anything. I don't think I'd even managed to mention that Dunne had brought Janet with him. I went into the kitchen to make some coffee and heard all hell break loose. By the time I got back into the lounge Andy and Janet were toe to toe. Dunne was pretending to look out of the window. When I asked what was going on Andy burst into tears and ran for her room.

'I found out, bit by bit, that she had greeted Dunne by, quite literally, jumping on him. Arms round the neck, kisses on the lips: the works. Janet was furious. Apparently Janet has struck up a deep and meaningful relationship of her own with this bloody Dunne since I last spoke to her. She took exception to Andy's enthusiastic welcome and bawled the kid out. That was when I came in and Andy ran out.

'So I bawled both Janet and Dunne out for being so stupid as to come here at all if they were playing games. They were very defensive – well, Janet was. Dunne didn't say one word.

'While I was defending my offspring, the girl was phoning Katie. God knows what she told her – I mean, it was Katie's mother that Andy had fought with for Christ's sake. But Katie's such a sensible girl. She turned up about fifteen minutes later – must have called a cab.

'By that time Janet had – serially – turned on Dunne, then me, and was having the vapours and a stiff medicinal scotch in the kitchen. Dunne was sitting in the lounge staring at his hands and looking gloomy. I wondered how the hell I was going to get rid of them. Then Dunne suggested that he should go up and have a word with Andy. I put my foot down at that.

'I was commuting between the three camps when Katie arrived. I sent her upstairs to see if she could talk some sense into Andy. Janet was still insisting that Andy must promise never to bother Dunne again. Andy and Katie came downstairs just in time to hear Janet sounding off. Andy squared right up to Janet and said she wasn't *bothering* Dunne, and told Dunne to tell Janet how things really stood. Janet started to paw at Dunne and Katie told her mother not to embarrass herself. Janet had done some serious damage to the whisky bottle and was becoming 'tired and emotional', as the phrase is. Andy flounced off into the garden. I expect she wanted Dunne to follow her, but he didn't – he couldn't get past Janet, who was now howling her head off in the kitchen.

'So Katie went outdoors to Andy. And while I was trying to get the whisky away from Janet and calm her down, Dunne left.

'The girls came in just after he'd gone. I expect they heard the front door close. I got a bit more sense out of the two of them after Dunne had gone. Andy clearly felt that Janet had no business moving in on 'her' David.

'I expected a bit more rationality from Janet – she is a solicitor after all – but she'd had too much whisky by then to be making any sense.

'Neither of them seemed to twig that it takes two to tango. Dunne was gone by then, so he couldn't be cross-examined as to which one of them he wanted. I'm sure he'd have tried to appease both. Fancy coming round with one woman on your arm to apologise for having stood up the other one! The man must be completely without a moral compass.

'Anyway, Janet and Katie left together soon after. I called them a cab. Janet was in no condition to drive. And if she *had* got into her car I'm sure she would have gone looking for Dunne.

'Katie came back about two hours later. She'd got her mother to have a lie down, and wanted to see how Andy was doing. To which the answer was, not well. Katie and Andy stayed upstairs all evening. In fact, Katie stayed the night. I shall have to go and get them up in a minute or they'll be late for school.'

Fergus sipped his tea and smiled.

'Marvellous,' he said.

'It wasn't at the time, but I understand what you mean.'

'This must have put her off him, surely?'

'I wouldn't put money on it, Fergus. Even though Katie – she's such a good kid – let slip that Dunne stayed over after the dinner party her mother gave on Friday night, and had spent Saturday and Sunday nights at their place too.'

'Here's something you may not know about Katie – she had the hots for the bastard Dunne too. Looks like his relationship with her mother has put her right off. Thank God one of them has seen the light. I'm glad she's on our side now. It should help.'

'I'm glad to see that *your* relationship with Katie has become purely conspiratorial, Fergus. Although it's a very strange game when one lecherous old coot is in league with a teenager to get rid of another lecherous old coot.'

Mary was right, bugger it. But at least Katie had not also been sacrificed to the Moloch Dunne. He remembered how she and her mother had behaved around Dunne at the supper party on Friday, and shuddered. And now she was having to minister to the other two dupes. Poor, sensible Katie. She was right – she never did get any fun.

After the phone call Fergus headed for his car, and his nine o'clock meeting, with a light step. Today was going to be a good one. He could feel it.

*

The nine o'clock departmental meeting went surprisingly well, for a departmental meeting. Under 'Any Other Business', Petra surprised those present by raising the forthcoming deanship elections as a departmental matter. She pointed out that, being a small department, they had never felt any need for a deputy head of it. But might it be useful, she enquired coyly, to have one in place in case the substantive head should be called to Greater Things – things which she would be happy to countenance.

Cunning cow. She *must* mean him. She was offering to make him deputy head (which would become acting head on her elevation) in return for his support for her candidacy as dean. Well, it was no more than Nick Bonetti had intimated the previous week. It would certainly raise his profile in the eyes of the faculty if Petra was willing to make him acting head. He and Petra had hated each other for years. He was on record, some eight years before, as saying that she would never get a senior lectureship at Ariel, and now she was head of the bloody department. The whole corridor had heard that conversation, even though it had been conducted in his office with the door closed.

Nobody else round the table said a word, though they must have been curious as to what he was thinking and whether he would take the deal thus obliquely offered.

Fergus had always found Petra to be a poisonous individual. This was the first time he had ever seen a spark of generosity in her. Well, perhaps not generosity – deviousness captured it better. How much nouse did it take to see that he was an influential member of faculty that she should cultivate if she wanted to be dean?

As Petra brought the meeting to a close, Fergus felt his longed-for personal Chair become solid enough to sit on.

Petra smiled at him, a scary sight. He smiled back.

And thus the pact was made: the deanship was to be delivered to Petra and the department to Fergus.

Smiles all round.

He was just about to take them all for lunch to celebrate Petra's bombshell when Nick caught him in the corridor. Behind him stood the most gorgeous bit of totty that Fergus had seen in a long time.

This must be a new lecturer in Art History. He rummaged around in his memory to disinter the reason why this goddess was a stranger to him. Ah, there had been interviews for a new lecturer in Nick's department while he was in Alexandria in the autumn. He and Nick usually invited each other onto their interview panels to play the objective outsider. Experience had shown that each had a good eye for things that the other tended to miss in a candidate. They made a good team. But Fergus remembered now that Petra sat on the panel which appointed this dream.

Why on earth would Petra have agreed to the engagement of such a vision? She liked serious minds, and believed external appearance reflected the person within (hence her own power suits, with their alarmingly padded shoulders). She believed that the beautiful must also be frivolous. She had, indeed, written a paper entitled 'The curse of beauty'. Had she, perhaps, been ill on the day and missed the interviews?

The classicists were still bunched up behind Fergus in the doorway of Petra's office. Fergus looked back to see if Petra's face might reveal a clue to the mystery of this beautiful art historian. Horror of horrors, she was smiling at him again. Twice in one day?

And suddenly he knew. This girl was for him, his Helen of Troy. Something to keep him in line while Petra was dean; something to hold over him should he fail to support Petra in the manner she expected. And Petra would be smiling her awful smile at him for a long time to come.

He turned again to Nick and the vision. She was exquisite. Her demure first-day-in-the-new-job frock was a figure-hugging dress in silvery grey jersey. It was bias cut and flared from mid-thigh to just below the knee, emphasising her hips. Such hips! Blonde hair tumbled down over her breasts. Her long face was full of features – strong nose, Pre-Raphaelite mouth, huge blue eyes the colour of a deep ocean. Could she really be so lovely, right through to her bones? Perhaps her voice would grate? Perhaps her mind would be uninteresting, banal? No. He was quite certain all of that would be exquisite too. Petra had seen this candidate and immediately knew she was perfect. Petra had smiled her lupine smile as the girl entered the room for her interview and Petra had done this to him.

He was insulted and entranced in equal measure.

His face smiled at Nick and the girl as his mind raced. This vision in silver grey was simple insurance. Petra knew Fergus well enough to be sure he would not be able to resist this Silver Girl. And he couldn't care less. He would walk the path clearly signposted 'Here Be Dragons' and he would fear nothing. He was Fergus Girvan, revitaliser of classics in the modern university, respected innovator of distance teaching methods in his and many other disciplines; soon to be, at long last, Professor Fergus Girvan. They would say, as they gave him his Chair, 'we can't understand how you've been passed over for so long'. And he would have this glorious girl.

How wonderful was his world.

Mere moments had passed. He blinked to clear his head. Nick had got almost as far as the name in his introduction and sure enough:

' ... meet Sara Somerton, our new lecturer.'

Nick moved aside and Sara Somerton stepped forward. Fergus's hand was already on its way forward to shake hers. By the time the girl was in front of him he was ready. He took her half-proffered hand, tenderly, as if it were a tiny frightened creature. He held it warmly, firmly, raised it a little as though about to kiss it, inclined towards her and spoke softly and fervently,

'Welcome, indeed, Sara. I hope you'll be very happy here. If there's anything you need, *anything* I can do, you have only to ask.'

Throughout his customary little speech to new staff he held her gaze – not in a predatory way, but warmly. Very warmly. She stood still, returning his grip, not removing her hand, not taking her eyes from his. And what eyes!

'Hi,' she said simply and smiled broadly, still looking him in the eye.

He began to feel slightly dizzy – as if, perhaps, a spell had been cast upon him which he didn't fully understand. The skin on the back of his neck crawled. He found he had to withdraw his own hand first – but lightly, as if he had noticed nothing, as if he hadn't, actually, been electrified. He dropped her hand and turned, expansively, to the people of his department. He raised both arms shoulder high, filling the corridor.

'Lunch!' he boomed. 'We have something to celebrate! Nick, Sara – you must join us. Petra? Will you grace us with your presence?'

Petra muttered something about pressure of work and retreated through the press of bodies into her office. She didn't look quite so pleased with herself now she had watched his performance as the centre of attraction. She would have to get used to that, thought Fergus happily.

He strode out of the faculty and towards the bar, like a colossus, trailing his little band behind him.

*

They had a wonderful lunch. Fergus was in scintillating form. Ted and Veronica laughed at his jokes, Nick kept his glass full, and made sure that he had all the openings he could desire for his wicked and witty reminiscences by throwing him lines of the 'do you remember ... ?' variety.

Sara proved to be a devotee of red wine and matched him glass for glass. Not, of course, that it was a contest. She laughed at every one of his stories as the empty bottles on the table multiplied. She watched him almost constantly. It was to her that he played all through lunch. Her steady gaze, ready smile and happy laugh were invigorating. At last, a youngster who knew how to enjoy herself, whose education had not soured her. Here she was, fresh out of college on a piddling temporary contract without tenure, which meant she couldn't make any real plans for her life, and what was she thinking? What a good time she was having; how good life was. Petra might find she had unleashed more than she'd bargained for with Sara Somerton.

Long past closing time they rolled back into the faculty, like a wave, raucous and jolly.

*

It wasn't until he was on the motorway going home that he realised the day's jollifications had left him with a considerable headache. This led him to review his lunch-time activities, which resulted in a mental picture of the number of empty bottles on their table in the bar and his participation in their emptying. Which led him to get out of the fast lane and stick to a more modest 65 mph. Tedious precaution, but necessary. Without his driving licence life would, for all practical purposes, cease.

Getting into his flat he headed for the kitchen and put together the makings of a big pot of coffee, with which to wash down several aspirins. Then he noticed the saucy light on his answerphone was winking at him again. He pressed play.

'Fergus? It's Mary. Call me. Soon as you can, please.'

Things must be bad. Mary never said please, not to him anyway. He called her right away.

Things were bad indeed. Andy had run away. There had been a note and empty spaces which normally contained the girl's favourite things awaiting Mary when she got home from school.

'I knew straight away, when I came through the door, something wasn't right. I could *feel* an emptiness in the house, as if it were ringing.' Mary sounded punch-drunk.

Fergus felt anger at his child for, possibly, the first time. He also felt desperately sorry for Mary; not an emotion he'd ever applied to her before. He was aware that he had no map for the place that he was in.

'Where do you think she's gone?' he asked.

'To be with that bloody man – where do you think.'

'So where's that? I'll go and get her.'

Mary sighed.

'I've no idea. She hasn't left even a phone number. Here: I'll read you the note. It says "I can't stand this any longer. I just want to be with David. He understands. No-one else does." It doesn't say when she'll be in touch; nothing.'

Fergus heard the catch in Mary's voice.

He hated inactivity. If there was a puzzle, a problem, he wanted to solve it, right away. He was good at solving things. But currently there was no action possible. Except ...

'Should we call the police?'

Mary was quiet for some moments.

'Mary? Should we?'

'Yes, I suppose we should. But let's leave it until tomorrow.'

'Why, for Heaven's Sake?'

'I don't know. It just feels so ...'

Awful. That was how it felt. It felt like Andy was dead. And perhaps she *was* dead to them. Perhaps this was how it was going to be now.

Could it be he'd had all the time with the child that he was going to get? He wondered if this was what Mary thought. It was a terrible slap in the face for both of them – to Mary most of all. She said,

'She's a sensible girl at bottom, Fergus. She's got somewhere to go, or she wouldn't have gone. She won't be sleeping on the Embankment.'

'No. She'll be sleeping with that bloody man ...'

'She's been doing that anyway. We ought to wait,' and now she broke down. 'but it's so hard.'

For some moments nothing more came over the receiver. Then Mary said again,

'We ought to wait.'

Her voice was thick with tears but more collected now.

'If you think so.'

This time the silence ran on. Neither of them wanted to hang up, to be alone with the news. Finally Mary said,

'I'll stay here, of course, in case she calls.'

'Shall I come over?'

But she didn't want him to. Strangely that hurt, but he knew why. Mary would be doing a lot of weeping and cursing tonight and she wasn't the sort of woman who wanted a witness to her weakness.

'Call me if I can do anything. Promise?'

'Sure.'

And she was gone.

Fergus's lovely bubble of a day burst around him, showering him with icy drops of apprehension. He had planned a quiet dinner at home and some solid work on a commissioned piece about Euripides's Trojan Women. But that was out of the question now. The reference materials on his desk reproached him as he picked up his coat and headed for The World's End. He needed company if Mary didn't.

The barmaid sorted him out some aspirin for his headache, but it didn't stand a chance in the circumstances. It was very late when he got back. No message awaited him on the machine. He felt wretched and went to bed expecting to lie sleepless, but fell unconscious almost at once.

Tuesday 15 December

Fergus came to and wondered, blearily, if it was possible to feel worse and not be dead. He looked at his bedside clock and discovered, to his dismay, that it was ten o'clock. He found it hard, even so, to move. His first action was to stretch out a hand to the bedside phone and call the university. He pleaded food poisoning and asked Marion to cancel his appointments for the day. That done he lay a while longer, thinking.

Andy's disappearance lay like a physical weight in about the place his breakfast ought to go, if he could face any breakfast, which he couldn't. After struggling to the kitchen he finally succeeding in making the pot of coffee he'd started the evening before. He consumed about a pint of it, strong and black, and felt well enough to wash, although shaving still defeated him. The beard looked particularly seedy, garnishing the ruin of his face. He put his tongue out at the mirror and regretted it; he looked like a corpse fished out of water.

He had to assume that no word from Mary meant no word from Andy – but he phoned Mary anyway, at work. They pulled her out of a class when he insisted it was urgent. She arrived breathless at the phone and was quite cross to discover that he hadn't rung with news but in search of it. As he feared, she had heard nothing. Fergus agreed to check in with her again at home around five.

By lunchtime he was halfway through a bottle of wine and had turned out his kitchen, chucking away out of date store cupboard staples and scrubbing until every surface, utensil and corner was pristine. His cleaner would be surprised. It was a revelation to Fergus what lurked in the further recesses. Patently it was also a mystery to Tracey. He would have a word with her about that.

The afternoon stretched long before him. Spring cleaning the rest of the flat would be ridiculous, given that Tracey was due on Thursday. The pile of drafts for the architecture course meeting the following day still teetered on the edge of his desk, unread. They required much more concentration than he could currently muster. Instead he started on his paperwork. He sorted and filed the heap in his desk drawer – some of it, he noticed, was over six months old.

At least he had achieved something, he thought morosely, as he slumped into a chair with the dregs of the wine at four o'clock, feeling extremely fragile.

This last hour before he could call Mary crept by on leaden feet. In the end he was reduced to watching the hands on his desk clock moving, infinitesimally, towards the hour. His only sensible action as he waited was to switch on the lamps

Finally it was time. He called Mary. She had still heard nothing.

The non-news hit him like a blow. He didn't know if he could take any more inaction. Whatever he and Mary did, severally and together, as two concerned parents (even allowing for the serendipitous events which had recently conspired with them) it seemed Andy was impervious to everything but this, her first Grand Passion. The child was completely out of control. It was so unlike her that it frightened him. He thought back over many years, many relationships of many kinds, many women. Had he ever felt as Andy apparently did now? Felt that, against all reason, he *must* be with someone? The image of Sara Somerton wafted into his mind, ethereal, enigmatic, silvered. He could almost believe it possible with her. But that was such a set-up. What did they think he was, a man who thought solely with his dick? They under-estimated him.

Was it just sex, though, with Andy and this bloody man? Or was it, perhaps, to do with having something of her own, like the puppy Katie wanted? Dunne as puppy was a risible idea, Dunne as dog perfectly credible. He gave a snort of laughter. It rang hollow through the flat. He realised that he had barely spoken, except to Mary, for twenty-four hours. The flat rattled with unexpressed angst.

Into the rattling silence thrust the bleating of his telephone. It made him jump. He realised that he was still at his desk. He had not moved since he spoke with Mary at five.

A myriad thoughts rushed through his mind in the time it took him to lift the receiver. His heart was hammering in his chest so hard he thought for a moment he might be having a coronary.

'Hello?'

'Fergus? Hi ... it's me.'

He had a moment of confusion, then one of re-orientation, then he realised he could delete his worst fears because this was –

'Andy!'

He opened with a phrase he hoped was a fair approximation of the approach of better parents than he in such a situation.

'Are you alright?'

'Yeah, of course.'

There was a touch of asperity in that last remark. How very far they had come from her calling him 'Dad' in moments of crisis.

'Well, if you're OK, what's going on? Have you rung your mother?'

'No. I called you first.'

That made his heart swell with pride, for a moment. She went on.

'This is what's going on. I've got a flat and David and I are going to live in it together. I sorted out the flat today. That's why I had to cut school. The flat's in Balham. We're going to pick up the rest of my stuff tomorrow. David's got a van.'

Fergus's brain was so full of questions that his mouth refused to make words.

'Fergus? You see, everything's all right.'

It was, of course, so far from being all right that Fergus didn't know where to start. He supposed it was his inexperience as a parent that left him floundering. He hated to flounder. He did his best:

'Andy, sweetheart, I love you, and your mother loves you. Is this flat on the phone? Good. Give me the number. I'll call your mother. Keep in touch – and I mean daily. If anything happens – anything – call one of us. Don't try and do this all on your own, OK? Talk to us.'

'Thanks, Dad. I knew you'd understand.'

Oh, Christ – now he was her bloody accomplice! What could you do?

'Let's be clear on one thing, Andy – I do not understand. But at the moment I don't think that's the issue. I – we – want you to be safe.'

'We'll have you over for dinner as soon as we're settled.'

Holy Hell.

'Great.'

'OK, then. Bye.'

He sat at his desk in the little pool of light from the lamp and worked his way quietly through all the swear words he knew. As he was fluent in five languages (two of them dead) and effective in the vernacular of three others this took a while. Eventually, when he felt a little calmer, he called Mary.

She was as stunned as he had been, and the conversation was short. After they had rung off Fergus thought of several questions he should have asked Mary. And, indeed, several he should have asked Andy – for an address to go with the phone number of the rat-ridden love-nest in beautiful Balham for one thing. These, however, would have to wait. His whole body cried out for something physical to do. He needed mischief.

He called Janet.

'No, I don't want to speak with Katie.' He let a certain grimness colour his voice. He intended to unnerve her and could tell her was succeeding. 'I need to speak to *you*, Janet.' He paused for effect, then administered his coup de grâce. 'It's about Dunne, Janet.'

She hadn't been expecting that. A sort of gulp came down the phone. He let her sweat for a moment, then,

'You see, Andy ran away from home yesterday and we've just learned that she's setting up home in some dump in Balham with your David Dunne.'

There was a silence, then she said,

'But that can't be, Fergus. It just can't.'

'Why can't it, Janet? I've just had a telephone conversation with Andy. She was most explicit. She gave me the telephone number of the flat. The flat that they are sharing.'

He was being brutal, he knew. But he – and Mary – had suffered quite horribly today, and now someone else was going to suffer too. He couldn't make that someone be Dunne without some detective work. This was the detective work. He couldn't think of a good reason why he shouldn't vent some of his spleen while he was detecting.

An eloquent silence rang in his ear as he pondered how very shitty it was of him to vent his spleen on Janet, whose only faults in all this (of which he was aware) were gullibility and an inability to handle whisky in quantity. As the silence lengthened he weakened. Janet really wouldn't do as a punch-bag. As he began to think through ways of withdrawing from the sticky web he had started to weave, Janet spoke.

'Could I trouble you for that telephone number, Fergus, do you think?'

Fergus's hunting instincts re-asserted themselves. He could scent there was a deal to be struck here.

'Of course, Janet. While I'm looking it out, there are just a couple of things you might be able to help me with.'

The phone number of the Balham hutch was on the pad in front of him. Trade goods. There was another silence as she worked out whether further embarrassment was worth the phone number.

'All right.'

How to put this? If he really offended her she might just hang up on him, then he'd have to go round there and schmooze her. Oh hell, not that. She'd be weeping on his shoulder in no time flat.

'Janet, I'm sorry to have to ask, over the phone, the kind of questions that will help me locate Dunne. But I badly want to talk with him before he moves in with Andy. I'm sure you understand?'

'So, I'm sorry to be indelicate but ... just what is your relationship with Dunne?'

'Well, he's got that wonderful gallery. I've bought several pictures from him. When he brought them round we ...'

She trailed off. Her words conjured up a mental image of Dunne delivering his wares, so to speak. It was not agreeable.

'Not so wonderful now, Janet. It's empty. I think you must have been one of the few to ... ah ... patronise him. What, really, is your relationship with him?'

'David and I are good friends.'

'How good?'

'Er ... well ... as the saying is, very good.' She gave a small embarrassed laugh.

'And is this a recent development?'

She sighed.

'Yes.'

'Could you expand on that, please? I am sorry to press you but I'm trying to understand why my daughter and this man should suddenly be setting up home together.'

'Yes. Yes, I can quite see that that would be a concern for you. But this is very difficult for me – particularly over the telephone. Could you, perhaps, come over?'

Bugger. He'd been hoping to avoid that.

'Katie's out. There's an extra-mural class this evening at her school. She won't be back until quite late.'

Double bugger.

But he had realised, as the conversation progressed, that Janet could perform an even more important service than providing him with a current address for David Dunne.

What Fergus needed from Janet was that *she* should do the dirty deed – confront Dunne about his relationship with Andy and insist that he leave the girl alone. This shouldn't be too hard for her – there had already been the scene at Mary's. Janet obviously believed that Dunne belonged to her. She had money which she might be persuaded to lend and a comfortable home which she might be prepared to share. An ultimatum from her would carry tangible weight. Not least because it gave Dunne better options. It would only hold him until the next, more lavish, meal ticket came along of course. But Janet did at least constitute a meal; Andy could not be considered more than a light snack. If he could get Janet to put her foot down it would leave him (and Mary) truly innocent when railed at by Andy for having messed up her Grand Passion.

This was getting to be a good plan. He'd better get over to Janet's and start implementing it.

He looked at his watch. It should be simple enough to get a cab now.

'Yes, I can do that. I'll be round in about an hour and a half.' He softened. 'We'll get the business out of the way and then have a bite of supper. My treat.'

'All right.' She didn't sound very keen.

Mind you, the conversation Fergus wanted to have would kill anyone's appetite. He still didn't have much himself, after the awful day of waiting and then the shock of the phone call. But his diet had been exclusively liquid today so far. Ought to eat something soon.

She, however, returned to the devil's bargain they had struck. 'You won't forget the phone number, will you?'

He was dealing with a solicitor here – it would pay him to remember that. She was an intelligent woman. It was only Dunne who caused her to lose all sense. The bloody man appeared to be everybody's aberration – even including Fergus himself.

'Rest assured. I will not forget the phone number.'

They parted with mutual expressions of insincerity. At least, Fergus assumed they were mutual. He certainly didn't feel the warmth for the woman with which he had managed to honey his goodbyes.

He at once dialled the number Andy had given him. The phone rang for a long time before her voice came on the line, breathless. Christ – had they been in bed?

'Hello? Fergus! Hi! I was up the ladder, painting. It's great. It's going to be fabulous. I can't wait for you to see it. We're doing it three shades of blue; Wedgwood blue walls and ceiling, bright navy in the alcoves and the dado rail, and baby blue woodwork. We spent ages with the shade cards. David insisted I make the final choice. It was a toss-up between Wedgwood and fuchsia, but Wedgwood is classier don't you think? David's got marvellous taste. Just like you. We've got this wonderful antique bedstead and ...'

There was quite a lot more in a similar vein but Fergus missed it, thinking through the implications of sharing good taste with David Dunne. Surely only a manic depressive or an aficionado of the Regency period decorated a room in three shades of blue. He didn't think Dunne was either. Romantic nest-building in blue certainly struck Fergus as a contradiction in terms. He entertained a small and malicious hope that a cold-looking flat would quickly chill Andy's enthusiasm for her situation.

It was likely Dunne had put her up to this choosing of colours and painting of walls to deepen her attachment. His interest would be in getting her firmly attached to the love nest. He probably wasn't much bothered by her colour choices as he was unlikely to spend much time there. Buggeration. Was Dunne that cunning? Undoubtedly. Was this how Fergus would, himself, have behaved in a similar situation? Absolutely not! He had, categorically, never encouraged any young woman to leave home (with or without parental permission) and set herself up in a flat for his convenience. He had never contributed to any such arrangement. In any way. No.

But thinking of Andy trying to make the best of this fabulous dump in Balham reminded him of the reason he had called – apart from checking that this really was her new number.

'Andy, love, I was so relieved to hear from you when you rang before that I forgot to ask almost all the important questions.'

'Oh.'

She sounded crest-fallen. This needed tact. She felt like a grown up right now and he would get a lot more out of her if he could build that up. It would be a good trick given the questions he needed to ask. He gave it his best shot.

'I was just wondering about the rent – for the flat. Do you need an allowance?'

'Oh Fergus – you are a dear. That would be such a help 'cos the flat's in my name. David said it would be difficult for him to sign a lease right now.'

Now and until the end of time probably. Bankrupts had trouble with things like leases.

'There's his wife, you see. He says that if he's seen to be able to lease a flat *she'll* say he can afford to pay her more maintenance. He's living in this grotty bedsit at the moment, so he can pay his share towards the children, but she's always on at him to pay more, and she won't let the children stay with him at the bedsit. You should have seen his face when he explained it all – so sad! So I said let's get a flat and then they *can* come and stay. He loved the idea. And after all, he's got to live somewhere, hasn't he? A man like him, in a bedsit – it's dire.'

'He's living in a bedsit? Where is it?' Fergus couldn't keep his eagerness to acquire the address out of his voice.

'I don't know. He says it's so awful he won't let me come round there.'

Was there yet a chance that Andy and Dunne were still only at the heavy petting stage? Unless Dunne had a bed hidden away somewhere at the gallery, yes. Here, finally, was something to be glad about. Possibly.

'She's been beastly about the separation, he says. She's using his children as a weapon against him. She sounds like a real cow. I hate her.'

Fergus took no pleasure in having been right about the inevitable existence of a wife and children.

'Have you met her?'

'No, but David's told me all about her. How she hardly ever lets him see the children. How she's always whining for money, never says thank you; never says anything nice. I've met the kids though.'

'And how did he introduce you?'

'As a friend.' She sounded a little defensive for a moment, but quickly rallied. 'David had them last weekend, for the afternoon. We took them out. They're great.'

'How many children?'

'Four, all boys. She wouldn't use birth control, although David begged her to. She's Roman Catholic, you see.'

Fergus railed inwardly. Dunne's poor bloody wife! It takes two to make babies, after all. Was there no end to the man's manipulations? How did he get away with it? Women seemed completely unable to resist him.

Fergus suppressed a pang at the thought of Andy talking so glibly about birth control and what happened when you didn't use any. He made a mental note to encourage Mary to get Andy down to the local Family Planning Clinic. Urgently.

'Let me see – they're two, four, seven and eleven. They're so cute. We played football. They really liked me.'

He made a mental note to look into this family of Dunne's. He'd start by asking Janet about it.

Then what she'd said about the flat being in her name finally registered.

'Andy, how have you managed to sign the lease for a flat, love?'

'Oh, I used you as guarantor, Fergus. I knew you wouldn't mind.'

'Shouldn't I have signed something?'

'Well ... er ... you did.'

'You forged my name?'

'Well, yes. That's OK, isn't it?'

'No, of course it's not OK. It's illegal, you idiot.' But curiosity would out. 'Was it a good forgery?'

'Pretty good. I practised first. I am an artist, you know!' He could hear her grin down the phone wire.

And once again they were partners in crime (quite literally this time). The little minx wouldn't have dared try this with Mary. But then, that had always been his function – when Mary said no, Fergus fixed things. That was a basic strand of their relationship he now realised. He undermined her mother and that way bought Andy's affections. No. That wasn't fair. The affection was real enough. Sadly, so was the undermining.

Just occasionally Fergus wished he was part of a normal family. He was wishing it again now. No normal family got itself into this kind of mess. Did it? And he had a feeling that the depths of this particular mess had not, even now, been fully plumbed.

'How much is the rent, love?'

He whistled when she told him. He went to sit down, then realised he already was.

'I thought this was Balham? For Christ's sake!'

'It's a nice part of Balham.'

'Sweetheart, there *aren't* any nice parts of Balham! I hope Dunne's going to give you his share,' he said, without any such hope.

'Oh, I'm sure he will. But with his wife taking all his money I'm not going to bug him about it.'

'So how are you going to manage?'

Even as he asked, Fergus felt his stomach slither down towards his kneecaps. Dear old Dad – that was how she was going to manage. There was no other possibility. To keep the flat in light and heat and Andy fed would take almost as much again as that extortionate rent. Then there was the phone, of which Andy was very fond, fares, clothes, and some sort of social life. These were grown-up sums they were talking here: a lot of families had *mortgages* smaller than this. It was going to be a serious financial drain on him until this mess got sorted out. Dear God, let that be soon!

Holy Hell, he'd thought of something else.

'Andy, what did you do about the deposit?'

'I used my Post Office money.'

Was there no end to it? There had been over three thousand in that account. He ought to know – he'd put most of it in there. That money was to help her through university, and after, when she started out on her own. It wasn't supposed to be thrown away on this.

'Did you pay it straight to the landlord?'

'Yes.'

At least Dunne hadn't got his hands on it. He went for damage limitation with a touch of blackmail thrown in.

'Andy, I'm going to start an account for you. I'm going to put a thousand in it, and I'll put in another six hundred each month but – and this is the condition – Dunne is not to touch *any* of the money in that account. Not a penny.

'I'll help you set up standing orders for the rent and the utilities and show you how to do a household budget.

'Dunne may *benefit* from the money, but the money itself he may not touch. Is that a deal?'

There was a silence, then,

'But what if ...?'

'No "what ifs". This is the deal. You must promise me.'

He waited for her reply. It did not come immediately.

The thought came, unbidden, that Andy's promise might no longer be the solid rock he had always known it to be. He had to trust her in this, and he didn't, not really. And that was the worst thing of all. Finally, grudgingly, she said,

'I promise.'

'Give me the address then. I'll set up the account tomorrow and then come over and we'll work out a budget for you. OK?'

'OK.'

'When will Dunne be out?'

'Well, he's not actually moving in until the weekend.'

'So he won't be there at all until the weekend?'

There was a silence, which spoke volumes.

'I don't know. He said he had some things he needed to take care of this week.'

So Andy was there on her own, in her wildly over-priced flat, waiting as forlornly as Ariadne on Naxos, for a man with a thousand golden excuses who never came. It broke Fergus's heart to hear her defend the callous bastard.

'I'll be over about nine in the evening then, if that suits? Will it give you time for your homework?'

'Oh! I guess.'

Another awful suspicion crept into his mind.

'Andy, you are still going to school, aren't you?'

'Well ... until you offered to stake us – me – I thought I'd need a job, to pay the rent and ... things.'

'And how did you think you were going to make that kind of money?'

Silence.

Fergus couldn't find anything to say either. It was too much. Every apparently anodyne enquiry produced a new hurt. He felt as if he was wading in blancmange that had been seeded with razor blades.

'Look, we'll talk about it tomorrow. I'll bring your mother.'

'Do you have to?'

'Of course I do! We *both* want to help, love. We've been worried witless.'

'I suppose you'll tell her everything?'

'Unusually, yes. I have already told her what I knew before you and I had this conversation. And as soon as we're done here I shall tell her the rest. She's your mother, for Christ's Sake!'

'Is her coming another condition of the money?'

Andy sounded miserable and defeated. Well, bloody good job too. Better she suffer a bit of a defeat at the hands of her family than a catastrophe born of ignorance out in the real world.

'I'll see you tomorrow at nine. Give me the address.'

There was another perceptible pause before she gave it to him. Reliable Andy, truthful Andy was watching what she said. He could hear the change in her, the calculation. It cut him deeply. He would have to warn her mother that the girl might not be straight with them. Sweet Jesus – let there be a time, and soon, when his lovely Andy would re-emerge. He ached for that lost girl and, whisper it soft, was almost afraid of this one.

He was afraid to ask anything more, every chance remark was another step into the razor blades. He didn't want to push her into something irrevocable. He took his leave gently, as one would of someone sick, and put the phone down. He noticed that the hand that had held it was curled into a claw.

He was out of his depth. He needed to talk to Mary.

But then he remembered Janet, and that there was possibly good information to be got from that source. He rang for a cab.

While he was waiting for it he washed and rang Mary. He gave her a precis of his conversation with Andy and an outline of his fears dully, without emotion, glad he was strapped for time, unable to bleed any more; unable to empathise. Mary was monosyllabic too.

He hoped she understood the cause of his own taciturnity was simply that he was at the end of his tether. And he still had La Crouch to deal with! He recalled the ancient Chinese curse: 'may you live in interesting times' and prayed silently for life to become much less interesting in the very near future.

He arranged to eat with Mary early the next evening, during which they would make a plan of action, then go round to the flat in Balham.

'This is awful, isn't it?' Mary said, finally.

'Yes, it is. And it's going to get worse.'

'But then it will get better?'

Accustomed as he was to giving Mary an expedient reply, he couldn't bring himself to say 'yes', just like that. He was silent. She sighed. Their goodbyes were gloomy.

He rode the forty minutes or so to Janet's trying not to think about Andy and failing completely. Lines of possibility merged together, tied themselves in knots, ran away into unspeakable futures. The taxi driver didn't say a word, just when Fergus could have done with some diversion.

Squaring his shoulders for what was to come, he put his hand on Janet's front gate.

He had called Janet out of devilment, which mood had long since passed. Now he was just tired, and very, very sorry that he had rung her. But if she could help him locate Dunne then he was in the right place at the right time.

He felt a headache pressing against his temples. God, he needed a drink.

However, never let it be said that Fergus ever failed to rise to a challenge. Show him an audience – even (or, perhaps, especially) an audience of one – and he was at once the showman.

He knocked and Janet opened so quickly that she must have been lurking behind it. She had on something long and loose. Not the sweeping thing she had worn for her supper party: it was much less formal than that. It looked like a kimono with a satin negligée under it. It was not, certainly, something in which most women would consider entertaining someone they didn't know well. In the hand not concerned with the door she held a glass containing a couple of inches of amber fluid. The fluid did not look like apple juice.

'Fergus!' she said, and made an expansive, welcoming gesture with the glass, spilling some of its contents over her wrist. She giggled and licked it off.

Fergus read the signs. Retreat was imperative – and impossible. Not least because the taxi had gone. He was in big trouble. The woman was pissed: extravagantly, libidinously pissed.

She let go of the door and leaned forward, took his elbow, drew him inside, gave a smart about-turn and kicked the door shut without letting go of him. Having got him inside she finally let him go and put her drink down carefully on the hall table, then she held out both arms to him.

'Let me take your coat,' she said.

They were, somehow, ominous words.

Fergus meekly took it off and handed it over. Janet took it and looked about her, apparently surprised to find there were no coat hooks in the hall, just a chair beside the little telephone table she had put her drink on. She folded the coat with great care, bent over (displaying a prodigious cleavage), laid it across the chair and patted it.

'There!' she said.

Fergus could feel his mouth drying as his eyes tried their damndest not to stare at Janet's breasts. He had wanted a drink. It looked very much as though he was going to get it. He suspected that drink was, indeed, about to flow like the Trevi Fountain. It became very clear to him that he should not imbibe. Janet was, patently, already not responsible. The two of them being irresponsible together could be a very dangerous combination.

Janet wafted into the lounge with Fergus in her wake. Over her shoulder she purred,

'I see you came by taxi. How sensible.'

Fergus was already feeling that the taxi had been an error of judgement. He hoped he would be able to avoid making any more.

He sat as invited, but not on the invitingly patted sofa. He occupied an easy chair across the room from that particular trap. A glass of red wine was put into his hand and the bottle by his elbow. He waited until Janet had turned away to refresh her own glass – which he noticed was brandy – before taking a restorative gulp of his own drink. It was still on its way down when he began to feel a little less ragged. He took a second large mouthful and began to feel almost comfortable. He wriggled a little in the chair, leant back into its cushions, crossed his legs. OK. He could do this. Where to begin?

Janet sank onto the sofa with a sigh which might have been theatrical, or simply a result of the unplanned suddenness with which she landed. She was bright of eye and cheek and smiling broadly. Fergus was aware that this was as good as she was going to get tonight. With a quantity of brandy inside her, on what was almost certainly an empty stomach, things would be going downhill from bright and smiley to maudlin and weepy shortly. Nevertheless, this was a big change from the upset and reticent woman he had spoken to on the phone a couple of hours ago and he should take advantage of her better mood while she was still inhabiting it.

It did not look, however, as if he was going to get the promised supper.

'What shall we drink to?' she asked.

Fergus felt mischief stir within him once more. He raised his glass.

'To honesty,' he said, and drank without waiting for her to respond.

She drank, although she didn't repeat his toast, holding the glass to her lips and looking at him archly over the top of it, as if he had proposed something far more risqué. It was unnerving, but nothing he couldn't cope with. He set his glass down, to be business-like, noticed it was almost empty and refilled it absent-mindedly while he thought through his best approach.

Old: that was the thing. He should appear old and pedantic, and narrow-minded. He must strive for an authoritative air. He should be standing.

He stood. He moved the two steps to the fireplace and turned to stand with his back to it, hands clasped behind him, leaning forward earnestly – the image, he hoped, of Victorian rectitude. In front of him was the bay window, the sofa and his audience. He began.

'The thing is, Janet, this business with Andy; it's got her mother and me in rather a state ...'

Janet's eyes narrowed, the smile got less broad. She didn't let him get any further.

'Very awkward for you both, I can quite see. Running away like that,' she tutted. 'I'm just grateful that Katie is more sensible.'

Fergus reflected briefly on his recent tête à tête with her daughter, wondering at the mother's confidence. If ever there was a pot ready to boil over it was Katie.

But, of course, it wasn't Katie who had boiled over. It was Andy.

'But I don't see,' Janet continued, 'how *your* problems with *your* daughter have any bearing on David Dunne – or my relationship with him. Andy has a schoolgirl crush on him, nothing more. He teaches her on an occasional basis, I believe?'

'He has promised her free, private tuition.'

Janet leaned back into the sofa's cushions.

'He has taken a professional interest in her, as an artist. She has responded inappropriately.

'Perhaps you are unaware, Janet, that Andy has taken a flat which, she tells me, is where David Dunne intends to co-habit with her as from this weekend. He is, apparently, giving up his bedsit because his wife won't let him have his children to stay with him there.'

Janet's smile disappeared and her sultry expression was replaced by a narrowing of eyes and mouth.

'Wife?'

'And four children.'

'Impossible.'

'Fact.'

Of course, Fergus couldn't prove in any way that would satisfy a legal mind like Janet's that Dunne had a wife (although the children were almost proven) but he didn't let that worry him.

Janet looked sullen now. She had not changed her voluptuous position on the sofa, but the allure had gone out of her. Her head was still laid back on the cushions, but tilted down now, the better to peer at Fergus. There was the definite suggestion of a double chin, and perhaps a need for glasses when close inspections such as this were called for.

However, Janet was not lacking in pluck. And her stocks of alcohol were plentiful. She levered herself off the sofa and made for the sideboard to refresh her glass.

Fergus realised there were two important things about Janet which he did not know: how much she had drunk before he arrived and how much more she *could* drink before becoming incoherent. Before she became incoherent he needed to convince her to make it impossible for Dunne to move into the Balham flat that weekend. He was certain she could do it, if she believed it was in her interests to do so. Thereafter he hoped Mary would come up with a plan to keep Andy away from Dunne on a more permanent basis. But his plan would fall at the first hurdle if he only got Janet onside when she was too drunk to remember tomorrow morning what she had promised to do this evening.

Janet poured herself another large brandy and returned to the sofa via the rear of the chair Fergus was sitting in. He felt a hand brush his shoulder. The lounge began to feel like shark-infested waters.

The frisson passed, as did Janet. Her landing on the sofa was less happily managed this time and the result was less languorous, more slumped. Fergus estimated that half an hour, and the brandy now in her glass, would render further sensible discourse impossible. He was about to try and further his agenda when she forestalled him.

'David is not currently married.'

Fergus could only shrug.

'Andy believes he is.'

'Andy is a child,' Janet went on, 'rather confused and – forgive me – runs wild. The girl was a latch key kid until she met my Katie and benefitted from our stabilising influence. Andy is wrong.'

Fergus felt his teeth begin to grind, but made no retort. The game was afoot now.

Janet was not a solicitor for nothing; she continued,

'Have you met this wife?'

'No, but Andy has met the children.'

'Simple hearsay, Fergus.'

She made a triumphant gesture with her glass and lost some of its contents to the sofa cushions. She appeared not to notice, something had obviously occurred to her.

'You have the phone number and address of this flat of Andy's? I have David's contact details.'

Fergus felt covetousness flow through him. If the phone number and address which Janet had were not those of the gallery, they could lead him to the mysterious bedsit. This was the chink in Dunne's armour for which he had been searching.

'I have been to David's flat, Fergus. It is a bachelor pad. Wifely touches were entirely absent. The bedlinen was a manly black and grey. There were dishes in the sink, there was dust everywhere, there were no children. Nor any room for children. Not a toy, not a sock, not a satchel, not a Beatrice Potter porringer was to be seen.'

'Janet, I would very much like the address of that flat.'

'I'm sure. And in the interests of getting this misunderstanding cleared up, I am prepared for an exchange of information. But,' she actually wagged her finger at him, 'I do not want you bothering David.'

Bothering? That was a polite word for what Fergus had in mind. To avoid making any unfortunate remark to this effect out loud, Fergus finished his glass of wine.

Janet had changed from silk to steel. Fergus felt much safer. He rose to get the precious slip of paper bearing Andy's new address from his trouser pocket. A twinge from his gammy knee as he got up echoed a twinge from his conscience. Andy was going to be seriously displeased when La Crouch turned up on her doorstep. However – no pain, no gain.

Janet also rose and sailed out into the hall where, presumably she kept her address book.

Fergus refilled his glass and realised that was the end of the bottle of wine with which Janet had so thoughtfully supplied him. While he waited for her return he finished this final glass, preparatory to an exchange of addresses, the calling of a taxi and an end, at last, to this endless day.

His mind was busy with the potential information about Dunne's flat, and how this could be fitted together with the rest of the information he had gathered about the wretched man. Thus preoccupied, Fergus ceased to concentrate on the potential dangers in Janet's lounge. This was a mistake. He was still standing in front of the chair, empty glass in hand, when Janet returned.

Janet's return from the hall was sudden. The brandy appeared to be affecting her braking as well as her steering. She stopped finally well inside Fergus's personal space. Her hands were clasped together in the region of her bosom in what, in other circumstances, might have been a gesture of prayer. She held a small Post-It leaf. There was writing on it.

Fergus peered closely at the little piece of yellow paper, eager for a glimpse of Dunne's location. As soon as he realised what other things he was now peering closely at he was aware that he should have stepped discreetly away and waited for her to hand it to him. As it was he knew himself instantly and seriously compromised by the proximity of Janet in general, and her breasts in particular, between which rested the precious Post-It.

He tried – too late – to avert his eyes from her bosom and take a step backwards. But as he tried to find something else to look at, his gaze met hers. Her eyes were very wide, the pupils large and lustrous. Her mouth was parted. Everything about her said 'moist'. His tardy step backwards was his final undoing. Behind him (unfortunately, less than a step away) was the armchair in which he had recently been sitting. He lost his balance against the chair and caught his foot in Janet's robe as he tried to regain it. In attempting to halt his fall he somehow ended up with his arms around Janet. They both fell into the chair, Janet on top. The trap had been neatly laid – and quickly sprung.

'Oh Fergus,' she breathed, and kissed him.

Cursing inwardly Fergus tried to restrict his response to a level of simple politeness, while he located the current whereabouts of the Post-It. It was difficult; he wanted to shuck her off his lap and make a run for it, but that wasn't an option. He could not leave without the address of that flat with the black and grey bedlinen and no porringers. He had known the stakes. This was for Andy he told himself, and lay back and thought of family.

After a while he thought he should show a little animation for the sake of his reputation, and thereafter instinct took over. It seemed like no time at all before he was undoing Janet's kimono with one hand whilst pulling the curtains in her bedroom with the other. He knew he was going to regret this – hell, he was regretting it already. He just hoped she wasn't the kind to kiss and tell. With luck her memory of the event would be hazy and her participation ditto.

However, as evening became night Fergus was first surprised then alarmed to find that Janet, far from becoming weepy and then comatose, was becoming more co-ordinated and energetic. He was keeping up fairly well, he thought, considering. Nevertheless, around midnight he found himself wishing fervently for Sukie and her relatively short attention span. As he lay back briefly on the pillows before summoning up the energy to go to the lavatory he reflected that if sex with Sukie was analogous to a fiercely fought five-a-side game, then this with Janet was more like an all-day knock-out tournament.

When he came back from the lavatory Janet was missing. He blessed his fortune and was gathering up his clothes when she reappeared with a tray.

'A little supper,' she said, 'to sustain us.'

Supper was not unwelcome. It had been a long time since lunch. There was a lot of fishy stuff and salad. All good for the libido, he supposed. He was pretty certain that the only thing good for his libido would be sleep, but he got back into bed, ate with relish and did his part with the bottle of Asti Spumante that accompanied it.

During supper he heard the sounds of the front door being opened. Katie. There were noises from downstairs for a while, then footsteps on the stairs. The girl called out a goodnight to her mother. Mercifully she then went on past the door. He realised that he had stopped chewing as he listened to the clomping coming closer. He must have held his breath as well because when the steps began to recede he recommenced both to breathe and chew. Inevitably he started to cough as part of his libido-enhancing supper slipped down the wrong way. His eyes watered with discomfort and mortification. Janet chuckled sympathetically.

'Katie's a good girl,' she said. 'She takes me as she finds me. Relax.'

She patted his bare shoulder and Fergus had to accept his situation with as much grace as he could muster.

After supper he leaned back contentedly, aware he'd over-used certain muscles and of a certain stinging discomfort beneath the bed clothes – but, overall, feeling pretty good. Janet put the tray on the floor and snuggled up close to him. The trick in such situations, as he knew very well, was to separate the pleasure of post-coital intimacy from the actual person involved. As if idly he switched off the bedside light with one hand and lightly stroked her hair with the other. It felt like wire wool.

She stirred, and her hand began to creep down his belly towards the site of the stinging discomfort.

'Shhh,' he said, catching the hand sleepily and bringing it to his lips. 'Plenty of time.'

Then he knew no more.

Wednesday 16 December

Somehow it was morning.

Fergus had a crick in his neck, a bad taste in his mouth and a moment of disorientation as he came to surrounded by pink wallpaper which he couldn't remember ever having seen before.

Aches and pains in various parts of his body quickly reminded him where he was, what he had done and with whom. He felt the hot blood rush of shame and applied to it the ice pack of necessity – there were no innocents in war.

He looked at the clock radio; seven thirty. After a few more groggy moments he realised it must be Wednesday.

He could smell fresh coffee. At once it arrived, in a cafétiere borne on a tray by Janet. She was dressed, which was a relief. She kissed him warmly all the same, which made him uncomfortable. And as the kiss was not unpleasant he examined the events of the evening before and the facts of the case, to be sure he had allocated the right people to the right sides in the current conflict. Whose side, exactly, was Janet on? He found it difficult to be precise about that. Her own, probably. He was, at any rate, sitting up in the woman's bed, drinking her coffee so it would pay him to be civil.

As he had nothing else to wear at the moment, he put on a smile. It felt a bit lop-sided, but seemed to serve.

He sipped the excellent coffee and thought about Katie. The thought of bumping into her on the way to the bathroom made him cringe inwardly. What would she think of him? He tried to analyse what about the situation bothered him. Katie must have met her mother's boyfriends before; must have run across them coming out of the bathroom, at breakfast – everywhere. Janet was an attractive woman; not his taste, but attractive. Boyfriends – stupid term, but less salacious than 'men friends' somehow – she must have had aplenty. But, moving swiftly to the nub of the cringing, neither Katie nor her mother had any idea that Fergus would rather have spent last night with Katie than with Janet. So there was no cause for cringing, simply for regret. Fergus could not now postulate a scenario that would enable his relationship with Katie to move from paternalistic friend to lover. Katie would never take him seriously. And Janet would kill him.

He sighed and sipped. The coffee was doing its work; he felt rather better. Bits of him still ached and stung, but his head felt clearer – clear enough for him to start thinking about the day ahead. Oh shit: here he was, across town from his diary on a day when he was definitely supposed to be at the university. He had a game of squash at lunchtime for certain, but what else? A more immediate need was revealed by his tracing the source of one of his aches to his bladder.

Thus galvanised he got quickly out of bed and immediately regretted it. A groan escaped him. No matter what else he did today he needed to apply lots of soothing warm water to his body first.

Thinking of Katie he slipped on his trousers, which immediately made contact with all his sore bits. After a moment's thought he pulled on his jacket as well and ran Janet's comb quickly through his hair. He looked ridiculous but, hellfire, he was only going as far as the bathroom.

Cautiously he opened the door – and heard someone coming up the stairs. It was Katie, munching toast. Retreat would be inelegant, he must brazen it out. He straightened and emerged fully from Janet's bedroom.

'Hi, Fergus,' said Katie, and moved along the landing.

Fergus was taken aback. What had happened to the shyness, the awkwardness in his company? She sounded completely at ease greeting a semi-stranger, with a naked belly sticking out from his jacket, in the doorway of her mother's bedroom. Somehow his change of status seemed to have legitimised their relationship. What a shame the relationship that had put her at her ease wasn't going to last.

'Morning,' he called cheerily after her retreating back, thinking black thoughts.

He made it into the bathroom safely and locked the door. Ten minutes in a hot shower made things look much rosier – himself included – and he fairly bounced down the stairs when he had dried and dressed. More coffee awaited him, smiles from both women, and breakfast.

Then it was time to step back into his life and wonder what changes last night were going to make to his future.

It wasn't until he was halfway home that Fergus thought to check his pockets for Dunne's address. It wasn't there. Buggeration. He checked again, squirming around like a man who has just discovered a poisonous snake inside his clothing. He found neither the precious yellow Post-it nor the slip of paper with Andy's address on it. Devious witch – had she abstracted it to make sure that he would have to call on her again? ('Oh, perish the thought,' said over-used parts of his anatomy.) Or had she been playing Mata Hari all the time – seducing him just to get what she needed? He should have remembered that where sex was involved anything was possible. He felt rather silly, even naive. Fergus hadn't felt naive since – oh, puberty.

Back at his flat he hastily checked his diary and rang Marion to re-arrange his morning, citing a 'minor domestic crisis' – that euphemism for all manner of life's peculiarities.

'Don't give my apologies for the course meeting, Marion. I ought to be able to make that, and I don't want to miss it.'

He felt disorientated – he almost never played away from home – and spent half an hour doing unnecessary chores which involved touching all his favourite things. Thereafter he made a mental note to tell Tracey about the accumulations of dust he had found on them. Then he chucked the hefty pile of unread drafts for the meeting into his briefcase, grunted when he tried to lift it, got the Jag out and headed for the university. He'd have to skim through the drafts during the meeting. And – damn and blast – he hadn't written up an outline of his Alexandrian Pharos material for their consideration. Never mind, he'd give them the gist verbally: probably more entertaining for them than yet another bloody paper anyway.

When he hit the motorway he flew up it like a hawk with its tail on fire.

*

At the university things began to move entirely too quickly for someone in his delicate condition. He was barely late for the course meeting, but he didn't feel he had a grip. The hernia-inducing stack of papers in his briefcase reproached him as he lugged them to the meeting room. He had been going to read them quietly the night before with a nice bottle of claret and some Vaughn Williams on the stereo – but events had put a stop to that.

This meeting was an important one. The faculty's new inter-departmental, second level course on architecture promised to be a major addition to its profile. Petra was chairing the committee charged with creating this course. It was, Fergus reflected sourly, safer than letting her write any of it. As author most of her text would consist of diatribes against the thieves of Greece's ancient marble marvels.

Fergus's newly developed theories on the construction and composition of the Alexandrian Pharos, upon which he had been working very hard, was going to make a wonderful addition to it. He could start on a draft immediately – all the material was bubbling in his head, just waiting to be released onto paper. He had the thrust of his chapter already worked out, the teaching points, the examples to support them. He, Fergus Girvan, could set this course on fire with something completely original. The course would become a trailblazer. His work would cause everyone to rethink their approach to the subject. Only Dr Fergus Girvan could inject this kind of fire into Classics. Only Girvan could make Classics exciting and dangerous. He wanted this badly.

And his research and resultant contribution to this course would make two fine strands in the fabric of his upcoming promotion submission. That submission was beginning to come together nicely, what with the Acting Head of Department pretty much in his pocket, and the possibilities of an excellent new PhD student still to come.

He had kept the thrust of his current research quiet in case colleagues in other universities showed an interest in pursuing it. He had worked fast partly because the material was so fascinating, but also so that he wouldn't get gazumped. It was only a matter of time before somebody else looked in the right section of the British Library's catalogue and found the same obscure bundle of scrolls that he had. He certainly didn't want to call attention to it. In the nineteenth century the bundle been used as packing for various Turkish artefacts found by an amateur archaeologist called Huntingdon in Constantinople, and sent back to the British Museum for evaluation. Fortunately, someone had realised what the papyrus rolls might be and handed them to the British Library, where they had been given the most cursory of catalogue entries. It was sheer, dumb luck and wilful curiosity that had caused Fergus to request the '33 papyrus scrolls, unopened. Possibly remnant of Alexandrian Library, via Alexandrian Serapeum, via Imperial Library of Constantinople'. When the librarian realised what they were, some time was lost while the library got them photostatted, which at once piqued Fergus's curiosity even further.

During the month he had to wait for the material to be rendered into a form that they would allow him to touch, Fergus ruminated on the happy chance that had brought those few scrolls to his attention. When Julius Caesar fired Alexandria in 48 BCE, diligent clerks in the Library gathered up what they could and made a run for it. Many strange armfuls of knowledge had survived various fires in Alexandria in this way: this was only the most recent to surface. There was another paper to be written on how the clerks had decided what to save from the flames, what the cataloguing and reading systems must have been to allow them to snatch such a multifarious cross-section of items.

This was why Fergus had been keen to make the meeting. He had a little glow of anticipation – or it might just have been the adrenaline rush of his dash up the motorway – as he slid into a seat.

It was a long morning (even though his had started late). The ideal place for his material on the Pharos would come late in the course, so he bided his time, contributed sparingly, occasionally set straight those embarking on wild or dreary flights of fantasy, while he hastily skimmed through the enormous pile of papers. He wasn't alone in this; several others were only one paper ahead of the agenda. It was a sobering thought that the course plan might well evolve from the reading solely of first and last paragraphs by those present. People should keep papers shorter. His were never more than one sheet of paper, often less. It was matter of principle with him to be succinct. Time taken by a paper's author to trim it down to its bones was time saved for all the people who had to read it. Blaise Pascal put his finger on the nub when he said, 'I only made this letter longer because I had not the leisure to make it shorter.' Make the time, people!

Lunchtime drifted close, and then past, and still they were gabbing. The meeting had a ghastly stop-go quality induced by everyone grappling frantically with the reams of paper. Fergus's belly was starting to grumble quietly to itself. He could cut and run, but he wanted this opportunity and had little confidence that it would come his way without a good pitch on his part. Not long now, surely!

At last (at half past one o'clock: there wouldn't be a single sandwich left on the whole campus by the time he was done here) the agenda item for which he had endured much was next up, 'Chapter 14: Architecture in the Ancient World'.

Petra introduced the item, praising the stamina of her hollow-eyed listeners and promising them a break as soon as it was concluded. That should make his pitch easier, Fergus thought – everyone was eager to be released. He sat up in his seat and prepared to speak ex tempore – always his strongest suit.

But Petra didn't stop talking, and it quickly dawned on Fergus that he had played his cards too close to his chest. The daft bitch had made other arrangements – and somehow there was a paper headed 'draft outline of Chapter 10: the Alexandrian Pharos' on top of the pile in front of him. He had not written this paper. Why, in the name of the Sweet Creeping Christ, hadn't he read these bloody papers last night? A glib phrase from the one and only management course he had ever attended tolled in his head 'fail to prepare; prepare to fail'. Shit, shit and shit.

'Given that no-one in my Classics Department, or on this team, has any particular expertise in this area which would enable us to illustrate the teaching points required, I have obtained faculty's permission to use a consultant from outside the university to prepare this material for us. I have had a most satisfactory – I may even say exciting – outline from David Dunne. His résumé is Paper 10a. I think you'll agree that his credentials are most satisfactory. The outline which he has submitted for our consideration – Paper 10b – is eminently suitable and will provide students with an excellent grounding in the area. To illustrate the teaching points as per our brief, he has chosen to investigate the ancient lighthouse at Alexandria. The research is quite novel and, I must say, exciting. It will be a feather in our academic cap that we have such innovative work to demonstrate our thesis.'

Fergus's stomach stopped grumbling and began to whimper. Dunne. Again. How could this have happened?

Mercifully there wasn't much more to the meeting. It was in his mind for a moment to try and talk them out of it, but he could hear his own voice in his head. It would have to go something like, 'but Petra, I was going to ...'. He had nothing in writing. Not here anyway. All his paperwork was at home. All the chits recording his use of the primary sources at the Library were there. It was his own fault. He should have had his own outline prepared and circulated ahead of time with the rest of the papers. Why hadn't he? 'Minor domestic crises'? Christ on a tricycle! How could he have let things slide so badly?

Suspiciously there was little discussion of either Dunne's credentials or his outline, and the acceptance of both went by Nem Con, with Fergus glowering but speechless.

People had been nobbled, that was clear. Nobody could have heard of the wretched man Dunne before this. Architecture wasn't even his area. People had been briefed to agree that Dunne was A Good Idea. It might, of course, have been an innocent attempt to save time, but Fergus didn't believe that for a moment.

Who had known what he, Fergus, had been working on? Who would sell a colleague's research down the river like this if they did know? And why, oh why, oh why would they do this to him for a middle-aged Lothario with a very iffy professional background? Surely Dunne's credentials couldn't stand up to any kind of scrutiny? Could they?

The answer to the first of his questions was definitely Nick. Nick was a member of this course committee because he was representing the Art History Department in general. He was also, specifically, its expert on modern American architecture. Nick was also the only person in the faculty who had known what Fergus was currently working on, so the leak must've come from him. Fergus resolved to ask him for answers to the other two questions as well. Suddenly he felt much more need for those three answers than for his lunch. His whimpering stomach had turned into a small, hard, spiky knot. He hoped a couple of glasses of Chris's special burgundy might help it, otherwise he would need to have recourse to Marion's Milk of Magnesia again. Christ alone knew why he kept on with this bloody university. It would give him ulcers in the end.

The meeting sputtered to a halt with a few of those items of Any Other Business which are, actually, major but which no-one has the concentration left to deal with. They were put onto the next agenda for a full debate by which time, of course, they would be fait accompli, or passée, or some other French cliché. Oft-times Fergus would have championed those AOBs, enabled them, insisted on timely progress. Today his own problems were overwhelming him.

Nick was gliding purposefully towards the door when Fergus grasped him firmly just above the elbow. Nick tried, idiotically, to shake him off. Fergus's hand closed hard, nails digging in to the soft bit of Nick's upper arm where, on some people, one might expect to find muscles. Nick winced, pulled up short in surprise and turned around. The opening gambit having set the tone, Fergus got right on with it.

'I need a word with you,' he hissed in Nick's ear.

Fergus had become an immovable object. He and Nick were blocking the doorway. Traffic was backing up behind them: traffic that wanted its lunch. The traffic began to make 'excuse me' noises and push forward. Nick had to give ground. Being Nick he gave it on all fronts at once.

'You'd better come to my office,' he said, sliding into the corridor, 'after lunch.'

Fergus slid with him, grip unchanged. A set, wolfish grin decorated his face to disguise his grip and his purpose.

'Now,' said Fergus, knowing very well that 'after lunch' Nick would have left the faculty and not be seen again until the New Year, this sort of vanishing act being his time-honoured method of turning wrath.

As one they marched to Nick's office – some fifteen synchronised steps. Nick unlocked his door while Fergus stood behind him like a gaoler. They slipped inside as one. Fergus was taking no chances.

Nick adopted an innocent, casual approach. Fergus was operating from a baseline of disbelief, and the result could be heard in effing and blinding detail all up and down the corridor. At this juncture it didn't matter to Fergus whether he was right or wrong, whether Nick was involved in the carve-up or not. He, Fergus, was seriously pissed off so someone was going to get it in the neck and Nick was always a suitable candidate.

On this occasion, however, it rapidly became apparent that Nick was also the right candidate. Prevarication and placation rapidly gave way to feeble explanation under Fergus's tirade. Nick put his hand up to all of Fergus's accusations and excused his behaviour by saying that he had felt sorry for Dunne.

'Sorry?' Fergus repeated, in little more than a whisper. 'Sorry? For a bankrupt Lothario like him? Do you realise what he's done? Do you realise what you've done?'

Nick looked mortified. As well he might.

The minor mystery of why Nick should have known enough about Dunne to feel sorry for him was soon explained. One of those strange and often unhappy quirks of fate had thrown them together in a theatre interval, where they realised that they had been at college together. During the nine minutes of that conversation Nick had set up the whole unfortunate business by mentioning the course, the angle it was taking, the level, and the subject areas being covered. It all came rushing out with some pride as Nick was himself writing a double chapter on Frank Lloyd Wright – Nick adored Frank Lloyd Wright. Dunne had mentioned his poverty as the first bell was rung. Hearing the sad saga of all the little Dunnes existing on bread and scrape while Mrs Dunne fended off the bailiffs, Nick had promised, as they parted to return to their seats, to 'see what he could do'. Dunne had delivered the coup de grâce by mentioning that he knew another member of the faculty quite well – old Girvan, good chap. Sure he'd stand as a reference.

Nick righteously pointed out that he had only been trying to do an old friend a favour. Fergus countered by pointing out that he had, by the same act, done a current friend a serious disservice.

'I thought we had an understanding about that research,' said Fergus. 'You were the only person who knew what I was working on.'

'We did,' said Nick. 'But David said you were a friend. So when his outline came round and it was about the Pharos – well, I thought you must have been collaborating, and you'd okayed him using it.'

'Sometimes, Nick, you're just such an arsehole. Of *course* I didn't OK him using it. We never even *talked* about it. This is original work I've been doing. I know it's to support second level study, but it's ground-breaking. There was a good paper in it as well – several, perhaps. I don't understand how he could have got all this material from talking to you. Does his outline cover *all* my stuff?'

'How should I know. You've had as much access to Paper 10b as I have,' said Nick, sulky now. 'Haven't you read the bloody thing? The paper's been circulated for over a week – it's not like I sprang it on you at the last minute. You never showed me anything like as much detail as David has in *his* paper.'

'This has been a particularly difficult week for me.' Fergus held up a hand as Nick, seeing a way of changing the subject, opened his mouth to enquire and commiserate, 'It's too long a story to go into now.'

A further damning indictment occurred to Fergus. 'You didn't think to mention the similarities in approach to anybody – me for instance – before circulating it, though, did you?'

Nick coloured, but said nothing more. He seemed to have accepted blame and defeat.

Fergus had a thought.

'I suppose you do actually *remember* Dunne from college?'

'Well, I suppose so. I don't think we were ever bosom buddies, but he seemed to know all about me.'

'Remembered your name right off, did he?'

'I don't know. It took a few minutes before it clicked that we'd been at Suffolk at the same time. But he knew old Quentin Bell and all the right people. Yes. I suppose I remember him.'

But Fergus had remembered something. Triumphantly he crowed.

'But he didn't go to Suffolk. He went to Dublin. My nincompoop of a daughter told me so.'

'Daughter?'

'Never mind. That's another long story.'

'Well perhaps he went to both. People do. His Master's might have been at Trinity.'

Fergus grunted. He felt it likely that Dunne's alma mater changed to suit the person to whom he was talking, like his place of residence. And his Master's degree was probably no more than a figment. Nick seemed disinclined to investigate the truth of Dunne's educational claims any further. Instead he tried to play down the disaster.

'So all this is just a horrible misunderstanding allied to an awful coincidence?'

'Is it, bollocks. I need to think.' And where better to think than ... 'D'you want a drink, Nick?'

Nick held up both hands.

'I'll pass,' he said quickly – obviously delighted to be seeing the back of his abrasive visitor and an end to their most uncomfortable interview. 'Lots to do. You know.'

Fergus snorted and hoofed swiftly to the bar before Chris called last orders. He had a suspicion and an indigestion which he was hoping wine would, respectively, hone and ameliorate.

Chris had his burgundy breathing, but called time before he could do much with it. She let him keep both bottle and glass when she evicted him from the bar.

Something niggled at the back of his mind as he wandered through the little wood between the bar and his office. Two squirrels were sitting on a windowsill demolishing a digestive biscuit. As he watched a woman opened the window at the other end of the sill and cautiously placed another biscuit within reach before shutting the window again. Another, smaller squirrel seized the new biscuit and ran off with it.

Now who did that remind him of? Dunne. Andy. Bank account! Fortunately, on campus there was a little sub-branch which had special dispensation to process any bank's business. Fortunately it stayed open until shortly after the bar closed (Fergus had frequently had recourse to it after particularly lengthy and expensive sessions). He changed course for the bank, scattering greedy squirrels as he went.

Inside, he set down his bottle and glass on the counter and set up Andy's account for her. The only thing lacking now was the girl's signature.

Back in his office, still clasping full bottle and empty glass, he made a start. The first glass was purely medicinal. It cleared his thinking passages a treat – and relaxed his dyspeptic stomach, which was just as well as there was now no prospect of it receiving any lunch to keep it quiet.

Fergus worked through the wine and the morning's disaster during the afternoon. He locked his office door and primed Marion to keep visitors at bay. Around half past three he was slumped in the sickly pool of light provided by his desk lamp, still very little further forward. He gave up cudgelling his brains for a solution and swivelled his chair towards the window to watch the sky redden over the water meadows.

By four o'clock he still had no idea what to *do* about the day's debacle, but at some point while he was watching the sun go down he found he had developed a theory as to how it might have occurred. He might even owe Nick an apology. And if he was right it was too late to get Mary to have the birth control talk with his darling daughter.

He dialled Andy's new number. He expected that the attractions of rendering the love nest three shades of blue would've won out over school. They had.

'Dad!'

He had, as intended, caught her off guard. He pressed his advantage.

'Andy love, I need a sensible, objective answer to an important question. The sort of answer that only my daughter can give me.'

Her reply sounded wary, but that was only to be expected.

'Sure, Fergus. Any time. You know me.'

She tried a casual laugh as punctuation to this, but it didn't come off. No reason why that should mean much, he told himself. Kid had a lot on her mind right now. Any one of half a dozen things could make her dread Twenty Questions with the Old Man. Fergus plunged on, respecting this.

'Andy, have you and ... uh ... David ever been to my place when I wasn't there?'

There was a silence that went on heartbeat after heartbeat. It spoke volumes.

'How many times, love?'

'Fergus, we had nowhere to go, what with his wife ...'

'That's OK. Just – how many times, and when.'

He was trying very hard to be gentle, but he was so restrained that he was scaring her, he could tell. Fergus was not a man who was often restrained.

'We used your spare room a few times.

'How often?'

Silence.

'Maybe ... six or eight? A dozen, tops.'

'When?'

'Through October and November, when you were away in Alexandria. Then David asked me to go and live with him and said he'd found us a flat. So we agreed we'd wait until we moved in together. Make it special.'

He had it now. Had it and could never prove it. Dunne had found, and used, his material on the Pharos when he had been roaming about his, Fergus's, flat (probably in his bloody underwear) fucking his daughter, fiddling with his favourite things and reading his research! How hard he had then worked to find a way to use it Fergus could only surmise. He presumed that someone who lived on his wits the way that Dunne did had a sufficient quantity of guile to enable him to get by. To scrape an acquaintance with Nick wouldn't be difficult for someone like Dunne, making connections was what it was all about for a hustler like him. Dunne's sort always knew someone who knew someone who had a friend in the right business. Dunne must have known that he only needed to get into conversation with someone else from Fergus's faculty and the stolen material could be used. By the time he, Fergus, caught on it would be too late to do anything sensible. Dunne had obviously been close enough to genuine academic research at some time in his life to know how difficult it was to prove plagiarism before publication. Bastard.

Oh yes, at finding and using Dunne was good – the teenager, the father, the old college friend, real or conjured. Not to mention Janet and Katie Crouch (doubtless he could always make use of a solicitor, given his modus operandi). The man was good at what he did alright. Not *very* good or there wouldn't be an abandoned gallery in Fitzrovia where his business used to be. But his real gift was to be completely unbothered by the hurt he caused. Knowing and uncaring. Double bastard.

The silence that accompanied Fergus's working through of this scenario had obviously alarmed Andy. He became aware of her voice repeating his name.

'It's alright, love. I just needed to know if he'd been to the flat.'

He refocussed his attention on his daughter with difficulty.

'It's not the sex, love. That's not it at all. It's just that I found out at work today that David has acquired something – some research: *my* research – that I thought only I knew about. And I needed to know how he might have come by it. Now I think I do, and I intend talk to him about it. You don't need to worry. Although I'd be very grateful if you didn't say anything to him about this. OK?'

'You think he's capable of anything! It's just 'cos you don't like him.'

'I just said, love, I'm going to talk to him ...'

'No you're not. You don't know where he is. You can't talk to him because I won't tell you how to get hold of him. You think he's an awful person, don't you? Well, don't you? And you won't believe anything he says, or anything I say either. I hate you.'

And she hung up on him.

Fergus sat for a few moments with the receiver purring in his ear, wondering why it sounded so pleased with itself, then put it back on its base.

That didn't seem to have gone awfully well.

He collected his stuff together – including Papers 10a and 10b – and started for home numbly. Every time he thought about one facet of the muddle that was currently his life it led onto something else, equally awful or worse. There seemed no end to the confusion, no solution.

He hit London's rush hour at the North Circular and wove his way through the traffic single-mindedly, grimly, giving and asking no quarter. But the mechanical task did not clear his mind as it usually did.

He was very glad when he finally drove down into the Stygian gloom of the underground parking at his apartment block.

By the time he got in it was nearly six. His answerphone was winking at him. The message was from Mary. A Mary with weariness in her voice. He called her at once. It was nothing, only that she wanted someone to talk to with whom she didn't have to pretend to be cheerful.

'You haven't told anyone about all this, then?'

She sighed.

'No. It's such a complicated saga; it would take so long. Who has time to listen?'

She had a point. Fergus tried to jolly her out of her funk (funny how it was always easier to cheer somebody else up, no matter how dreadful you were feeling yourself) but she just swore at him.

'Shall I come over now?' he said. 'We said we'd get something to eat before going over to Balham. And talk through what I've done to hold the fort and the brilliant plan you're going to come up with to solve the whole stinking mess.'

This blatant attempt to lighten the mood did not make her laugh.

After a moment's thought she said,

'Can I come to you? I just don't want to be here a moment longer.'

'Of course. Or I could meet you half way?'

'No. I'll come to you.'

Things in his life were getting odder and odder. Mary had *never* been to his flat.

'Do you know where ...?'

'Oh yes, Andy's told me all about your little eyrie next to the Heath. I expect you flap out of the lounge window on dark and moonless nights and go and scare small rodents.'

Well, she wasn't feeling completely hopeless, then – she'd sworn at him, and made a joke at his expense. The least he could do was laugh at it. He did so.

*

While he was waiting for Mary the phone rang. Usually at this time of day the only people who rang were pathetically cheerful cold callers trying to sell him kitchens or double glazing. Just in case it was Andy he picked up before the answerphone cut in. It was. She was in a call box and a mite breathless.

'Dad? David's come over. I've come out to get fish and chips – and to tell you not to come.'

But this was a golden opportunity that Fergus had been angling for ever since he'd found out about Papers 10a and 10b. He couldn't quite keep the grim glee out of his voice when he said,

'Oh, I don't think there's any need to cancel.'

'But you said he wasn't to have anything to do with the money.'

'Yes, but ...'

'So if you come over and start working stuff out on a calculator then he'll know.'

'Yes, but ...'

'And now you think he's stolen your stuff on top of everything else. It's going to be really weird if you come over. I just want to see him.'

'Andy I just ...'

'Dad! *Please* don't come. I haven't seen him since last week. I want this to be a lovely evening, not spoiled by you two rowing.'

She sounded close to tears. He tried to soothe her.

'Andy – I'm not going to row with him.'

'Yes you will. And if you don't Mum will.'

How well the child knew her parents. Bugger.

'Did you set the account up?'

'Yes, of course. I said so. All you need to do is go into any branch of my bank and give them a specimen signature.'

'OK. I'll make sure to do that tomorrow. Did they give you a cheque book?'

'No. When they've got a signature on file for you, you can use counter cheques, from any branch, until it comes through.'

'OK. Give the calculations to Mum. She can give them to Katie and I'll pick them up from her.'

Suddenly Fergus realised something. It didn't matter whether Dunne was at the flat or not. Andy didn't want – couldn't afford – to have the two halves of her life come together at present. The new life was not yet robust enough to cope with an intrusion from her old one. He would have loved to have popped the bubble that she'd built round herself in that bloody awful flat in Balham, but he could find no way to say to his daughter, baldly, 'we're coming anyway'. He couldn't cause her that kind of distress, not now he understood why she was so upset. Sadly he acquiesced. He hoped he wasn't strengthening the hold Dunne and the flat had over her – he hoped he was being a wise and caring parent. But really he had no idea *what* he was doing, except sparing his child all the hurt he could.

Mary was over in record time. He hadn't long hung up from talking to Andy when she was at his door. He told her the latest. She was both crestfallen and relieved. It seemed that nobody had been looking forward to meeting.

'Let's make a pact,' she said. 'Let's not talk about ... The Andy Thing tonight – please?'

'Fine with me,' he said. 'If you think we can manage it.'

By seven o'clock they were sitting in The World's End and arguing about what they were going to eat and who was going to pay for it. Mary was keen on Chinese, and wanted to pay. Fergus felt like Greek, knew a good place, and also wanted to pay. Mary, as usual, got her way. The meal was fine. Mary had been right in her choice. Something piquant and in small bites was just right for two people whose digestive tracts had suffered from excessive stress in the recent past. They had a pleasant evening.

Fergus invited Mary up to the flat for a night-cap before she went home. They stood in the dark with the curtains drawn back and admired his moonlit view over the Heath from the lounge window. It looked peaceful and beautiful and lonely. Looking over London, the lights of the cars, the streets and the dwellings, reminded Fergus that there was a world outside his own little round. He didn't know what it said to Mary, but she was quiet and thoughtful. Mind you, she'd been quiet all evening. This thing was taking its toll on both of them. They might have stuck to their pact and not talked about The Andy Thing, but they were certainly thinking about it. And now, mixed up in The Andy Thing, was Dunne's plagiarism. He wanted badly to tell Mary about it, but it would have broken the pact. And he didn't want to add to her worries.

Fergus was slightly surprised that Andy hadn't phoned her mother to complain about his latest attack on Dunne. Andy usually pitted one parent mercilessly against the other when she wanted her own way. Perhaps she'd got her own way: simply to be left alone. She must know that couldn't be allowed to last. But it would do for now.

Mary said she must go home. As Fergus helped her into her coat she turned to him. It always unnerved him to be eyeball to eyeball with Mary. Usually it meant she was spitting invective at him. This time she looked at him deeply and said,

'Thanks, Fergus. You've been very good through all this. I don't know how I would have managed without you.'

She brought her hand up and just cupped his cheek. Fergus managed not to flinch as he caught sight of the hand rising towards him. He got the distinct impression that Mary would not have objected if he had kissed her. Indeed, she was swaying on the balls of her feet in a way that made him think that she might be contemplating such a move herself. Fergus wondered if she would feel differently if she knew that Dunne's theft of his work, caused entirely by his giving Andy a key to his flat, underpinned much of the trouble she was experiencing.

The moment passed and Fergus walked her down the stairs, keeping his distance in case a similar moment should occur when she got to her car. It didn't. But the odd occurrence upstairs made Fergus question the very foundations of his world as he plodded back up to his flat.

Thursday 17 December

On Thursday morning, first thing, before any more familial disasters could occur, Fergus read Paper 10b.

It didn't take long; it was only two sheets of paper – rather poorly presented he noted, with pleasure. It looked as though Dunne had done his own typing.

It was definitely Fergus's material, some of the primary sources he had consulted were cited, all the theory was there, all backed with examples. Damn him.

It looked, however, as though Dunne had constructed the paper from memory and a few hasty notes made while he was at Fergus's flat.

But how had he intended to flesh out this outline into a full chapter? Invite himself to dinner? Burgle the flat? Make it up?

Dunne was, of course, a man who lived on his wits. The events leading to this outline were likely to have been serendipitous. He almost certainly hadn't come to the flat with the intention of stealing another man's work – but had spied a potential profit, just lying there on the desk, and been unable to resist. Dunne probably didn't know himself how he was going to follow through. It was all carpe diem with Dunne. Doubtless he wouldn't think twice about not fulfilling his contract for the Pharos chapter if fate didn't provide him with an opportunity to acquire enough additional material to do so. The standard university contract specified payment be made in stages as the work progressed. Perhaps Dunne had only ever intended to bag the first payment for the outline and then make some excuse. What

Fergus sighed. Would it be possible for him to offer to complete the work when no first draft was forthcoming? No. No, no, no. That would put him in a most invidious position. Questions would be asked. Christ – they might accuse *him* of plagiarism! Through his own stupid fault he had lost control of his work. What a bloody mess.

He picked up Dunne's résumé. Might as well see what *this* work of fiction contained. And, of course, there, right at the top of the paper was the address Dunne wanted the cheque sent to.

Fergus sat and stared at it, while a smile slowly spread over his face.

The address was of a flat in Balham.

How many different addresses did that make? There was the gallery – although that might have been repossessed by now; somewhere there was the house containing Mrs Dunne and offspring; there was the bedsit – location also unknown – with the black and grey bedlinen which Janet had visited; there was the flat with a Balham address which Andy was painting blue.

This address was in Tooting but, not the same as Andy's flat. Dunne's stamping grounds were becoming clearer now. Fergus got out his A-Z and pored over it. Tooting: Balham – neighbouring boroughs of similar character.

He was tempted to drive straight over there, but he had learned the hard way that Dunne was a tricky adversary. This time he, Fergus, would be fully prepared.

He read the rest of the résumé. There wasn't much he hadn't expected. Dunne claimed to be a Dr – well, one would in the circumstances – which might give credence to Nick's theory that Dunne had done a postgraduate degree at Trinity; although it was unlikely, in Fergus's opinion, that he had attended the college or achieved a doctorate. He had given Nick as an academic referee. Presumably Nick knew about that (although in Fergus's experience all sorts of inappropriate people put one's name down as referee without having the courtesy to ask if they might). If he *did*, it suggested a greater acquaintance between Nick and Dunne than Nick had described. Or maybe Dunne had just *assumed* Nick wouldn't mind, and Nick hadn't liked to make a fuss: that was more likely.

The address given for the second, character, referee was a private one: the name wasn't known to Fergus. Although it soon would be, if such a person existed. No telephone number was given, which only increased Fergus's suspicions. It was an Irish address – clever – which would make it more difficult to check, but that was a far from an insuperable obstacle.

There followed an impressive list of publications, time listed both at Sussex and at Trinity, and a teaching post in Limerick which had ended some years before. He mentioned the extra-mural lectures at Andy's school. Finally as 'current occupation' he gave 'art dealer' as his profession and the gallery as his major area of concern. It all looked wonderful. Fergus glowered. It was a pretty bubble; he would very much enjoy bursting it.

The man must have known that he, Fergus, would see both the résumé and the chapter outline. What did Dunne think Fergus was likely to do about the theft of his daughter and his research? Which led Fergus to ponder what kind of a half-wit Dunne thought he was and how the man could imagine Fergus was going to let him get away with any of it.

Fergus snorted. He picked up the A-Z and headed for the door, sweeping his coat off the peg as he passed.

*

A lot of the terraces in Tooting had a certain fin de siècle charm. The house at Dunne's contact address was not one of them. He drove past it first, then drove from there to Andy's flat, to clock the distance. He didn't linger outside the flat in case Andy thought he was spying on her. He wanted his next contact with his daughter to be a carefully controlled event which resulted in her finally seeing some sense. By that time he would have so much evidence of Dunne's perfidy that even a love-struck teenager wouldn't be able to deny it. He was almost at his wits' end to know how to get through to her. It hurt a lot that she saw him, her good friend and frequent partner in crime, as the villain in all this. Everything Fergus did to try and save her from pain, pregnancy and penury got turned around and used against him.

Fergus put that resolutely out of his mind and looked at his mileometer. He'd driven a mere eight tenths of a mile between those two addresses of Dunne's. Cheeky bastard.

He drove back to No 9, St Anselm's Close, Tooting. It lurked round the back of a hospital, in a warren of similar little streets. It was a gloomy, narrow, run down, mid-terrace house of three stories, held up by similar dwellings on either side. The Jag stood out among the bins, fly-tipped furniture and disembowelled rubbish sacks lining the kerb like an emerald wedged into a dunghill.

No 9 had a tiny front garden surrounded by a broken down fence and gate. In it were two boy's bikes with various bits missing and an easy chair with its stuffing coming out. Fergus made it past the ruined gate and the other obstacles and walked the two paces to the front door. The bell seemed to be broken and there was no knocker so he used his knuckles on the glass in the door. It hurt, but made a significant racket. If anyone was in he would make them hear. No-one came, so he knocked again. The glass rattled in its frame.

Inside he heard a child shout for its Mum, a muffled woman's voice, then a loud, childish 'there's someone at the door', then a commotion of feet hurrying and internal doors banging until, finally, the door was scraped open a few inches.

A woman stood inside, with a child on her hip and another, presumably the shouter, peering round her at knee level. It looked like something out of a Victorian lithograph and might have been captioned 'wife and babes of wastrel face the bailiffs alone'. Poor cow, thought Fergus fleetingly, as he wondered how to begin.

The woman was no help, she just stood and looked at him. He looked back. She was nondescript from head to foot. Indeed, she was spectacular in her nondescriptness. Fergus had never seen anyone, man or woman, have so little about them as this woman had. She could have been any age from twenty five to forty. Her hair was neither long nor short, neither brown nor blond. It straggled. Her clothes were brownish, shapeless. There was a cardigan and a skirt and a pair of house shoes. The baby was grubby around the face, but only with recent food. Fergus wondered if he had interrupted its meal. There was an odd smell coming through the door, constituent parts of which he identified as damp and curried vegetables. His heart bled for her, but he staunched the flow and cleared his throat.

'I'm sorry to trouble you, but I wonder – am I speaking with Mrs. Dunne?'

The woman gave a short laugh with no humour in it. It reminded him of Mary's cynical bark.

'Yes.'

'I wonder if I might have a word? It's about your husband.'

This time she sighed. Fergus rather thought she must hear those words a lot.

'You'd better come in,' she said.

She stepped back, treading on the larger child who yelped and was shushed. Fergus did his best to squeeze into the house without turning his entrance into an intimate encounter. The hall was very narrow and full of coats, shoes, toys and a chest of drawers; it also contained this woman holding her baby at Fergus's eye level and that second child somewhere down by their feet.

They slid into a tiny lounge, which was also full. Mrs. Dunne put the toddler into a play-pen, which was wedged between a TV and a ratty sofa covered with a moth-eaten throw. A dining table piled with papers and surrounded by three chairs occupied the rest of the room. The ratty sofa, obviously a mate for the defunct chair in the garden, stood in front of a rather nice upright piano on the hall wall. A bookcase stretched from the table to the door. Something very worn covered the floor. The play-pen was plentifully supplied with bright plastic things to do if you were one year old or less, and open picture books covered most of what floor space there was. The only brightness in the place was strewn about the floor.

When the second child eased into the room as well Fergus began to feel distinctly claustrophobic. The boy hung onto his mother and she, absent-mindedly, kept peeling him off. The clinging and peeling continued all the time Fergus was there.

Mrs. Dunne straightened the throw on the sofa and turned to Fergus – a good trick in itself. She said wearily,

'Please sit down. What's he done now?'

This was a promising opening. But it left Fergus rather in the position of a child in a sweet shop: so much to savour, where to start?

'Your husband seems to have several addresses, Mrs Dunne. Could I be very ... er ... personal and ask, which one he actually lives at?'

'He hasn't lived with me since I was six months pregnant with Michael.' She indicated the baby in the play-pen. 'He's got a flat within walking distance, so that he can come and see the kids, take them out, you know. It also means he's close enough to come round when he wants to borrow money or just be a nuisance. I don't lend him money any more, but it's more difficult to stop him being a nuisance. The kids like him.'

Fergus was putting two and two together and making a resounding four out of them.

'Is this a flat over the newsagent's on Cromwell Road, with a Balham address?'

'Yes. He entertains there, if you know what I mean. He entertains rather a lot. Then when he's tired of them he comes round here and asks me what he should do.'

'And ... forgive another personal question ... are you divorced?'

'No. David's a good catholic.' She laughed, a sad sound. 'And I converted when we married. He's stuck with me.'

'And you're stuck with him.'

'Oh yes.'

There was a brief silence. She hadn't asked why Fergus needed to know all this. She demonstrated a sort of dignity in her humiliation. Fergus felt obliged to share the humiliation as far as he was able.

'The reason I'm asking these ... awfully personal ... questions is that – well, he's set my daughter up in that flat.'

'Yes. I gathered he had someone new.'

'Would you *know* if he had another flat, somewhere else close by?'

'Oh yes. He tells me everything.' She sighed. 'That's his only other residence.'

'So, he's reassigned the lease to her?'

'Looks that way, doesn't it? Not the first time. He's always broke. Always got an angle. Always one step ahead of me, the police, the fraud people – you.'

Her calm acceptance of the situation he had revealed rather irritated Fergus.

'My daughter is a minor, Mrs Dunne.'

'Yes, she would be. He likes them young. Obviously somebody was silly enough to stand as guarantor for her when she signed the lease.'

Fergus coloured. He hoped she thought it was anger at her husband.

'And what happens to these girls?'

'Not much, if they're sensible and take precautions. When he's flush once more he'll chuck her out, get the flat back and start again.'

'And what about the gallery?'

'Oh, he's got another gallery has he? I *didn't* know about that. He'll have been sleeping there if he's short of money again.'

'The gallery's in the past tense, really. He seems to have done a bunk from there and taken the best stuff with him.'

'Of course. You never get anything back from David.'

Fergus almost wanted to shake the woman. To say to her 'why don't you ...?'. But what good would it do? She was this man's victim for life, the children too. God alone knew how she kept it all together. And the boys thought their father was wonderful. Bet he always brought toys and sweets, and bought them treats when they were out, but never contributed a penny to feed them at home, or buy their clothes, or to pay the rent on this awful little house. Mrs Dunne needed to believe in a vengeful God. And Hell.

There seemed nothing left to say, and Fergus was beginning to feel quite breathless in the over-furnished and over-populated lounge, so he thanked her for her frankness and began to pick his way towards the front door. The three of them inched down the hall, avoiding the various obstructions, in line astern. Fergus managed to get the door open, and turned. Mrs Dunne – did the woman even have a name of her own? – stood like a shabby Madonna with one hand up to her throat and the other resting on the hair of the child still clinging to her skirt.

Fergus couldn't wait to leave, but something prompted him to stick out his hand. She looked at it a moment, then took it. Her hand was hard and dry, her grip firm. He hoped she'd be all right. He rather thought she would.

It was almost lunchtime. Fergus's next port of call was mapped out for him really – it would be silly not to see Andy, since he was in the neighbourhood. He had some interesting information for her, if she would listen.

He drove the short distance to Cromwell Road and found a parking space not far from the flat. It had started to rain and become very dark. Cromwell Road looked almost as gloomy as St Anselm's had done. He wondered how it felt to move into a down-at-heel flat in December with Christmas looming. Dispiriting with any luck.

The bell outside the street door had no name under it. Dunne covered his tracks well. He rang and soon heard feet clattering down carpet-less stairs. He smiled.

Andy had on her painting smock which was now covered with splodges of emulsion in various shades of blue. So was her hair, which she had scraped back in a knot. She looked pinched about the face and ten years older. She stood in the doorway with her hand on the door-handle for quite a while when she saw who her visitor was. Fergus just stood and smiled. When he judged that she had had time to gather her wits he asked himself in.

'Well, it's a terrible mess upstairs. I've been painting ...'

'I can see.'

She looked down at her clothes and put her spare hand up to her hair. The hand was covered in paint too.

'It's more difficult than painting pictures. I didn't think it would be.'

'I don't mind about mess. I was in the neighbourhood and it seemed silly not to pop in.'

'In the neighbourhood, Fergus? This is *so* not your sort of neighbourhood.'

'I've been to see Mrs Dunne.'

Andy thought about that. Finally she said,

'How did you find her?'

'Why don't I tell you about it over lunch? You look like you could do with a break.'

'Yes. But I can't clean up. There isn't any water. I need to go out and call them about it.'

'Isn't there a phone here?'

'Yes, but it's disconnected.'

'How about electricity and gas?'

'They haven't been connected yet.'

Couldn't the child see that the utilities had been cut off because someone hadn't paid the bills? Although – a change of tenant did often produce this sort of snafu. Presumably the letting agent blamed the previous tenant when Andy enquired, and hadn't hurried himself to get the name change sorted out. The utility companies certainly weren't going to make the necessary changes this close to Christmas. What the letting agency possibly didn't know was that the same unsatisfactory tenant who had left the flat trailing debt behind him was about to move back in. Someone – probably Fergus – was going to have to ride the utility companies hard and pay through the nose to get the phone, electricity and gas reconnected if Andy was to live here. That would make quite a comfortable Christmas for the bastard

Dunne. He wondered if there was any point telling the letting agency about Dunne's way of coping when he was broke. Or was there a pretty girl in the agency's office who was also familiar with the black and grey bedlinen?

'Come on then – we'll go back to my place. You can have a bath and then we'll go down The World's End for some lunch. How about it?'

The temptation of getting clean and warm was obviously too great to resist.

'OK. That'd be good. Thanks, Fergus. I'll just go and get my bag.'

She might have thought he would stand there at the door in the thin rain, but she was wrong. As soon as she turned he was through the door, casually but determinedly, took it from her and closed it behind him. She mounted the stairs with him her very shadow. He really wanted to see this flat. He hoped it was the only time he'd ever have to come here, but that depended on her deciding not to come back here. Convincing her would not be easy.

A steep flight of bare wooden stairs led up to the living room, which was at the back of the house. It looked large, but Fergus quickly realised that that was because there was hardly any furniture in it. The good thing about it was that it wouldn't get the street noise. The bad thing was that it was very dark, as the only light came through from the kitchen, where a half-glazed wall and glazed door divided the kitchen from the living room. There were candles on plates and saucers all around the living room and a big Calor Gas space heater in the middle. Against one wall, covered in an old sheet to keep the paint off it, was a sofa. While Andy rummaged around under the sheet for her bag Fergus moved quickly across the landing to the other door in the room. In there was a brass double bedstead and mattress, made up with the famous black and grey bedlinen, currently much rumpled. This room had been divided along the same lines as the living room and kitchen. It also had no natural light, except what it borrowed from the bathroom via a frosted glass wall and door. An estate agent would call it ensuite. On the floor by the bed, bent over as if in sorrow, was an old Anglepoise lamp with no bulb in it; against the outside wall a built-in wardrobe stood ajar. Fergus pulled its door further open. There was nothing inside but a smell of mould. In the corner between the wardrobe and the bed was a pile of Andy's stuff: books, a suitcase with clothes spilling out of it, her portfolio, her guitar.

While his heart bled for his daughter his mind was working overtime.

He returned to the living room. A single bare bulb hung from the centre of the ceiling. It was gloomy, but he could see enough to gauge the results of Andy's efforts at decorating. She was right, she had found it hard. There was emulsion everywhere – on the walls, sure, but also on the woodwork. Drips from the ceiling marred the walls because she had done the walls first. Basically it was a mess, as she had said. The kid needed help. Fergus really couldn't see any way round it but to move her out or move professional decorators in. Jesus H Christ.

Andy straightened up, having found her shoulder bag. Her hair was half down now. She looked a mess alright, and not just a painty mess: she looked as if she could turn into Mrs Dunne given a little more of David's attentions. Fergus regarded her anxiously for a moment. Never had he been more glad of the ability to bluster which he had cultivated over the years to cover the awkward moment, the pregnant pause.

'Come on – let's get you clean, then lunch on me.'

She started to move, and his arm landed around her shoulders in an unplanned gesture of pathos that undid his attempt to get through this by not letting his real feelings show. She stopped, aware of what had just happened, and looked up at him. She was closer to him in that moment than she had ever been. She said,

'It's a mess, isn't it?'

Almost he was tempted to be honest. But he wasn't going to risk it now. He reverted to jolly bluster,

'Nothing we can't sort out, love.'

'But I shouldn't need you to sort it out. I should be able to cope. David's coming tonight. What's he going to say?'

She was angry; whether with herself, or with circumstances he wasn't sure. He toyed with allowing himself the luxury of saying 'who gives a shit what he thinks?' but he sensed matters were at a delicate juncture. A deep and devious game was afoot. It wasn't Andy who was other player: it was Dunne. He, Fergus, had not started this, had not wanted it and was not sure what the rules were, but he would play it out. He was good at games. Unfortunately Andy was now only one of several prizes at stake. Fergus was playing for his daughter, his research and his substantial deposit on this rancid flat. He had no idea what he had done to piss David Dunne off so completely, but this ongoing campaign against Fergus and his family was really beginning to get to him.

He, Fergus, must out-manipulate Dunne on all three fronts. Poor Andy was right in the middle of it all, and was seemingly everybody's dupe. Fergus's heart bled, but his head was resolute.

He broke eye contact. He kept it simple.

'I don't know, love.'

And he pressed with that encircling arm until she started moving towards the door. It didn't take much pressure.

As they got into the car she looked back, as if she'd never see the place again. He hoped fervently that she wouldn't, but the look of misery on her pinched face hurt him deeply.

He reminded himself that this mess was not of his making.

*

When they got back to Heath House she was hungry – surely a good sign – so they went straight to the pub, before it stopped serving lunches, and ordered pie and mash twice. Fergus badly needed a drink, which he ordered as soon as Andy went to the Ladies to try and get some of the paint off. He asked Sue for a pint of Winter Warmer – although the chill he was feeling had little to do with the weather. He got them a table by the fire. He was doing his best.

When Andy came back she looked much less like Mrs Dunne. She had taken her hair down, got the worst of the splodges of emulsion off and looked pinkly scrubbed. Fergus was glad of the transformation, although he dreaded to think what the roller towel in the toilets must look like. He smiled at her as she made her way across the bar and got a tiny smile back. She didn't say anything when she sat down.

Their lunch soon arrived and Fergus got a small cider for Andy and a second pint for himself to accompany it. He was beginning to feel human again.

Andy demolished the food in short order and sat back with a sigh. It was the first sound at their table, except for the polite clatter of their knives and forks, since they sat down. Fergus had determinedly kept silent as he consumed his food and beer, as being a more productive way forward than further conversation. Lunch done, they sat and watched the fire.

He risked a glance at Andy. She was flushed with the heat and the food and did not look unhappy. However, he was reluctant to explore her state of mind. Too often recently it had been quite incomprehensible. It had led to misunderstandings. Fergus could usually deal with misunderstandings, providing they were of his own making. He purely hated, however, hanging onto the tail of somebody else's tiger. Usually he was the tiger.

Finally he broke the silence by asking her if she wanted another drink. She said yes, so he went and got her a second half pint, and another pint for himself. He was hoping a little alcohol might loosen her tongue. He wanted her to talk to him but he didn't want to be responsible for the direction that talk might take. He'd got into trouble doing that before.

The silence between them was becoming more strained than companionable when Sue called 'time'. Fergus risked raising a quizzical eyebrow in Andy's direction. It was the eyebrow that used to say 'let's do something wicked'. He had no wickedness in mind – he had had a surfeit of wickedness connected with Andy – it was just an overture.

He was astounded to see Andy's lower lip start to quiver and her eyes fill with tears. Concerned but uncertain what to do, he handed her one of the paper napkins that had come with her lunch. Still they exchanged no word. Fergus reached across the table and patted what of her he could reach – an elbow – in as fatherly a fashion as he could, while she tried not to give way. He really didn't care about the embarrassment: if you needed a good cry you needed a good cry and that was that. But a teenager would probably find it awkward, in front of her Dad, in the middle of a pub, so he said,

'Shall we go?'

They went, Andy very quickly, he after having settled up at the bar.

Sue often saw young women in Fergus's company. Although Fergus tried to make sure they were old enough to drink in pubs (which Andy, actually, wasn't quite yet). Sue was somewhat frosty. She obviously thought the silent lunch and the tears were his fault. Fergus almost let her think what she liked, but it was a very good pub, no more than a hundred yards from his home, so he jerked his head towards the doorway where Andy could be seen blowing her nose, and said shortly,

'My daughter. Boyfriend trouble.' And tutted in that way which says, "kids, eh?".

He had the satisfaction of seeing Sue revise her opinion of him as he turned to go. It was a bit like watching a goldfish inhaling.

That Fergus had a daughter would be common knowledge to the Public Bar crowd by closing time tonight. Bugger.

He joined Andy outside. The afternoon had become no less gloomy since his whistle stop tour of Tooting and Balham. There was sleety rain in the wind. Andy looked very wan, despite the food and cider. He smiled and put his arm around her, which set her off crying again. So he marched her briskly round the corner to his flat. As soon as they got into the lobby Andy flew up the stairs.

As soon as he got in Fergus sat her by the ersatz living room fire, put some Vaughn Williams softly on the stereo, ran her a bath and busied himself assembling towels and a robe. Soon he could announce,

'Your bath awaits, Ma'am.'

She gave a small hiccupy giggle.

The Vaughn Williams had been a calculated ploy. He was calculating hard this afternoon. He had sat her there, tears barely dry, warm and comfortable, and was playing mournful music at her. Christ, he was a cad. He just hoped it would work.

He saw her safely into the bathroom and waited until he heard splashing before dialling Mary's work number. He felt like a conspirator – which, indeed, he hoped he shortly would be. Mary, fortunately, was between classes and he didn't have to negotiate very hard, or very loudly, to get to speak to her.

'Mary,' he hissed, 'it's me.'

'Fergus? Why are you whispering?'

'Andy's in the bath.'

'In your bath?'

'Yes.'

'Oh, well done!'

'Dunne's due at the Balham flat tonight. God knows if he'll turn up – I mean, it's a hell hole; no light, no heat, just candles and a Calor gas thing with no bottle, and the place is running with damp.

'Oh good!'

'But if he does turn up I want to be waiting for him – alone, without Andy.'

'Ah. You want me to come over?'

'Yes. Do you think it'll look too obvious?'

'Yes, but what else can we do?'

Fergus sighed.

'I've never been so conscious in my life of making it up as I go along.'

'Oh, I don't know, some of your lectures in the old days ...'

'Were never as 'doorknob' as this! I wasn't expecting to get this far. I just popped round to see how she was and get a look at the inside of the flat. She was in such a state that getting her to come out for a break from painting was easy. Then I fed her and got her warm.'

'And wormed your way back into her confidence ...'

'I'm just hoping that I don't make a mess of it. There may not be another opportunity. If we lose her confidence this time there'll be hell to pay.'

'True enough. But 'bravo' all the same. I'll be over as soon as school's out. I'll bring her a change of clothes, that might help make it look as though we've spoken but are just trying to be helpful.'

'No it won't.'

'No. I suppose not. It'll all depend on just how much of a state she's still in. If she's really miserable we'll just be Mum and Dad and she'll be clingy and grateful. If she's recovering it'll be more difficult.'

'I know. I'm working on keeping her depressed.'

'Good man.'

They rang off.

Only an hour or so, then, until the cavalry arrived.

Fergus hoped that Andy was enjoying her bath, and would remain in it indefinitely. He had more plotting against Dunne to do. And, truth be told, he was running out of platitudes and silent sympathy. This was no time to realise that his repertoire of interactions with his own daughter was so limited, but it was so. And the Vaughn Williams was depressing him too. He couldn't get the image of the mould-scented bedroom at the flat out of his mind.

He boiled water for tea that he didn't really want, and tried to compose himself. He was relying on Mary to come up with some ideas on how to keep Andy away from the flat. To have a confrontation with Dunne he needed Andy to be out of earshot.

It hadn't taken much cleverness to track Dunne down, or to make the connections between the apparently separate parts of his life. How he had been so successful in his interference in Andy's life? And Fergus's? Was there something Fergus was missing? Something that a full and frank exchange of views might shake loose?

Andy took her time in the bath and emerged very pink and scented and enveloped in one of his robes. She sat by the hearth to dry her hair by the fire. Fergus made the tea he still didn't want and they sipped companionably, cosy. The Vaughn Williams had long since given way to Britten's *Peter Grimes.* Tortured stuff, severely lacking in comedic bits. The afternoon grew older and darker. They remained silent – Fergus was still finding it hard to come up with a plausible topic that didn't have some connection with Dunne. The man ran like a poisoned vein through their lives currently, damn him. But he sat and smiled and sipped like a paragon, because it *was* going to be all right: he *would* make it so.

It was unsettling, though, to find Dunne's influence in his life at every turn. Fergus was sure he had the measure of the man now. And his blunt commonsense (Fergus prided himself on his blunt commonsense) combined with a little light blackmail, would clear the air and shift the revolting con artist out of their lives for good.

A tiny warning bell tinkled away back in his mind, but he didn't know what it might mean.

*

At last Mary came. She brought an overnight bag with some of Andy's things in it, and tried to make out that she'd just happened to have them in her car against this sort of eventuality. She even went so far as to return to her car to fetch them. Andy didn't seem to smell a rat.

The two of them went off to Fergus's spare room to investigate the contents of the bag and, presumably, to have some girl talk. Soon Fergus could hear Andy crying again: great, earth-shattering, caterwaulings of misery. He was glad. She needed to get the pain and confusion out of her system. It saddened him slightly that she hadn't felt able to have a proper cry in front of him but, hell, what are mums for? He was no good with tears anyway.

He wandered about the flat, tidying his already tidy kitchen, squaring piles of papers, picking things up and putting them down somewhere else. When the Britten had finished he put on Sarasate's *Carmen Variations*, loud, to see if he could lighten the mood. If Andy felt a little more light-hearted and secure after her cry she might agree to go home with Mary, leaving him free to go round to the Balham flat and await Dunne's arrival.

Fergus looked at the time: five thirty. Andy would be hungry again soon. He had long ago discovered that teenagers need regular injections of carbohydrates. He smiled. There was nothing like your Mum's cooking in times of crisis. He looked into the fake flames of his fire, remembering back to crises of his own, thirty five years ago or more, resolved with homemade bread and fresh eggs and tea strong enough to crack the pot and a lumpy old green eiderdown.

It was full dark when they emerged from the spare room. Nobody seemed to remember the paint-ruined clothes in Fergus's bathroom and he didn't mention them. They were just another tie back to Dunne best left forgotten. Andy seemed composed, if subdued. Mary was trying hard to match her mood, but she was flushed and her eyes flashed. Fergus knew that look of Mary's only too well. He knew she scented triumph, or at least blood, and was trying not to show it. Mary said,

'Andy's going to come back with me, have a bite to eat, and then we'll sort out some stuff for the flat. I'll take her over there later on.'

'But we'll have to be quick Mum. If David comes and I'm not there ...'

'Well, it's going to take a while to get a meal together and sort out those rollers and brushes and stuff, dear. Why don't you write David a note and Fergus can drop it over now, so that David won't worry when he comes? You don't mind doing that, do you Fergus?'

Fergus had to work hard to keep the grin off his face.

The note was soon written, carefully sealed, and pressed into Fergus's hand with many injunctions about its delivery. The women departed. Fergus was pretty sure Mary's deviousness was equal to the task ahead.

He quickly put on his coat and headed out himself, then stopped and went back to the kitchen. He brought the kettle back to the boil and steamed open the note; it said simply:

Dear David,

I'm sorry about the mess. It just wouldn't go right. I've gone to Mum's to get some brushes and rollers and stuff. I'll be back as soon as I can. Please don't worry.

I love you,
A

Fergus noted she hadn't mentioned the intervention of her parents at all. So now Andy was lying to Dunne (at least by omission). Good. After the many lies of omission (and commission) Andy had told himself and Mary about her relationship with Dunne, it felt like a step forward if Andy was now lying to Dunne about her current relationship with her parents.

He wondered whether to reseal the note. It looked a bit secondhand now. Did Dunne deserve this note? No. But Fergus fully intended that he would shortly receive something that he did deserve.

Fergus wove his way south skilfully through the theatre traffic. It had started to rain; lights shattered and dazzled in his windscreen and on the slick black tarmac. He was glad when he got through the West End and across Chelsea Bridge, but he still needed to keep his wits about him. Endless ribbons of Christmassy shopping streets confronted him now, shredding his concentration. Their gaiety grew more tawdry as he moved south, which made him pretty certain, without recourse to his A to Z, that he was getting close.

Strange what a different city it was after dark. Reality somehow receded – or perhaps it was being in the cosy cockpit of the car gave that illusion. He found that his anger had largely dissipated owing to his need to concentrate during the drive. He had developed a headache on the road. Adrenalin, he supposed. Also that endless shattering of lights in his eyes and the hypnotic swishing of the windscreen wipers. He tried practising what he would say to Dunne when he found him, but got little further than 'look here, Dunne...'

before some minor crisis on the road would demand his full attention once again.

As a result he had no clear idea of what he was going to do or say when he arrived at the Cromwell Road flat in Balham. He sat in the car for a few minutes to gather himself and – what was the phrase? – case the joint. There were no lights showing, but would candlelight show through to the front windows? What should he say? Should he go for broke and say that Andy had seen the error of her ways and wouldn't be coming back? The thought of Andy's reaction to that kind of intervention made little cold prickles start around the back of his neck. Should he say that he, Fergus, knew all about the scam with the flat (that he, Fergus, was now standing guarantor for) and that Dunne would never see a penny? That approach was fraught with potential disaster if Andy, despite their best efforts, were to decide to return – which was still horribly likely.

Should he broach the matter of the stolen research? The theft would be difficult to prove. Fergus's hand-written notes weren't dated – who took that kind of precaution? If Dunne were to laugh in his face what could he do? He could threaten to expose the truth about the wife and four to Andy. But Dunne already had a version of that story playing with Andy that she believed.

Hmm, perhaps the shit's success as a charlatan wasn't as much down to dumb luck as Fergus had thought. Catching him out in any meaningful way was like trying to grasp smoke.

Fergus sat and thought. None of these revelations was going to matter a good goddamn to Dunne. He would wriggle and smile and give his damnably reasonable explanations. And if Fergus wasn't very careful Andy would turn up in the middle of Fergus's confrontation with Dunne and accuse him of betraying her trust Again. That mattered to him more than any of the rest of it. He had just won her back with the bath, the sympathy, the hot meal, and no moralising; he was loath to jeopardise it all again. The Andy who had gone home with Mary was the one he knew and liked. The one he loved. He didn't want to meet the other one again – the one that was Dunne's conniving creature. Meeting that calculating young woman had upset him deeply.

He began to realise how dangerous Dunne was: he had a gift for putting everybody in the wrong except himself.

Damn and blast.

Thus Fergus sat, and pondered, and waited. The time ran on and nobody came. He hunted through his CDs for something to listen to. Most of his driving music was sweeping, expansive stuff for the open road, or for cutting through traffic. But he did find, at the bottom of the pile, a CD of the Tallis Scholars doing Russian church music which seemed to fit his mood. Thus accompanied he watched, and listened, and fretted. The hands of his dashboard clock moved inexorably onwards. The Gregorian chants droned seamlessly on.

It got to be nine o'clock, and then ten. Still nothing.

Keyed up as he was, he would not have thought it possible that he could doze off. But one minute he was sitting up, watching and listening; the next he was slumped in the car seat, a crick in his neck, and it was after midnight. How had this happened? Blood pumped; his heart lurched and he thought for an awful moment that he was about to have a coronary. He struggled upright and stared at the flat. His headache was worse. His neck also ached now. His eyes felt gritty and his brain had turned to cotton wool. What had he missed?

He looked up at the windows. Still no light showed. Damn and bugger. Angrily he pulled the crumpled note from Andy out of his pocket, hobbled across the road in the rain, and jammed it through the letterbox.

Mary was going to be cross.

Back across London he drove, berating himself all the way. How could he have been so stupid? It was, of course, entirely probable that Dunne had not come. But he should at least have been awake to document that non-event! He felt bested. Again. So much for having gained control of the situation. Reason told him he was no worse off than he had been when Andy and Mary left his flat but, nevertheless, the sour taste of defeat filled his mouth.

When he finally got home, and to bed, of course he was unable to sleep. He gave up tossing and turning around five, made a cup of Earl Grey and sat watching the dark trees dripping on the Heath until dawn came up. He could seldom remember feeling more miserable. There had been no telephone message from Mary, so he hoped that things at her end were going better than they were at his. Dawn was not a good time to ring and make sure.

Uncertainty added to his misery.

Friday 18 December

Friday began very well, considering what a disturbed and disturbing night it had been.

Fergus spent the morning most productively in the British Library. He arrived depressed, without much hope of being able to concentrate on anything, but that had not lasted long. An off the cuff enquiry of the librarian on duty in the Reading Room revealed that they did, of course, keep a record of all the slips presented to them and it was possible – although not easy – to know who had used which documents when. Fergus couldn't understand why he hadn't thought of this before. *Of course* they would record the slips; libraries loved to record things. Fergus exerted all his considerable charm on the librarian, and she promised to have the list for him by the following Thursday, Christmas Eve. With that list a happier Christmas was in prospect.

He would, after all, have a dated record of when he consulted the British Library's original source materials for his Pharos research. This precious information he would keep close to his chest until it was time to use it. It was not, surely, possible for Dunne to have such a record? Dunne had never consulted the materials: the materials had never been in Fergus's flat. Nor could Fergus remember referencing the scrolls in his notes – all his work had been done on the same 33 scrolls, why would you bother? However, it was almost scary how Dunne managed to acquire what he needed. Which thought reminded Fergus that he really ought to get the locks changed on the flat.

Much cheered, he went home via The World's End. Fuelled with a ploughman's lunch and a couple of pints, he set about solving his Dunne problems with enthusiasm.

On his way up to his flat he stopped at the concierge's desk and asked that his lock be changed at the earliest opportunity.

When he got home, he telephoned International Directory Enquiries for a telephone number to go with the name and address of Dunne's second and unknown referee. There was no such listing in Ireland, so he called an old friend who had been at Trinity and began tracking the elusive referee through friends of friends. It didn't take long to establish that no such person had ever been connected to the Dublin university in any capacity. Dunne had obviously relied on Ariel taking his credentials at face value – as one well might with Nick's imprimatur attached to them.

Next he made a call to the Editor of *History Today* and was delighted to find that they were planning a themed issue on architecture the following May. The would be happy to use his piece on the Alexandrian Pharos, subject to the usual reservations. They were very pleased at the prospect of a piece on the ancient world with a new slant. He promised a synopsis in the New Year and hung up gleefully. That synopsis would be written, dated and in the hands of the magazine's editor long before Dunne's stolen material could be worked up for the architecture course at Ariel, if Dunne actually intended to do any work on it.

In the New Year Fergus would show the reading requests from the British Library to Nick and enjoy the fireworks when Nick showed them to Petra. At best they should have been more careful. At worst it would look like collusion. Let joy be unconfined.

Fergus was so cheered by his day's work, he wondered what he would do for excitement once Dunne stopped plaguing him.

He was so pumped up that he started work on the article for *History Today*. He knew the material so well that it flowed out of him. Indeed, he had been longing to share what he knew on the subject for several weeks now. The noise in his private life had seriously undermined his professional life. He loved what he did for a living. Who wouldn't enjoy making sense of the past? When you weren't dealing with wayward daughters or faculty politics what could be more rewarding? It was just a pity it didn't do more to inform the present.

Around three o'clock he sat back in his chair and stretched, satisfied for the first time in a while.

As his joints popped and cracked the doorbell rang. He opened the door to Fliss.

Immediately his mind whirred. There was a reason she was here. If only he could remember what it was. She spoke.

'Every time I call on you, Fergus, you hang onto your front door with your mouth hanging open like an ancient spinster who's been sent the Chippendales as a kissagram.'

Still he couldn't remember.

'Die Meistersinger?'

'Oh shit! I forgot.'

'Good job I'm early then. You *can* still make it, I suppose?'

'Yes! Yes, I wouldn't miss it for the world. I would have been looking forward to it only ... it's a long story.'

'Well, I'll drive and you can tell me all about it. I love a mystery. Do you want to change or shall we get right off? Curtain up at four thirty and I won't go in late.'

A half-remembered line from a song swam into Fergus's mind. Something about lady tramps. He smiled. He noticed she didn't look at all like a tramp. He said,

'Did you go to work like that?'

'No, I had a night-shoot last night, so I haven't been in today. Today I have slept, bathed, eaten and dressed. Nothing more. It has been wonderful.'

And wonderful indeed she looked. She had on a long russet cloak that picked out the auburn lights in her hair. Under that he could see a choker of wonderful beads in green, plum, amber and milky white that could have been agate, and a wisp of green fabric the colour of his Jag – British Racing Green. The line from the song swam into focus:

'She loves the theatre, but never comes late. That's why the lady ...'

'Fergus, you're staring again. I'm sure it isn't news to you that a chilly wind whistles up these stairs of yours. And it's finding its way up under this cloak.'

'Oh, hell – yes, of course – come in. I'll put something on and be ...'

Her shoes were green too, suede, with chunky little Twenties heels and a strap. They moved past him into the lounge.

She twisted her cloak off in a practised fashion and it came to rest over the back of a chair. No wonder she had been getting cold. The dress she was wearing had no back and very little front. A woman who still dressed for the opera and 'never arrived late': marvellous!

He moved towards the bedroom, casting over his shoulder;

'I'll be quick.'

But at the doorway he had to stop and turn and say;

'You look stunning.'

Then he fled into his bedroom and closed the door.

He leapt swiftly into his best suit short of a tux; a very suave double-breasted grey number with a rust-coloured thread through it. He had a rusty coloured bow tie that went with it and found it, to his relief, without too much rummaging. It had been a while since he'd needed it. It needed tying – and it had been a while since he had done that too – but he could wrestle with it on the way.

Seven minutes after leaving Fliss to be stunning all alone in his lounge he rejoined her, suited and booted, tie in hand.

She'd helped herself to a glass of wine from the opened bottle on his drinks table. She had obviously expected him to take longer. He felt absurdly pleased.

'I always seem to be doing quick changes when you come,' he said lightly as he picked up his keys and wallet. And then he realised she'd only been round twice. It felt like more.

'I'm glad you're driving,' he said. 'I've got this bloody thing to wrestle with.' He held up the tie.

She looked at her watch, then held out her hand.

'Let me,' she said.

Her hands fluttered briefly at his throat and it was done. His face must have demonstrated some disbelief. She gestured to the mirror over his fireplace.

He looked. She had tied it perfectly. He put up his hand to straighten it, as you do, but it needed no attention and his hand dropped again. He wondered whether she was naturally dextrous, or if it was a learned thing. And if it was learned, who she had learned to do it for. He thought about that as he admired her handiwork.

'Beautiful,' he said. 'Let's go.'

She took a big swallow of her wine and made for her cloak. He got there first.

'May I?'

He wrapped her in it, and was alarmed at the tenderness he felt whilst doing so. She smelled nice: not perfumed, just nice. She smiled at him over her shoulder, picked up her bag, got out her keys and jingled them at him. He picked his good coat and silk scarf off the pegs by the door and they swept out.

*

They were just a few minutes early, giving Fergus time to nip up to the bar and order them a G and T for the intervals. Wagner was never short, and always needed a little help. By the third Act he knew he'd be glad of a little anaesthetic around his posterior *and* it would've been a jolly long time since lunch. But the queue to order the Light Supper between Acts II and III was long and he knew he'd never progress to the head of it before curtain up. Why had he told Fliss he was looking forward to this? Sure it was the kind of thing everyone should do once, like going to Wimbledon or Brands Hatch, but he *had* done it, donkey's years ago, in Bayreuth. He didn't need to do it again, now.

Nevertheless, he could feel the aura of anticipation in those around him and found it quite irresistible. He fought his way out of the packed bar to rejoin Fliss, who was waiting for him in the lobby. There were people everywhere, chatting on the stairs, waving to each other across the auditorium. Many of the men sported velvet jackets and floppy bow ties that looked as though they had started life as part of a Bunthorne costume in a production of *Patience*. Fergus felt vaguely under-dressed. Everybody talked at the top of their voices about Wagner, about the opera, about other Wagner operas, about the singers, about the production, about each other. Many carried large bags which clinked and rustled seductively – picnics! He saw several people he knew and several others whose faces looked famously familiar: wasn't that Bernard Levin vanishing into the Gents?

When he got back to the lobby, Fliss was checking her cloak and bag. He added his coat to the hanger. She still smelled nice, despite the overpowering whiff of mothballs coming from the massed fur coats in the cloakroom. Furs didn't get out much these days. Fergus found he was glad Fliss hadn't worn one. For some reason he blurted out,

'Have you got a fur coat?'

'Good God, no!'

He was strangely pleased.

They went up to their balcony seats, which were as good as she had said. Fergus even had an aisle seat and would be able to flex his gammy knee without kicking the person in front of him. He felt a little guilty as Fliss was, actually, taller than he; and could have made a good claim to this blessed leg room. But she offered it up and he accepted. Guilt and tradition prompted him to nip out again for a programme.

It was pleasant to be sitting next to an attractive woman in the semi-dark, warm and comfortable, with towering music to look forward to which would demand that he think of nothing but the now for the next four and a half hours. The famous Covent Garden horse shoe auditorium was spread out below them in all its red and gold finery. He surrendered himself to the evening in prospect and noticed, in a pleased sort of way, that his arm and that of Fliss lay together on their communal arm rest.

The orchestra's Leader entered to polite applause, the orchestra ceased fiddling with their instruments and Colin Davis came on to a warm wave of appreciation from the audience. Fergus smiled to himself in the warm dark. Davis raised his baton.

The fabulous overture began. Fergus allowed the figures and fugues to flow over him. He had seldom listened to the whole opera at a sitting, but he was familiar with the story. Overtures being the 'best of' bits of any opera, the whole story swam swiftly by, a taster of what was to come.

But Fergus was finding it difficult to be in the 'now'. He tried deep breathing, but it came out a little heavy and Fliss used her spare hand to pinch his arm where it lay alongside her other one.

'I wasn't asleep,' Fergus stage whispered. But he might as well have been. The past fortnight was catching up with him. *Die Meistersinger* came too close to his own recent experiences: the Guilds of hidebound artisans, their creativity subsumed under so-called 'traditions'; the posturing middle-aged men competing for the favours of young Eva. This was what the opera was about, and Fergus was currently living through something very similar. His conscience wouldn't let him alone. He thought he had snuck out without it, but he was wrong. However, there was the triumph of selflessness, youth and vitality to come, thank God.

The curtain rose on a set that looked like a Brueghel painting. The colours were ruby, chestnut brown and honey; deep royal blue; the glowing green of trees in high summer. A chorus of jolly, bustling townsfolk scurried onto the stage. Fergus's over-worked conscience finally shut up.

*

After enthusiastic applause at the end of the Act Fergus and Fliss made for the bar to retrieve the first interval gin and tonics that Fergus had set up. Fergus was embarrassed to discover that his stomach was making loud, empty noises. This would only get worse the deeper into the four and a half hours of the opera they got. On their way to the bar he became aware of rustlings and poppings around him in the corridors. Picnics were emerging. Indeed, the bar was not the crush he had expected. A few people were unwrapping sandwiches and pork pies there, and munching as they drank. No-one remonstrated, despite the provision nearby of that 'Light Supper' he had seen advertised earlier. Doubtless management realised that if everyone depended on the Light Supper to assuage their hunger the theatre couldn't possibly have fed them all.

How he wished he had persevered, and ordered the bloody supper. The evening stretched long and hungry ahead of him without solid nourishment.

Then Fliss said,

'Hang on to this, I'll go and get it,' thrust her drink at him and was gone.

Fergus remembered now that, as well as her clutch purse, Fliss had had a larger bag with her, which she had checked into the cloakroom with their coats. He found he was salivating hopefully. He hoped he hadn't misheard. She might have just said she was going to the lavatory.

She was gone some time. As the bar was accessible Fergus took the opportunity to freshen their drinks. When she still hadn't returned he grew concerned, and freshened them again.

Finally she wafted across the bar towards him, carrying a substantial holdall. He noticed that her gown moved as if it had been made for her. Perhaps it had. He was suddenly glad that he wasn't here with some callow Eva of his own, attempting to teach her something about the arts. Such a girl wouldn't have wanted the sort of gown that Fliss was wearing, wouldn't have known how to wear it, how to carry it off; such a beautiful classic would have been wasted on such a one. Fashion held the young in thrall. They wore black a lot, with black eyeliner and very red mouths. They wore denim, big hair and big shoulders; and ra-ra skirts (he rather liked ra-ra skirts). Recently they tended to wear Doc Martens boots with everything. He found Doc Martens difficult to come to terms with. Not to mention difficult to get off and prone to ripping holes in his silk sheets. But bugger all that – right now a beautiful, classically dressed woman was walking towards him, swinging a bag with a picnic in it. He couldn't decide which he wanted more.

This was turning into an extraordinary evening.

'How many have you had?' She said, when she reached him. 'You're brick red!'

'It's warm in here,' he said. '*You* haven't got to wear a jacket.'

'No. Evening dresses do have an advantage. Do you want to eat in the corridor? Get a breath of air?'

'Good idea.'

He rationalised the glasses of gin, gathered up the bottles of tonic. They made their way to the top of the stairs, where there was a little breeze.

Fliss delved into the bag and brought out two plastic containers. She handed one to Fergus.

'I packed a tea each – it's easier than being polite. Dig in.'

Fergus eased the top off the container and saw a cheerful array of sandwiches.

'It's all Marks and Spencer's,' she said attacking a prawn mayonnaise triangle with some care. 'Sorry.'

'Don't apologise – this is marvellous. You have no idea how I was dreading another three hours on an empty stomach.'

'Three and a half, actually. You're forgetting the second interval. We're still going to be starving by the end. I don't know why sitting still all evening should give one such an appetite, but it does.'

She bit into a smoked salmon sandwich. Fergus attacked his own prawn mayonnaise.

He remembered now a picnic at Bayreuth. He hadn't provided that either. Who had? Somebody's mother? Yes. He had gone over to visit a German girl he had formed an attachment to in his final year at Oxford, and her parents had taken them.

University was where he had realised that the world contained pussy and music, literature and good food, wine and art. He and Ingrid had done their finals and were awaiting their results in that haze of laziness that never comes again. They had screwed like rabbits all summer, whenever her parents left the house. The only German phrase he could manage in those days was 'Kondome, bitte?'. It had been a relationship perfect in its time and place. They had gone back to Oxford for their Convocation hand in hand. He had never seen her again after that.

He munched on his own smoked salmon triangle and washed it down with gin. Such a time for learning that had been. It had felt so good he had vowed he would never stop. And he never had. He had always felt that the least he owed the world was to have a continuing curiosity about it.

'You're very quiet,' Fliss said. She took a sip of her gin. 'Holy Crap! This is pure gin. Where's the tonic? How many are in here? I've got to drive after this, don't forget.'

He had forgotten. All he had remembered was that *he* was off driving duty for the evening and could enjoy himself. He passed her one of the bottles of tonic.

'We can always get a cab,' he mumbled round half a ham sandwich.

She laughed, added tonic to her gin, lifted the glass to toast that idea, and drank deeply.

'Of course we can.'

Fergus responded with his own glass and smiled broadly.

*

The opening of Act Two quickly threw Fergus back into the confusion he had felt during Act One. He railed at himself silently, inside – why could he not just enjoy this wonderful music with this very attractive woman, full of gin and a Marks & Spencer's picnic, in this good seat which had come his way gratis? But no: the similarities with his own life once again reared up, not to be denied. Here was Sachs deciding that he must be the nubile Eva's platonic friend, despite his desire for her. He would promote the cause of the whippersnapper, Walther.

Fergus had always had difficulty with self-sacrifice. And Sach's was making a meal of his.

He found he had both fists clenched and his left leg had gone to sleep. His mind was a whirlpool of this current performance and picnic, and that long ago summer in Germany. He was a mess of conflicting emotions. He felt on edge, restless. He began to wriggle to try and ease his leg and clear his mind. He noticed that the person behind him was having trouble too. He could feel a couple of knees through the back of the seat.

But now the music developed a comic bounce; it stuck its tongue in its cheek. The knees behind stopped jabbing him and he lost his own desire to fidget. Beckmesser sang and Sachs hammered. Fergus found all the complications flying around in his brain blown away, and he sat and chuckled. Fliss's arm lay on the seat, he felt it warm alongside his own. The scene became a riot as Sachs marked Beckmesser's song ever more harshly. The orchestra wound down like a locomotive slowing, became pensive, with a rising cadence foreshadowing hope and dawn. Fergus found he was holding his breath. Fliss didn't remove her arm from alongside his until she needed it to clap with at the end of the Act.

They returned to the bar for the second interval. It was crowded this time. Fergus felt quite conservative in his good grey suit. Outlandish outfits were commonplace. A few tiaras were out, as were plenty of Bunthorne berets, floppy bow ties and smoking jackets. Cigarette holders were popular. Fliss hissed,

'Look at the fans. Now they've had their sandwiches they can concentrate on being seen.'

The noise was stupendous: people hailed each other across the bar; laughter was loud and prolonged. The word 'marvellous' could be heard everywhere. The whole thing was very camp and a lot of fun. The real Wagner fans formed a sort of club (the sort you needed serious money to join) by dressing like Wagner, or at any rate in the style of audiences at his operas when they were first performed. Fergus and Fliss chatted, and sipped, and watched the eccentrically dressed falling on each others' necks.

Fergus wondered who Fliss knew who had provided such 'marvellous' complimentary tickets. Had she been let down by a boyfriend? She seemed so honest, surely she would have mentioned a relationship? Perhaps she just didn't see him as the sort of person to whom she needed to make such a declaration. But then, with her schedule she hardly had time for romance. Fergus realised he was a fine one to talk, as he suppressed another lurid picture of the current complexities in his own life. What a cat's cradle! But hang on. Was he contemplating starting something romantic with Fliss? Was he?

It was now dinner time in the real world. Fergus found he was hungry again, and there was still another substantial act to go. There was no possibility of storming the bar for nibbles in the time available. He said,

'What shall we do about supper afterwards?'

'I know a nice place just round the corner.'

He had to ask.

'How often do you come here?'

'My ex is a partner with Coopers & Lybrand. He loves the opera, and persuaded C & L to become a patron, but he's away abroad so much now that he doesn't get to use the complimentaries. He's about the only one who likes to go, so he passes them on to me when he can't use them. Good, isn't it?'

'Marvellous, darling!' They both laughed.

The five minute bell rang and they separated to find the lavatories.

*

The third Act fairly leapt along to Fergus's surprise, despite the hunger pangs nibbling gently in his belly. This time he found he was able to lose himself in the glorious music and spectacle. Walther's 'Morning Song' was, as always, so lovely that the hairs on the back of his neck stirred.

He was completely engrossed when Fliss waved something in front of his nose and then popped it into his mouth. Fruit pastille; blackcurrant. He wasn't usually a great sweet eater, but there, cosy in the dark, sharing a bag of pastilles, making just the tiniest rustlings, took him back to the innocent days of Saturday morning cinema.

The hairs on the back of his neck stirred again as the whole company brought the production to its climax with its reprise of the 'Morning Song'. The curtains closed and the appreciation of the audience was instantly deafening. The curtains opened and flowers began to rain onto the stage. The complicated business of giving everybody their due began. The ovation was still in its infancy when Fliss dug Fergus sharply in the ribs and hissed;

'Let's go.'

He lurched to his feet and into the aisle. They'd been sitting down a long time and his gammy knee was as stiff as a poker. Fliss overtook him at once and set off for the exit like a woman who has just remembered she left a cake in the oven and hopes she may yet anticipate the fire brigade. Fergus followed, stumbling and ricocheting in the dark, wishing blood would return to his extremities.

He made up some ground on her when she stopped at the cloakroom. There was, of course, no queue so she was off again in short order, leaving Fergus with one arm in his coat. The pins and needles in his feet were now fierce. Nothing daunted, he picked up speed again and reached the front steps just in time to see her disappearing round the left side of the building. He followed her into something little better than an alley. He was, he was pleased to note, gaining on her slightly when she emerged from the alley into a little square, shot across that, and into a pub on its opposite corner. Fergus was confident that this was her goal. If she'd run in the front and out the back things had got too bloody silly and he wasn't going to play any more. He slowed to a walk to let his breathing return to normal and his pins and needles work their way out.

And there she was, sitting at a table near the fire with a bottle of red wine and two glasses in front of her, holding a menu. She waved when she saw him come in. When he had caught up to her she said,

'This is the place I told you about. But they stop serving food at ten thirty. Everybody comes here, or to the White Lion up Floral Street. I didn't think you'd mind missing the audience participation at the end. It's bound to go on forever, it was such a good performance. I've ordered us the Special, OK?'

Fergus looked at his watch: 10.25 p.m.

'Bloody well done,' he said. 'Should I get another bottle before the hordes arrive?'

'Good idea.' Fliss poured. The wine gurgled opulently into the glasses.

Fergus nipped over to the bar and caught the barmaid's eye just as the door opened and a large party entered. It was the first of several.

By the time he got back to the table their Specials had arrived: bowls of lamb stew smelling strongly of garlic and onions, with big hunks of brown bread on the side. It smelled wonderful.

More people were pressing into the pub all the time. Fergus toasted Fliss's forethought across the table with the last of the first bottle, and they started to eat. The stew was as good as it smelled: garlicky lamb, pearl barley, onions, root vegetables, mint and rosemary, and a great deal of pepper.

When they finished their supper they tucked into the second bottle and began to talk about the opera. Fergus tried to describe his view of Hans Sachs;

'*He's* the hero of the opera, not that wet Walther. I always think Walther's a bit petulant. Or perhaps he's arrogant. The young are. More so now than ever.'

'I see Sachs as the catalyst. After all, nothing changes for him as a result of what he's done. He's the deus ex machina.'

'Deus, yes. He's good and honest and rational – but he carries such love for youth and beauty inside him. It makes him a wonderful teacher; a good friend to the young ones. But how can you say he's not changed by what he's done? There's a deep sadness in him at the end. He has to come to terms with losing Eva.'

'She was never his to lose.'

'She could have been, if he'd entered the contest he'd have beaten Beckmesser.'

Fliss laughed.

'How can you possibly know that? It's just a story, Fergus. It's not real life. And if you *want* to treat them all as real people you *could* say that Sachs is as bad as the rest. He *knows* he has more power than the others. And people with power always go the same way, ultimately: they abuse it. You could argue *he's* the arrogant one, not Walther – 'fixing it' for the lovers like that.'

'But he cares deeply for Eva. Surely it's a selfless act, what he does?'

'Cobblers. He's just an old lecher like the rest of them.

'It sticks in my craw, by the way, that even in something make-believe like opera a man can give away his *daughter* as a *prize*. That was unacceptable even when Wagner wrote the opera, the old proto-Fascist.

'The whole thing is about power, not love.'

'Well, I've always thought of it as a very touching love story that reaches across generations. It's not even so much about the jeopardy the young lovers are in: anyone can see that will be resolved. It's the sadness in Sachs as he enables their love to flourish and creates something good for his artform too. He respects the tradition of the Singers but knows there must be renewal. Grow or die. That sort of thing.'

'Double cobblers. Sachs loses in the end. He's doomed to repeat what he's good at. He's as hidebound as the rest of them. That's what's sad.'

Fergus found her well-argued case a conversation stopper. As he identified strongly with Sachs, he hoped she was wrong. He had been feeling warm, contented, expansive: happy, in fact. Now he just felt hot.

He excused himself and went to the loo. Splashing water on his face helped, but he realised he was quite seriously diddled. Too much wine had hit his stomach before the stew. And of course there had been all that gin earlier on.

The toilet facilities were not the pub's best feature. He looked into the cracked mirror over the sinks. It was not kind.

A man of middle age who thinks he might make a pass at the attractive woman he has just escorted to the opera should not look into ill-lit mirrors. That man is likely to see Time's Wingéd Chariot hurrying near. As here. He dried his hands, combed his hair and left quickly.

He pottered back to the table by the fire, too diddled to try and hide his dejection. Fliss saw the change in him straight away.

'What's the matter?'

'Nothing. I'm just tired. It's a long show.'

'It's time we were going anyway. They'll throw us out any minute.'

Fergus noticed that the bar had emptied completely while he had been gone. The clock behind the bar said ten past eleven.

'Do you think we can get a cab? I've had far too much to drive.'

'They'll be like hen's teeth at this time of night.'

'Bus?'

'Oh, God!'

The following hour was, indeed, gruesome.

It started to rain with some enthusiasm as they left the pub. Fergus made several valiant attempts to hail a cab, but all of them were busy.

Fliss knew almost as little about bus routes and schedules as Fergus, but she was determined. An hour to get from Covent Garden to Camden Lock struck Fergus as insupportable, but it was certainly eventful. It took them three buses (the first one going the wrong way). After that first directional error, Fliss threw them on the mercy of the bus drivers and things went better. It was remarkable to Fergus that one could get so very wet travelling by bus. Bus shelters seemed to be a thing of the past and what missed you coming down was given a second chance when it was splashed up in tidal waves by passing traffic. His shoes were quickly sodden and the bottom foot or so of Fliss's beautiful cloak began to look bedraggled.

Fliss's flat turned out to be what she called a garden apartment, by the canal. It could have been in Timbuktu – they had been travelling so circuitously that Fergus had lost all sense of direction. When they got inside, Fergus could see greenery thrashing gently in the rain outside French windows, so the garden bit was probably accurate. Beside the French windows was an enormous cat flap excavated through the outside wall, which let in a prodigious draught. The penny dropped: it was, of course, a medium-sized dog flap. Fliss pulled a pair of warm, floor to ceiling curtains over the whole arrangement. A little later Bracken made use of her private access. Fergus experienced the rain once again as the dog brought quantities of it back in with her. Fliss laughed and went to get a towel.

Fergus put off calling a mini-cab for a few minutes, shed his coat and accepted Fliss's offer of coffee. While Fliss sorted out dog and coffee in the kitchen Fergus looked around her living room. It was very comfortable. Nothing matched, and yet everything did. She obviously had an eye and enjoyed junk shops. Of course – Camden. There were plenty of junk shops, and the market, nearby. Three big book cases stood round the walls. Two contained novels: everything from Austen through Pynchon to Waugh and Woolf he noticed, all arranged by author. A smaller one contained works on history, biography, photography, the stage and television. In the hall were two more bookcases which held the most eclectic collection of reading material he had ever come across. Books on the Middle East rubbed covers with extracts from the Domesday book and Celtic customs. There were several books about African art, and an atlas of the ancient world. He was still trying to work out what sort of person would need such a magpie collection of stuff when she emerged from the kitchen with a tray of coffee and caught him bent double, reading spines, in her hallway.

He took the proffered mug and sat carefully in an easy chair by the French windows. Fliss descended elegantly onto the sofa. She kicked off her wet shoes, swung her legs up under her and cradled her hands round her mug. Fergus had a brief déjà vu of his recent evening with Janet Crouch and suppressed a shudder.

'Was that a helluva evening,' she said, 'or what?'

She suddenly sat up again and let her feet back down on to the floor.

'But I upset you in the pub, didn't I?'

Fergus was amazed she had noticed, or remembered. It felt as though the moment had been a long time ago. Remembering the bus journeys they'd been on since then, it was. He shrugged, but the mention of it, the concern in her voice, and the déjà vu moment he'd just had of being trapped in Janet Crouch's lounge on Tuesday evening (was it really only three days ago?) brought the beleaguered sensation back strongly.

'There,' she said. 'I did.'

She sighed and leaned forward on her knees.

'I can be an aggressive bitch when I'm not being an assertive, decisive executive.'

Fergus chuckled, he couldn't help it. She smiled when he laughed and it was a beautiful thing. Not that she didn't smile often. But somehow that one was special. It dispelled his gloomy mood. With sudden bravado he got up and went and joined her on the sofa. He didn't want to talk about what the opera's subtext was any more. He didn't want to delve into his wine-washed mind and pull up the reason why he had been upset. All that was gone: she had magicked it away with her smile.

Soon their coffee was abandoned. Some time after that they managed to get from the sofa to the bedroom, leaving a trail of small items of clothing along the way.

Saturday 19 December

When Fergus woke up things felt strange. After a while he worked out why that was. His right foot was wet. There was, indeed, a sensation – surely quite mad – of it being scrubbed vigorously.

With difficulty he pushed himself up on one elbow and looked down the bed. The duvet was in a tangle and several bits of him poked out from under it, including the foot. Working on the foot, as upon an icecream cone, was the resident spaniel.

The sight of Bracken woke Fergus properly. He remembered where he had ended up last night. And with whom.

He at once checked the other side of the bed for occupation, and found none. His bladder was insisting that he move *right now*, so he scrabbled around the bed for his trousers. As he zipped (with care, given his lack of underwear) he noticed the dog slink out of the door with something in her mouth; he suspected a sock. He followed after her as fast as he could on a mission of his own; rummaged about in the passageway for the bathroom, found the broom cupboard and the airing cupboard first, but the third door was the charm. Blessed relief!

Thereafter he wandered through to the living room, to find out what Bracken was dragging about and say good morning to Fliss. What he found was Bracken under the dining table, growling softly and chewing on one of his socks, which she refused to part with. Of Fliss there was no sign but a note. It read: 'Very sorry. Early shoot. Will call you. F'. His day began to sag.

The sock, when finally retrieved, proved to be now more hole than sock. He threw it in the kitchen bin, showered and dressed. His bare foot in its shoe was soon cold and chafed.

He felt at a loose end. Stupid in a man of his age, with his many interests and extensive acquaintance. It was Saturday, the whole day was his to do as he wished. Saturdays tended to be a low point of his week. His girlfriends had things they did on Saturdays that did not include him. Saturday was a family day. But Fergus's family was of an unconventional sort. He and Andy sometimes went on a cultural exploration of some kind, but there was nothing regular about it. His Saturday was usually spent doing domestic chores, watching the footie and having a couple of pints in the World's End. He used it as a day of respite when he could recharge his batteries. This had always suited him, in the past. He was at a loss to know why it should grate on him now.

There was nothing for it but to go home.

He used Fliss's phone to call a mini-cab. Its ETA gave him time to make himself a cup of instant coffee and drink it. There was nothing to eat: no bread; nothing in the fridge; a lonely, wrinkled tomato sat in a dish on the counter; he found a couple of tins of baked beans in the cupboard accompanied by copious amounts and varieties of dog food.

He got the ruined sock out of the bin and gave it back to Bracken. She seemed grateful. Fergus watched her rend it into shreds until the cabdriver blew his horn outside. He patted Bracken and remembered to drop the latch on his way out.

*

He felt better back in his own place. He had a long bath and made himself some breakfast. As he carried the tray into his living room, the day already felt like an anti-climax. He did, of course, have a pile of things to do. To prove it he moved the pile of things that needed doing from one side of his desk to the other. It didn't help.

He could start on the article which he had promised somebody in a bar somewhere in a weak moment, but in which he had subsequently lost interest. The deadline approached, but inspiration did not. He could begin that today. It would soon fall into place once he got started. He dug out the beer mat with the brief written on it: it was illegible. He put it on the top of the pile on his desk, then he moved the pile back to its original position.

He considered starting on the outline of his Pharos material for the architecture course that he should have written last week. But that horse had left the stable at speed. What was the point now? After Christmas, maybe, if the reading request slips had the desired effect.

Feeling oddly aimless, he sat at his desk with his breakfast and the latest History Today. His toast had gone soggy and his coffee was lukewarm. On his way back to the kitchen with the tray of disappointments he noticed the red eye of his answerphone winking balefully at him again.

The voice on the tape was Mary's, and he would swear she was crying.

That woman never ceased to surprise him of late.

'Fergus. Fergus? You bloody old tom cat, are you there? Fergus, please pick up.' There was a silence while she waited for a response that didn't come. 'Well call me as soon as you get this, OK?' The message had come in while he was on his way home from Fliss's flat.

What could possibly have reduced her to such a state? It must be Andy. Something must be terribly wrong with Andy. Did he want to learn about it on the phone? Not bloody likely. He grabbed his coat and his car keys and was out of the door before the message tape had finished rewinding.

He arrived at Mary's place in a record twenty eight minutes. As he drew up outside he thought it would serve him right if she was out. At the hospital perhaps, or the Police Station – it didn't bear thinking about. He tried to compose himself as he locked the car and walked quickly up the short path. His heart was knocking at his ribs.

Mary took a long time to answer the door. His imagination was ranging again over the gruesome places she might be if she wasn't here, when the door opened. She *had* been crying, but had made an effort to cover up the ravages.

'What's the matter?' he said without preamble. 'I picked up your message and came straight over.'

Mary's lower lip began to tremble. Her eyes filled.

'Oh, you dear man,' she said and threw the door open. 'Come in.'

Fergus was not used to Mary calling him a dear man: tom cat, yes – and worse – but endearments for Fergus, from Mary's lips, were unheard of. Even in this new, generally more positive, phase of their relationship. He was wary.

She held onto the door and he squeezed past her into the little hall. She closed the door and came the two steps to where he lurked, uncomfortable, by the door to the living room.

'Let me take your coat' she said. Her voice was wobbly.

He didn't press for information. Tears were his least favourite thing, and he could sense they were imminent. It would, without doubt, all come out soon enough. He started to take his coat off, no minor undertaking in a space as cramped as Mary's hallway. She slithered round behind him and began to tug it down over his shoulders.

'Stand still,' she said. 'Let me.'

The sliding became a caress. Fergus knew the signs from his night with Janet. He felt panic close over his breakfast. This was not what he had expected. It was much, much worse. Mary wanted company, comfort – love. And she had decided to fulfil these requirements with the devil she knew: Fergus. He should shuck himself back into his coat and make a run for it. But he didn't. He never did the sensible thing. A flashback of Janet leading him upstairs flicked through his mind like an animated film. Each separate frame showed a moment when he could have extricated himself, but hadn't. Anything for a quiet life. Never turn down an opportunity. The homilies came easily to him. It wasn't exactly that his dick constantly led him into trouble, as that he just couldn't bear to say no to women. Why was that? And then last night, with Fliss …

His reverie ended as his coat was taken from him. She'd hung it up. Too late. Again.

'I'll make you a nice cup of Earl Grey,' she said. 'Come and talk to me while I do it.'

Nice? Cup of tea? 'Nice' was not usually a word that featured in Mary's acerbic vocabulary. She had never made him a cup of tea. He had, after all, only been past the front doorstep twice before. Neither of those occasions had been pleasant.

She went through to the kitchen, Fergus followed slowly, his mind working overtime. The message hadn't been about Andy, he realised now. However, it *was* why he had come. He must try and put straight what was obviously a misunderstanding. He tried,

'You sounded upset on the phone. Has something happened to Andy?'

She shot him a look over her shoulder as she filled the kettle. There was something of the old Mary in it. He realised he preferred the old Mary. But then she turned back to the kettle and said,

'No. Andy's fine. She's going back to school after Christmas, with a note. I'll say there's been a family crisis.'

Which was no more than the truth.

Mary chatted on about Andy while she made the tea, cut lemon, put up a tray. She didn't look at him once. Fergus reflected that she was no better at seduction now than she had been eighteen years ago. Yet for some reason he didn't understand, he couldn't seem to leave.

Finally the tea was made and carried through to the lounge.

'Sit down,' she said. There was a touch of the old Mary in the command. He sat.

As she poured the tea, still not looking at him, she said:

'I was talking to Janet yesterday.'

Fergus did not claim to understand women. He loved them unquestioningly, blindly, physically; but most of all he found them to be complete mysteries. He loved them for that. But even he could tell where this was going.

'She said she was surprised not to have heard from you.'

'Oh?'

'I said that we'd had this … family crisis, and that you'd been tied up with that.'

'Ah. Yes. True enough.'

'She asked me to tell you that Katie would like some more help with her project.'

'Ah.'

'You slept with Janet, didn't you?'

There was a silence that felt, to Fergus, like a very important silence. Possibly the one that comes before a storm.

'Well, yes.'

Mary sighed.

'At least it was the mother, not the daughter. Well?'

'Well what?'

'Are you going to call her?'

'Not bloody likely.'

'You callous bastard.'

This was better. Perhaps he had misread the signs. He shrugged.

'You know me,' he said.

'I wonder if I do,' she said.

He had not misread the signs.

'So, why did you sleep with her?' she asked.

'Would "mind your own business" be an acceptable answer?'

'No.'

'It seemed like a good idea at the time?'

'No. You like pullets, not mother hens: I know that much. What's changed?'

'Nothing's changed. She ... I ...'

He stood up, walked across and put his cup on the tray. He tried again. 'Nothing's changed. It was a ... thing of the moment.'

'Yes?'

'We were both under a lot of stress, I suppose there was an element of mutual comfort in it. She was ...'

He walked over to the window. There was nothing out there but a mirror row of identical houses on the other side of the street. He wondered if the lives of the residents included conversations like this one. He turned, feeling rather like a stag at bay.

'It was a mistake,' he said.

Mary was grinning. He must have said the wrong thing.

'So you're fancy free, as it were, at present?

He realised she didn't know about Fliss. This gave him a jolt. He had been *thinking* about Fliss a lot, so much so that it felt as though she had permeated his life. But he realised now that he hadn't been *talking* about her. He had never been one to kiss and tell. He kept his relationships very private. No-one would be interested in Fergus's new relationship in an altruistic 'I'm so happy for you' sort of way. Except perhaps Andy.

He could think of a couple of people who would take a most unhealthy interest in his new relationship. He was with one of them, and she had been talking to the other. He decided to keep quiet about Fliss. He shrugged again.

'What's that supposed to mean?'

The old Mary was definitely reappearing now. If he could really piss her off he might yet get out of this in one piece. Perhaps he should tell her about Fliss after all? No. He didn't want Mary to hate her from the outset. Fergus had begun to hope he might be seeing quite a bit of Fliss in the future, which would mean Fliss would be spending time with Andy. If Fliss was going to spend time with his bizarre family it would help if Mary could be civil to her. And he could sound far more of a scoundrel if he opted for:

'You know me. I always like to have something on the go, as it were.'

'Since Janet? But it's only been ...' she counted on her fingers ' four days.'

'I told you, Janet was a mistake.'

'I think it's horrid to refer to someone like that – like an unwanted pregnancy.'

Fergus sighed. Hyperbole really was most unpleasant when used as a weapon.

'The incident has nothing to do with pregnancy. It was a one-off evening of mutual consolation. I thought Janet understood that. I am sorry if she doesn't.'

'You surely haven't had time to start anything else up, what with Andy and everything?'

He smiled his most wolfish smile.

'I manage,' he said.

Was this the moment to call her bluff? He didn't get the chance. She stood up and collected the tray. On her way out to the kitchen she said gaily,

'What a busy life you must lead.'

She was gone for a while. Some minutes later he detected a whiff of smoke. Mary must be having a sneaky cigarette in the kitchen. Andy hated her mother smoking, Fergus didn't like it either. And it never boded well. Mary only smoked when she was really miserable. The conversation so far hadn't cleared the air at all. Rather the reverse. She was making out that he'd rather fuck any woman than her. Which was true, but not for the reasons she seemed to think. He toyed again with the idea of making a run for it, but she was the mother of his child and he wanted to make what peace with her he could. Short of ... He shuddered. This was a mess. He sighed and stood. Time to get it all out in the open. He headed down the passage and into the kitchen.

The back door was open and Mary was leaning in the doorway, puffing away, ashtray in hand. The room was cold.

'Lurking in the doorway with a fag just sucks the smoke in, not out. If I can smell it in the living room it must be wafting up the stairs too. Andy will be furious if she comes downstairs and catches you.'

Mary looked at him through narrowed eyes. He suspected she had smoke in them. She had never been very good with cigarettes.

'Why this interest in my love life all of a sudden?' he said. 'You don't give a toss what I do, or don't do, with Janet. You're not remotely interested in fixing me up with her. What's going on? I rushed over here when I got your message because I thought Andy was in trouble. Well, for once it's not Andy, it's you. I can tell that much.' He indicated the cigarette that Mary was trying, unsuccessfully, to extinguish. 'So let's have it.'

She looked up at him while she poked and prodded at the smoking ashtray. Her eyes filled and her mouth wobbled. It wasn't smoke this time.

'Oh Fergus,' she wailed. She clattered the ashtray over to the draining board, rushed across the small space between them and buried her head in his shoulder.

He patted and soothed awkwardly. He tried to disengage her, but her grip was strong and his attempts only made her wail louder. The whole soggy saga floated up to him, muffled by his tweed jacket:

'When Janet told me that you and she ...' There were a couple of gulps before she went on, 'I felt such *anger*.' Sobs prevailed again for some moments. 'Then I realised I was *jealous*. Janet was telling me about her plans for you to have Christmas with them, and I thought of me and Andy sitting here looking at each other over a miserable little chicken again. It was so unfair! And then I realised that *I* wanted you.'

Her head came out of his shoulder. Hair got up his nose. Two alarming eyes – blood-shot, wide open – fixed upon his own.

'You want me to spend Christmas with you?'

She stepped back, still holding on to his forearms.

'Not just that. That's just an example. I want us to be a proper family.'

Icy fingers began to toy with Fergus's intestinal tract.

'But you don't even like me.'

Alarmingly, Mary began to attempt to flirt with him. It was not a pretty sight.

'Silly man. Of course I do. I like you very much. I love you. I always have.'

Fergus thought of saying it would have been helpful if she had mentioned this eighteen years ago. Then reflected what a bloody good job it was that she hadn't.

He thought he had experienced everything that the women in his life could possibly throw at him over the past two weeks. He had been wrong.

Gently he disengaged her grip and sat her down on the nearer kitchen chair. What could explain this volte face? Had she been drinking? He sniffed surreptitiously. She had. And it was only eleven in the morning. Usually Mary was abstemious. From that moral high ground she gave him a lot of grief about his own drinking habits. He himself would have thought twice about alcohol at eleven in the morning unless it was a special occasion – say champagne breakfast in bed. Mary said,

'I've been up all night thinking about this.'

Ah! Lots of drink and brooding through the sort of long winter night when hearts stop from the sheer effort of having to face up to another day. Not good.

He pulled out the other chair, moved it round close to hers, sat down himself and picked up her hands from where they lay in her lap. They were very cold. He began to rub them gently.

'Mary,' he said. 'Janet was a one night stand. It was something I did not choose, but could not avoid.'

He winced inwardly as he recalled how easily Janet had led him upstairs, despite his current protestations.

'She was upset. I was there, Dunne wasn't. She just needed comfort. I went over to get a contact number for Dunne. One thing led to another. I stayed the night. There is no possibility of a repeat performance. Do you understand?'

Mary got up and fetched the kitchen roll. She wiped her face and blew her nose. She blew lustily. It was not, Fergus thought, the sort of noise you make in front of a man about whom you are thinking romantically. They had a real relationship already. Admittedly it was of a rather peculiar nature. Nevertheless, it was the kind of – he hesitated to use the word, but realised, for the first time, that must be what it was – *friendship* that would permit a woman to trumpet into a piece of kitchen roll with him watching. He hoped the mopping up meant that there would be no more waterworks. She looked very vulnerable. He had never seen this side of her before. It tugged at something inside him: a heartstring?

'You've had a rough night,' he said.

She looked at him; face very pale, eyes and nose very red. She looked devastated.

'And I've got a dreadful headache.'

He grinned despite himself

'What were you drinking?'

'Dubonnet. There wasn't anything else.'

Few things gave such a vile hangover as fortified wine. He patted her hand.

'There's always that bottle of Dubonnet at the back of everyone's cupboard. Could you eat some breakfast? It would help.'

She managed a small smile. It was good to see.

'What have you got? Eggs, bread, milk, coffee?'

She nodded.

'Direct me then. I'll whip us up some scrambled eggs.'

She directed. He whipped. While he whipped, toasted and percolated he told her about Dunne's theft of his research on the Pharos, just for something to talk about. He made it light and amusing. It felt like an anecdote now, even to him, the injured party. He had, after all, fixed the bugger: or would do very soon.

Mary was outraged. Less on his behalf than because it revealed Andy had been sleeping with Dunne for much longer than Mary had been aware of.

Every problem impinged on something else, currently. Solve one thing and you created another difficulty, or made some other part of the puzzle worse. Men like Dunne lived on that. Dunne obviously reckoned that no-one would bother sorting out such a Byzantine mess of tiny misdemeanours. There was, indeed, a strong temptation just to let it all go hang, but Fergus knew he couldn't do that.

It was unfashionable, in the Eighties, to retain a sense of justice. Greed was good. Anything you could dream up to make a few bob was 'entrepreneurial'. But Dunne had reckoned without Fergus. Fergus well knew he himself was no knight in shining armour; but if he didn't put this mess right he would be no better than Dunne. Fergus couldn't quite define how or why that should be, but he felt it deeply. A perfect example was unfolding right now: he had made an amusing story out of his predicament with his stolen research to take Mary's mind off her own angsts, and she had immediately latched onto the element of it which demonstrated that Andy had been lying to her mother for months. Now Mary had something else to stew over – as well as, not instead of, the thing that had caused her to put away a bottle of Dubonnet last night. Anything touched by Dunne was pure poison.

Fergus exerted himself over eggs, toast and coffee. Soon the kitchen was full of tasty smells; not least the invigorating scent of freshly brewed coffee. It certainly made Fergus feel ready for anything. Although he wasn't the one who had spent the night downing Dubonnet.

Mary began to shiver. He shut the back door, got a coat from the hall and draped it over her shoulders. With a sleight of hand of which he was rather proud, he managed to palm her cigarettes and ashtray on his way past, and leave them outside on the window ledge.

The results of Fergus's culinary efforts were excellent. When he dished up she started on her eggs at once. They sat companionably, she munching, he with a cup of coffee. Mercifully, as far as he was concerned, if Mary was eating she couldn't be talking. Fergus offered nothing by way of conversation. Anything he said just seemed to make things worse.

When she was fed, and calmer, Fergus said,

'About Christmas. Why don't you both come to me?'

She smiled at him – not flirting, not sneering, just a smile – and he knew he had said the right thing for once. He thought about leaving it at that, but his stupid sense of fair play drove him on.

'As for the rest of it, Mary, think about it some more. I'm not a family man. I don't think I ever can be now. Maybe I'll regret that in the years to come. Maybe that's just how I am. This thing with Andy – and you – it means a lot to me. And it works. The kid gets a good deal out of it, anyway.' This wasn't coming out *quite* as he intended. It sounded as though he was pricing, not valuing, but he ploughed on. 'If you stop throwing things at me I'm sure our friendship will grow – but ...' He was stuck, momentarily, then continued hesitantly, staring into his empty mug, 'there *is* somebody I'm growing fond of. It's not Janet.' He looked up to make sure that she believed that, then went back to staring into his mug so as to get the rest out. 'I met someone at Janet's dinner party. It might be something, it might not. She's away a lot. Her job ...' He lumbered to a halt and looked up again.

Mary was looking at him. Just looking.

'Christmas would be lovely,' she said. She got up and started clearing away the breakfast things. 'The eggs were delicious.'

She put the dishes down on the draining board, turned and came round behind him. Then she put her arms round him where he sat, and hugged him.

'Thanks,' she said. 'For putting things in context. And for not taking advantage.'

She shrugged the coat off and went and started the washing up. He found a tea towel and dried.

The worst seemed to be over.

*

On his way back he popped into the World's End for half an hour. He had a large medicinal brandy and then, as the peculiar sensations left by Mary's unexpected behaviour still hadn't settled, he had another. They didn't help. He found himself staring at the optics behind the bar, his mind wandering. Again. On his way back from Mary's he had decided to start knocking his Pharos material into shape after all. But his mind felt like a bag of cats, and refused to be persuaded into academic mode. He kept thinking of Mary's swollen, bloodshot eyes searching his as she said she loved him. Hellfire, he was fifty years old – far too old to start being a family man in any conventional sense. Fifty years old. Shit.

But the most important part of his odd little family – Andy – had fallen for this turd, Dunne. What was that all about? Was she looking for the father figure missing for the first fourteen years of her life? If that was so, then it was Fergus's fault that Dunne had been able to spot the weakness and weasel his way in on the strength of it.

And Mary. She had said that their Christmases were miserable, just the two of them. Did she have any family? He'd always thought her parents were dead, and that she was an only child. In much the same case as he was himself. You had to have family at Christmas. That was the social convention. Friends wouldn't do: friends were busy elsewhere – with family. So, Mary was lonely. And Fergus, if he was honest, was often lonely. The bubbly girls on his arm were becoming fewer, gave less satisfaction. Oh, the sex was still all right. But the girls had become less interesting, somehow. All girls giggled, but now they seemed to do nothing *but* giggle. He started on his third (a single) brandy and realised he had been lonely for years. If his professional standing had risen as it should have done, perhaps that would have been enough. He had come a long way from humble beginnings: a working class boy from Glasgow on a scholarship. But what heights could a boy from the Red Clyde really aspire to? It led to a feeling of disjunction. He often felt he wanted to *return* to something, but there was nothing to return to. Literally. They'd demolished his childhood home years ago.

An idea occurred to him: he could marry Mary. It wouldn't last very long, of course. But perhaps that wasn't the point. He would have done right by her and Andy. He would have given them both his name and, when his time was up, a bit of an inheritance. He swallowed the last of the brandy at a gulp. What was driving his thoughts in this maudlin direction? What could Mary and Andy possibly gain from such a marriage, except a lot of evidence that he was not the person he had always claimed to be? Everybody had several people inside them. He had always tried to give Andy the best of his many personalities. Mary had seen a slightly broader cross-section during their brief relationship. But that had been a long time ago. During her night inside the Dubonnet bottle, perhaps Mary persuaded herself he had changed.

There was a new thought. Perhaps he had.

Today's Mary was one he hadn't met before. After all, he knew very little about the mother of his child. The only time they had spent together was their whirlwind romance, deep and hard, out of time and place, at summer school. They had both been running on adrenalin throughout the week; pissed and exhausted most of the time. At some point during those few days they had started a child. All things considered the child had turned out better than they had any right to expect. Although, wait a bit, Andy had been conceived in something more than lust. She had, actually, been conceived as a sort of primordial *and* intellectual reaction to stimuli. Their shared love of learning, of communication, had culminated in Andy, as the embodiment of the purest kind of communication there was! Andy had been created out of the best of him. And Mary too, of course.

But even if he could ever articulate that in a way they would understand, it wouldn't take long for them to forget it, seeing him every day, warts and all, unshaven, hungover, being selfish, losing his temper, staying out on a whim, lashing out with the acid tongue that got him into so much trouble. Not long.

When he first met Andy, more than three years ago now, he had had to tease her life story out of her, straining it through a lot of bitterness, to reach the easy – if fragile – relationship they had now. Mary had had no kind word for him either, wouldn't have him in the house. Until Andy took up with Dunne. Mother and father had pulled together then, for the first time. They made a pretty good team. But it was a big leap from there to Mary's recent declaration that she had always loved him. Loved the *idea* of him, perhaps.

She had a bloody odd way of showing it, that was certain.

The brandy, which he had intended would provide clarity, wasn't helping at all. Marriage couldn't be the answer, could it?

It would be a huge responsibility, and Fergus didn't deal well with responsibility. Not in his love life. Never had. A man of fifty couldn't change just like that – or at all, could he?

And now, too, there was Fliss. Was she becoming a complication, a responsibility, an intruder? She certainly didn't feel like one; though she had made most of the running, as he recalled it now. As had Mary, all those years ago, and again now. Fliss. Mary. Then there was bloody Janet and her big mouth. And Janet's daughter Katie with her own Dunne fixation (thankfully fixed, albeit painfully, by having had to watch him fawn over her mother). In a different but connected circle of hell the Gorgon Petra and her creature, Sara, revolved. His life had become nothing more than a constant rolling boil of females wanting a piece of him. He didn't seem to be meeting uncomplicated girls any more. He missed them.

The attraction of uncomplicated girls was that they prattled and giggled, but didn't think of him as a long-term proposition. He was nice dinners, good sex, a little culture: a good time on the way to something settled, permanent (boring). They wrote about him in their diaries, perhaps, and kept his phone number in their little black books. Each for other soon became a pleasant, romantic memory. The giggling girls for whom he put the black silk sheets on the bed were nothing like this world of sexual politics that he seemed to have stumbled into.

He realised they had called time some time before and were urging the last of the lunch-time crowd to 'drink up now, please'. They locked the door behind him. There was nothing for it but to go home. He walked the two hundred yards or so to his block of flats, while the afternoon and his mood settled on him like a heavy, damp blanket. He climbed the stairs wearily, like an old man. He opened the door reluctantly, and the sound of it closing behind him was like the clanging of a prison door. For the first time in many years his home and his work provided no comfort.

The Pharos material was definitely not going to get started on today.

'Jesus H Christ,' he said aloud, 'get a grip, Girvan!'

But he still couldn't settle. He pottered about, found the research he had done for the uninspiring article, washed his breakfast dishes, wiped the work tops, tidied things away, but it didn't help. In the end he slumped in his favourite chair, with a cup of strong coffee, to watch the trees on the Heath. They looked bleak, not grand or wild. He got up and pulled the curtains on them, although it was barely three o'clock. He put on all the lights in his living room, some Wagner on the stereo, settled into a different chair. But none of it helped.

Perhaps this was what a guilty conscience felt like?

He would have given anything for a distraction, but the phone did not ring. He was quite alone.

*

He got up and switched off the unbearably poignant theme of the 'Pilgrim's Chorus': *Tannhäuser* had been a mistake.

Perhaps he should go and see a show? He looked in the paper for inspiration. The Christmassy offerings looked very lack-lustre. If you didn't want a pantomime (and he certainly didn't) there were the usual revivals, lavish musicals and earnest, right-on efforts being performed in refurbished (or even unrefurbished) warehouses. Fergus was currently anti warehouses. They reminded him of Dunne. Almost everything did at present. Fergus was a man renowned for his dislikes, but Dunne definitely came top of his substantial list. Dunne seemed intent on destroying something which Fergus had taken years perfecting and of which he was very fond: his life. The ease with which the wretched man had done it was astonishing. Fergus found it particularly unpleasant to have it so clearly demonstrated how fragile his beloved lifestyle was.

Was there nothing light and witty to take him out of himself? Ah – there was a Stoppard on. That would do. But who could he take? He and Andy often went to the theatre on the spur of the moment. He could ask her if she would like to come, but his hand fell away from the telephone. If he called Andy he would have to invite Mary too, and she was currently in more of an emotional funk than he or Andy were. The Andy and Mary thing had become so complex! The whole point of going to the theatre tonight was to take him out of himself.

Did all parents go through this kind of angst with teenage daughters? How in the name of God's Holy Pantihose did they cope? Was he just particularly weak? A particularly poor parent? Was his lifestyle too fragile to cope with a family crisis? He feared the answers to his own questions.

He should phone Mary, anyway, to see how she was. But what if she took it as a sign that he did, after all, reciprocate her recently expressed feelings? He had thought about all that, briefly, in the pub; but that was just the brandy and a momentary depression talking. He couldn't marry Mary. It was a mad idea.

Above all else he mustn't make things worse. Best to leave them alone tonight. He'd call Mary tomorrow. Give her time to pull herself together. And Andy was there, of course. They could have a girls' night in; talk things through.

He had started to telephone for a single ticket for the show when he thought of Fliss. She would enjoy Stoppard. He thought of her naked body lying against him: post-coital but not clingy, just *there*. He thought of Bracken destroying his sock. God, was it only this morning? He thought of their evening at the opera, their supper after. He thought of her kindness. He smiled. He dialled her number instead.

He got the answerphone. But then, over it, came her voice, real and slightly breathless.

'Hi. It's Fergus. I wondered if you'd like to come to the theatre tonight. I know it's short notice, but I ... well, I've been staring at four walls most of the afternoon and I'm a bit ...'

Shit! What was this rubbish coming out of his mouth? She didn't want to hear him gibbering on about his problems. Good times and no complications were what kept a relationship going.

There was a silence. He had overstepped, come over as pathetic. She was thinking up a graceful way to cut him loose. Oh double shit. The silence lengthened. Finally,

'What's happened?' she said.

Fergus began to think he might not have been benched after all, and the breath he'd been holding gushed out of him with relief, straight down the receiver.

'Oh god – is it that bad?'

And suddenly it wasn't. Nor was it something he needed to bury or be awkward about. It poured out of him and he realised what a wonderful thing it was to have someone to talk to, with whom one didn't need to watch what one said.

He found he had a lump in his throat when he came to the end of the tale. Then he remembered who he was talking to and hastily added an addendum with a chronology onto it, in case Fliss – even sensible Fliss – should take exception to the possibilities of his two-timing her with Janet. When that exposition had also run its course, she said,

'Jesus, Fergus, you've had a bitch of a fortnight! No wonder you've looked a bit preoccupied from time to time. I'd love to come to the theatre, but I just can't. It would be playing hookey. I've only just started marking up this script, and we're shooting it on Monday. But I can meet you for supper after. Where's the play?

'Piccadilly.'

She laughed.

'Wonderful! I'll meet you under Eros. I've always wanted to say that to someone. We can go to Chinatown.'

'Good. Look – I'm sorry about unloading on you. I don't usually ...'

'I know, it showed. Don't worry. Everybody's got baggage. Hell, I've got loads. It's ghastly when the universe decides it's all going to get dumped on you at once. Even if you deserved it. Not that I'm saying you did. Or that you didn't. I know you well enough to know you might have! Try not to brood. It sounds as though you behaved very well this morning, considering. There's nothing more you can do today, anyway. And perhaps it will cheer you up if I say you behaved very well last night too ... ? I'll see you later. Ten'ish. Under the statue.'

They rang off.

He felt a lot better now. He phoned the Criterion theatre and had a ticket put aside, called for a cab and went to change.

Looking through his wardrobe for something suitable for supper with Fliss he found all his clothes suddenly dull and far too formal.

*

The Real Inspector Hound – for it was he, paired with another of Stoppard's shorts, *After Magritte* – had been a good choice: light, but exquisitely performed.

But as Fergus took the few steps across a lively Piccadilly Circus to the statue he thought about the clothes still strewn about his bedroom. He only went clothes shopping when strictly necessary, and had not ventured into the minefield of gentlemen's outfitters for some time. It showed. He bought good when he bought, but somehow it was all too tight, or too short, or the lapels were wrong, or the legs flapped too wide. And it was all jackets and trousers: so formal! He was an observant man. He kept abreast – why had he only just noticed this? Why had nobody told him? Andy, for instance? Or Sukie? The first afternoon he had to himself he must shop until he had a selection of clothes that fitted and flattered and were at least remotely fashionable.

Then he saw Fliss standing under Eros, holding a single long-stemmed red rose, and his worries evaporated.

As he came closer he could see that that her chestnut hair took the light from the multi-coloured neon signs and broke it down into wonderful, subtle colours – mauve and green and an iridescent blue. The colours played in her hair as he walked up to her. She held out the rose to him. He smiled and took it and kissed her on the lips. Jesus, it was like something out of *Brief Encounter*. She smiled back – a smile that went in at the eyes, squeezed the heart in passing and finished up hugging the soul. His belly and various other organs lower down constricted pleasurably. God, it was good to see her. Was it really less than 24 hours since they'd last been together?

She took his arm and they crossed the square, headed up Shaftesbury Avenue and into Chinatown.

She suggested a place with a spicy Szechuan cuisine. The place was busy, but they only had to wait a few minutes for a table. Soon they were sipping Chinese beer, awaiting their meal, in a quiet corner.

'Now,' she said. 'Tell me.'

'I told you,' he said, 'on the phone.'

'Yes, but now tell me the whys and wherefores.'

So he told her. He drew for her the line from his childhood in the west of Glasgow to the man that had made him; he drew others from his many successes to his painful failures, from the heady week at the end of the summer term at UEA with Mary to Andy's discovery of him nearly four years before. By the time their food came he had told her about his whole life and was glad of a reason to shut up.

The food was exquisite, as she had said it would be, and hot enough to make his eyes water and his nose run. The chilli and spices felt good, cleansing somehow. The dishes bubbled on the little hot plate in the centre of the table, waiting for them to select another perfect morsel. The flavours remained with him after, warm and comforting. He felt a great deal better.

'Life,' she said when they had finished eating. 'It all piles up, doesn't it?'

He looked at her quizzically.

'After you've been doing it for a while. All those mounded experiences. Nothing's isolated, is it? Everything piled up *here* makes ripples – waves, sometimes – somewhere else. One gets a lot of cross-currents. You more than most, I should imagine. You tend to lead with your fists.'

He saw that this wasn't judgmental, simply an observation.

'I don't think I handled it well,' he said. 'I don't have much of *that* kind of experience.'

She snorted into her beer.

'What kind's that? How do you classify? No. Unless you've prettied up your part in it, I think you've done the best you can, all things considered.'

'What things?' he said glumly.

'You were in a lose-lose situation. That's, actually, quite rare. Usually in human interactions the natural outcome is win-lose. But what *you* need is a win-win outcome. That's the hardest kind, but I'm sure you can pull it off.

'It seems to be human nature that someone always wants to pull a stroke. They gain an advantage all right, but they just pile up grief for themselves later because nobody trusts them. You need for Mary to feel she can trust you and that she's gained something, without you feeling you've had to give away something you can't afford. And you need not to change your mind after you've told her what you're going to do.'

Fergus felt it was time to mention Christmas.

'What a good idea,' she said. 'That'll help.'

'I'd hoped that you and I might ...'

'That would have been lovely, but I'm away over Christmas. I've got ....'

'Don't tell me – a shoot.'

Fergus tried to keep his disappointment out of his voice. He wanted to spend Christmas with her. Even if he couldn't be with her on Christmas Day, he wanted her to be close by. In the same country, at least. It was not a worthy thought. It was not win-win. Already he was failing. His dog in the manger whined softly as it slunk away.

Fliss grinned wolfishly.

'Barbados,' she said. 'I've swung ten days in Barbados over Christmas. What do you think about that? I'm abso-bloody-lutely delighted. It took some fixing, I can tell you. I've been chasing the co-production money for six months. Don't you just love it when a plan comes together?'

'New Year?'

'I am all yours for New Year.'

Around midnight she ran him home. On the way he tried to think of a way of asking her to stay that didn't sound louche or passé. He needn't have bothered. She got out of the car with him when they arrived.

'All right to leave the car here?' she said as she locked up and set the alarm.

He wondered, fleetingly, what he would have said if he hadn't wanted her to stay. But somehow he had no doubt that she would have known if he hadn't wanted her, kept the engine running, kissed him goodnight and simply gone. He was certain now: that would have left a most unwelcome hole in his complicated life.

Then he thought about his bedroom, knee-deep in discarded, sartorial possibilities ...

Sunday 20 December

Fergus was awakened on Sunday by the smell of fresh coffee that he hadn't made. For a moment he panicked. Then he remembered. He looked at his bedside clock and groaned: it was only seven thirty.

Seven thirty was not a time Fergus liked to see on a Sunday. However, he rallied when Fliss brought in breakfast on a tray. She was wearing one of his shirts that he had discarded as unwearable the evening before. On her it was just long enough to tantalise. When she put the tray down he noticed she hadn't bothered to button it. Parts of him were waking up fast.

Fliss had found croissants and runny honey. They had a lot of fun with the honey after they'd given up trying to make it stay on the warmed croissants.

By nine o'clock the bed and Fergus were a sticky mess and Fliss was in the shower. At some point during the honey episode she had apologised for the early start.

'I have to get back for Bracken. You can go back to sleep ...'

Fergus had demurred, but while she was in the shower he must've drifted off. When he next woke it was nearly eleven and he had a honey-sticky shirt over his face. He thought he had dreamed the morning sex until he rolled onto a rubbery croissant and realised that he had, indeed, had a period of intense and pleasurable activity earlier in the day. And Fliss was long gone. How did she burn the candle at both ends like this?

As he came to properly he saw the state of his bedroom: clothes and bits of croissant everywhere; honey on the bedding, which had become a giant, sticky, snaky thing. When he tried to roll out of bed the bottom sheet came with him, stuck to his arse.

What an unholy mess. He looked at the room. If Tracey saw this ... or, worse, Mary or Janet, or – even worse – Andy! They'd think he was debauched. Fergus began to grin. Quite right too. They'd had an orgy, he and Fliss. And he'd bet a pint that even the indestructible Fliss would need an afternoon nap today. He'd given a pretty good account of himself, as he remembered it.

Still smiling to himself he toddled off to the shower and began to scrub the honey off. After that he scrubbed the honey off the shower. Then he stripped the bed and chucked it all in the washer with the shirt Fliss had made breakfast in. He got some black plastic rubbish sacks from the kitchen and threw the clothes on the floor into them. He went through his wardrobe and drawers and dumped into the black sacks various other items that screamed 'Seventies' at him. He even found a few things that growled 'Sixties'. Fortunately he found nothing of 'Fifties' vintage. His second best suit had to go (those lapels!). And he promised his good suit a demotion as soon as he could get to the shops. Some frayed underpants, holey socks and a handful of kipper ties with sentimental value but no remaining sartorial raison d'être completed the pogrom.

He made up the bed with fresh linen and subsided onto it, thirsty. He looked at his watch. Noon: they were well and truly open. He dressed quickly – there wasn't much left to choose from – and started for the front door.

Shit. Mary. He must phone. He dialled. He held his breath. He got the answerphone. Immeasurably relieved he left an affectionate, concerned message and immediately regretted it. However, as it could not now be retrieved he picked up his coat and set off for The World's End to wash the taste of kindness out of his mouth.

*

He approached his front door again, carelessly and full of bonhomie, some two hours later. Some gentle music – Debussy perhaps – and a quiet afternoon in the chair by the fire. He had some journals to catch up with. He still felt a bit emotionally frayed, so decided he'd give himself a little holiday from work today. The uninspired article could wait until Monday. The Pharos outline could wait until after Christmas. He'd read, watch the trees fade out on the Heath, doze a little. Perfect Sunday.

He stopped six steps short of his landing, from whence he got a first sight of his own front door. Mary was sitting in his doorway.

Fergus felt the hot flush of panic. That bloody message he'd left on her answerphone! The happy little alcohol molecules that had been wafting about inside him gave a collective squawk and retreated to a small area behind his left temple. Never had he known a headache appear so fast. Could he be developing an allergic reaction to Mary? This wasn't on. He must be firm.

'Mary!' He held out his hand and helped her to her feet. 'How are you feeling?'

'I'm feeling perfectly awful, thanks for asking. I'm still hungover from that filthy Dubonnet and I feel a complete idiot.'

Helping her up had made his head thump. At least he hadn't had to fend her off. Yet.

'Oh?' He stuck with 'non-committal' in case he had misread the signs. His judgement hadn't been very reliable of late.

'Can we go in? It's bloody freezing out here.'

'Oh, yes, of course.'

She didn't move, so he had to brush past her to get his key in the door. She didn't seem to make anything of it, but it made his temple throb anew. When he got inside he strode across the room to the window before stopping and turning, just in case. She stood just inside the door.

'It's all right,' she said. 'I'm not going to jump you. Take your coat off and stop looking so hounded.'

He grinned weakly, a primitive baring of the teeth denoting submission, and did as he was told. He took her coat too and hung them both on the rack by the door. He needed paracetamol.

'I'll make some coffee, shall I? And perhaps you'd like some paracetamol?'

A gruesome thought occurred: the family that takes paracetamol together stays together. He squashed it firmly. That way madness lay ...

'I've got half a bottle of painkillers inside me as it is. Any more and I shall pass out. But I'll take the coffee thank you. I was half an hour sitting on your perishing doorstep. It's the least you can do.'

And the most, hopefully, thought Fergus as he headed for the kitchen. He didn't need to turn to know that she was right behind him. She stopped in the doorway and leaned on the jamb, arms folded.

'Why don't you put the fire on,' he said. 'Go and get warm.'

Mercifully, wordlessly, she went and started tinkering with the controls. Fergus dismissed a momentary vision of a small, problem-solving explosion as uncharitable.

He took his time over the coffee, and took two paracetamol while he was making it. But the throbbing in his temple was only slightly diminished when he carried the tray in. Bending over to put it down he thought for a second that his left eye was going to pop out into the cups. He sat down quickly on the opposite side of the hearth.

'Warmer?' he said.

'Yes much.' She sounded less angry. 'You winced when you put the tray down. Are you all right?' She made it sound like an accusation.

'Bit of a headache, is all.'

'Drinking at lunch-time,' she said.

Fergus forbore to point out that his headache (if it wasn't the shock of finding Mary on his doorstep) was more probably connected to the various tremendous bouts of lovemaking he had engaged in in the past few days, plus the energetic clearing up of his bedroom and de-junking of his wardrobe this morning. He just plunged the cafétiere and poured the coffee.

Mary picked up her cup and curled her fingers round it like a child. She was hunched over in the chair. She stared into the coffee as if it was the most fascinating stuff she'd ever seen. Here it comes, thought Fergus. His temple throbbed sharply. Mary looked up at him. He tried not to flinch.

'I'm so sorry about yesterday, Fergus.'

'Oh, don't ...'

'No. I was completely out of order, and you were a brick. You made all the right noises, put food in my stomach, stayed beyond the call of duty and left me with my dignity.'

'Oh. Well ...'

'I'm very sorry, and I'm very grateful. And if I hadn't seen you behave like that with my own eyes I would not have believed you capable of it.'

Fergus was quite overwhelmed and attempted to cover his confusion by picking up his own coffee cup. Mary put hers down and leaned forward. Fergus leaned back. He feared there was more to come.

'It reminded me of that end of term at UEA when we had our Thing. In the kitchens after the bar shut, when you made coffee and toast and put a big slug of whisky in it because we had no milk. And there was nothing to put on the toast.'

Ah yes, Norwich: the bloody ziggurats – lovely to look at and misery to inhabit. Mary had had a study-bedroom in one of those ziggurat accommodation blocks. The beds were pre-formed concrete shelves built into the wall. The shelf was narrow, the mattress thin. Nevertheless, they had managed.

They had ended up in her room (UEA was modern – you didn't have to share a room), munching the dry toast, still jawing on about which was the most wonderful of the Seven Wonders of the Ancient World; they kissed and discussed, stripping each other's clothes off as each argument stood or fell. Those ancient architectural wonders had always been Fergus's favourite field of study, whereas Mary was a first year student. His superior knowledge of the subject meant she had become naked rather quickly. She had stood there, proudly, still holding up her end of the argument, glowing with enthusiasm and lots of wine, her breasts jiggling up and down as she made a final point. Then he'd pulled her down onto that excuse for a bed and they had explored an eighth wonder that left the others for dead.

It had been special. Not that it was the first, or last, time something like that had happened to him. The first year students were always so enthusiastic, had such a need for debate and to test their hypotheses. A young lecturer, such as himself, was always a target. If you played your cards right, as guru, fantastic experiences could be had for the plying of a few drinks and the taking up of some extreme academic position the seeds of which were available in the first year work books. He loved it and he was good at it. Oh yes.

That had been his final term at Norwich, he recalled. He had already accepted a post at the nascent Ariel University. She was going down for the long vac after her first year, and he was going to start a new phase of his life. It had lasted only a week or so, but it had been intense.

But Mary had been special. Not just because he found out, all those years later, that it had resulted in Andy. No. *At the time* it had been special. If she hadn't been so bitter towards him when they were thrown together again by the child, the gloriousness of those few nights might have started what she had just called their Thing up again. But bitterness is very unattractive, no matter how apt, and nothing had happened.

Now Mary was talking about his kindness! If anyone had asked him about his good qualities, kindness would not be the first one he thought of. Wit: yes. Passion: definitely. He had always thought it was his enthusiasm, his energy, that made him attractive. But perhaps kindness is not an appellation one applies to oneself? It seems like a feeble thing – and Fergus never thought of himself as feeble.

So she had thought him kind, had she, preparing Scotch coffee and dry toast for her. It just went to show that Burns had the right of it. We do not see ourselves as others do. There is the problem.

And he had certainly needed all the energy he could muster. It had been an exhausting week, teaching all day; drinking and fucking all night. That final week of the academic year was always a concentrated experience, outside real time, containing more hours in each day than could possibly exist – the wall to wall parties, the general air of hysteria... But that week: wow. He had gone down with a virus when the term ended and Mary waved him a tearful farewell. He'd begun to pack for his move to London, dragging about his flat with armfuls of newspaper and packing cases like an old man. He remembered it distinctly because he was so seldom ill. If he hadn't gone down with the bug would he have called Mary that week? Truly? No. How could a proper relationship ever live up to such a breath-taking start?

He had always dreaded the occasional fallout of such episodes. Someone would turn up at the university, wanting to continue on from the high point he and she had reached; didn't understand that all the passion between them had been compressed into that tiny time, that such a beginning was also an end in itself.

Fergus became aware that Mary was still looking at him. How long had he been wool-gathering? Seconds, minutes, longer? He felt embarrassed.

'Penny for them,' she said.

'Oh, just thinking about ...Christmas,' he floundered. But he could see she wasn't fooled.

'It *was* good wasn't it? Sometimes I think I misremember; that I've coloured it better over the years – but it really was *that* good, wasn't it?'

'Yes,' he said. 'It was.'

And now here they were, knee to knee across his coffee table, clutching tea cups like shields, remembering their passion, and the electricity arced between them once again. After eighteen years, and all that bitterness, it was as if they had been romping around in that scruffy study bedroom at UEA just last week.

It was astonishing, unexpected, alarming. But he knew what he had to do, what needed to be done. He put down his cup and saucer.

'Something good came *out* of it, too,' he said.

'Our lovely Andy.'

Our lovely Andy. She had never included him in the family before. She had always implied he was an interloper, thief, free-loader. Our Lovely Andy.

He reached across the little table and took away her tea cup, her last defence.

'I think we have some unfinished business,' he said, took her hand and led her into the bedroom.

*

It was different, of course. Time had seen to that. It was less energetic. There was no frenzy. They were gentle with each other. Clothes came off slowly. He paid her compliments with his body that they hadn't had time for eighteen years ago. They gave it time and space and commitment, because this was the last time. They both knew that, and they wanted it to be the best it could possibly be. Neither spoke a word.

Fergus was glad they were taking it slow. Three days on the trot was asking a bit much from a man of fifty. He blessed the impulse that had made him change the bed linen *before* he went to the pub. When at last he slid into her the moment was so perfect that he almost wept. They lay still for long moments before moving, aware that this was the zenith, everything after this was moving towards an ending.

When the ending came it was marvellous. So often the climax is anything but; you've done all the preparatory work and then it just slips by before you have a chance to grab hold of it properly. But this was absolutely right. He didn't even think of suppressing the cry of joy that came. Mary wept and smiled. He stroked her face and kissed her. They lay together for a long time, still saying nothing. Fergus dozed. He was woken by movement. Mary sat up.

'So that's what's been wrong,' she said, leaning over him. 'I understand now.'

Languidly he caressed her nipple where it hung over him.

'We seem to have worked it out between us,' he said.

'A coda.'

'Exactly.'

She leaned over and kissed him. Then she straightened up and leaned back against the headboard for a moment.

'I'm going to get dressed now,' she said. 'You don't need to get up.'

But he found he wanted to. Something very proper had just happened; something had been expiated. He wanted to bustle. He wanted to wrap Mary warmly into her coat and send her off into the dark evening with a hug.

And he wanted never to do this again. He saw his way clearly now. He had a brief palpitation when he thought that Mary might not see it the same way, but he felt reasonably sure they were on the same page. He looked up at her, a little quizzical.

'One door closes,' she said, 'another opens.'

She got out of bed and started gathering up her clothes. He did the same.

Fifteen minutes later he swathed her in her coat and hugged her, and she went off home.

Well, he thought, as he closed the door, this has been quite a weekend. I would not have expected this kind of revelation at my age – or two women in one day either.

He put on Bach's *Toccata and Fugue*, very loud, as he cleared away the tea things and washed up. He conducted expansively with a teaspoon. He changed the bed for a second time. Then he returned to the World's End for an hour. There was no way he was going to get anything sensible done today now. He grinned broadly throughout. Sue behind the bar remarked upon it at closing time.

'It's been a helluva weekend,' he said happily and limped erratically off home.

Monday 21 December

Barely recuperated, Fergus made his way up the M1 to the university the following morning. The weekend seemed, already, like something in the distant past. The last few days before the university closed for Christmas were always hell. Hardly anyone came in and, conversely, everybody who *was* in wanted to do urgent and important business with those who had already fled for the holidays. When they found somebody, anybody, in the building they off-loaded said urgent and important business willy-nilly. It was called 'clearing your desk for Christmas'. In addition there were always crises in distant admin departments to do with the many exam results which were about to be posted out, or had already arrived. The usual gatekeepers had invariably done a runner this close to Christmas, so student queries were allocated quite randomly to any extension that picked up. Students didn't want to hear that there was nobody about to sort out their queries: it made them tetchy, it spoiled their Christmases. One got odd telephone calls forwarded from desperate clerks all over the campus. It was an edgy time.

The only reason Fergus was braving the faculty today was that he had an appointment with his prospective research student. Such busy lives did students live these days that only on a brief stopover between a working holiday in America and a family Christmas in Budapest could she fit him into her schedule. It would have made a good deal more sense if she had simply come the much shorter distance from Heathrow to Fergus's flat, but protocol demanded that both of them should travel up to the university. So now he tried to push his extraordinary weekend from his mind and concentrate on Irena Jardanyi. She would have to be shown round the campus. Fergus hoped that Marion would be available to deal with the guided tour, but somehow he doubted it.

As he strode up the steps from the car park his mind clicked cleanly into the appropriate gear. By the time he reached the corridor on which his office lay, he had the meeting planned out, his questions ordered, the answers anticipated. At that moment his day disintegrated. Petra barred his way.

'Fergus, a word.'

She turned and walked back towards her office, obviously expecting him to follow. Fergus would have been angry had he been able to marshal enough of his wits to have a cogent thought. Why did she always have to wade in like a cross between Wackford Squeers and

Margaret Thatcher? She probably only wanted a contribution to the department tea money.

Despite pretense to the contrary, a hierarchy existed in his department. Petra was at the top of the, soi disant, pyramid. How he longed to change that. But failing overthrow of the tyrant, he wished that the tyrant would find a way of dealing with her underlings without coming on like the Queen of Bloody Sheba.

His brain cells were functioning fine again now, but the plan for his meeting with Irena Jardanyi was no longer there. It had all been straight in his head, and now it wasn't. Petra was a first class bitch. He made a face at her retreating back and then dutifully followed her down the corridor.

They went into her room. She didn't close the door, so Fergus did. Petra enjoyed having embarrassing conversations at high volume. The office walls were mere plaster board, but one did what one could to minimise the damage.

Why she was doing this he couldn't imagine. Nor what her purpose could possibly be. Yet here they were. He'd take her on at whatever game she was playing. But they must play it quickly – Irena Jardanyi was imminent.

'Coffee, Fergus?'

'Thank you. No.'

He stood. Ordinarily he would have sat down, invited or not, but this was to be 'a word', and he *really* wanted it to be brief.

'I'm just making some ... are you sure?'

She started to measure coffee and water into a cafétiere. He had never seen anyone put coffee together so slowly. She switched on the kettle. Now, he thought. then she began to rummage in a desk drawer.

'I have some biscuits, somewhere. Would you like a biscuit?'

'Thank you. No.'

'Made time for breakfast did you? How wise. No point in trying to start the day on an empty stomach. Although I always find interviewing research students rather trying, rather indigestion-making. You don't?'

'Petra, was there something?'

She continued rummaging, tried other drawers. Fergus began to fidget.

'Perhaps I should come back when you've had your coffee,' he said waspishly.

'No, no. I'm sure they'll come to light in a minute. Do sit down Fergus. You're twitching.'

The kettle boiled. She filled the cafétiere. Fergus remained standing. Mercifully she didn't start the hopeless search for biscuits again. She sat down, put her elbows on the desk and steepled her fingers in front of her chin. The gesture compressed her lips to a desolate, thin line.

He realised that she must have been watching for his arrival this morning. Her office overlooked the car park. Anyone who thought Petra was anything other than Machiavellian did not have long to live, professionally speaking.

He waited. The silence stretched on.

Finally she deemed the coffee brewed and poured a cup out. She handed it to Fergus.

'Thank you. No.'

He put his hands behind his back. Nothing would induce him to take that cup, that poisoned chalice. Petra put it on the corner of the desk nearest to him and poured a second cup for herself.

'Milk?' she asked.

Fergus maintained what he hoped was a dignified silence. He must not lose his temper now or he would lose whatever battle was to come. Her softening up tactics were pitiful. He could get through this. He tried hard not to shuffle, planted both feet firmly and kept his hands clasped behind his back. He felt like Alec Guinness in *Bridge over the River Kwai* facing up to Colonel Saito.

'I can soon run up the corridor for some ...?'

'*Nothing* for me, Petra, thank you.'

She eyed him for some moments, obviously wondering how much longer she could string this out. Fergus was desperate to look at his watch, and his two cups of breakfast Earl Grey were beginning to press on his bladder. He was beginning to wonder, now. *Was* there something? *Had* she got something on him? Surely not. He thought through the faculty events in which he had been involved over the past couple of weeks and remembered no transgression. Then he thought, that's what she wants me to do, and made himself stop worrying.

He was just beginning to reconstruct his plans for the interview to come when she started again.

'What are your plans for Christmas, Fergus? A single man like you, no ties – the world your oyster. Are you going away? Abroad?'

Fergus swallowed a snort of derision with difficulty. Was this really what she had called him in to talk about?

'I am similarly fortunate, of course. I have no family. Several friends have suggested I spend the time with them, but ... I prefer to do my own thing at Christmas, don't you?'

She sipped her coffee, regarding him all the while over the rim of her cup. If the look had come from another woman Fergus might have described it as 'arch'. As it was, it reminded him of a raptor regarding a meal. He looked at his watch, not bothering to be surreptitious.

Petra ignored the gesture. She sat back in her seat, cradling her cup in her hands. She continued to look at him. He was beginning to find it disconcerting. And he really didn't want to keep Ms Jardanyi waiting. He tried to wriggle free,

'Well, it's been enchanting, chatting with you, Petra. Now if you'll excuse me?' His right foot swivelled towards the door, but he got no further.

'Nevertheless, Christmas is more fun with companionship. I'm sure you'd agree with me there?'

Was there to be no end to it? He searched for some inconsequential repartee that might ease him out of the door. His best get-out-of-jail-free lines, he realised, all involved sex and alcohol. He struggled to create one that didn't. She had total recall of the weaknesses he had been careless enough to show her over the years. She stored them up to use at critical moments – like a Promotions Board. It had happened before.

'I was sure you would have marvellous plans for the holidays. Are you completely at a loose end? Contemplating the lonely preparation of a chicken for one?'

Well, of course he had plans. But he wasn't going to tell Petra about them. The faculty had no idea Andy existed, let alone her mother. He would have loved to tell Petra he was planning a festive family Christmas with all the trimmings. But such a revelation would undoubtedly come back to bite him. He found himself almost tongue-tied with wrath at her making him late like this while he knew there was a perfectly innocent truth that he could not trust her with. Any number of half-truths which were now springing to mind would land him in hotter water than that in which he currently seethed. She would file away whichever one he used in the steel cabinet she called a mind and throw it back at him at a time when he least needed to hear it. Bugger the woman.

'Of course I haven't booked my trip abroad yet. I was relying on a last minute deal to somewhere warm.' She raised her cup to her lips again but, instead of drinking, giggled. It was a horrible sound. 'So much easier to put up with all the tinsel and sentiment when one is lightly clad and sipping something long and cool on a veranda, don't you agree?' She lowered the cup and her face fell. 'Although these days one has to go very far afield to find somewhere without dried out turkey and party hats.'

She sighed and put her cup down on its saucer in front of her, her hands around it, as if it were a precious thing. She looked up from the cup to Fergus. It looked as though whatever it was she had called him in to say was coming now. He hoped it was well worth bloody waiting for.

'If you have no plans perhaps we might spend Christmas Day together? I would be happy to forego my trip.' Her face gave a wriggle which Fergus feared was supposed to indicate coyness. 'People have been kind enough to say that I am a very good cook. We could avoid turkey – I have a very good recipe for venison that I've been dying to try. Apparently it's very low in cholesterol ...'

He was enormously relieved when she fell silent; he had no idea what more she might have offered in the way of self-advertisement but was afraid that he would shortly have found it impossible to keep a straight face if she had continued. He wasn't sure why he found it funny. There was nothing funny at all in what he had just heard: he had just been propositioned by his head of department. Even if one accepted it all at face value – a simple invitation to share a Christmas dinner with a lonely woman who liked to cook – he was in a terrible spot. Obviously he couldn't go. Even if Andy and Mary hadn't been coming, he couldn't go. He would rather spend the holiday in an unheated monastery in the high Himalayas than eat Christmas dinner with Petra.

A terrible suspicion began to grow within him. His synapses made links across a range of experiences he had endured with Petra. It all made sense now – the carping, the advice, the constant put downs: the bloody woman fancied him! Fergus was rocked to his foundations.

'What an enchanting idea. I'll check my diary and get back to you, Petra. Must fly – Ms Jardanyi awaits. The Hungarians are such punctual people. We don't want to make the department look bad ...'

And, with a sickly grin plastered to his face, he fled.

*

Fergus regained his office with relief and closed the door firmly. He glanced at his watch; he had five minutes before the Jardanyi girl was due. A generous-hearted soul might have supposed that Petra had felt shy of inviting Fergus to Christmas dinner and had taken time to work up to it. Fergus had, over the years, experienced Petra's gamut of emotions (how did the phrase go? From A to B?) but had never noted shyness to feature among them. She would not coerce him into Christmas dinner à deux, but she *had* succeeded in making him late. Despite his need to concentrate on Irena Jardanyi he found himself wondering at Petra's contradictory behaviour. He was woefully distracted: his beautifully structured (but sadly, not written down) plan for the interview had disappeared as soon as Petra had collared him. He felt flustered and under-prepared. There was no time now to look out the more relevant of his own publications with which he had hoped to impress the girl. There was time only to try and render his office into a welcoming environment. This he accomplished by dumping the pile of papers which lived on his 'guest' chair onto the floor and wiping all flat surfaces within reach with a handful of damp paper towels he got from the kitchen

He well aware that this was not the only interview the Jardanyi girl had. She was good enough to have her pick of supervisors. Her potential, when turned into a good thesis and the several publications which would, doubtless, follow it, would redound very favourably to the credit of whoever mentored her achievements. Fergus very much wanted her to choose him.

There came a knock on his door, and Marion's head poked round it wearing a quizzical expression. The girl was early! Shit, shit and shit! He threw the filthy paper towels into his waste basket and ran his fingers through his hair.

'Ah, Marion, and Ms Jardanyi, I presume?'

The two women moved into the room.

Irena Jardanyi was a bizarre young woman to look at. She was tall and thin. Her hair was cut into a precise pageboy; that and her strong eyebrows were very black – a Gothic, Transylvanian black. Her skin was beautiful, pale and creamy, as was her silk blouse. Everything else about her – from her lips and eyelids to her expensive-looking high-heeled ankle boots and briefcase – was a shade of oxblood. She looked a bit like an animated liver.

Halfway across the space between them he encountered a hand with oxblood coloured nails held out towards him, stiffly, like a spear.

'I am Irena Jardanyi. You are Fergus Girvan.'

She did not smile. Bad sign. Fergus found himself girning enough for both of them.

'Yes – Girvan, that's me. Come in, come in! Sit down here,' he patted the back of the dejunked chair invitingly. 'Marion will bring us some coffee, or would you prefer tea?'

The girl continued to regard him without expression. It was unnerving. He knew he was prattling. He knew she knew. A glance at

Marion confirmed that she knew too, although her efforts to control her face were almost successful.

'Thank you; hot water only, for me,' said Irena.

Fergus's eyebrows did a little dance. Ascetic as well. A beautiful, forbidding, vampiric beauty who drank, not blood, but hot water? Fascinating.

She continued,

'It is so good for the system. Nothing else do I take until luncheon. Only then do I break my fast.'

Who ate 'luncheon' these days? Strange girl – no: a girl in a foreign country doing her best.

Marion went to boil the kettle. The girl subsided into the chair prepared for her. Fergus worked his way around to the chair behind his desk (carefully avoiding the new pile of papers on the floor). He put his elbows on the desk and steepled his fingers in what he hoped was a thoughtful and distinguished manner. A silence ensued. Even with the security of his own desk before him and his publications ranged behind him in his bookcase, Fergus had difficulty knowing how to begin. It was absurd. He had conducted interviews – many interviews – for years. But, somehow, he felt he was the interviewee here.

Marion re-appeared with steaming cups on a tray (but no biscuits, damn it). Fergus was grateful for the small diversion, which gave him a chance to rally his thoughts. He thought of Buck's Fizz and oysters for breakfast. He thought of Fliss and honey. These things enabled him to find a proper smile and wear it as if he meant it.

By the time Marion closed the door behind her he had, he felt, regained control. He picked up his cup and saucer and leaned back in his chair, regarding Irena as solemnly as she still regarded him.

'Well, Irena – may I call you Irena? – what exactly is it that you feel you have to offer Ariel?'

At once she became the earnest student. She put her own cup and saucer down and folded her hands in her lap, where her fingers at once began to intertwine like a little nest of snakes. A flush rose up her cheeks and neck. Fergus was entranced. The girl was nervous! Thank God. Although it was still a toss-up which of them was the more nervous of the two.

She gave him a pretty speech which had obviously taken her time and research to prepare. Then she bent to her briefcase and, without rummaging, pulled out a neatly stapled pair of pages which outlined her thesis. She handed them to him to read. She still didn't smile. She stared at him constantly – but Fergus had her measure now and the constant regard no longer discomfited him. He took the proffered outline and put it on the desk in front of him. Very gently he said:

'Why don't you *tell* me your premise?' It was a rotten trick, perhaps. But he wanted to gauge her passion for her subject, find out how much she knew without recourse to books and other people's papers.

Now she was flustered. She hadn't expected this, it was not in her carefully prepared plan.

'Yes, of course ... I ...'

She took a minute to arrange her thoughts, pull up the most interesting and salient points and make them into something for a conversation, then she launched into it.

It was fascinating; a truly original approach to an ancient conundrum. It was potentially provable. And it could plug a genuine hole in understanding of the ancient world. He had known the general thrust already, of course. It concerned the whereabouts of The Hanging Gardens of Babylon supposedly built by Nebuchadnezzar. The bloody things were patently nowhere near Babylon, or somebody would've stumbled across them by now. Irena intended to show, by re-translating, re-interpreting and cross-matching ancient texts in Greek, Cuneiform, Arabic and Latin, that they were actually built by the Assyrian king Sennacherib at Nineveh in historical Mesopotamia, modern Iraq.

The lack of any trace of the Gardens had led a number of Ancient Wonders' scholars recently to seek to have them demoted. Fergus felt it would be a pity to lose them on a technicality. Even if the technicality was that the Gardens were the only ancient wonder for which no archaeological evidence had ever been found. More importantly, he couldn't help feeling that as so many ancient writers had taken the trouble to marvel at the Gardens, there had to be a grain of truth in them.

At the end of Irena's exposition he probed gently to see how far she had taken her planning. There was nothing he could ferret out that she hadn't thought of. He was impressed. At length, he told her what he thought of her proposal and was finally rewarded with a smile. Suddenly words burst out of her, unprepared, unscripted.

'I want you so much for my supervisor. Many people want me to fail. I do not want to study under them. I have heard you are not afraid of controversy.'

Fergus felt a warm glow begin deep inside himself.

'You are brave, they say. You will stand up for me, I hope, against those who think my premise is not worthy.'

'It will be my pleasure,' said Fergus.

'I am so glad. I have read all your books.' She blushed again. 'You are required reading in my country. I have dreamed of meeting you since I was very small.'

Fergus felt his own face begin to warm. A prophet may be without honour in his own country – but in Hungary, apparently, he was the bee's knees! He held up a deprecating hand, but she continued.

'And it is so wonderful a thing, your Ariel. In America education is so expensive. Here knowledge is accessible. At home education is free to everyone, but subjects are strictly controlled and we only learn what is deemed proper. In *your* country also there are marvellous English eccentrics like Waugh, like Carroll – like you. The best work comes always from *original* minds.'

Irena's smile was now a beaming, beautiful thing. Fergus was entranced – and gratified. Thanks to Petra he had had to busk his way thought this interview, but it had turned out all right. Things were, indeed, much better than all right. Irena liked him. She liked his work, his reputation for eccentricity, his championing of classical underdogs, and she wanted to him for her supervisor. He was absurdly pleased.

After that it was easy. As the interview had run on rather he suggested lunch in the campus refectory. On their way out she paused and looked around his office.

'Do you have no computers here? In my family we use e-mail all the time – between institutions, to talk to each other, and to know what is happening in the world. It would be very good if you and I could talk through the computer. Then I could study from my home In Budapest, from my brother's home in America – anywhere.'

Expansively Fergus reassured her,

'No problem. The faculty uses them all the time. We can soon get ourselves set up with the necessary.' That's going to come back to bite me, he thought. Now I'm going to have to learn to use one of the bloody things – and find somewhere in the office to put it.

*

In the Refectory she ate the watery plat du jour with gusto, although he couldn't persuade her to share the bottle of too-cold Côtes du Rhône which was the best he could coax out of the girl at the till. They toasted the prospect of her official arrival at the university in the New Year with wine and tap water.

After that he walked her round the campus. Its furthest reaches had expanded since he last provided a guided tour, and in some cases he found he had no idea what might be going on inside a particular building. She was excited by the size of the place, its grounds, its sculptures, its banks of shrub roses, puzzled by the lack of students (although he had explained the reason for that a couple of times already) and entranced when they saw the grey squirrels playing in the little patch of woodland outside the bank.

Eventually he got her a cab and waved her off to the station. Then he got out her file and reminded himself where else she had applied. The only serious competition appeared to be Oxford – and they would want her to be resident. Fergus rather thought that his track record (and the acrobatics of the squirrels) together with her desire to live away from the university (after all, Ariel was a distance teaching institution) had swung it.

Elated, he began rationalising his piles of papers, during which he unearthed several long overdue library books he'd forgotten he had. An agreeable number of papers could now be filed WPB. The others he made into short, categorised, over-lapping stacks on his desk.

A couple of hours later Sara knocked at his door. Without waiting for a 'come in' she swung in on his door handle and hung there, all hair and legs.

'Petra said you were in. Have you heard?' she said. 'There's a train strike. Someone's put it up on Con-Sys.'

Fergus indicated the absence of computing equipment in his office.

'What do you expect,' he said. 'It's the week before Christmas.'

'Wow! How do you manage without a computer?'

'People talk to me. Or they send me a note.'

Fergus pointed to the various short stacks of paper on his desk. They looked much more business-like now than they had two hours ago, when he would not have wanted to use them as a testimonial to his communication system.

'Wow,' she said again. 'Computers are great. You just have to let them know who's master. It's only like using a pencil and paper really – and a calculator and dictating machine, and library, and dictionary and ...

He remembered Irena.

'You understand the bloody things?'

'Sure. Essential tool these days. I get more than half my research done on the Internet. If you need to crunch numbers, a computer makes it a doddle. And I send almost all my memos electronically. Would you like me to set it up?'

Would that she were offering to initiate him into something more exciting than the joys of computing, but Fergus was a realist. And his love life was already sufficiently complicated.

'That would be very kind.'

'Anyway,' she went back to her original topic, 'there's nothing running to London tonight.'

'Thanks for letting me know, but I've got the car.'

'Then, if it wouldn't be a terrible nuisance could you give me a lift? I *could* stay somewhere local overnight I suppose, but there's my cat ...'

She gave him a big smile. Sara's big smiles were serious knee-tremblers – the sun came out; he felt heat-stroke imminent. And he well knew there was nowhere local to stay overnight.

'Of course,' he said.

'Great! What time do you want to go?'

'If there's a strike the roads will be hell. Would half past three be too early for you?'

'No, as far as I'm concerned we can go now if you want. I'm easy.'

She did a little twirl in the doorway. Happy and carefree, she was; just how he liked them. Happy and carefree, earnest, ingenuous, gorgeous – and *not* easy he suspected. Despite her light-hearted remark.

'I've still got some stuff I want to finish up. Three thirty is good.'

'Okay.'

With a flash of thigh and teeth she was gone.

Fergus's heart rate settled slowly. His office still pulsed with something – pheromones? No, something less animal. Fergus suspected it was pure joie de vivre. Sara Somerton was what Pollyanna turned into when she grew up.

She re-appeared a few minutes early with a huge satchel that made her look like a schoolgirl. She sat in the newly cleared chair without being asked. Her short skirt, thick tights and clumpy shoes reinforced the schoolgirl image. The chair was low and she tall, so her knees stuck up in the middle of an expanse of black clad thigh. Fergus found it hard to concentrate on the last little tasks he wanted to complete. There wasn't normally anything titillating about woolly tights. But, like Marilyn Monroe, Sara would look sexy in a sack.

*

The motorway was still moving when they joined it, and they made reasonable time. Sara prattled cheerfully about her experiences in the faculty to date; how much she admired and liked Nick, the view from her office ('the sunsets are wicked'), the course work she was engaged on, the quality of the teaching materials she'd seen and so on and on. Ten years ago he would have been joining in with anecdotes of his own about their collective and individual achievements. Instead he concentrated on his driving and contributed only the occasional 'hmmm' and 'aha'. It should have been exhilarating to hear all this, to know that the incoming, young ones could still find that sense of achievement and wonder in their work. Instead it depressed him mightily. Twenty years ago he *was* this bright-eyed newcomer, in a faculty full of the same. The world had been theirs to mould to their will – and look what a fucking mess they'd made of it

He was dragged back to the present when he heard Petra's name.

'What did you say?'

'Oh. Petra. She had me in for tea this afternoon. She wanted to know what I was doing for Christmas.'

Fergus laughed.

'What's so funny?'

'Let me guess – an interview about your seasonal plans and an enquiry into whether you like venison?'

'I'm vegetarian.'

'If you told her that, I imagine teatime was short and sweet.' His memory of Petra and beverages was both fresh and raw.

'It took her *ages* to make it.'

Fergus's hands clenched momentarily on the steering wheel.

'I don't know why she doesn't get her secretary to make it – like you do.'

Why indeed. Petra's tea and coffee making rituals were a strange addendum to her already complex agenda.

'Anyway, while she was making it she let slip that the university was putting together an enhanced early retirement package. She was ever so upset when she realised what she'd said – she said it was confidential until the details had been worked out with the union and that I wasn't to tell anyone.'

She paused a minute, obviously bothered that she had just let it 'slip out' too.

'But I'm sure it's all right to tell you. You're discreet. Petra said so.'

Fergus reflected that if Petra had been speaking of him as 'discreet' that it was unlikely she was referring to his ability to keep schtum about confidential faculty matters. More likely she had been referring to his campus affairs. Next year there was the possibility of a dalliance with the new secretary, Angela, whom he had taken to lunch a couple of weeks ago. Although he doubted that it would come to anything more, this time, than a certain frisson when he went into the typing pool and an easier time of it when he needed something keyed or copied urgently. And, of course, there was the possibility of something developing with Sara, except that she was Petra's stalking horse. Or perhaps he might find romance closer to home. In Camden, for instance.

Having begun her indiscretion Sara was, apparently, eager to unburden herself of the rest of it. She continued:

'She said it wouldn't affect Art History, because we are all so young, and the department has a big course replacement programme over the next few years. But she's worried about Classics because her department tends to contribute to other courses in the profile and not make whole ones of their own. She said Ted Pater's *bound* to be offered a package. And you *might* be. She said she didn't know if there'd be anyone left to act as Department Head if she becomes Dean in the New Year, the way things are shaping up.

'I thought that, since you're in Classics, I ought to tell you. I guess Petra can't. Not until the scheme goes public.'

Let slip indeed! Petra was a devious bitch.

'It must be awful,' Sara continued 'to be fingered as dead wood and paid off like that. Not that I need to worry for about thirty years.' She gave a little giggle.

Fergus thought, 'and what happens when your two-year contract comes up for renewal?' He said nothing, however, and Sara rattled on,

'The scheme only comes in at fifty five. Although Petra said it is *possible* to make exceptions for people as young as fifty, if you were interested.'

Fergus felt his stomach squirm. He managed a small non-committal noise. Anyone who had turned fifty was past it, now, it seemed. This was what happened to education in Thatcher's bloody Britain. Experienced, tenured teachers tossed out in favour of recently qualified kids on temporary contracts. The worst of it was, he would probably have been all for this survival of the youngest and cheapest twenty years ago!

He had no doubt about Petra's motives in telling the girl about the early retirement scheme. He had no doubt that Petra had engineered this lift home at some level – she must have blessed the train strike. The invitation to Christmas dinner didn't feel so much like a bumbling attempt at a date now. It felt more sinister than that. Perhaps the invitation to a venison dinner had been Fergus's last chance. Nothing Petra did surprised Fergus, but he had *thought* they had an understanding that their usual hostilities would be put on hold while she got herself elected Dean, and that he would be keeping her Department seat warm for her for the next three years. Hadn't Nick told him as much? Now it transpired that the first thing Petra did when the information about early retirements being in the offing crossed her desk was go to his personnel file and check his birth-date.

Fergus found himself sweating and opened his window a little. The wind noise made it difficult to hear what Sara was saying. However, as she hadn't shut up since they got into the car and had now dropped her bomb, aimed by Petra, he felt little compunction to listen. Instead he began to work through possible scenarios that might get him nobbled as a candidate for this bloody early retirement nonsense. It would be a good trick to show that Fergus Girvan wasn't pulling his weight, professionally speaking. He was, after all, working on two courses in production, writing innovative teaching material for both of them, fulfilling his obligations on time and to length.

But nobody had liked his final draft of the material about the Minotaur of Knossos for the 'Myth and History' course. (Although they'd seemed to like the previous draft just fine.) And the chapter he had been about to propose on the Pharos of Alexandria for the new course on architecture had been given to Dunne. Had both those commitments been cursed by Petra somehow?

In the new year he was scheduled to contribute a chapter to another new, inter-faculty, course with the working title 'How to Make Discoveries' He was going to use Agamemnon's death mask (so called) found at Mycenae to show how dangerous it is to make assumptions when dealing with primary sources. He hadn't really started on that yet. After that he didn't have anything lined up except supervision of Irena Jardanyi's thesis on the whereabouts of the Hanging Gardens of Babylon. That could take several years, if she was going to get stuff re-translated and go through it all with the rigour he suspected (from the carefully matched oxblood outfit) was one of her strengths. He'd better make damned sure that came through, then.

But surely a man of fifty with so much potential was worth ... As he rummaged for a superlative he realised that to be fifty and still trying to realise his potential rather made Petra's case for her. How had the years slipped by so fast? The end of his working life was so much closer than he realised, and he hadn't even noticed it dribbling away.

The traffic ahead was motionless. He took his foot off the accelerator and switched on his hazard warning lights. They came to a halt beside Gunnersbury Park. Just when you thought things couldn't get any worse! Cold rain was spitting on him through the open window. He closed it.

Sara was still talking. About Christmas now. Keeping his voice neutral he asked,

'When does the early retirement scheme start?'

'February, Petra said.'

'So soon? But it's not been to Faculty Board yet.' Fergus could not prevent some heat from creeping into his voice, but Sara didn't seem to notice.

'It's coming to the February meeting. "For information", I think.'

How convenient. Faculty Board met on the first Thursday of every other month, so the people would hear about it mere days before it was to be implemented. And the February meeting would be almost completely given over to the Deanship elections anyway. The Arts Faculty was nothing if not parochial. They would immerse themselves in their own concerns and then wonder what the fuck had happened when the university started cutting out – what was the phrase Sara had used? – dead wood.

Ted would be glad to go. You could see in his face that he didn't know how he was going to make it through to sixty. He wasn't well. Everybody said so, although nobody knew what ailed him. Ted was just fading away. They hardly ever saw him in the faculty any more.

Earlier in the year Ted had come in specially to ask Fergus if he could possibly see his way to giving an old colleague a hand – apparently Ted's course committee had been hounding him for a promised draft for over a month and he was embarrassed that he hadn't been able to complete it. Ted had rummaged in his briefcase for the couple of crumpled sheets of paper which constituted his outline of the chapter,

'It's all in here somewhere. I know where everything is, you see, because I keep it all in here.'

Ted's briefcase bulged with papers. It was difficult to close, dangerous to open. As Ted rummaged papers spilled out. Ted muttered 'oh dear, oh dear' as the papers got into a muddle, spoiling his system. At last he straightened up, clutching the relevant pages, close to tears.

'It used to be all here, you see,' he said, tapping his forehead, 'but now it's here.' He put his two hands on the top of his briefcase, protectively. 'And if it *isn't* here, I don't know *where* it is.'

Fergus had helped him gather it all up again, concentrating on the task, not meeting Ted's eye, giving him time to compose himself.

Ted is only eight years older than me, Fergus thought. Please, God, don't let me go like that.

*

The traffic began to crawl forward: Fergus crawled with it.

But the others ... Fergus ran through them, department by department. The only real candidates were Ted and Patrick. Patrick wouldn't need to worry about being squeezed out. The immediate past Dean could call in a few favours to turn the sword away. If he wanted to. He *might* consider his Deanship the zenith of his career: be glad to shuck off all responsibilities at the end of his term, and bugger off to enjoy lucrative consultancies with other institutions. Could Fergus do the same? In the way of that solution stood the old problem about his star never having risen high enough. His theories were sound, all of them proven. He was scrupulous in such matters. But, as his field was the ancient world, he'd worked over a lot of old ground through the years. Old ground tended to have theories already attached to it. The people whose theories he had debunked tended not to take the debunking well. He was considered combative because he didn't sugar-coat his conclusions. Why the hell should he?

It wasn't the money, so much as the work. What the hell would he do with himself all day if he didn't have projects to work on? And if those projects didn't have the imprimatur of an institution of learning attached to them, research would be much more difficult. He needed access to libraries around the Mediterranean, for a start: Alexandria, Athens, Istanbul. No letter of recommendation? No entry.

He still couldn't understand why Petra had decided he was to be the sacrificial lamb. But wait a minute. Was it that, as Dean, she knew she would have to offer up a candidate for this infernal scheme? And it was true that most of his colleagues were in their forties or younger. Too young to be targets.

What had happened to all his contemporaries? Gone on to greater things elsewhere. Ariel's Young Turks had been head-hunted aggressively in the late Seventies by institutions anxious to update their teaching methods and course structures, and jump on the distance teaching band-wagon. Somehow, as so much else, all that seemed to have passed him by.

It was plain to him now that no Chair would be forthcoming. He'd be lucky to keep his job.

The car began to steam up and he cracked the window again. Cold air hit his face. He looked across at Sara and saw that she had fallen sleep. Her hair was all over the headrest in a shining swathe. She looked like a heroine in need of saving. What she actually was, of course, was Petra's mouthpiece and an inveterate chatter-box. Part of him longed to touch her cheek, lean over and feel the soft breath from her parted lips before he kissed her awake. But then she would start talking again. Much better to let her sleep. Time enough to wake her when they arrived somewhere.

The weather and traffic both continued to get worse as they inched towards central London. As they crept up Hanger Lane towards the North Circular Fergus woke Sara up. He didn't need to outline their predicament.

'I'm going to tough it out to Hampstead,' he said. 'Shall I drop you at Willesden Green Tube?'

She looked beleaguered, still half-asleep, pushing her hair out of her eyes.

'Oh Christ, it'll be a nightmare trying to get to Harringay from there.'

'How about if I drop you near Bounds Green?'

She brightened, but then put two and two together.

'But you'll be going miles out of your way!'

It had started to sleet. Sloppy flakes lodged on the windscreen between the languid strokes of the wipers. Fergus thought of the warm and cheerful fire at the World's End, a dark pint of Winter Warmer and one of their excellent steak pies.

'No problem,' he said heroically.

The North Circular stretched clogged and motionless in front of them. The sturdy old Jag continued to creep forward when it could. Fergus put on Radio 3 for a while. It was a profile of Michael Tippett. Not only was it beguiling, it also encouraged Sara to stay quiet. At length the painfully beautiful spirituals from *A Child of our Time* filled the car.

Fergus sat in the fuggy dark next to a beautiful and oh-so vivacious girl. Sleet settled on the windscreen. His career was in tatters. The World's End seemed accurately located. The voices sang 'Deep river, I want to cross over into camp ground'.

Fergus could've wept.

*

Eventually he was able to drop Sara at Bounds Green. It seemed almost churlish not to take her all the way home, but he had had enough of company (especially hers) and wanted to be by himself for a bit. He wanted to be *home*; without chatter, back-stabbing, duplicity or arguments. And when he got there he was going to step outside the box of his life, think hard and long, and see if there was anything in that beloved box that he could save.

He got out his A-Z and plotted a route through back streets, while waiting to get to the Park Avenue turning.

It was nearly seven o'clock when he got home. In the underground garage, he switched off the engine with a sigh and sat for a few moments, before climbing the stairs to his flat. Inside, he fingered his favourite objects, waiting for his usual contentment to re-assert itself. It didn't.

Almost fearfully he glanced over towards his evil, red-eyed answerphone. Sure enough it was winking at him. Pure masochism drew him towards it. Whatever had happened now, he must know the worst.

It was not good. It was Janet. It was an invitation to yet another Christmas dinner fraught with complications. Everybody, it seemed, wanted a piece of Fergus Girvan. Couldn't they all just leave him alone? A kindly portion of his mind reminded him that Janet might simply have thought she was doing him a favour – a man on his own over Christmas might be a sad and lonely being. The sharper portion pointed out that Janet had an agenda which doubtless included a reprise of the rumpy-pumpy in which they had engaged the previous Tuesday night. Obviously Dunne had not re-appeared in Janet's life. Such a pity he was still deeply embedded in Fergus's own.

Almost he felt sympathy for the lonely woman who had invited a lonely man for Christmas. *Almost* he dialled her number. But his constitution was not equal to the task. Today had already been more than enough. He would call her tomorrow and make his excuses. He *might* even pay Janet the compliment of telling her the real reason that he couldn't accept her invitation. It was, after all, in present circumstances, nice to have friends.

He put his coat back on and made his way through the sleet to the World's End for the anticipated beer and steak pie. The pub was warm and cheerful, the ale good, the food excellent. He stayed for a second pint, exchanged inconsequential banter with Sue behind the bar, but his mood wouldn't lift. A line from Tippett's arrangement of 'Steal Away' ran through his head like a mantra: 'I ain't got long to stay here'. He drained his glass and bade her goodnight before nine o'clock.

He finished the evening with a bottle of Laphroaig that had been lingering in the cupboard long enough. Fergus wasn't a whisky drinker and this had been a misjudged gift. As he unscrewed the cap he knew that this was not good use of a twelve year old single malt – but he needed the expiation that only whisky, in quantity, can give.

It gave.

Tuesday 22 December

The alarm woke him at seven the next morning. He was still fully clothed and knotted up in the duvet. He felt like hell. Again. He was getting too old for this.

It was still dark. His bladder insisted he got up right away. Then he stumbled into the kitchen looking for rehydration, trying to remember what day it was and what, if anything, was on his schedule. After he had downed a pint of orange juice and two paracetamol (too little too late, but what the hell) he shuffled over to his desk and consulted his diary.

Damn and hell. He was due at the university *again*: that source of all his misery. Here was the bottle he had attacked the night before. About half of it remained, and he had replaced the cap, he noticed. Funny what shreds of reliability remain to us in extremis.

His diary told him that today was the faculty Christmas party. He groaned. In most universities, Christmas parties meant dozens of students getting legless on cheap beer and cider as they marked another milestone in their university careers: rather pleasant. At Ariel, of course, there were very few students, all of them post-grads. Terms started and ended at odd times of the year: nobody went down, or came up. The academic year delivered no peaks or troughs, so the party would consist of the usual faculty faces, the usual boring conversations. He toyed with the notion of going back to bed; but some part of him was reluctant to do so. He had long ago learned to listen to his instincts so – wearily, gingerly – he went through the motions. Breakfast was a bridge too far. Even the making of coffee was beyond him, so instead he finished the litre carton of orange juice, hoping that all that Vitamin C would cut the alcohol (and hurry up about it).

He suspected there was still enough alcohol in his system to put him over the limit. But as there were certain to be no trains today he would just have to drive carefully. And he'd better not have any more alcohol at the party. The very thought of booze made his stomach flip flop. No. No alcohol today. The faculty Christmas Party and no alcohol. Was he really sure he wanted to go? But half an hour later he was on his way to the M1. And two dreary hours of stop and go later he arrived at the university.

As he sidled along the corridor to his office Marion was passing with a big bowl of something that might have been vomit but was more likely to be potato salad.

'Crikey, Fergus,' she said, 'what's happened to you? You look like hell.'

'Thank you. I feel so much better now.'

'Oh, I didn't mean to make you feel worse, but you should see yourself.'

'I shaved this morning, so I know how bad I look. It wasn't an experience I want to repeat until things stop hurting.'

'Ah. Hangover. I thought for a minute it was 'flu.'

Marion really did know him entirely too well. Well enough, indeed, to abandon the bowl of puke and go and make him a mug of strong coffee. Fergus retreated into his office and awaited the restorative.

The coffee smelled wonderful when it came. He was effusive in his gratitude. Marion tipped a couple of paracetamol into his hand and departed to retrieve her bowl of sick.

By the time the party was officially supposed to start Fergus actually felt up to putting in an appearance. He went into the lavatory and splashed some cold water on his face. As he was alone he also straightened his bow tie, combed his hair and checked his smile in the mirror. This last was slightly marred by the fact that he hadn't shaved very effectively and his eyes seemed to have disappeared into his skull. But you have to work with what you've got. He was ready.

*

Fergus was known to be a party animal and his arrival was greeted enthusiastically. A glass of red wine was immediately pressed into his hand by Angela. He was going to have to work hard, he realised, to live up to his reputation without drinking any more alcohol. The glass in his hand contained – to all intents and purposes – poison. He took a deep breath and began to apply himself to the project at hand. Soon he had gathered quite a gaggle from the secretarial pool and screams of girlish laughter were washing over the room. Nobody seemed to notice he was in a delicate condition. As he warmed to his task (and the paracetamol cut in), his jokes got first better, then bawdier, and his audience laughed more and more uproariously.

Of course, a good time cannot be had with impunity at an office party. There are always watchers and listeners who do not take part but instead take notes which they can use later. Fergus was as sober now as when he had come in (which wasn't saying a great deal) and fully aware of which quarters he had to watch. He didn't bother watching his language; everybody knew it was colourful. He used expletives as exclamation marks, to signal the denouement, the climax, the punch-line. His audience now included several junior lecturers. These, together with Nick and Veronica – who was currently the size of a small blimp – roared with laughter in all the right places. Fergus was in his element, and able to ignore the nagging pain in his temples.

Just as pleasure was taking over from pain Fergus heard an inevitable voice:

'Fergus, a word. When you've finished your amusing anecdote, of course.'

Petra stood at his elbow, face as stony as her name, suit as navy blue as always, enlivened for the occasion by a tiny enamel Christmas Tree pinned to her lapel. Her interruption deflated the yarn that Fergus was halfway through about the first bra-burning at which he had been present. His listeners melted away to join more congenial groups that didn't contain Petra.

Nevertheless she had a right to an answer to her Christmas dinner invitation today. Had he been compos mentis he would have popped his head round her door before coming down to the party. It was irritating to have been back-footed by her again like this. He thought that, for devilment, he might shock her and tell her the truth, as like he was intending to do with Janet later on. Damn the consequences!

Petra turned and walked towards the window wall. He strolled, apparently casually, in her wake, wondering whether to lose his still full glass somewhere. As Petra already considered him a toper there didn't seem much point. If he was seen without one, someone was almost certain to press another on him. The cheap red wine was conflicting with the whisky hangover, and making his gorge rise.

Petra arrived at the glass wall that looked out over a drab little courtyard garden planted in memory of the first Dean. The designer had thoughtfully placed radiators along the knee-high brick footings which supported the single-glazed wall. Fergus was immediately roasted up to his knees and chilled from there up. His fragile bodily equilibrium didn't take kindly to this kind of treatment. Blood was flowing much too quickly away from his brain as urgent summons were sent by his lower limbs. He began to feel distinctly woozy again.

Petra turned towards him.

'Have you had a chance to consult your diary yet, Fergus?'

'Diary?' His brain had been expecting the word 'Christmas' and was anyway wrestling with the strange temperature effects on this side of the room.

'My invitation.' She batted her eyes at him. 'You can't have forgotten.'

'Christmas!' That was the word he needed. 'Such a kind offer. Unfortunately – not possible. I find I have, after all, a prior engagement.' He put down his glass of wine to get away from the smell. He really wasn't feeling well. A cheeky gremlin in his hind-brain suggested he was allergic to Petra. He could only agree with it.

'You forgot you are already engaged for Christmas?' Petra was plainly disbelieving.

'No, not really. But my private life is important to me. And private.'

Further than this he was not prepared to go. That little half-truth would have to do. Nobody here would believe the whole truth even if he were to tell them about his family, which he found he still wasn't ready to do.

He managed what he hoped was a deprecatory smile. It was a strain. He felt as though all his blood had now collected in his feet, which were over-hot and sweaty. Cold rills of air were creeping around his neck and shoulders and down his back. His hand was shaking; little waves of nausea were washing over him. He needed to sit down. Right now.

He realised Petra was speaking. He had long ago learned to let her ever-urgent voice roll over him. He could wool-gather very well through meetings at which she presided. Now was not the moment to indulge, however.

'I'm so sorry, Petra – what were you saying?'

'I was asking you how you thought it had gone with the Hungarian girl.'

To this Fergus was able to respond positively. He gave her a precis of the interview, including Irena's desire to have him as her Supervisor because he wasn't afraid of controversy, and was able to conclude,

'So I think it's in the bag.'

Petra's face was hard and pale. He had seen Petra's face set like that before. Something bad was coming.

'I've been wondering, Fergus, whether it is quite fair to add the supervision of this girl to your burdens.'

'Oh, don't worry on that score, I'm looking forward to it. Her résumé is – well, brilliant isn't overstating it. Her premise is intriguing. It's really got legs. Tremendous feather in the Department's cap, you know, to get her. She could have her pick.'

'Very well – you force me to be blunt. Your reputation with young girls in the faculty has been, shall we say, colourful. It would be a terrible embarrassment if something untoward were to happen to Ms Jardanyi.'

'What could possibly happen?'
Petra sighed impatiently.
'Do I have to spell it out, Fergus?'
Fergus felt his chin begin to jut.
'Yes, Petra, I rather think you do.'

She had the grace to colour. She tried to find some euphemism. Her mouth opened and closed several times, giving her a peculiarly fishy demeanour that Fergus found almost amusing.

'This is, perhaps, not the place.'

'No. It certainly isn't, nor the time. I can't think of a time or a place, myself, when this conversation would be appropriate or pertinent.'

Fergus didn't keep the anger out of his voice. It had become apparent after his conversation in the car with Sara yesterday, that no Chair would be forthcoming, research student or no research student. He would be lucky to keep his job. But Irena had told him that she wanted *him*, *because* of his reputation (as a man unafraid of taking up cudgels in a good cause). Now bloody Petra was trying to deny him that by implying he would have his hand up the kid's ox-blood skirt before she'd got settled in her office. Petra was, of course, unaware that Irena was not going to occupy an office at Ariel but, rather, continue to commute between Hungary and the USA. He turned to leave in as much of a huff as he could muster, but it seemed Petra wasn't done with him yet.

'There is a further problem with your potential supervision of this student, Fergus. You fear change, and change is what the university world is about now. The *survivors* in the academic world that is to come will be fitter and leaner than their less fortunate colleagues. It's about numbers now, Fergus, and per capita funding – not ivory towers, however romantic and pleasurable a concept they may be. I myself do not see a long term future here. After I have served a term as Dean, should I be fortunate enough to be elected, I shall be looking to get into museum work. That's where the future is for anyone with ambition – in media and PR; in entertainment; in the provision of accessible and inexpensive history capable of being consumed in small bites by people with the short attention span a sophisticated society creates. Knowledge for its own sake is a dead duck.

'You will, doubtless, be encouraging Ms Jardanyi to produce a dry and erudite thesis on some shard of pottery or bit of statue from the ancient world. You will not be doing her any favours.'

'Ms Jardanyi has a ground-breaking premise worked up. It is a proper field of study for a Classicist and will change the way we view the ancient world. I shall be delighted to help her realise the full potential of what she has begun. The result will be brilliant, and it will be a game-changer.

'I do not produce "dry" work, Petra. My intention has always been to excite and stimulate my students.' He couldn't resist adding, 'And I have always been led to believe, by those who use the materials I produce, that I have a considerable talent for that. My work for the university has always carried a high student retention rate and top notch marks for both interest and clarity. May I remind you of my two best-selling ancient history books, *Wonder of Wonders* and *Naked Knowledge*? People actually understand what the word "gymnasium" means now. I take much – nay, all – of the credit for that state of affairs, Petra.'

'You can teach anybody anything if you put enough nudity and sex in it, you smutty little man.'

'Name calling will not alter the facts. Knowledge is never going to go out of fashion, Petra.'

She smiled sarcastically.

'Knowledge has *already* gone out of fashion Fergus. It's not about knowledge any more – it's about power. Once knowledge *was* power. What people need now is data, and training in how to interrogate it. That's where power resides now – in information. That information will be disseminated by computers. Do you even *have* a computer? No. I know you don't. You've threatened to throw up the barricades if the computing people try to install a machine in your office. I've heard you.

'I shall be re-assessing my position on the computer. Irena said it would be a useful way for us to communicate, as she spends most of her time in America and Hungary.'

'Ha!' Petra expostulated. People turned their heads. '*Now* you try and drag yourself into the Eighties! It's too late, Fergus. Much too late. I assure you.'

He really had no idea where all this angst of Petra's was coming from, and even less where it was going. Everybody's lives are enriched by knowing about the past aren't they? If you want to know what's ahead, look behind. "Those who do not learn history are doomed to repeat it", that misquote of George Santayana by F D R was still crucial. What *has* happened (be it in the ancient past, in Greece, or Egypt or Rome, or more recently in the everlasting wars humankind seemed unable to wean itself off) must inform what *will* happen. If she couldn't see that ... well, he wasn't about to debate it with her today.

Of course, this might not be a theoretical discussion. It certainly felt more like a thinly veiled threat. Ah, how deadly the female of the species, spurned, could be. Was all this outpouring consequent upon him refusing to have that bloody dinner with her? He said;

'You must please yourself what you do about this supervision, Petra. But I'm quite certain that if she can't have me, Irena will look for a champion at a different institution. She didn't seem to think anyone else around *here* had any balls.'

He made his farewells at once and headed for home. Concentrating on the drive was difficult. He kept turning the row with Petra over and over in his mind. It was always infuriating to be wilfully misunderstood like that. He still didn't understand what she wanted from him. Perhaps she simply wanted him gone. On the other hand, she only saw her future with Ariel for another three years, then she'd be gone. Perhaps she'd go earlier if she didn't become Dean. What was that tiny spark of an idea somewhere behind his headache? He tried to catch it: Petra not elected, Petra in a huff, Petra taking her power shoulders and campaigns for the return of Grecian artefacts elsewhere: problem solved ...

The drive home was even more tedious than the drive up had been. The train strike continued to launch a myriad frustrated commuters onto the roads in and out of London. Why didn't the buggers just stay home? Why hadn't he?

He realised he hadn't seen Sara at the Christmas party. Perhaps, having done her bit, she was keeping a low profile. (Amazing how paranoid being shafted made you.) Well, 'nil illegitimi carborundum'.

*

When he got in he phoned Mary to make sure all was well with his Christmas arrangements.

'Oh Fergus.' Mary sounded exasperated. 'The silly girl won't come. She wants to spend Christmas Day with That Bloody Man,' Fergus could hear the capitals down the phone line, 'and when I suggested he could usefully spend the day with his wife and children she flew into hysterics and rushed up to her room. That was yesterday and I haven't seen her since. I was going to call you as soon as I thought you'd be in.' She thought for a second. 'Why are you in? It's awfully early.'

'A particularly bloody Christmas party.'

'Ah.'

Mary obviously understood about Christmas parties.

'What's to be done, then?'

'I don't know. Why don't you talk to her. You seem to have better luck with her recently than I do.'

Fergus reflected that he wasn't fit to take on a kitten, currently.

'Sure. Where do you think she is?'

'At that bloody flat, I shouldn't wonder.'

'She did promise she wouldn't go back there.'

'I don't think her promises are worth much at the moment. Anyway, she says that my "appalling behaviour" means all bets are off.'

Mary sounded dismal.

'It's not your fault, you know.'

'I know. But sometimes knowing that just doesn't help.'

She was worse than dismal: she was tearful. He could hear it in her voice.

'I'll come over. We'll scour the streets together. She won't be expecting a search party at this time of day. We'll catch her unawares.'

There was a hiccup at the other end of the phone which he took for agreement.

He remembered Janet's invitation to Christmas dinner on his answerphone, and called her next in the hope of being able to leave an anodyne message. Katie answered. Of course: school holidays had started. He should have remembered that. He was still gathering his wits when Katie said,

'Did you want to talk to Mum? She's at work.'

'Er ... yes.'

'Is it about Christmas? I can take a message.'

'Um ... thanks. Would you tell her that I'm grateful for the thought but that I'm having Andy and her mother over for Christmas.'

'Yeh, right.' She sounded disbelieving.

'It's not that I wouldn't *like* to spend it with you and your mother, Katie. It's just that ...'

'Oh, I don't mind who you spend it with. But Andy's going to spend Christmas Day with David, she's told me. I wasn't best pleased. We usually get together Christmas Night and play music and stuff. But now she's in the middle of this stupid affair she says that's for kids. Mum wanted to ask David to come here for Christmas. I don't know what I ever saw in him. He's a bit of a creep, isn't he? I didn't really want to meet him in his underpants on the stairs again so I got her to ask you instead. Andy's going to end up in terrible trouble, isn't she?'

'We'll see,' said Fergus grimly, made his goodbyes and rang off.

*

Fergus took a handful of paracetamol and another of breath mints, got the Jag out again and went over to Mary's place. Together they set out in search of their daughter.

Although he didn't *want* to believe Andy would be there it made sense to check the Balham flat first.

She was there. She looked pinched and miserable, but her jaw set and her face whitened when she saw who was at the door. They had heard her clattering down the stairs in a great hurry, so she must have been expecting someone she wanted to see. Her eagerness had lulled her into not looking out of the window to check who it was before coming down. It couldn't be Dunne she was expecting; he would have a key.

Sure enough:

'Oh shit, it's you two. I thought it was the electrician.'

Mary looked bleak at the casual curse. Even Fergus, foul-mouthed since his early teens, was taken slightly aback at the sound of the word in Andy's mouth.

His heart bled at the sight of her, looking so hard and miserable. Why was she putting herself through this? This was no way to grow up.

Fergus didn't really know where to start. Andy gave him a clue by continuing:

'*She's* not coming in. I've had enough. I'm not talking to her any more.'

Mary looked as if she'd been slapped. Fergus looked quizzically at her. She gave a half nod.

'I'll wait in the car,' she said, and left them without another word.

Fergus turned his attention back to his daughter. Would he have got involved in family life if he'd known it was going to lead to this? Who was he kidding. He wouldn't have missed out on all this for anything. He felt alive: useful. OK then, time to prove his worth.

'That really hurt her you know.'

Andy stopped glaring at him and looked down at her scuffed Doc Martens.

'I know. I'm sorry about that. No – not sorry, sad.'

'This is a sad time. In so many ways.'

She looked up at him again, still hanging onto the front door like a shield. For a second she reminded him of Sara – careless, happy, always chattering Sara, for whom downers like Dunne did not exist. He made a mental note to tell Nick not to introduce Dunne to Sara.

'*I'm* sad too, you know,' she said.

'Yes, I can see you are.' He took courage and continued, à la Marion. 'You look like hell.'

'Thanks, that makes me feel *really* good.'

'Can I come up for a few minutes? It's cold.'

'It's cold up there too. The heating's gone, and the lights. That's why ...'

'The electrician?'

'He said he'd be here by four o'clock.'

'It's well after that now.'

It was most unlikely she'd get anyone to come out before Christmas, whatever the problem was. Even electricians had their Christmas shopping to do. Come to that he had his own to do. What happened here would determine what he needed to buy. So: onward and upward.

Shall I see if it's anything obvious?'

Reluctantly she opened the door properly and he trudged silently up the stairs behind her, their footsteps echoing on the bare wooden treads. When they got upstairs it was as cold as it had been down on the street. She showed him the fuse boxes. They were on the landing, high up where there was no natural light. It was dark outside now anyway, and positively Stygian inside the flat.

'Have you got a torch?'

'No, but there are candles.'

'Get me one, please. And a chair.'

This was madness. If he'd been thinking more clearly he wouldn't have tried it. There was a flight of steep stairs right behind him and, if the chair broke (which was very likely), he could easily end up at the bottom with a broken leg, or worse.

The chair and candle scraped and flickered towards him. Andy's face, in the yellow light, was shocking. She looked so thin. The candlelight threw sharp shadows and the pinched look to her face looked like bone standing out.

'Haven't you got the Calor gas fire on?'

'The cylinder ran out last night. David going to bring a new one when he comes. There's a little blow heater in the cupboard – but, of course, there's no electric to make it go.'

Fat chance of Dunne arriving with a gas cylinder, thought Fergus. He'll spin her a line about them having their love to keep them warm. He obviously cared nothing for Andy at all, otherwise he wouldn't keep her in this slum of a flat, cold, dirty and probably hungry too. He felt his hands begin to clench. He wished Dunne's neck was within their grasp. One day. One day very soon ...

Fergus positioned the chair and clambered up onto it. Andy stood by with the feeble glimmer. When he had oriented himself, he asked her to hand it up to him. Holding onto the light gave him one less hand for holding onto anything else, which didn't make him feel any more secure. The chair creaked, but held. So far so good. Candle wax dripped hot onto his hand. He peered at the meters and fuses. Why, in the name of God's Holy Cheeses, didn't a culture that could put a man on the moon make electricity easier to see to? When did you ever want to look at a fuse box in good light? You only went near the bloody thing when there was a problem – and the problem was always, by its very nature, to do with darkness. How anyone was supposed to get to grips with something so tiny and obscure in almost total darkness when wobbling about on a chair, Fergus couldn't understand.

He pulled each fuse out in turn and examined it as well as he could by candlelight. He didn't find anything amiss. Perhaps rats had chewed through something important.

But wait,

'What's this other box – the small one, under the fuse box?'

'I don't know.'

Andy sounded cold and fed up. That made two of them.

Fergus raised the candle and peered at the second box. There was a slot in it.

'Andy, how do you pay for the electricity here?'

'David said it was a meter. Just like anywhere else.'

'I think this is a prepayment meter.'

'A what?'

Of course, the child had never come across such a thing. He well remembered being sent out to the corner shop for shillings to feed the one in his childhood home. He hadn't, indeed, seen one himself for many years, but that was what he was looking at, he was certain. What did one feed them on nowadays? Looking for a clue he peered closely at the size of the slit. Smallish, and quite broad. Pound coins? Could it be so simple? The child had been freezing all day because the shit Dunne hadn't fed the meter, or thought to tell her she would need to?

'Hold onto the light for a minute, love. Let's see what I've got in my pocket.'

Relieved of the candle he went through his change. Nothing larger than a fifty penny bit.

'Right. You need to go and see if your mother has any pound coins.'

Andy shook her head vigorously, but said nothing. With a gusty sigh Fergus got down from the rickety chair.

'All right then, *I'll go.*'

He gave her the lit candle, inched his way carefully down the stairs and out into the night. It was warmer outside than it was in the flat.

Mary was huddled up in the car, with the CD playing *Madame Butterfly*. That wasn't going to make her feel any more cheerful. Sure enough, when he opened the door, he could see she was crying. He suspected Andy might well be doing the same thing inside. He hoped this pound coin thing was going to work. If he could cheer Andy up she might condescend to talk to her mother, and then things would be on the way to being fixed. Fergus knew *he* couldn't fix what had gone wrong between them, he could only mediate. At the moment he was mediating like crazy, and all he had to show for it was two weeping women.

'Have you got any money on you?'

Surprised but docile, Mary opened her bag. First some crumpled tissues, then a purse emerged. Fergus switched on the courtesy light.

'I need a pound coin.'

She held one out.

'Good girl.'

He took the coin and patted her hand, switched off the overhead light and returned to the black maw that was the flat's open street door.

Back upstairs all was as he had left it, except for suspicious sniffling sounds coming from Andy. He took the candle back from her and returned to the meter, fed the coin in, turned the only knob on the box in the only direction it would go and held his breath. The light in the lounge came on.

'Thank Christ for that.'

'Dad! What did you do?'

'Fed the meter.'

'What?'

'Long story. Let's try and get some heat on in here, shall we? And then I'll go and get some more coins. A pound's worth of electricity isn't very much these days.'

*

Half an hour later the miserable little slum was – well, not warm exactly, but at least condensation was running down the windows instead of frozen to them. Fergus checked to see if Andy had something to eat in the flat. He found a half-eaten tin of beans and some mouldy bread, some tea bags and sugar. Next he looked to see if the pub on the corner was open. As it was, he had a swift half to test it out. It tested fine. In the pub he parked a very cold Mary with very red eyes and nose. He left her with a large, strictly medicinal, rum and black and went to the corner shop. He bought two boxes of chocolates with a £20 note and got his change in coins. He went back to the pub and gave one box of chocolates to Mary, then returned to the flat once more. There he gave the other box of chocolates and the coins to Andy and explained the meter to her.

'You've got to feed it regularly, otherwise this will happen again. I shouldn't worry about cancelling the electrician. I don't suppose he had any intention of coming out this close to Christmas.'

Andy hugged him, which almost made it all worthwhile – but he still had the other one sitting, soggily, in the pub. Gratitude was a wonderful thing. He didn't want her to retreat to the position she had taken up when they arrived. But it was time to collect.

'Andy, Mary says you want to spend Christmas with Dunne.'

At once her face hardened.

'His name is David. And yes, I want to spend Christmas Day with him.'

Fergus felt a compromise coming on. It was a most peculiar feeling for a man who was used to getting his own way.

'Well, how about if David comes too?'

'What? To your place? For Christmas dinner?'

'Yes.'

That took her aback. She had been expecting another attempt to talk her out of her heart's desire – mention of the Dunne children, of Christmas being a family time, an appeal to her good sense. She had not expected this. Fergus wasn't quite sure why he'd said it. Always expect the unexpected when you're dealing with Fergus Girvan. Andy might be his daughter and have all those getting-your-own-way genes, but he'd been at this game a lot longer than she had. As he stood there with an innocent smile on his face his mind was working hard. An angle, that's what he needed. It didn't take him long to find it.

Andy said nothing for a while – obviously trying to spot the catch, but Fergus was a wily bird. His face gave nothing away. When Andy found out what he was going to do to her precious Dunne she probably wouldn't speak to him for a month. But by that time Dunne would be gone, embarrassed out of existence. And even Andy would have seen what a consummate shit the man was.

'OK,' she said cautiously. 'Thanks.'

Fergus's apparent capitulation had left her no other avenue. She had to accept or appear unreasonable. Fergus knew his mark; she wouldn't want to appear unreasonable when she was working so hard at being an adult in an adult relationship.

'Splendid! Come over at noon. We'll eat about one, after we've done the present thing.'

'But there won't be anything for David. Only my present.'

'Oh, there will. I'll make sure of it.'

He tried to keep the purr out of his voice and hoped she thought it was simply the gesture of a superlative host planning a wonderful time for his guests. It was going to be wonderful alright. His step was light as he made his way down the stairs.

*

When he retrieved Mary from the pub she was rather the worse for several rum and blacks but significantly more cheerful having eaten half the chocolates. She bucked up even more so when Fergus told her that Andy was now coming to Christmas dinner. When he told her Dunne would be coming too she was furious. When Fergus explained what he was going to do to Dunne when he came, she was rapturous – very loudly. Fergus removed her from the pub and took her home. Back at her place, he put her to bed and went to make her a cup of tea. When he came back upstairs she was asleep and snoring gently – which he took as a good sign – so he rolled her onto her side and left her to sleep it off. He doubted she'd had much rest recently. He anticipated she would blame him for the inevitable headache when she awoke. Rum, like Dubonnet, was a bad hangover in waiting.

When he got home there was a message waiting for him. It was from Fliss.

'I'm off to the sun tomorrow. Can we meet tonight?'

He dialled her straight away. She answered so quickly that he could let himself believe she had been waiting by the phone.

'Just picked up your message. Can we still get together?'

'Of course. Marvellous. Where? When?'

For a woman with a busy schedule Fliss was certainly uncomplicated. Was this her charm? Fergus usually enjoyed the games that went with dating. However, the rest of his life was over-filled with complications currently, and Fliss was a refreshing change of pace. He found himself grinning broadly into the telephone and wondered what on earth it was about this woman that was so attractive. Perhaps he could work it out when he saw her.

Arrangements concluded, Fergus went to change. The state of his wardrobe didn't seem to bother Fliss, but it bothered him. As he couldn't go for style, he went for colour. From the clothes he hadn't yet thrown out (pending that shopping spree that nobody would leave him time to have) he unearthed a pair of sea green trousers, with a barely perceptible flare to the slightly too-short legs, and a green shirt. An oatmeal sweater seemed to tie the two together. He had the devil of a job finding socks that did anything for the ensemble. He failed to find a complementary bow tie, so went with a green paisley cravat. The only pair of shoes that worked were an ancient pair of beige desert boots he discovered under the bed, where they had escaped his previous cull. They needed a good brush. At the end, although his bedroom once more looked like a charity shop, he was pleased with the result. He bundled all the discarded items into the wardrobe and under the bed – in case he had company later – then set off with great anticipation.

He had left the choice of venue to Fliss, and was meeting her at a jazz club in Camberwell. Either her instincts as to what he might like were good, or they had jazz in common too. (The list of commonalities was growing each time he saw her.) The place was ideal for his mood dark, smoky, raucous, and the beer and music were both excellent. She hadn't dressed up, knowing where they were going, and had on cream trousers and shirt, with an ochre jumper. Fergus couldn't take his eyes off her. The jazz was straight from New Orleans – just how he liked it; visceral, sexy. He wished he still smoked. He wished he was twenty years younger and twenty pounds lighter. Finally taking his eyes off Fliss, he paid some attention to his surroundings. The band members were all about his age, as were most of the audience. He suddenly had a suspicion – it had been a week for suspicion and the habit was becoming ingrained.

'Do you come here much?'

'Oh yes. Whenever I can. I love it.'

So she hadn't brought him here just so he could be with other old fogies. It reminded him, though, that she must be fifteen years younger than he. Although she was a lot older than his usual dates. He still wondered how they had got together at Janet's supper party: Janet's seating plan, Fliss's determination, his curiosity? It didn't matter. He was just glad she was in his life. The beat of the music was primal, somehow. It made his feet and fingers move. Now his whole body wanted to be moving. Christ, it was good to be alive.

The musicians took a break and Fergus joined the scrum at the bar to get another round. When he came back there was a little parcel on the table in front of his seat.

'I don't usually do this,' Fliss said. 'This is a gruesome time if you're not part of a conventional family. I don't spend it in Britain if I can help it. I don't do cards, presents or decorations. I don't like turkey, and plum pudding gives me heartburn. Happy Christmas.'

She gestured at the parcel. It was wrapped in glittery tissue and tied with a silver ribbon. This was embarrassing. In all the excitement he had forgotten that she would be gone before he got around to present buying. Before picking up the parcel he told her this. She waved an airy hand.

'So what? It's just a little fun thing. It's the wrapping makes it look pretentious. I can't help my artistic nature.'

The "little fun thing" turned out to be a shot silk bow tie which was gaudy or tasteful, festive or sombre, according to which way the light caught it. He was touched. He would wear it for his complicated Christmas dinner. It would remind him of her in the midst of his tribulations and he would smile. He told her this. It was difficult to be certain in the low light, but he thought she blushed.

*

Afterwards they were hungry. Only fish and chips would do as a coda for that kind of evening. They had to walk a long way before they smelled what they were after but, finally, they found a late night chippie. He hadn't eaten chips from the paper for years.

'Are you sure about this? You don't want to be ill on the plane.'

'Relax. Enjoy. It'll be great.'

And it was. He felt like an old fart for suggesting it might not be. He realised that new things made him uncomfortable these days. Andy's liaison made him angry partly because it was a new departure in their relationship. She was nearly grown up now. He had been prepared for university and boys to drive a wedge between them. He had been bracing himself for that. It was inevitable. He just hadn't expected it to happen so soon. However, some new kind of relationship would emerge; he might not like it. And it would be hard work. But there wasn't an end to family.

'Do you believe there's a reason for everything?' he asked Fliss.

'Of course. There must be a cosmic plan. You leave yourself open to opportunities and they appear. All my best jobs have come by accident, although I do put myself about, make sure people know I'm there. Then I wait for the phone to ring. It always has so far. See, if I hadn't gone with Steph to that dinner with – what's her name? Janet? I wouldn't have met you. I rest my case.'

'Well, what's the reason for Dunne?'

'Ah. I thought you were quiet.' She sucked thoughtfully on her fingers for a moment as they continued to stroll back to their cars. 'I have no idea – but there is one. Be confident of that.' She thought some more. 'Perhaps it's got more to do with your daughter than with you, some sort of rite of passage for her.' She thought for a moment. 'Perhaps that's what it is for you, too.'

She had confirmed his fears: something in the universe thought it was time old Girvan had a wake-up call. He wondered how much more the cosmos expected him to take. And what lesson he was supposed to be learning.

He crumpled up his chip paper and stuffed it into an overflowing rubbish sack as they passed. Fliss did the same. Then she took his arm and gave it a squeeze.

'Try not to worry,' she said. 'She's a sensible girl, from all you've told me. She'll be fine.'

They walked in silence for a little way. Fergus could see the Jag and Fliss's hot hatch just down the street.

'I suppose you need to get back?' he said.

'I'd better. I've got to pack yet, but the plane's not until mid-afternoon tomorrow. Will you come back?'

'Sure,' he said as they arrived at her car. 'Lead the way. I'll follow you anywhere.'

As soon as he said it he hoped she thought he was joking, but knew very well that he wasn't. For two pins he'd fly out with her tomorrow and to hell with his complicated plans for Christmas. But where would you find two pins after midnight in Camberwell?

Wednesday 23 December

He was awakened by very loud classical music. He fought for consciousness and realised it must be Radio 3 on the alarm. Strange how a perfectly pleasant piece of music can sound like several cats being strangled when you're less than half awake. His own alarm emitted a peremptory pinging that got louder the longer he ignored it. He couldn't be at home then. A wet tongue in his ear confirmed that he was, indeed, at Fliss's flat and that Bracken was doing her morning duty – making sure the guest was washed and up, in that order.

He could hear running water and assumed Fliss was in the shower. A faint smell of coffee was in the air. He smiled. Life was good. Well, last night and this morning had been. Given recent events, perhaps he shouldn't push his luck.

Fliss was moving determinedly, she kissed him warmly but briefly and then began to gather up stuff she needed while she was away with one hand while sipping from a mug of black coffee held in the other.

'Do you always pack like this?'

'I always *get up* like this. It's a nightmare isn't it? I call it just-in-time management, but really it's *just* that I hate getting up in the morning and I'm always about ten minutes behind schedule by the time I persuade myself to get out of bed.'

'I'd better go.'

'Afraid so. I shan't be bearable today until I've caught the plane, and I've a mountain of jobs to do before then. Have coffee then go, there's a love.'

Fergus did as he was told. He too had a heavy day in prospect. Today he must shop. Tomorrow he must cook. Then on Christmas Day he could plot and plan.

And at some point, he supposed, he must worry about his career. He suddenly realised he hadn't told Fliss anything about his conversations with Sara and Petra. The most recent Andy incident had overtaken all that the day before. He didn't particularly *want* to tell Fliss about his possible, enforced, early retirement. It made him sound sad and old. Fliss would sympathise and then he would feel worse. He would work something out first, then tell Fliss. Perhaps if he managed to hang onto his job he wouldn't tell her at all. The prospect of dating a low-income pensioner must, surely, wipe the smile off her face. He really didn't want to spoil the fun they were having. He was really going to miss her.

*

As soon as he got home he called the British Library. Yes, Dr Girvan's documents were ready for collection. He was profuse in his thanks. Those documents were an essential ingredient of his Christmas dinner.

He went to the British Library first, then to Oxford Street, and finally wriggled the Jag through appalling traffic to Knightsbridge and Harrods food hall. He intended it should be a memorable Christmas. At the end of the biggest shopping spree of his life, he leaned wearily against the car as Harrods minions packed enough food into the boot of his car to feed his entire building. The back seats were already full of presents.

He had found a lovely warm winter coat for Andy and a decent sound system for her mother. He had agonised long over what to get Fliss and eventually found, in Liberty's, a beautiful cashmere wrap the colour of autumn leaves. It was excessive; he knew that. It was all excessive. There had been an element of throwing money at the problem of Christmas in order to solve it as quickly as possible. Tomorrow was, after all, Christmas Eve, and he had been buffeted by problems which prevented him from concentrating on the Christmas meal he had rashly promised to provide, let alone the presents he felt should accompany said meal. But he was feeling exceptionally well-disposed towards the women in his life at the moment, and saw no reason why they shouldn't know it.

He had also bought himself some new clothes: two pairs of pleat-front chinos, one beige, one lovat; half a dozen shirts in warm colours; a jacket in a coppery brown with a hint of padding in the shoulders and much narrower lapels than he was used to; a suit that made him look half a stone lighter and two inches taller. All that, with sundries (socks, underwear, a couple of bow ties, a belt and some hankies) came to a large enough sum to make his credit card wince. However, although the size of the bill was frightening, the effect was most pleasing. Goodbye to flares and spaniel-ear collars.

What the hell, he told himself. Spend it while you've got it! He might not have money to throw around soon.

Back at the flat he had trouble stowing all the food. His kitchen had never seen such an invasion of comestibles. As well as a goose, there were the obligatory spuds, sprouts, parsnips and carrots; stuffing (sage and onion, no faddy stuff); ripe Brie and Stilton; Bentinck's bitter chocolate mints; brazil, walnut and hazel nuts; two bunches of sweet white muscatel grapes and a big net of satsumas; candied fruits; two boxes of chocolates (one milk, one plain); an enormous plum pudding;

canapés for appetisers; smoked salmon parcels for starters; a tin of biscuits for cheese; a pack of Harrod's freshly ground coffee; two pints of cream and four pints of milk (full cream and semi-skimmed); custard powder; unsalted butter for the brandy butter, salted butter for the veg and biscuits; gravy browning; apple sauce; and a bottle of brandy for the brandy butter.

He hoped that his guests ate at least some of this mountain of food. One of them might leave early. He hoped it would be only one.

He tried on his new clothes again, in different combinations, and remained pleased with the effect. He tried not to look at the price tags as he ripped them off. When Fliss came back she'd see a different man.

After such a frenetic day he felt like a beer, but not like cooking – he'd have enough of that over the next two days – so he mooched over to the World's End for one of their steak and kidney pies and a pint. The pub soon filled up. People were in a cheerful mood. He chatted amiably with the regulars he knew. During a lull in conversation he looked about him. Nothing had changed in this pub, not even the paint, in the years – how many, fifteen? – that he had lived round the corner from it. Bloody good job too. One could have too much change. What was wrong with things staying the way they were for five minutes? The World's End was a *traditional* English pub – OK, specifically it was Victorian if you wanted to be pedantic about it; but that was usually accepted as 'traditional' in Britain – and if 'traditional' meant inside plumbing, electricity, gas and water that you could drink without boiling it, he was all for it. Further back than that he didn't feel a need to go.

He was all for 'traditional' tertiary education as well. Even in a university like Ariel that taught its students in the comfort of their own homes – a radical departure in itself – you could still keep up the quality of the teaching and the rigour of the courses in Thatcher's Britain surely? Not according to Petra. There were just too many people (sadly, in powerful positions) who knew the cost of everything and the value of fuck all. He still didn't understand how wanting to keep standards up qualified him as being out of date. There were modern ways of teaching Classics. Not only had he developed them, he was using them daily! If Petra wasn't so focussed on her bloody marbles she might see that he was the mainstay of her miserable department. When people at Ariel pointed out that Classics only had two courses of its own, it would behove them also to enumerate the several modules and many chapters in courses elsewhere in the Arts Faculty, not to mention courses in the Social Sciences and – once – the Maths Faculty, contributed by the Classics Department. And who had prepared these materials? Dr Fergus Girvan. He had been very proud indeed of the chapter he'd done for the mathematicians – 'From Thales to Eutocius: a thousand years of mathematics'. To make the history of mathematics engaging in less than 50 pages is no small achievement.

But then again, the wind of change was certainly blowing through his life. For example, all those old clothes of his that should have been purged many years ago. It was difficult to decide what to keep and what to throw out when people said it was time for change. Babies got thrown out with bath water; Girvan got flushed down the toilet.

His troubles at the university crept in as soon as there was nothing else to occupy him, like a family crisis, or a night of pleasure. What was he going to do? Buggered if he knew. He rather wished unsaid his parting sally to Petra. Would she call his bluff, or see he was right about Irena Jardanyi? When you got right down to it, nobody was indispensable. Much depended on whether Petra really believed the department could survive her years as Dean with no Fergus Girvan driving it in her absence. If she was prepared to present him as an early retiree to the Molochs of the university hierarchy, then he was done for.

He managed to catch Sue's eye and got another pint in, then gave himself over to the trivia being talked around the bar. It was good to belong somewhere.

Thursday 24 December

The next morning he rose and bustled. No way was he going to get up at six tomorrow and have to get this most important meal ready in a panic against the clock. He would break the back of it today, calmly. Then he would be able fully to enjoy the events which he had planned for Christmas Day. Reconciliation for Andy and Mary. Nemesis for Dunne. Fergus was glad the man was coming. Inviting him had been a good idea.

He breakfasted and cleared up in the kitchen ready for the assault. Cupboards, fridge and freezer bulged. He got out the Delia Smith cookbook that he used for sexy suppers and looked through it. It was little help; it told him how to make a plum pudding – but apparently he should have done it in October. And he had bought a very nice plum pudding from Harrods. The instructions on the cellophane wrapper said it could be micro-waved. Good. He investigated other wrappers and discovered how long he needed to cook the goose for and how to make up the stuffing. He knew what to do with the vegetables and how to roast potatoes. He put the plum pudding back in the cupboard and started on the rest.

He washed and dried, pared and chopped, decanted things into bowls, discovered those bowls weren't big enough and decanted the things into other, larger, bowls that lurked at the back of cupboards and needed washing first. He mixed and stuffed; whipped and chilled.

By lunch-time his little kitchen was completely covered with tomorrow's Christmas dinner. This marathon was a far cry from the tasty little suppers for two that he was used to preparing. He prided himself that he spent no more than twenty minutes on preparing and cooking a meal. Even washing up was now beyond him; the sink was full of vegetables and the draining board was covered in dirty bowls. Something was amiss with his system. He decided to go to The World's End for an hour and puzzle out what it was.

*

The pub was a peaceful haven after the uproar in was his kitchen. He drank a pint, had one of their ploughman's lunches and felt much better. In a minute he would return to the mayhem he had left in the flat. He had another pint, and then another. On three pints Fergus was prone to reflection. How did families manage? How did parents cope with the endless feeding of offspring. He thought of baby birds, mouths constantly agape; wanting, wanting, wanting. A nightmare.

This was his first attempt at feeding his family. Mary had been doing it all Andy's life *and* she had a full-time job as well. He lived alone and had a cleaner and a microwave. The capacity of mothers to do so much astonished him, now that he thought about it. He asked Sue if she had a family.

'Yeah, two kids, no husband – you know; usual set-up.'

'How do you manage?'

'I've got Mum.'

Mary presumably had no Mum. Actually, he had no idea what might have happened to Mary's Mum. But surely if you'd been a Mum, and raised the demanding brood, the last thing you wanted was to have to raise the brood's brood? There still seemed to be an assumption that women were satisfied by cooking and cleaning and child-rearing. All those pretty, delicate, girls that he had made love to over the years – were they all doomed to a daily kitchen full of woe? And then, when comfortable middle-age approached, doomed to have to do it all over again?

His chaotic kitchen presented itself in his mind's eye. He was only making one meal for four people. If you made meals for two every day – say, breakfast and dinner – did the same order of mess ensue? If, for instance, he were to be living with someone (an image of Fliss swam into his mind, slopping towards the kitchen in his bathrobe and slippers) would his kitchen *always* be in such a state? And what about the rest of the flat? Surely that would be affected as well? A shudder passed through him. Commitment, it seemed, equalled housework.

Fergus had never been a particularly tidy man, but his cleaner kept his worst excesses under control. Tracey, if left to her own devices, would put into neat piles things that looked like they had a relationship: so, in order to avoid her arbitrary piling, he had long ago learned to tidy up himself before she came. What would it be like to share space permanently with someone else – their piles, your piles? A Tracey with Fliss's face flitted into his mind. He shuddered.

*

Back at his flat the state of the kitchen perplexed and depressed him anew. Perhaps, he thought, if I just start at one end ...

The evening was well advanced by the time he finally achieved order, but all his vegetables were prepared and bagged, his cream was deliciously whipped, the stuffing was in the bird, bowls were full of nuts and fruit, smoked salmon parcels were plated and cling-filmed in the fridge. It still didn't look like his kitchen, but it was workable now.

Traumatised he disinterred the nice Wiltshire ham, rolls and vine tomatoes he'd bought in Harrods (which he'd got for his lunch, except that he couldn't find them at lunchtime), ate them in front of the telly, and dragged himself to bed, exhausted.

His opinion of Christmas had not improved one whit. Bloody awful time of year. He had almost forgotten, in the mountain of vegetable parings, plastic bags and washing up, of his primary goal on the morrow. He set the alarm for eight thirty (the wretched bird was going to take forever in the oven) and pondered that tomorrow might not be a *culinary* triumph (although if results equalled energy expended, it bloody well ought to be), but it would be a triumph all the same when Dunne received his gift from Fergus.

Friday 25 December

Fergus didn't feel much goodwill towards anybody the next day as he applied heat to his many ingredients. However, about ten o'clock he allowed himself to lubricate his travails with one of the nice bottles of claret he'd got from Harrods.

When he put his glad rags on, he cheered himself up with a glimpse of Fliss's bow tie under his chin whenever he passed the mirror over the fireplace in the lounge.

Things were going reasonably well, if messily, by half past eleven when the doorbell rang. His schedule didn't allow for interruptions. And he still had on Tracey's pinny over his new shirt and chinos.

He opened the door with a scowl which he managed to turn into a smile almost quickly enough when he realised who stood there. Mary was early. She gave him a big hug.

'Happy Christmas!'

He returned the hug enthusiastically. Hugs meant friendship; kisses would have been another matter. Their recent closeness really did seem to be turning into something workable and lasting. He was pleased.

She stood back and brandished a carrier bag at him.

'Present for you, wine too. Thought you might need a hand so I came early.'

This was considerate. He certainly could use some help. This was, after all, his first Christmas dinner as cook. The meal had completely taken over the kitchen and he was rather at a loss to know how to gather it all together for dishing up.

'Good thought. Come into the kitchen.'

For the next half hour they cooked and drank and laid the table and drank. All was poised on the brink of readiness at twelve.

'Do you think we've peaked too soon?' Fergus asked his advisor.

'Nah, nothing here that won't hurt in the oven for a few minutes. Turn everything off and shove it all in there.'

'It won't fit – there's a goose the size of a small car in there.'

'Ah. Stand aside and let me at it. I've done this sort of thing before.' She grinned up at him as she opened the oven door and leaned down to size up the problem.

Despite Mary's confidence Fergus was becoming jittery. What if it all got dried out and over-cooked?

His other guests were only a few minutes late. Fergus hurried to open the door. On the threshold stood Andy, with a face like thunder. Fergus smiled a welcome while hoping the ill-temper might be aimed at Dunne, who stood at her shoulder trying to look pleased to be there.

He got them inside and took their coats. He sat them down with drinks and canapés and went to see what Mary had managed to stuff into the oven.

Everything seemed to be satisfactorily on hold, so they went into the lounge and joined the love birds.

The love birds were silent, sitting at opposite ends of the sofa. So it was a row. Fergus could hardly prevent himself from rubbing his hands with glee. Such timing. It quickly became a struggle to make small talk, so Fergus said;

'Let's eat!'

He shepherded them all to the table, which looked very congenial if he did say so himself. He sat them down with refills of wine and excused himself to fetch the starters. The smoked salmon parcels might be shop-bought, but they were Harrods, and he had made a hollandaise sauce to cheer them up a bit.

They were, indeed, very tasty. Just as well – the conversation remained non-existent.

Andy was obviously intent on teaching Dunne a lesson (and not for worlds would Fergus have discouraged her). Mary and Andy had not, of course, had a chance to make up yet so there was little chance of much chat between them. Dunne was looking very wary, unsure why he had been invited and expecting ground glass in his food.

Slowly the party began to polarise. Dunne began to flirt gently with Mary and Andy devoted her attention to Fergus. Occasionally Dunne would attempt to include Fergus in some hearty male thing; presumably he was trying to come across as a right-on sort of chap. Fergus didn't mind. In fact, he responded positively to every sally.

As the wine worked its magic Dunne became less reticent, more expansive. Soon the man looked positively at home, offering wine and filling water glasses as if he himself were the host.

Fergus permitted Dunne's manipulation to continue with a small, private smile on his face.

After the salmon had been eaten Fergus picked up the plates and excused himself again.

'Can I help?' Andy asked.

Fergus was just about to refuse, when he saw the look on her face.

'Of course – thanks.'

They had barely stepped through the kitchen door before she was hissing at him.

'Do you know what he did? Can you believe it? He's going round to see his children later and he hadn't got them anything. Said he couldn't afford it this year and that they'd understand. I said *I* certainly wouldn't have understood at that age. Not so much as a stocking with a few little presents in it! He only told me yesterday morning, so I went straight out and got them something.'

The man's timing was, as usual, inspired, Fergus reflected. There would have been no point telling her this *after* the shops had shut.

'What did you get?'

'Just a Christmas stocking each and a few toys to fill them up, and some sweets and wrapping paper. The whole fun of it is the unwrapping, isn't it?'

'What did you use for money, love?'

She blushed.

'The money you gave me for housekeeping.'

'What? All of it?'

'Toys are expensive. I was surprised.'

Fergus had to smile at this world-weary remark from a girl of seventeen. Such a mixture of the feckless and the dutiful she was.

'It's not funny, Fergus.'

'No. It isn't. It's very sad. You did a good thing.'

'And I said to him about the meter and why hadn't he told me about it. He said he forgot. And *I* said, well it was jolly cold and dark. Then I went to feed the meter this morning and I found that all the pound coins had gone, so I had to get more for today and tomorrow. It gets through a lot. I bet he's bought me a present with that money.'

Fergus would confidently have bet against that.

'He should have spent it on the *kids. I* don't need a present, I know he loves me and that's all I need. They must be very confused. He should have spent it on them.'

A rift within the lute. Good. But far from a fatal one. Well, he had something that might just bust the bloody lute wide open.

The bird required to be carried through for dismemberment, so he loaded Andy up with the vegetables and sent her on ahead, while he wrestled with the golden brown beastie.

*

Fergus attacked the goose with various sharp implements from his kitchen drawer and wished he had thought to buy a carving knife and fork while he was in Harrods. As he shaved the meat off the bones Mary arranged it on the plates. Vegetables were handed, also gravy, apple sauce and stuffing. Delicious smells filled the flat. Whatever triumph was to come later, Fergus was delighted to realise that the meal was a culinary triumph too!

At last it was time for the pudding. There seemed no point in suggesting a break from the table, given the tensions surrounding it, so he cleared the dirty crockery away, flamed his pudding and brought it straight in. Mary brought in the custard, cream and brandy butter. Dunne was fulsome in his praise as the pudding arrived. Fergus smiled until his face ached.

Everybody had a little pudding and professed themselves stuffed. Fergus moved them into more comfortable chairs before proffering brandy, coffee and mints. The best was soon to come, but it had been hard work getting to it. Dunne's attentions had soured Mary's mood, and his constant prattle had taken its toll on Fergus. Despite having looked forward very much to this part of the day, Fergus felt very flat. He also felt over-full and slightly acid, having been up and down all through the meal serving this, clearing that and checking on the other. A couple of those after-dinner mints and a lie-down was what he felt like, but this day had a long way to run yet. He rubbed his belly and got up, one last time (he hoped), to go and fetch the parcels which were lurking in his bedroom.

The parcels were heavy, lifted all together, and he inched back into the lounge gingerly. He bestowed to each, remarking:

'And positively no shaking, OK?'

This generated, as he had hoped, a flurry of reciprocal parcel-fetching and discussion of what could be in parcels that couldn't be shaken. While his women were thus engaged, Fergus paused before Dunne and took a smart envelope out of his inside jacket pocket.

Dunne accepted it with alacrity, demurring that Fergus really shouldn't have. He obviously thought there was a cheque in it. The sound of tearing paper and squeals from Andy made Fergus turn to see just how well his gifts were going down. When he turned back he could see the avarice shining in Dunne's eyes. Dunne waved the envelope:

'Perhaps I should open this later, old man?'

The scheming shit didn't want Andy to see him take money from her father.

'Oh, I think it's safe enough for you to open it now.'

Bugger this being a Christmas present for David Dunne: this was Fergus's Christmas present to himself.

Ruined wrapping paper lay all over the room. Andy and Mary were entranced with their new things. They wanted to give hugs and kisses and Fergus was very happy to accept them. Then they got out parcels of their own and presented them. The disguising wasn't very good and Fergus was pretty certain both contained paintings. Before handing hers over Mary held up a warning hand:

'Now the thing is, Fergus, Andy and I didn't consult about these until yesterday and, given the nature of what's in these packages, it was a bit late to do anything about it then.'

Intrigued Fergus started to unwrap Mary's present. Under the paper was bubble wrap (confirming his suspicion that this was a painting) and under that, there was tissue (now he was sure: Andy was right, half the fun was in the unwrapping – he hadn't realised) and under the tissue was a pastel of Andy, looking demure and mischievous at the same time. The artist had caught her vitality wonderfully. A slight breeze stirred her hair, hinting at the wild side of her nature which Fergus always felt she got from him. It was stunning. Fergus looked from the representation to the original. It was a good likeness, beautifully executed. Things like this took time to do. Mary must have had this planned for a while. Long before their recent ... intimacy. Fergus was touched and said so. It took some time for him to get the words out and then there was a lot more hugging to be done. Then he realised something and bent down to look at the signature on the picture.

'It's your work? He said to Mary. 'You've started painting again. I'm so pleased. So very pleased.' And there needed to be more hugs after that revelation.

While Fergus drew breath before starting on his other parcel he glanced over towards Dunne. David looked pretty pissed off. He looked up from studying the gift he had received from Fergus and their eyes met.

'I suppose you think this is funny?' Dunne said.

'Well – yes, actually. You thought I'd given you money to spend on our daughter. And you weren't going to open it here so that Andy didn't know you were in funds. But – as you've just discovered – there isn't any money in that envelope.'

The bonhomie in the room ended at a stroke; the last parcel was forgotten. Fergus could feel the tension. His lounge suddenly felt like the pub just before a fight started. He hoped Dunne wasn't going to get violent about this, but he didn't really care if he did. Full belly notwithstanding he'd had a bitch of a month and would welcome something he could solve with his fists.

Dunne lifted the photocopied sheets that had been in the envelope and shook them.

'What do you think this proves?'

'It proves you're a cheat,' Fergus said calmly. 'Perhaps you're not familiar with the workings of the British Library? That wouldn't be surprising, as you're not a member.

'That's a list of all the sources I used in the British Library while I was researching the material you stole. You can see my name and the various dates. That is the record the library keeps of each use of every item it holds. Your name does not appear, as it could not – you not being a member there. Ipso facto the outline paper on the Alexandrian Pharos that you presented to the university on the sixteenth of December was pure, provable, plagiarism. And plagiarism is the big no-no, Dunne. Nobody likes an intellectual thief.'

Fergus was aware that he was sounding smug. Not to mention precise. He had rehearsed this speech in his head rather often. It had sometimes come out less pompous than this – but it was all true, and it was about bloody time.

'Oh Dad,' said Andy. 'Not now.'

'You should have thought this through, Girvan, before you started it. You think you've been clever, do you? So what do you think you're going to do with these?' Dunne shook the photocopies at him again.

'I'm going to take the originals to the Dean when the university re-opens and have your contract terminated.'

Dunne laughed. It was not a pleasant sound. Andy said;

'Oh, stop it. Please.' She sounded tearful.

'And what do you think the Dean is going to say? They want you gone, Girvan. When the severance package is announced in the new year you're history.'

'How do you know that?'

'I've got friends at the university. Well-placed friends. The Dean isn't going to pay any attention to this – not when he's got Petra leaning on him to let you go. Petra knows where my piece came from, Nick told her.' He laughed again. 'Nobody wants you. They want a team player who doesn't fight them on every issue. You're a dinosaur, Girvan. You're stuck in the Seventies. You're a has-been and a nay-sayer. The university wants a man who can adapt, someone flexible, eager to embrace the changes coming to education. That man is not you. It's me.'

Fergus stood on his dignity.

'I don't see what any of that has to do with theft. I don't think so many changes have afflicted the university that plagiarism is now acceptable. Whose stuff are you going to pinch next? Petra's? Nick's?'

'Go tattling to the Dean, by all means – but don't say I didn't warn you. Petra and Nick know that I don't usually do this sort of thing.'

Fergus snorted in disbelief.

'They know that I was desperate. They understand. They don't kick a man when he's down.'

'Oh don't they? They seem, according to you, to be perfectly happy to kick me. So do you.'

Dunne flounced onto the sofa.

'Oh, for Pity's Sake, Girvan – you're not on your uppers. It's just a bloody course text. They're only paying me a couple of thou.' He grinned. 'You can work your research up into whatever you like after the course is out.'

'It's my original work!' Fergus felt himself to be spluttering and somewhat higher pitched than usual. 'Those sources have never been tapped before. Anything I write after some course unit of yours on the subject is published will seem derivative – as if *I* am the plagiarist. It was *my* research. It *is* my research. As you have pointed out, academically I *am* on my uppers. This theft of yours is likely to end my career. Unless the truth comes out.'

Dunne laughed.

'Don't be such a sad sack, old man. Share and share alike, eh?'

'Bollocks.'

Dunne leaned back on the sofa and stretched his arms out along the back of it. He looked confident. He was still smiling, but his eyes had narrowed.

'Girvan you're "The History Man". That's what they call you at the university behind your back. You're a joke, with your womanising and your drinking and your bellowing and bellyaching. Nobody likes you. Nobody wants you there. You don't have an ally in the whole faculty.'

There came a cry from Andy.

'Leave him alone!'

Dunne stood and held out his arms to her. She leapt off the sofa and threw herself into them. She was crying.

Fergus felt it all fold in on top of him, like a soufflé collapsing – the silent, unappreciated lunch, the betrayal by Dunne (from whom he would have expected no less), his colleagues (from whom he had, foolishly it seemed, expected more) and now his daughter. There really didn't seem to be much of anything left. His gifts lay abandoned on the carpet. His daughter clutched at the man she loved whom he, Fergus, hated. Mary sat silent on the sofa. How could he expect support from her, the way he'd treated her down the years?

He was, it seemed, a pariah. The spectre of unwanted early retirement loomed large now, alongside his very own ghost of Christmas Present. Somehow his marvellous hatchet job had been turned on himself and it was Fergus himself who had been struck down.

He sat down, heavily, on the easy chair behind him. He watched Dunne wrap his arms around Andy and nuzzle in her hair. The man looked over Andy's shoulder at him. There was a foxy triumph in Dunne's eyes, as well there might be. Fergus's coup de grâce had rebounded on him, that was certain. Never go armed with something that can be turned against you; his mother – who had grown up in the school of hard knocks – had taught him that. Stupidly, Fergus had not seen how this could be turned. And although he had expected Andy to hate him for his revelation he had expected her to see the truth of it, to accept it. Not this.

But then he saw that Andy was struggling in Dunne's arms. She pushed herself back from him and began beating his chest with her fists, still crying. Having made herself a little space in this way she started kicking at his shins with her Doc Martens. Words came out of the melee of fists, hair, feet and tears.

'You shit. You shit. Leave him alone!'

Who was she calling a shit? Who did she want left alone? It wasn't so clear now. Dunne tried to laugh it off, but the face Fergus could still see over Andy's shoulder looked less pleased with itself. It looked in pain, for one thing. Dunne tried to catch Andy's hands and dodge her feet, which caused him to start doing a little jig on the spot. She should have been easy to overpower – and had this happened Fergus would have hit Dunne, or tried to – but she held her own. Fergus watched the little power struggle playing out in front of him. Finally Dunne released her completely and stepped back out of range, knocking over Fergus's fireside table and the lamp that stood on it. The sound of the crash stopped Andy's attack.

Dunne was paying all his attention to Andy now, perhaps to try and gauge what might be salvaged, what tack to take to bring her round. Or perhaps in case she started beating on him again. Andy didn't let him say a word.

'You'd better go,' she said.

It was obvious she wasn't intending to go with him.

Fergus became aware that Mary was at Dunne's elbow, carrying his coat. She handed it to him without a word and went and opened the outside door. She stood beside it, waiting. Dunne had no choice. He went.

After he had gone there was silence. The quiet was a relief but also somehow, for Fergus, an accusation. Could they find nothing to say to him? Had *he* not been told to leave only because this was his flat? He supposed they would shortly make their excuses and go.

He watched Mary go to Andy, enfold her and brush the child's hair back from her face, in that time-honoured gesture of mothers offering comfort. This simple act was too much for Andy and she began to sob again. Their heads bent together for a moment as Andy recovered herself. Finally the storm of tears eased.

'There,' said Mary. 'Better now?'

Andy nodded and began to push the tears around her face with the heels of her hands. She went over to the sofa and picked up the bag that had his present in it. Then she came and knelt beside his chair and pulled the parcel out.

'Here,' she said. 'After what's just happened, you may feel this is too much of a good thing.' She gave a watery sort of conspiratorial laugh, then sat back on her heels and waited for him to open it.

Inside was, as he had expected, another picture. Another portrait of Andy; this one painted by herself. The differences between this picture and the picture Mary had given him of the happy, pretty, mischievous child were enormous. This Andy was wan, gaunt, with enormous eyes surrounded by deep shadows; the palette was mainly blue and black with a little ochre. The face was sad, but there was strength there too. And in the background there was a lightness, as if better weather was on the way. She had obviously painted it very recently. Fergus looked up at the tear-stained face of the subject and painter and felt tears start in his own eyes. He put the painting carefully to one side and leant down and hugged her closely to him. As they clove together she began to rock gently on her haunches and he realised that his daughter was trying to comfort *him*. She had become a woman. At which revelation Fergus did, indeed, weep.

They had not been rocking long before Fergus was aware of another pair of arms around him. Mary joined the group hug. What a joy women were. All women, yes. But particularly *these* women. *His* women. What powers they had, to hurt and heal. He began to feel better.

*

When they'd both gone he put *Tannhäuser* on the stereo and started on the mountain of washing up. If he did a bit tonight, and some more tomorrow and so on, he reckoned he'd be finished in time for Fliss to come over at New Year.

It had been an odd sort of month, he reflected, up to his elbows in suds. In a few days a lot of time seemed to have passed – years and years. Andy had stopped being a child and become a woman. His career prospects had become zero. He'd begun to find young women boring. A mature woman (with no boobs to speak of) was fascinating him. The mother of his child had forgiven him. He'd cooked a delicious Christmas dinner.

His life was very different today from what it had been three weeks ago, when he had stood up at Faculty Board and sorted out Nick's trip to Florence for him. If he'd known then what he knew now he would cheerfully have left Nick to squirm!

He was bloody glad he'd remembered about the British Library reading slips. Whatever the slime ball Dunne claimed, however anti-Girvan the top brass of the faculty were, they couldn't ignore hard facts. He *would* be vindicated, academically. But none of that was to the point.

The point was that next year his life looked like being quite different. He wondered how he felt about that.

He disinterred the bottle of port from the debris on the table in the living room and managed to find a clean glass at the back of a cupboard. He brought the two together and poured himself a substantial slug.

'Happy Christmas to me,' he said, 'and many more.' He took a substantial sip and left the glass within easy reach as he went on with the washing up.

The end

About the Author

I live with a variable number of critturs beside the seaside (where I do like to be) in Dorset. Being a starving writer I couldn't afford a sea view – but when I round the corner of my road on a blustery day I am reminded that I only live some 100 yards from it. That'll do.

I came to Dorset via Milton Keynes, via west Wales, via Cornwall. In Milton Keynes I spent 17 years working for the Open University as a project manager, which was fun, if sometimes exhausting, work. In 1997 I left the university to write professionally. Over those 20 years my short stories and poems have wheedled their way into a number of anthologies and magazines and I have published a novel, a novella and a volume of some of my short fiction. Short extracts of these three books are provided on the following pages.

Between 2006 and 2013 I returned to the Open University fold as a part-time Lecturer in Creative Writing, which was a tremendous experience and also great fun.

I am now 'retired', whatever that means.

Actually, it means I'm working on my next two novels, contemplating a collection of poetry, and dabbling in far too many other projects (as always).

All my published work is available from FeedARead; Amazon worldwide (on paper and Kindle); Barnes & Noble and The Book Depository.

If you have difficulty sourcing any writing of mine in which you may be interested, please let me know at judimoore.wordpress.com.

Weymouth
November, 2017

Ice cold passion and other stories

The primrose way

'I had thought to let in some of all professions, that go the primrose way to the ever-lasting bonfire.'

(Shakespeare: Macbeth, Act II, Scene 3)

At the convent of St Nonna, Altarnun and Pelynt, Cornwall: May, 1972

They came to me as a deputation. They couldn't go on any longer, they said. It was too much for them.

'Perhaps we could borrow a rotovator,' Sister Kathleen said.

Sister Myrtle clucked her disapproval. 'No good. Never get it round the hedges. Have to have them all out. Months of work. Quite impractical.' Crisis always made her sharp.

'Perhaps ... a man, a strong man, just for the digging ...', Sister Iris suggested tentatively.

'And for the orchard.' Sister Cicely added. 'The tops need to come out of the trees this autumn and I've been wondering, Reverend Mother, just how we can ... the ladder isn't so good now and we ...'

She didn't go on. She didn't need to. I looked to Sister Adelaide. She could usually be relied upon to see a way through difficulty. Sister Adelaide said,

'A strong young man with no other calls on his time could soon get it in hand again. Yes, I think we need a gardener.'

They were silent, looking to me. I said,

'You realise what this means?'

Sister Adelaide nodded; the other three just looked at me, their eyes wide in their wrinkled faces and their gnarled hands fluttering about their rosaries. I sighed.

'I'll look into it,' I said.

*

It wasn't that we were unused to men about the place. Father Tyrone came to St Nonna's on a daily basis to say Mass and hear confessions; Mr Tyler the bank manager sometimes called – and was all too often in our thoughts; Mr Sanderson the milkman came whistling up our weedy path every morning, adding his strand of musicality to Prime; Mr Peebles the coalman came twice a month in winter; Dr Freeman called on an increasingly frequent basis. Men with a purpose, all – and a gardener would be no different. And yet the idea made me uneasy.

Perhaps my unease was caused by what our need for him meant.

We were getting older. Our last novice had taken her vows three years before. She had lasted a scant two more before she had come to me, her eyes swollen with weeping for her weakness, and begged to be returned to the world. We had never had a failure of that kind before. We were known as a reclusive Order, there were no late surprises for a novice to discover, nothing new to endure when the vows were taken. The withdrawal we brought to the novices was paced carefully. And in the modern world our seclusion could never now be total; we needed to interact with the community often, to buy our milk now we no longer kept a milch cow, to buy the foods we no longer grew, the clothes we no longer weaved and sewed ourselves.

I had prayed long and fervently to know what the Lord meant us to understand from poor Sister Joanna's abandonment of her vows, but had received no answer. None that I understood, anyway

And now: a gardener.

Later, as I watched my Sisters through my window, I reflected that it wasn't only the garden which was getting beyond us. The five of them moved low over the earth with their hoes, wimples whipping in the brisk spring breeze, tucked-up habits bunched around their calves. The window through which I watched had paint flaking from the frame inside and out. The gusts of wind which played with the Sisters' wimples reminded me of the slates which fell like leaves from the roof with every gale. Each was retrieved and tutted over, then joined its fellows, neatly stacked by the kitchen door. They made a goodly pile now. We put buckets and bowls in the attics to catch the rain when it came. Once we would have got out the roofing ladder and put them back ourselves. Now even all twelve of us couldn't get the ladder up onto the roof.

Everything here was past its prime.

I spoke to Father Tyrone about the problem of the garden after Mass the next day. He found the plan appropriate to our situation.

Accordingly, I made yet another appointment to see Mr Tyler. He is a kind and realistic man. He promised to increase our overdraft facility to meet the need. Only after we had enjoyed a cup of tea together did he throw into the conversation,

'At least this will increase the value of your one and only asset, Reverend Mother. Anything you can do to look after the bricks and mortar – and grounds – of St Nonna's will reap benefits in the long run.' He looked at me over his tea cup in a way that made me think he had made a more sophisticated remark than I had understood.

On my way home I made a detour via the offices of our local newspaper and placed an advertisement – 'wanted: gardener, two days per week, payment by arrangement'.

*

He slipped into our lives, when he came, like a splinter under the skin does sometimes – you know it's there, but it's not particularly uncomfortable so you wait for it to work its way out again, and grow used to it in the process.

One morning there he was, hovering outside the kitchen door when Sister Margaret went out to retrieve our milk delivery for breakfast. It gave her a terrible fright. She came for me at once, having left him on the doorstep with Sister Elizabeth to watch him.

When I got there Sister Elizabeth was in the open doorway, holding a broom as if she was about to shoo a hen out of the scullery. The unaccustomed commotion had communicated itself to the others and all twelve sisters crowded behind me on the steps. He stood quietly before me – us – with a battered hat in one hand, feet planted squarely on the flags of the yard, back straight, arms strong, not young, not old.

Oh dear, I thought, what have we done?

Little mouse: a novella

(Heroes come in many shades of grey)

PART 1: KRISTALLNACHT, BERLIN, 1938

Chapter 1

A tinkling sound woke him and drew him out of his warm bed, despite the November night-chill, in case there were fairies to be seen. Now he huddled on the end of his bed peering through the curtain and out of the window. The smoke of his breath turned to ice on the glass; he scrubbed a hole in the thin film with his fist wrapped in the too-long sleeve of his pyjama top.

In the distance a harsh baying had begun. The tinkling sound was getting louder and didn't sound so musical any more.

Through the branches of the bare black tree outside his window he could see a red glow over the roof tops. *Something* was happening in the next street. As he watched, a lick of bright flame cleared the tops of the buildings and reached up into the black of the sky. He drew back with a gasp. But curiosity quickly brought him back to his post. Dark figures were running ziggy-zaggy down the street. As they careered towards, and then past, his vantage point they smashed every window they could reach with stick or stone. His disappointment was complete: it was not fairy bells he had heard, it was these dark men in the street breaking all the glass.

He realised the street-lamps were all out.

He began to shiver. But he didn't want to get back into bed. Not yet. It was long past time for something good to happen: he had hoped this might be it. He could see a few figures running up his street. Above their heads bobbed flames on sticks.

He watched the people swishing their torches this way and that. Was this *Hanukkah*? *Hanukkah* was nearly a month away, surely? Mutti had been telling him all about it, saying that a big boy like he was now – he was nearly four years old – should know that not everybody celebrated Christmas. Some people had *Hanukkah* instead, and they were called Jews. One time, when Eva had come to play, she said that people like him weren't *allowed* to have Christmas – which seemed strange. And unkind. But she had flounced off to her mother Helga, before he could ask her what she meant. Helga was their maid and Eva was her daughter. He only got to play with Eva if she was off school, sick; or it was school holidays. Mutti didn't really like him to play with Eva. Nor did Helga. But he didn't mind it. She was six, so she knew lots of things he didn't.

But even at not-quite-four years old he knew that the *Hanukkah* torches should be in the Temple, not out in the street. He liked *Hanukkah*. All the bigger children took turns to spin the *Dreidel* with the letters on it, and Mutti had told him that this year he would be allowed to join in for the first time. The letters on the old top were very important, Mutti said. They spelled out a sentence in Hebrew: 'a great miracle happened here'. The miracle had happened once upon a time, in a place far away from Berlin. Mutti had told him that they played the game with the *Dreidel* to remind the children that Jews only survived in the world against great odds. He was going to ask Mutti what 'odds' were, when she wasn't so irritable all the time.

Mutti and Vati were always short tempered recently. There had been a lot of whispering and sighing when they thought he couldn't hear. And conversations that went on late into the night, which sometimes included raised voices when they thought he was asleep. Vati never usually raised his voice. He was a man with a voice as soft as Mutti's silk blouses.

But recently they kept saying to him 'Theo, be quiet' and 'not now, Theo'. These days there was a hard edge to their voices that Theo didn't like a bit. Vati had spoken sharply to him this very evening, when he'd complained that his hot chocolate wasn't sweet enough. He hardly ever had any of his favourite things to eat and drink any more. The bread was always hard, nothing was ever sweet enough and milk tasted thin and sour – nor was there much of it.

Perhaps this of the torches was a special *Hanukkah* celebration to ask for another miracle? And they had switched off the street lights to make it more special. That must be it. Theo watched the pretty lights reflect off the puddles of rainwater on the street. They poured water into bowls in the Temple to make the *Hanukkah* lights twinkle, too. Theo smiled and snuggled into the curtains to watch.

Suddenly a great crowd poured into the street, out of the alleys on both sides of it and up the road from the synagogue. They carried so many torches that the street was brightly lit by them – although it was an odd light; red and full of shadows. As the torches came closer he could see that they were carried by men, not children as they would be for *Hanukkah*. And the torches were great flaring dollops of fire at the ends of long poles.

Hanukkah lights were lovely, fairy things that fluttered in the least breath of air. These weren't *Hanukkah* lights. The men swished their poles through the air, and the fires made an angry, roaring noise. The men made an angry noise too. Their faces were distorted by the flickering fires they carried. Their mouths became big black holes in their faces. Bad words poured out of the black holes. Sometimes he thought he saw the red light shine on fangs in those gaping mouths. They looked like the bad wolves in stories. Theo became frightened: he curled himself further into the curtain, hiding now.

From downstairs he heard feet running, then Mutti's voice.

'Theodore – the synagogue. The synagogue is on fire!'

'Get the child. Quickly.'

His father's voice was barely raised, but there was something in it that the boy had never heard before.

Mutti came into his room too quickly for him to get back into bed. He turned to her to smile so that she wouldn't be cross with him not being asleep; but she gave a gasp with a scream in it when she saw him beside the window. She ran across the room, scooped him up and pulled the curtain back across the window properly. The room got very dark then, but Theo could still see the red flames playing on the other side of the curtains. Mutti held him tight in her arms, releasing her warm, lavender smell that always comforted him. He was always safe with Mutti, whatever bad things were outside.

Mutti went downstairs very fast with him clasped awkwardly across her chest. All the house was dark. Why was there no light? The house was always bright with light from the big windows, or from the electric if it was night-time.

At the bottom of the stairs Vati was waiting for them. He carried his walking stick with the silver dog on top.

'He was looking out of the window,' said Mutti. 'I don't think they could see him, but ...'

'*HaShem!* – he could have done for us all. Quickly now ...' He put one arm around Mutti to guide her, and with his other hand felt his way across the big, dark hall to the cellar door. He yanked it open.

'Hurry,' he said.

Is death really necessary?

1.1

On the 31st of January 2039 Teddy Goldstein left Dunster castle on the Caithness coast for the first time in two years. She was on her way to Edinburgh to bury her father. Theo's death had ended a father-daughter war which had degenerated into endless campaigns of petty spites and frustrations.

Teddy was wondering what she had left to live for.

The jetpod ahead of them, carrying her father's coffin, banked sharply as it entered city airspace. Moments later their own jetpod followed suit. Teddy glanced at the other two passengers – her son and his partner, Rory. She saw Ek give Rory's hand a squeeze as the jetpod lurched extravagantly onto its new heading. Rory was a nervous flyer, and the two loved to touch – any excuse would do. The little incident made Teddy smile wanly as she turned back to the window. The huddled roofs of Edinburgh slid beneath her, greasy-grey with rain. Edinburgh was pretty in the snow, but it never got cold enough to snow any more. Rain made the grey slate, granite and encrustations of city pollution that made up the façade of the city look dejected.

Very suitable, then.

The jetpod continued to turn. The city continued to rush by beneath her. It made her feel queasy – but almost everything did these days.

The pilot straightened up, finally, and began to follow the railway lines into the city. The restored and Listed tenement blocks loomed up like cliffs in front of them. Teddy cursed the pilot under her breath. These flyboys were always ex-military, burned out by tours in Afghanistan or the Middle East and craved the old combat rush of adrenalin every time they flew. This one had saved his kamikaze tricks until now, so that the citizens of Edinburgh could hear him power up the boost and watch him make this dangerously steep and completely unnecessary climb. They swept over the old tenements with feet to spare, the blare of their own passage thrown back at them from the stonework. She tutted to herself: it had been a cheap trick and as a result of it she felt *really* queasy.

Now they swooped down over the elegant roofs of New Town, slick in the rain. January was always grey, and January in Edinburgh was one of the gloomiest places Teddy had ever known. She'd spent plenty of nights in underpasses, weeks in cardboard cities: she knew gloomy when she saw it.

It had taken nearly an hour to fly in from Dunster – which Teddy had discovered to be more than enough time for the sort of introspection inevitable when burying your father. Although Rory was the poor flyer, it was her Ek that looked the more miserable of the two. Teddy and her father had started badly and worked at making matters worse for as long as Teddy could remember. But Ek had loved his grandfather. Theo Goldstein was, after all, the only parent Ek had had when he was growing up. Today would be hard on him.

Teddy sighed. She owed Ek. There was a lot that he should know about his mother. But they had to get the old man in the ground before she could think about anything else. Besides, a noisy jetpod piloted by a burnout with a death wish was not the place for the sort of conversation that begins, 'there are some things I've been meaning to tell you'. And, fond as she was of Rory, the conversation she must have with her son was one that should only take place between blood kin.

*

The noise from the jetpod's engines rose to a scream and everything began to shake. The pilot had reversed thrust for landing. Teddy realised that even the fillings in her teeth were vibrating. Perhaps the train would have been a better bet, after all.

The noise and vibration got still worse and she lost her train of thought. Then she realised that, not only did she feel very sick indeed, she was now starting a brain-stabbing headache. *How appropriate*, her father would have said.

Theo had always been so vital. He had already been over a hundred years old when she returned to Dunster castle two years ago – and far fitter than she. He'd still been putting in sixteen hours a day at The Works then. Most of his veins and arteries were plastic by that time, his heart was plastic, as were his lungs, kidneys and liver – all developed by his beloved company and a boon to private medicine. But this year the little explosions in the blood vessels of his brain had begun and even Gold's Prosthetics had been unable to devise a way of reconnecting the delicate little blood vessels running through that particular organ. The life had gone out of him, week by week: the trips into the Works had become a struggle, then a chore, then impossible.

When the infarctions in his head had rendered him speechless she'd begun to go and see him every evening. He looked so tiny in the hospital bed, flattened by the bedding. Last night the only life in his room had been the tell-tales of the machinery monitoring his vital signs, beeping and winking with counterfeit cheerfulness. The old man in the bed had been waxy white. And now he was gone.

About an hour after she'd gone back to her own rooms the LEDs on the monitors had ceased to flash and the beeps changed to a constant wail. One of the identikit starched white nurses had come and told her, solemnly, that her father was dead.

Teddy hadn't known whether to laugh or cry.